D1329624

THE MIDNIGHT LIE

An exclusive signed edition of

THE MIDNIGHT LIE

Signed by the author

MARIE RUTKOSKI

H

HODDER &
STOUGHTON

THE MIDNIGHT LIE

MARIE RUTKOSKI

HODDER

First published in Great Britain in 2020 by Hodder & Stoughton
An Hachette UK company

1

Jacket illustration by Lisa Perrin
Jacket design by Elizabeth H. Clark
Book design by Beth Clark

A CIP catalogue record for this title is available from the British Library

Hardback ISBN 9781529357479
Trade Paperback ISBN 9781529357509

Typeset in Perpetua Std

Printed and bound in Great Britain by Clays Ltd, Elcograf S.p.A.

Hodder & Stoughton policy is to use papers that are natural,
renewable and recyclable products and made from wood grown in
sustainable forests. The logging and manufacturing processes are expected
to conform to the environmental regulations of the country of origin.

Hodder & Stoughton Ltd
Carmelite House
50 Victoria Embankment
London EC4Y 0DZ

www.hodder.co.uk

This book is dedicated to my sons, Eliot and Téo

1

THERE WERE WARNING SIGNS in the Ward that day that anyone could have seen. The children must have seen the danger in their own games, in the crescent moons, roughly cut from tin, that they strung from fishing line on sticks and dangled to cast shadows beneath the pale sun. They knew, as I knew, that the festival meant the militia would be out in force, seeking to fill their quotas for arrests. They would find infractions enough in the Ward, whether from drinking or improper dress or any of the many offenses you can commit when you're Half Kith.

Maybe I should have been more careful from the moment I saw the bird from my little window in my little room in the tavern attic, so cold I had been going to bed fully dressed. Ethin—a pretty name for a city, and this city *was* pretty for the right sort of people—is usually warm, so warm that tiny purple indi flowers grow out of the cracks of crumbling walls. Thin green fingers dig deep into stone. A heavy scent thickens the hot air. But every now and then a wind blows from the west that freezes everyone's bones, Half Kith and High Kith and Middling alike. People say teardrops of hail spangle the pink-sand beaches outside the city. They say the trees beyond the wall become jeweled by clear pearls of ice, and that the High Kith drink bitter hot chocolate at outdoor parties where their laughter is white lace in the chilled air.

I had never seen the shore. I didn't know if chocolate was something I would like. I had never even seen a tree.

I woke because of the way the bird sang. The song was sparkling, limpid: a string of glass beads flung onto a polished floor. I thought, *Not possible* and *Not here* and *That bird will soon die.* Maybe I should have guessed then how my day would end. But how could I? When I came close to the window and palmed away the feathered frost, when I dug my nails into the window frame weathered from the times when the damp got in, eating the wood, softening it, I could not have known. When I saw the spot of red flickering amid the brown and white rooftops, I could not have known, because I thought I knew myself. I thought I knew the things I could do, and what I would not. Here is what I believed:

I would do what was expected of me.

I could trust myself now.

Anyone I missed would not come back.

I would die if my crimes were discovered.

So you tell me what would make a good, quiet girl get herself in trouble, especially when she had so much to lose.

Tell me.

2

"ANYONE COULD CATCH IT."

"With the crush of people out there for the festival? It will never fly down."

"True. Someone will have to go up."

"To the rooftops, yes."

I wrapped the hem of my apron around the oven's hot handle and opened it. Heat breathed over me. Morah's and Annin's voices rose. You could hear the longing in their tones. It was the kind of impossible wish you treat as though it is precious. You make a home for it in your heart. You give it the downiest of beds for its rest. You feed it the choicest pieces, even when the meat it eats is your very soul.

What they wanted was not the Elysium bird, but what the bird could bring them.

"A child could do it," Annin said. "I've seen them clamber up the sides of buildings along the gutter pipes."

I could guess what she was thinking: that she was light enough to try it. I hate heights. They turn my stomach inside out like a glove. Even if

I'm standing on something firm, being high up makes me feel like nothing is solid, like nothing in the world can be relied upon—except the fact that I will fall. I looked at her shrewd expression and thought that I could never do what she was thinking. And I didn't like the thought of *her* scrambling over the rooftops, either.

Morah shook her dark head. "Someone would be waiting at the bottom when the thief came down with the bird, and pounce, and take it."

The fire at the back of the oven, which had been burning all night, glowed dark red. It sucked on the fresh draft of air and blushed orange. I scraped the ash into the hod. Then, one by one, I used the long-handled wooden paddle to slide domes of bread dough into the oven. They were each a cream-colored pillow, scored with a delicate pattern that would reveal itself as the loaf baked, no two the same. The loaves would show scenes of rainfall, fanciful castles, portraits of pretty faces, flowers, leaping animals. An artist, Annin sometimes called me. Little did she know.

I shut the oven door and dusted my floured hands. "It will freeze before anyone catches it." The Elysium bird had surely escaped from some High-Kith lady. It would not be ready for life outside a cage.

"Even dead," Morah said, "it would fetch a fine sum."

Annin looked stricken. She had unusual skin for a Herrath—paler than most, even milky, with freckles that dusted her cheeks and eyelids. There was a fragility to her features (fair eyelashes, flower-blue eyes, a small mouth with dainty upturned corners) that made her look far younger than me, though we were close in age.

"Pit the cherries," I told her. "I need them for the pies." The tavern was lucky for the bushel of ice cherries. Who knew how Raven had managed to get them. The black market, probably. She had connections with Middlings who were willing to trade such things for wares made in the Ward. It was not legal—just as Half Kith couldn't wear certain kinds of clothes restricted to the upper kiths, we also couldn't eat certain foods. Half-Kith foods were plain and filling and the City Council saw to it that no one starved. But no food was tangy or sour or spiced or sweet.

The ice cherries wouldn't need sugar, they were so sweet on their own: pale golden globes with glossy skin that would melt away in the oven. I wanted to taste one. I would sneak just one in my mouth, let my teeth slide through the flesh to the unyielding pit, honeyed juice flooding over my tongue.

The kitchen seemed full of wants.

"The bird won't *die*," Annin said. "It is the gods' bird."

Morah sniffed. "There are no gods."

"If it died it would be *gone*," Annin said. "You couldn't do anything with it."

Morah and I exchanged a look as she wiped wet dishes dry. She was older than Annin and me, old enough already to have shoulder-high children. Her manner, too, suggested that some invisible child moved around her. Her gestures were always careful, her eyes sometimes darting warily to make certain everything around her was safe—that a fire did not burn too high, that knives lay out of a small person's reach. Once, I had glanced at her as she sat at the worktable, picking one-handed through a bowl of lentils to remove any leftover hulls. In her other arm, she cradled a baby. But when I glanced again, the baby was gone.

I knew better than to mention this. It had been my imagination. I had to be careful. Sometimes an idea took root inside of me—for example, that Morah would be a good mother. Then the idea would become too real. I would see it clearly, as if it *were* real. It would displace the truth: Morah had no children. She had said she never would.

She and I were similar in one way that Annin was different. Morah and I were good at managing expectations—I by not having any and she by imagining the prize to be more attainable than it really was. Morah had probably decided that a dead Elysium bird would not be such a miracle as a living one. Therefore, it would not be impossible that *she* would be the one to have its valuable corpse.

"There are its feathers," she said. "Its meat."

And its hollow bones, which play a lilting melody when you blow through them.

I cut butter into flour. "The bird is out there. We are in here."

Annin opened the one slender window. Cold came in like water. Morah muttered in annoyance, but I said nothing. It hurt to look at Annin, at her hope. The shape of her stubborn chin reminded me of Helin.

Annin swept crumbs from the worktable into her palm. I didn't watch her go to the window. I couldn't. There was an ache in my throat. I saw things that weren't there. Things I wanted to forget.

She sprinkled the crumbs on the open window's sill.

"Just in case," she said.

3

THEY SAY THAT THE SONG of the Elysium bird makes you dream.

They say that these dreams remedy the past, take the sting out of memories, dust them up along the edges, blur them with soft pencils, the kind of pencils whose color you can smudge with a finger. The dreams make what's missing in your life seem unimportant, because what *is* there suddenly entices.

Imagine the stars hung closer: spikes of ice. Imagine the simple comfort of an ordinary blanket gone gorgeously soft. How could you ever slip the blanket off, when it feels like the fur of a mythical creature that can read your mind, and knew who you were before you were born?

Its song holds the grace of a mother's first smile.

A kind stranger brushing rain from your shoulder.

A kite flown on the Islim shore, sky peeking through its vented slits: little slices of blue so solid in color that you feel you could catch them and carry them home.

Feeling someone's arms around you grow heavy with sleep.

They say the bird was blessed by a god, though we can't remember which one.

That the sight of its red feathers will charm people.

In the Ward, where we must live the whole of our lives, never leaving, never allowed to leave, the promise of anything different was enough to bring everyone out into the streets. Turn them into hunters. Demolish friendships. I wanted to tell Annin to shut the window. Don't go outside. This is the sort of thing people will kill for.

But I wanted that bird, too.

4

I FINISHED BAKING THE PRINTED breads. Raven would bring them up quarter, out of the Ward and into the city proper, which I had never seen. Raven had inherited the privilege to sell her wares in the outer Wards of the city, beyond the walled Ward that marked the city's center like the stone of a fruit. Raven was born a Middling and so was allowed to come and go beyond the wall. Many Middlings traded with us. Some of them even stayed at the tavern as paying guests, but Raven was the only one I knew of who had chosen to *live* in our Ward. That choice gave her a complex status among the Half Kith. Some people respected her more. Others thought her crazy. But—although this was a secret I could never share—I knew she had come to live here out of goodness. She had come to help us.

I had asked Raven once what it was like to pass beyond the Ward, what the rest of the city looked like. She told me to brush her hair and keep my questions to myself.

"Why can't I know? If only to see it in my mind."

"You don't have the right to know."

"Why? Why must Half Kith stay in the Ward?"

"It is as it is," she said, which was what everyone said to such a question. The answer was like threadbare cloth worn so thin that you could see light and shadow through its fabric.

"I took you in," she said.

The hairbrush was metal, bristles stiff.

"Gave you a home."

Her hair was an early silver, thick and strong and easily knotted. I brushed gently.

"When you first came, you had to name everything, even the hinges on a door."

She had said this before.

"It was as though, if you didn't know something, if you couldn't catalogue every bit of the world, it would vanish."

True, I thought, and was ashamed of how weak I had been, how confused. I used to look at her hair and see black instead of its true gray, hair as black as mine, black as a raven's wing. When I was new to the tavern, I asked, Are you called Raven because of your hair? She had stared hard. What do you know of my name? Cowed, I said, Nothing. Yes, she told me. You know nothing. Then she gentled and said, Raven is a nickname. I asked, What is your real one? She lightly tapped the tip of my nose. She said, Raven is real enough.

"Isn't it better now, without the nightmares?" Raven said. "You had them even while awake. Your trances. You said the strangest things. You've grown out of it, thank the gods." She didn't believe in the gods any more than the rest of us did, but we referred to them out of empty habit. If you had asked a Half Kith why, she'd shrug and say, It is as it is. If you wondered why we had a festival for the god of the moon when we didn't believe in the gods, we'd get a little tight around the eyes. We'd think, Will this be taken from us, too, our one holiday of the year?

I pinned Raven's hair into a spiral—too elegant for the Ward, a hairstyle no Half Kith could wear.

"You don't need to know what the city is like," she told me. "It will do you no good to know."

She was a warm-hearted woman. She had opened her home to three orphans. Morah and Annin and I had spent our tender years in the Ward's orphanage, though separated enough by age that we had not known one another there. "Lost ones," Raven called us—kindly, for there were other, fitter words for what we were, like *unwanted*, or *bastard*, words that name a person who brings you shame. Morah had the coloring and features of what we called Old Herrath: black hair, gray eyes upturned at the corners, curled lashes, low-bridged nose, light brown skin. She looked High Kith, which meant she was born out of wedlock. Some noble-born woman must have brought her to the orphanage and left her in the ventilated, lidded bin outside its doors.

I looked High Kith, too.

I came to Raven when I was twelve. "Difficult," she called me then, though I followed all her rules. When I cried out at night, she came to my bed, stroked my brow, and told me that it was all right.

She cut my hair and said, Isn't this neat and clean, isn't it better? I said yes, though my long black hair had been my pride. Helin had envied it. It shines like paint, she had said. Raven told me to sweep the shorn hair and said, Now you'll be sure to stay out of trouble.

Girls in the Ward usually kept their hair long. Hair was the easiest thing to give up when the militia arrested you. They could choose any tithe they like. Blood was the most common tithe, drawn with a needle and syringe. People released from prison spoke of the blood tithe with relief. Blood loss made you feel like a phantom, but not forever. It was not so bad. Giving up your hair was even better. They took your hair if they were feeling nice, and it was sewn into the natural hair of High-Kith ladies to make what they had seem fuller.

Men inside the wall kept their hair short out of pride. They wanted to show that they were not afraid of paying a higher price. This was a pride they could afford. The militia could take things from women they didn't usually take from men.

By cutting my hair, Raven took away my easiest tithe. I want to keep you safe, she said. Don't trust they will take something easy. Follow my advice, my lamb. Act as though you obey every law. Make the militia never doubt you, for now you know the truth: you can afford to lose nothing.

Raven was good to me in other ways, too. When she saw my first printed bread she did not scold me for being fanciful. She grew quiet and said, There's money in this . . . and more.

She gave me a set of pencils and asked to see what I could do.

I sketched her face.

This is better than good, she said. This is me. This is my very face in a mirror.

Can you imitate this? She signed her name.

I could.

Perfect, she said.

She taught me how to remove oil from her greased apron. When my blood first came and spotted the sheets and she caught me trying to launder them with hot water, she said, Cold water, my girl, not hot, and gave me a block of soap that made my sheets smell like indi flowers. That day she let me keep one soft, sugared biscuit that I had made. She cut and buttered it. As I ate this treat, so unexpected, given to me when I had been ready for punishment, she said, Would you like to learn how to remove stains from paper?

Ink stains? I asked.

Yes, she said.

The headmistress at the orphanage had taught me how to read and write. It was not a common skill for any of us to learn, but the headmistress saw something in me that made her set aside time, curl my fingers around a pencil, and be patient. I could copy each letter perfectly the first time after being shown. I never forgot a spelling. Sometimes, however, I might write a phrase that I regretted. She taught me to cross a line through it, or to blot it very darkly with ink, if I wanted to make sure that no one could read what I had written. I hadn't known there was a way to make ink vanish.

Vinegar, Raven said. Lemon juice.

It was magic, to see the ink disintegrate.

I thought: I wish.

How easy. Everything done became undone. If I didn't want to see something, I had the power to make it go away.

Show me more, I told Raven, and when she showed me all she knew, I asked for different kinds of paper, different kinds of ink. It took her a while to procure them. Such things are a luxury in the Ward. A Half Kith possessed paper and ink only to produce something worth selling beyond the wall, such as a printed book. Paper and ink were not for our own use. But Raven smiled when she gave them to me, and nodded with approval when I experimented with them in my room. I became very good at making ink vanish.

Nirrim, she said one day. What you are doing is a secret. You cannot tell anyone.

Who would I tell? I said. Raven had made clear to the Ward that I was under her protection, which meant that no one troubled me when I walked in the streets, but it also meant that few were friendly with me.

Ever, she said. This is our secret.

I agreed. I was twelve, then. It was my name day. My first name day was perhaps a year after I had been left at the orphanage as a new infant, small and large eyed. I seemed no different from the other infants who arrived and grew and sometimes died. A fever. A fading. Thinning down to the bones for no reason I knew besides neglect. But a year of life meant stubbornness, a will that had to be acknowledged, so the headmistress decided I was likely to live and therefore should be named the word that had been pinned to my swaddling cloths when I was abandoned: Nirrim, a type of cloud that is rosy, lined with gold, and predicts good fortune.

For your name day, Raven said, I would like to teach you something new.

What is it? I said. I liked being good at what she asked me to do. It pleased her. It made me feel safe.

To be quiet, she said. We were alone in the kitchen, seated at the table, which was pale from age and scored by knives. I was sucking a sugar cube she had given me. I shifted the cube into my cheek so that I could speak.

I can be quiet, I said.

I know, my girl. She tucked a lock of my chin-length hair into my cap. She said, But you can become even better at it. You could become the best. And if you do, I can teach you other things.

What kind of things?

Ah, she said. I cannot tell you yet.

What do I need to do? I asked. The sweetness of the sugar drizzled down my throat. The sharp edges of the cube dissolved against my gums.

We will start with something small, she said.

All right.

She said, Put your hand on the floor, palm down.

I did. I had to get down on my hands and knees to do it the way she wanted: palm fully flat, the fingers spread. The sugar cube had dissolved. My mouth was full of sweetness.

She got out of her chair, and I was confused. I thought that she would leave me in the kitchen, perhaps for hours on end, that solitude would be how she would teach me silence. But she did not leave. She positioned her chair so that the tip of one leg rested on the web between my thumb and index finger. It didn't hurt, but I saw right away how it soon would.

Now, my girl, not a sound.

She lowered her weight onto the chair.

5

ON THE DAY THE ELYSIUM BIRD came to the Ward, Raven sent me on an errand. She had me tuck a printed bread into a muslin drawstring bag that had been deftly embroidered by Annin to display the tavern's insignia: a lit oil lamp. Raven buttoned the top button of my coat, which was her coat and made with cloth finer than anything I owned, but its dark brown was discreet enough for a Half Kith to wear. "There will be a lot of nonsense in the streets," she said, "what with this wind and the festival and that godsforsaken bird. You keep your head."

"But Annin."

"Annin! She is made of dreams, that one."

"She wants the bird."

"She'd get herself killed going after it. You think I will let her out of my sight? I'll tie her up if I have to."

I nodded, but I felt a small sadness. I remembered Annin when she first came here. She was careless. She let food burn on the stove. She forgot to change the sheets of a paying guest, a Middling merchant. I once found Annin asleep in the kitchen, head pillowed on her arms at the table, knife nearby, onion skins floating to the floor, sandal untied. I brushed the dark reddish hair away from her face. Soft round cheeks. A doll's face. She drooled a little: a wet shine on her mouth. I knelt beside her and tied her sandal.

"Bring me back something nice." Raven patted my cheek. She gave me a little push, and I was gone.

When an ice wind comes to the city, indi flowers freeze along the white walls. Purple enameled petals chatter in the wind. Then the cold snap passes. Petals melt and fall from their stems. New flowers grow, fluffy and thick. I love the flowers. They are so strong. Really, they are a weed, and destructive. The vines cannot easily be ripped out. They must be chopped. Over time, they can crack and crumble a wall. But I love them for that, too.

The Ward is a puzzle of skinny streets that turn an ice wind into pure malice. A wind will gust through tall buildings, kick sand in your eyes, freeze your fingers into claws. They say more murders happen during an ice wind. Maybe it's because of the cold, but I think it's because the cold is temporary. People get the sense that everything is, and that there are no consequences.

I passed members of the militia, usually in pairs, men stiff in their starched red uniforms, a stripe of dark blue across the chest to indicate their Middling kith. I kept my head down.

They could take me if they wanted.

They could always find something I had done wrong. They could smell my breath and accuse me of having eaten something sweet. They could look closely at my coat, which was almost too nice. They could say the center part in my hair was off-center, that its natural wave was because I must have had it in small, illegal braids. I had looked boldly in their faces. My hands had been in my pockets. What did I have that I should not? Those sandals. That leather looked too good. They were sure of it.

Come with us, they would say.

We'll see to your tithe.

My chest always flooded with fear when I passed the militia. You are nothing, I told myself. No one.

Their glances slid from my face and left me, forgotten. Thank you, I thought. Yes, I thought. I am unimportant. Insignificant. A crumb to be brushed away.

Children ran past me, their breath pale streamers in the cold, their tin moons twinkling behind them.

The militia didn't stop me. They eyed the children. Then I saw the men's gaze float to the rooftops. They, too, wondered where the Elysium bird had gone.

The buildings of the Ward were brilliant with white paint. The Half-Kith men had given the walls a fresh coat of limewash, as was tradition every year on the moon festival. The tang of new paint sharpened the air. The Ward buildings were perhaps once beautiful. Raven said they were older than anything beyond the wall. Stone arches braced the stone walls at their height, bending over the narrow streets. The arches seemed to serve no purpose. I supposed they were architectural. Sometimes, though, I looked at them and saw canopies of sun-shimmering cloth draped over them, shading the walkways below.

But I would correct myself. There were no canopies. I didn't *see* them. I *imagined* them.

I emerged into an agora, one of the open squares. It bustled with people celebrating the largest full moon of the year, cooking salted fish over open fires, warming wind-dried hands. As always, they wore dull colors: brown and gray and muddied beige. The black-and-white diamond marble beneath my feet was soap-smooth and uneven with age, interrupted by large, deliberate holes. It looked as if objects had been gouged out of the paved ground, though no one knew what.

The holes made me think of the vanishings. Sometimes people disappeared from the Ward. Half Kith entered the prison and never returned. Far worse were the night-snatchings, which happened for no reason anyone understood. I sung him to sleep, a mother said. Tears slipped off her face and onto a tavern table. She said, I should never have left his side. Her words dissolved as Raven stroked her shoulder. I saw the boy in my mind: soft, fat cheeks, thick lashes like little black fans. A reaching shadow fell over his face.

Is it a tithe? the mother whispered. But I did nothing wrong. I am so careful. What did I do wrong?

There was never any answer. I occasionally saw that woman in the Ward, though I always looked away. All of us in the Ward lived our lives around empty spaces, but she became the emptiness.

One of the holes in the agora was slick with ice. Children skidded on it and slipped and laughed at their game. I was struck by how children, at least when they are small, can make do with whatever they have, even if it is not much, without the burden of realizing they are compensating for what they lack.

I wonder, I once said to Morah as we passed through the agora together, how this place used to be.

Her expression turned strange. What do you mean, she said, how it used to be? The agora has always been like this.

⌒

Before I saw to Raven's errand, I had one of my own.

I stopped at the home of Sirah, who was too elderly to shuffle outdoors for the festival, even if it weren't so cold. As I'd feared, her home had no fire and was freezing. Sirah lay under a mound of blankets. She opened her one eye. The other had been tithed from her when she was young. She had been arrested for wearing cosmetics on her eyelids.

She was lucky. They could have taken both eyes.

"Sleep," I said, and built a fire in the kitchen, but when I brought her a steaming cup of tea, she was wide awake.

"I have something for you." I produced a small loaf of bread that I had hidden in my deep coat pocket.

Her gray eye shone. "My sweet Nirrim," she said, which made me feel as warm as the tea, as warm as the fire. She said, "It will rain."

I smiled. "When?"

She squinted. The skin covering her missing eye was as wrinkled as a fig's. "Six days."

"Will someone have caught the bird by then?"

"Child, I only do the rain. No birds. Six days. It doesn't happen at night. I feel it in my bones."

She was never wrong. "I'll plan to stay inside, then, and bake another loaf of bread for you."

She smiled back at me, showing her missing teeth. I thought she'd lost them through age, not as a tithe, but I never knew for sure.

A vine of icy flowers hung over Aden's door. When he opened it, they chimed like a shopkeeper's quiet bell. He gave me a cocky smile and made a silent game of tugging at my coat sleeve to pull me indoors. This was in case the militia was watching us. They would see us not as criminals, but as lovers catching a moment for themselves before the night's festivities truly got underway. I smiled back, ready to kiss his offered cheek. He turned at the last moment and caught my lips with his.

"Aden!"

He pulled away. He was a full head taller. I didn't raise my eyes but kept my gaze on his tanned throat. His playfulness soured. If I looked up, I'd see his broad mouth thinned, light eyes narrowed. A notch always formed between his brows when he frowned. That would be there, too. He said, "As if you've never done it before."

It was true. We had kissed, and more, but I had put an end to that.

Sometimes I didn't understand things and felt stupid later. Like how his lovers' game to protect us from curious eyes hadn't been a game to him.

"Come inside," he said.

Normally, during an ice wind, it would be nearly as cold inside a Ward house as outside. Our houses weren't built for the cold, since it came so rarely. Aden dealt on the black market, which meant that his home had a few comforts others didn't. A brazier glowed with live coals. Orange light flared against the white, limewashed walls of the first room. Half Kith must keep the walls of their home white, just like they must always wear muted colors. Although some people in the Ward could carve sinuous chairs, shape exquisite sofas, craft tables with minute patterns of inlaid bone, such furnishings were sold to the upper kiths beyond the wall. Everything we owned must be plain.

I handed Aden the bread. He made a pleased sound to see its design: a raptor with talons outstretched. "You made this for me?"

Raven had chosen this masculine image, likely for the same reason I told Aden yes. We wanted to please him. We needed his skills.

It is important to make people feel appreciated, Raven said, and made certain to slip Aden a few coppers every now and then. She set money aside from the tavern's profits. We must do our part, she told me.

Maybe I should apprentice myself to the printer, I told her. I am good with paper and ink. I could earn a little.

But I give you everything you need, Raven said. I will always take care of you.

It was true. I was grateful. Although Morah, Annin, and I didn't earn money working for Raven, we never needed to.

I just wish I had money to contribute, too, I told her. For the documents. You shouldn't have to pay for everything.

She touched my cheek. Don't you worry your dear heart, she said.

"Do you have the heliographs?" I asked Aden.

"All business, I see. Little Nirrim, made of stone." He brought the bread close to his face and inhaled its fresh, sugared scent. My printed breads were soft inside, with an airy, melting texture.

The bread was a risky thing. Too sweet for people like us.

Aden set the loaf on a table that bore a bowl filled to its brim with seed. "Not you, too," I said. The seed was stolen, probably, from the upper Wards of the city, where ladies kept pet songbirds of all kinds. Aden had a Middling passport that allowed him outside the Ward's wall. The document had been forged by me.

But it would be a lie, I had said to Raven when she had suggested that I forge passports, which she would give to those who needed them most. I was anxious about the risk—to her as well as to me. And I didn't like lying. It was hard for me to tell what was real. Lies made it worse.

It is a midnight lie, she said.

A kind of lie told for someone else's sake, a lie that sits between goodness and wrong, just as midnight is the moment between night and morning.

Or a lie that is not technically false, like a misleading truth.

"I saw the bird fly away," I told Aden, which was true enough, but which I hoped would make him think the bird was gone.

"It's somewhere in the Ward, I know it." Aden's smile was back. He was—as Annin had reminded me many times—even more handsome when he smiled. He made a room warmer. When the day dimmed, sunshine always seemed to linger around him like bright vapor. Lucky, women in the Ward called me. "Don't be so disapproving," he said. "Why shouldn't I hunt the bird as well as anyone else?"

"You can't *hunt* an Elysium bird." A pet Elysium is raised from an egg stolen from a nest in the sugarcane fields outside the city. They say its shell is a glossy crimson. They say that when the shell cracks, it weeps a fluid that, if swallowed, will add a happy year to your life. "The bird can't be caught."

"I will be the first, then, to catch one."

"Even if you did." I shook my head.

"No one would take it from me. They wouldn't dare. I'd like to see them try." He leaned back against the table, large hands bracing its edge. He was well grown for his eighteen years. Aden had just the kind of body the High Kith would approve of in our kind: one made to work, all muscle and sinew.

"It's your funeral," I said. "The heliographs, please."

He reached into a breast pocket and produced them: small, thin squares of tin, fanned out between his fingers like a miniature deck of silvery cards. There was the scent of lavender. Only the face on the top tin could be seen clearly. It was Raven's face. I wasn't sure why she had asked Aden to make a heliograph of herself. A Middling passport was already hers by birth. We had never tried to forge a High-Kith one. Even if we had the proper Council stamp—which we didn't—passing as High would be impossible without a great sum of money. Even one day's outfit of High clothes would cost more than I could imagine.

I took the tins from Aden and shuffled through them. They showed families with small children. An infant. The baby's parents. A girl with wide, startled eyes. I made the tins disappear into a secret lining in the collar of my coat, where their stiffness, even if felt, would be taken for cardstock meant to make the collar rigid.

Aden had shown me how to capture someone's image with light and a bitumen-coated plate of tin, to wash the tin with lavender oil to make the image appear. He was good at it. His mother had been good, too, so good that when she decided to leave this city, and abandon Aden around the time when he was no longer a child yet not quite a man, she had thought that an excellent heliograph was all she needed to make her fake passport convincing. She was caught by the militia and sentenced to death. Aden never even received her bones to bury. When the City Council took your body, they took all of it.

Aden had made a heliograph of me. "We could go beyond the wall together," he had said, setting the small tin square in my palm, "and work in the Middling quarter." But I couldn't leave my home. I couldn't leave Raven, who needed me.

If I left the Ward, who would forge documents for others who wanted to leave? The ones who had seen the blank mother questing the Ward for her night-snatched son, and decided, Not me. Not my child.

"If I caught the bird," Aden said, "I would share it with you." His fingers brushed my cheek. They smelled of lavender. They touched my mouth.

A loneliness opened inside my chest. It was a kind of song that always sang the same thing.

He kissed me and I let him. Sometimes it can feel so good to give someone what they want that it is the next best thing to getting what you want. His hard body was warm as I leaned into him. His mouth was hungry at my neck, beneath the fringe of my chin-length hair. I pretended that his hunger was my hunger. I kissed him back, and the quiet inside me didn't feel so large anymore, so heavy.

I thought, This is not so bad.

I thought, I could be with him again.

I thought, He loves me.

But what I did surprised me. My hand reached around him and dipped into the bowl of seeds. I closed my fingers around a handful. Tiny and hard. I could feel their shine.

I kissed Aden back, and slipped the seeds into my coat pocket. For good measure, I took the embroidered bag, too.

6

YOU KNOW WHERE THIS IS going.

When I still lived in the orphanage, after Helin's death, I would spend hours at a window. One might have wondered what could keep my attention, since the view was only the brick of an opposing wall. I was looking not at the view but at my reflection. I pretended the girl I saw there was someone else. A friend. A sister. A High-Kith girl whose life I could only imagine, with silk slippers and pet foxes taken from the pink beaches and tamed, leashed with ribbons. Who could stack a castle of sugar cubes. Who slept in late. Who lived so tenderly it was as though she were housed inside a flower. This girl was afraid of nothing.

Sometimes the reflection seemed real.

I would grow frightened and stay away from the windows, from any mirrorlike surface, from spoons, from still water in a sink.

And then, though you would think I had learned better, after what had happened to Helin, I would return to the window. The girl in the glass would smile.

The wind whipped the edge of my coat as I walked home from Aden's. My mouth still tasted like his mouth. Things had gone too far.

I was the one who allowed that to happen.

And I was the one who thought, This will always be my life: kissing someone I don't love. Living in a city I will never leave.

And I was the one who saw the crimson bird perched at a gutter's edge.

But it wasn't me who stopped, sandy dirt scraping against the pavement under my sandals. It wasn't me who glanced around and saw— strangely, impossibly—no one. It wasn't me who felt a need grow inside my chest like a fruit and split its rind.

Nor was it me who set my hands and feet onto the metal struts that bound the gutter pipe to the building's wall. *I* didn't begin to climb.

It was the girl in the window's reflection.

So brave.

So foolish.

7

I GLANCED DOWN AT THE spinning pavement. The metal gutter pipe froze my fingers. I was robbed of breath. The bird above me trilled.

I forced myself up. I climbed past indi flowers twined around the gutter. I spied their roots in cracks that split the wall deep enough for me to dig my fingers into them. The cracks were sticky with fresh white paint. It grew colder as I climbed, the wind meaner. It tore off my cap. Hair spilled into my eyes, got into my mouth.

When I climbed up far enough to know—to know the fact deep in my body, in my trembling legs and dry throat—that if I fell I would die, I stopped. I hugged the pipe. The wind blew dust against the wall. My mind seemed to flip upside down. My sandals skidded along the pipe. Nausea rose up my throat and I had an image of vomiting out my insides, of my stomach coming out first, then my heart, my lungs. I imagined these organs blundering from my mouth and dropping one by one to the ground with soft thuds.

And that was stupid, so stupid. I couldn't let my imagination feel too real.

I forced my eyes open. I saw the pipe. I saw my bleeding fingers, tipped with white paint. I looked up into the sky. Gray lambswool clouds. It was getting dark.

And over my shoulder: a glimpse of the wall, solid and as thick as the length of a man from toe to top. I couldn't see beyond it.

Raven would wonder where I was.

There was nothing but silence above me. The bird had probably flown somewhere else.

But I thought: I don't know, not really, how large the Ward is compared to the rest of the city.

I thought: What harm would it do to see the High quarter beyond the wall? Just for a moment. Then I would come back down and be myself again.

I pushed myself up. My arms ached, my back ached, my right leg jittered like the needle of Annin's pedaled sewing machine. But I climbed.

Then I heard the bird again. Its song slipped fluidly inside me.

It occurred to me that the bird wanted me as much as I wanted it. That it knew I was coming, that it was watching, tiny, its crested head cocked, its tail plumes of pink and green and scarlet. In my mind I could see its short, inky beak. Its tiny emerald eyes. It sang to me.

I was confused, because I had never seen an Elysium bird up close. How could I imagine it in such great detail?

It didn't feel like my imagination.

It felt like memory.

I didn't want to glance up. But the song calmed my shaking body. It floated the hair out of my eyes and ran a finger up my neck, under my jaw, tilting my head up.

The bird circled over my head, red wings wide and crenellated. A feather fell. It pivoted in the air until its shaft stuck into a joining where the horizontal length of the gutter met the roof's edge.

Then the bird disappeared out of my line of sight, over the roof.

SOMETHING SEIZED MY FOOT. I jolted, and I would have come off the pipe entirely if not for my grip on the gutter's frets.

"Out of my way."

I glanced down. My heart got stuck in my throat. A militiaman was just below me, hand wrapped around my ankle. He shook my leg. "Please," I said. "Stop! I'll fall."

"The bird is flying away!" His face shone with sweat. "Get off, damn the gods!" He yanked at me. I slid, my hands coming off the fret.

My fingers snagged the indi flower vine wrapped around the gutter. It held my weight.

"You are blocking my way," he said, and when I glanced down into his face it was filled with grim determination and need. He *would* kill me, I realized.

Hands twisted in the indi vine, I begged, "Let me go."

He didn't release my ankle. "The bird is mine."

His final word echoed among the buildings, but in an otherworldly voice, higher than his own. It was the bird. *Mine*, it sang.

The roots of the indi vine gave a little, some of them tearing free of the wall, popping out of crevices. The gutter creaked.

Mine, the bird sang again, and it seemed to be singing to me.

I kicked the man's face.

He cried out. I felt him fall from me. The pipe, still in his grip, came off the wall.

I clung to the vine, which spun like rope from one anchored point. I heard the loud clank of the pipe and the thump of his body on the pavement.

He lay twisted below, legs splayed. I gripped the vine. Blood pooled beneath him. A veil of fear prickled over me.

The noise must have been heard. Other militiamen would come.

The alleyway rang with shocked silence. Then, in the distance, I heard cries.

Forget the bird, I told myself.

I had to hide.

9

I SCRAMBLED UP THE TWISTING vine and onto the roof. I wouldn't be seen from below, but I had to get as far away as possible. Fear coated me like paint. I ran across the rooftop, ducking around the cistern there to collect rain. Night had almost truly fallen, and the cistern was sheeted in thin black ice. I tore at the collar of my coat—Raven's coat.

Stitches ripped. The collar came off in my hand, the heliographs scattering at my feet. If I were caught, the heliographs could not be found. They would be traced to the people whose images they bore, even the children. The price for impersonating a member of a higher kith was death.

Shouts rose from below.

I punched through the ice in the cistern. I scooped up the heliographs and dumped them into the black water. Then I ran to the far edge of the roof.

I had always refused to consider things that could never happen.

What if you were on the Council? Annin sometimes asked me in the kitchen.

I wouldn't be.

What if you were High Kith? What would you do?

I'm not.

Don't you wonder, she would say, why things are the way they are?

It is as it is, I'd tell her, and find comfort in that saying. It pointed toward certainty. I might not like the world as it was, but at least it wouldn't change around me.

I didn't want to become someone I couldn't recognize.

Yet when I reached the edge of the rooftop, I became someone else. The reflection of that girl in the window. Another self. Someone who jumped across the narrow space.

I landed on the neighboring rooftop. I kept running, judging where best to bridge the gaps between roofs, hoping anyone below would be too distracted by the commotion in the streets to look up. The yellow moon, swollen to its full size, was rising. I might be seen, if someone thought to look.

But no one did.

When I had put enough distance between myself and the body, I slid down behind another cistern. My trousers were thin. My rear grew cold on the plastered stone and I shivered against the aged wood of the cistern, pulling the coat closer to my body. I should stay here, I thought, until the festival has ended. Maybe, soon before dawn, when everyone was asleep, I could clamber down another gutter pipe. Sweat chilled on my skin. I pushed my loose hair behind my ears. A lock of it was matted with white paint.

I could see, now, the whole city. The thick white ribbon of the wall wrapped in a snaking circle around me. Beyond it lay the upper quarters, their spires topped with silver and golden orbs. Dark, dense, waving blankets confused me until eventually I realized they must be treetops. The upper Wards glittered with colored lights. There seemed to be a pattern: some areas of the city glowed with pink windows, and others with green, still others with blue: a code, perhaps, that differentiated one quarter from another. High up on the hill, rooftops were not flat as they were in the Ward, but sometimes shaped into pointed towers with bellied windows and the black stitching of wrought-iron balconies. One large building bore ghostly figures that ringed an enormous dome brilliant with ruby panes of glass lit from within. People, I thought at first, dipped in white paint.

Strange, impossible.

Statues, of course.

I felt suddenly tired and consumed by cold. I had killed that soldier. I had done something terrible that could never be undone, that only proved that no matter how hard I tried to be otherwise, I was someone who made mistakes. Who looked at statues and thought they were people. Who looked at a reflection and thought it was another girl instead of only the image of herself. Who saw no other way out of a situation than murder.

I could have asked him to let me climb, I thought, or I could have sworn to let him chase the bird when we reached the rooftops.

There is always another way.

My girl, I imagined Raven saying. Do you think you can keep what you have done hidden?

The militia will take you away. You will never come back.

How I would miss you.

A scrambling feeling rooted around inside me.

No one, Raven said in my mind, can know what you've done.

I looked at the statues. They were of the gods, surely, but no one really remembered them. Maybe that was a blessing.

My eyes closed.

Are you hungry? I remember Helin asking. She was a little younger than I was, six years old, perhaps, then, her hand soft. She held an apple, its shiny skin red and gold.

How did you get that?

She shrugged. It's for you.

I took the apple. Why are you giving this to me?

Will you be my friend?

I bit the apple. Then I passed it to her. Your turn, I said. You take a bite.

We ate the apple like that, passing it between us, until we got to the core, which we also ate, the seeds sliding down our throats, the stem crunched between our teeth, our fingers and mouths sticky and sweet.

I huddled inside Raven's coat. I slipped between seeing the city before me and remembering Helin. I almost wished I could forget her the way everyone had forgotten the gods.

Cold came over me, but I was warm inside with guilt. The feeling nuzzled against me. It pressed against my heart like a soft animal and slept in my lap.

10

A LIGHT PRICKLE ON MY wrist woke me. I startled out of sleep, shaking my wrist hard, sure that I had been seen, I had been caught, a soldier was slipping a manacle onto my wrist. But the prickle disappeared, air beat against my face, and what I saw was not uniformed men but the Elysium bird launching itself from my wrist. It hovered for a moment in front of me before sweeping away.

It landed a few feet from me. It scratched the plastered roof, oddly chickenlike for such a glamorous bird, wings tucked close to its body. Now that I was so close, I could see streaks of green on its belly, speckles of pink on its breast, the black thorn of its beak, the tips of white on its red wings. It sang.

"Shh," I said, which was foolish—what bird obeyed a person?—but it stopped midsong. I reached into my pocket for the seeds—Aden's seeds. *Mine*, I remembered the bird singing. It felt not like it belonged to me, but that it was telling me that I belonged to it.

I scattered the seeds across the roof.

It pecked its way toward me, head tipping left and right, tail dipping, luxuriant feathers drifting behind it like the train of an iridescent dress. It ate the seeds, husks splitting beneath its beak and dropping to the roof. The moon was high and bright. I wanted desperately for this bird to be mine no matter what it could do for me, no matter if the stories were real, if only so that I could see it in full light and know its patterns and colors, to know it so intimately that I would see its details even when I closed my eyes.

It flitted closer, then landed on my knee.

You can't catch an Elysium bird, I had told Aden. Had anyone ever heard of an Elysium behaving like this?

Maybe it was because it was trained and had been raised from its shell.

Maybe hunger had overwhelmed it.

Whatever reason it had decided not to fear me, I couldn't question the peace that spread from where it perched upon my knee, drifting down my leg and up into my stomach, stealing over my chest. I dipped my fist into the coat pocket again and offered an open handful of seed. It jumped to the heel of my hand, feathers curling over my wrist, caressing my upper arm. It ate. The beak gently jabbed the palm of my hand, a tender little needle.

What are you? I wondered as I studied it. What are you, really?

What am I, that you chose to come to me?

Its body was only slightly larger than my hand but its tail floated long, the tip of it almost to my elbow. It warbled: a bubbling sound. I stroked its head and it allowed this, leaning into my touch. When it burbled its low music again, I stroked its throat. Beneath its feathers was a light vibration, like a purr.

I realized then what anybody in the Ward should have realized.

I couldn't keep this bird.

It wasn't possible to hide such a secret. Everyone in the tavern would learn, and then it would be only a matter of time before the Ward did, and before people began to wonder whether the death of a soldier on the day the bird flew into the Ward had something to do with me. It would be only a matter of time before the militia learned who had the bird. Then they would come for me, if not for the crime of murder, then for the crime of stealing a High-Kith pet. When the Council could sentence you to years in prison for dressing like a High-Kith lady, what would it do to someone from the Ward who had kept an Elysium?

The bird nosed among the seeds, looking for its favorites, which were slender black ovals.

The only way to keep it, I thought, was to kill it.

If I were to wring its neck, I could sell the feathers. I could see whether the stories about its meat were true. Its hollow bones.

A dead Elysium bird held so much value. It could be parceled out secretly and slowly. *That*, perhaps, could be kept hidden when a living thing—with its song, its rustlings, its need for food and water, its excretions—could not.

The bird looked at me. *Mine*, it sang, and I was so startled that my hand sagged and the bird floated up, wings stuttering. But it settled back into my palm.

It would be easy to snap its fragile neck. I had just killed someone. The murder of a bird would be nothing by comparison. And there was so much to gain.

A treasure, Raven would say when I showed her the limp corpse, its feathers as bright as a bouquet. *My* treasure, she would call me.

Who knew what comforts we could bring into our home through the sale of the birds' parts?

Who knew how many Half Kith we could save, with extra money to buy what we needed to make passports?

But the bird nestled into my palm, its feathers a warm cloud, its happiness thrumming into my skin. I had never felt or seen anything so beautiful, and it was only then that I realized how starved I had been for beauty. Its liquid green eyes studied me.

A thought came so slowly that it reminded me of Annin building a tower out of playing cards: the precision and care, the light touch, the slight shake of her hand lowering a card into place.

The Elysium closed its eyes and sighed. It grew heavy with sleep.

I could keep the bird, I thought, if I left the Ward. If I forged a passport for myself. If I went beyond the wall, beyond the city.

Fear flooded me. I couldn't kill the bird. But I also couldn't leave behind everything I knew.

I slipped the embroidered bread bag from my pocket.

I clamped the sleeping bird's wings to its body, and thrust it into the sack.

When I was certain that no one was passing in the alley below, I climbed down a gutter pipe, the jerking, squawking bag swaying from my wrist by its drawstring.

Moonlight painted the street. The alley was a quiet, bright river.

I walked until I spotted a pair of soldiers. Dread pulsed inside me, but I couldn't keep the bird and I couldn't kill it. It must be returned. I had to hope that the militia would be so distracted by the Elysium that they wouldn't think to link me to the soldier's broken body—which, after all, would surely look like a mere accident, especially with the fallen gutter pipe.

"Here," I said to the soldiers, holding out the bag. I remembered Helin holding out the apple and asking to be my friend.

One of them, staring, took the jolting bag. "Is that the Elysium?"

The other soldier seized my arm.

"But I'm turning it in." Panic darted up my throat. "To be brought back to its owner."

The soldier dragged my other arm behind me.

"It's unharmed!" I said.

I was arrested anyway.

11

THEY CAN TAKE ANYTHING from you.

You hear stories of surgeries, of how a slice of liver had been taken, or a kidney. Surgeries allowed doctors who worked for the Council to heal the High-Kith sick.

Sirah's missing eye.

Once I saw a woman whose eyelashes had been clipped to the lids. The lashes, I knew, would be crafted into fake ones for a lady to wear.

The pain of a lopped finger.

Sometimes it seemed that the tithe was not about physical pain or weakness or even shame, but fear. I was afraid that a judge might discover something I hadn't known I couldn't lose. Maybe I wouldn't recognize it as valuable until it was stripped from me.

For resisting arrest ("But I didn't resist") and defiance before a judge ("I am not defiant. I was *helping*"), I was sentenced to a month in prison. For daring to touch High-Kith property, I must pay a tithe of blood, one vial to be drained each day of my prison sentence.

"I was *returning* the bird," I said. "The property would have been lost if not for me."

The judge shifted, his rich red robe rustling. The court was a narrow little room that housed him, the two soldiers who had arrested me, and myself. There was no need for a witness, and although I had always wondered whether a court would be grand, this was a mere room attached to the prison, probably because it was a foregone conclusion that anyone who was arrested would be sentenced.

"Do you think yourself special?" the judge said. "Perhaps you think yourself too good for your kith. Perhaps, indeed, too good for any kith. Would you like to become Un-Kith?"

I had never seen an Un-Kith, but I knew they existed. They cleaned the waste from the sewers. They worked in the cane fields outside the city. It was a choice offered, I had heard, to the worst offenders in the Ward: death or Un-Kith? Sirah, who had been imprisoned more than once, said that sometimes the guards would sweep through the prison and randomly pull Half Kith from cells. She never saw them again.

The chair I had been shoved into smelled of sweat. A faint trace of urine permeated the leather seat. "No," I said. "I know what I am. I don't deserve anything. Please. I accept the sentence." I tried to twist my wrists in the straps that bound my hands to the arms of the chair, but they had been tightened hard, so that the bones hurt.

"The owner will be grateful for the return of this pet," the judge said, "but the law is what it is, and your impertinence is not appreciated."

I tried again to give him what he wanted. "I am grateful for the sentence," I said. "I thank you for your mercy."

He smiled.

What made him so different from me, aside from his birth? His eyes were a common Herrath color, gray, his skin no lighter or darker than mine, his nose a similar slender and long shape as Raven's, his mouth a humorless line. His true hair I couldn't see, because the thick rich black of it, set against his aged face, suggested a wig made from the hair of someone like me. If it was so wrong to be Half Kith, if my birth placed me within an encircling wall I could never leave—not even to go to prison, which was actually built into a portion of the wall as the orphanage was—why would this judge wear part of a Half-Kith's body? I wanted to ask why, but I knew the answer: It is as it is.

"Perhaps," said the judge, "I could see fit to forgive your behavior and waive the sentence if you were to help the Council and your city by telling me something worth knowing."

I hesitated. Sirah had warned me that prisoners were asked to denounce their fellow Half Kith, to offer up the crimes of their neighbors in exchange for a lighter punishment. I had asked Raven if she worried someone would denounce us for forging documents that classified Half Kith as Middlings, and able to leave the Ward. She shook her head. "The Ward loves me," she said. "No one would dare. And who would provide fake passports if we were sent to prison? Never bite the hand that feeds you."

"Well?" said the judge.

My strong girl, Raven sometimes said when she took the forged pages from me to stitch them into a palm-sized, pamphlet-thin book. She was the only one ever to call me that. It made me want to be how she saw me. My brave one, she said. All I wanted was to go home. I wished she were here now. She would say, It is only a month! A child could do a month.

But what if they forget me here? That happens. What if a month becomes more?

I will come for you, she would say.

You will?

I am Middling born. I still have friends in that world. I have favors owed.

And you would use them, for me?

My lamb, of course!

She would say: You are like a daughter to me.

She would say: I have never known someone so loyal, so true.

She would say: Whatever you did or were like before you came to me does not matter and never did, not to me.

"Well?" said the judge.

I could bear a month's sentence. The tithe was but a vial of blood a day. An easy tithe, a common one.

I said, "I know nothing."

"Did you know a militiaman died near the time of your arrest?"

Fear trickled down my throat. "No."

"You were not so far from where the body lay. Perhaps you saw something?"

"No."

"Really?" he said.

"I can't say what I don't know."

He rang a bell. The soldiers unstrapped me. Blood rushed back into my hands, making them sing with pain.

"Then this matter is concluded," the judge said.

⁓

"My coat," I said to the soldier who nudged me into the little cell. Cold bled through the stone walls. I wore only trousers, a thin tunic, and sandals, the clothes one normally wears year-round and that the Half Kith wear even during an ice wind, because we know the heat will still come again and cannot afford better for such a brief period of time.

"*My* coat," the soldier corrected.

"An old-fashioned cut," the other man said, "And a pity about the ripped collar. But good cloth. How could someone like you afford it? Be glad, girl, that we took it from you, or the judge would have had you for thievery, too."

"I borrowed it. I must return it." What would Raven say? I remembered the sting of her metal brush striking my cheek. But it had been so long since she had needed to correct me, and I worked so hard for her and our cause, that it wasn't her punishment I dreaded. It was her disappointment. "I already paid my tithe." Gauze wrapped my inner arm just below my elbow, where a needle had slid in and drained the first vial of blood.

"You can pay in other ways," said the soldier in the cell with me, his hand tight on my shoulder. He was older than me, the age of a man with children. He was thick with muscle, his beard neatly trimmed and shining in the light cast by the lantern in the hallway. I could smell the oil of his beard. I imagined him stroking it in the morning, trimming it just so, making his appearance neat.

It would rasp against my face. Maybe later, when he was done, my cheek would bear a rash.

But the skin would heal, I thought. And the kind of tithe he was imagining was no more than what any woman in the Ward might have to pay.

I would be all right, I told myself.

My strong girl. My brave one.

"Pardon me," said a voice that was neither soldier's, "but my cell is musty. It could use a good scrubbing. Perhaps one of you could see to that while the other fetches me a decent vintage of wine?"

The soldier's grip on my shoulder slackened in surprise. The soldier in the hallway turned. Beyond him I could see a shadow behind the bars of the cell across from mine.

"I am not fussy," the shadow said. "As long as the wine has aged at least ten years I won't complain. Oh, and what if you brought me some of those ice cherries? Such a delicacy."

"Mind your manners, thief," said the guard in the hall.

"Stay out of what doesn't concern you." The bearded soldier's grip on me doubled. The heat of his hand came through the thin fabric of my shirt.

"I spy with my little eye something gold," said the shadow, "upon someone's finger. Not every country has that custom, to be sure, but here I would call that a ring. I would say that here, such a ring means that one is married."

The bearded guard made a strange sound in his throat.

"There are few things I pride myself on," the shadow said. "But when someone makes an impression on me, no matter what kind, charming or repulsive, I never forget a face. I will remember you."

"So what if you do," said the bearded guard. "You'll rot here a good long while."

"Nooo. Check your roster of prisoners."

There was a silence.

"Did I mention one of my many other talents? I am resourceful. Would it be hard for me to find the wife of such a memorable man as our fine guard? Not at all. Moreover, I tell a good tale. Would it be difficult for me to engage her with the tale of an attack in close quarters? Would she listen? I think she would. Would she be pleased? I think not."

The bearded guard's hand slid from me. "I want a look at the roster," he said to the other guard, and stepped from my cell. When he locked the bolt home, my veins fizzed with relief. I felt suddenly, deeply tired. My eyes slid shut as I heard the soldiers walk away.

"Finally!" the voice said. "Company!"

I opened my eyes. I could see a bit better, now that the guards did not block my view, the shadow in the cell opposite mine. The light cast by the oil lantern in the hallway was dim, but still I saw the shape of a young man, hair cut close to the head, in trousers tighter than I would wear and a waist-length jacket with the short, stand-up collar allowed to Middling men. He lounged against the bars, a languid hand dangling through them, fingers slender and long. He was taller than me but not by much, the lines of his body fuzzy in the darkness, loose and lazy.

"Come closer," he said. "I can't see you."

"Yes, you can. You saw the ring on that guard's finger."

"I would like to see you *better*."

I was grateful that he had made the guard leave, and I was curious about him, too, but my curiosity unnerved me. Curiosity is too much like wanting. It comes from feeling dissatisfied, and I knew well the danger of that.

"It's only neighborly," he said.

I moved back into the depths of the cell.

"My name is Sid," he said.

That was a strangely short name, and I told him so.

He hesitated, the first time I had seen him pause at all. Thus far, he had spoken so quickly after the end of someone's words it was as though he had known long ago what that person would say. Finally, he said, "I don't like my longer name."

"Why?"

"It doesn't suit me."

"Why?"

"Persistent thing. And curious. Aren't you curious? Come closer, and you'll see me better, too." His voice, husky yet light, had lowered a little.

"A cheap trick." He had dropped his voice to a whisper with the intention to make me instinctively draw nearer.

"But if a trick is so obvious, is it really a trick? If I know that you will know it? I think it's *trusting*, actually. If I trust you to see through my trick then I have placed great faith in your intelligence."

"Flattery."

"Honesty!"

"Flattery disguised as honesty."

"Flattery just means that I like you."

"You don't know me," I said. "You are playing a game, and it is with me."

There was a mortified silence. "I didn't mean to. It was silent here before you came. That's no excuse, I know. Should I be quiet? I can be. It will be hard."

"No." Like him, I didn't want the frightening silence of the prison. His voice was supple and clever. It hid the corridor's empty echo. It meant I wasn't alone.

"Will you tell me your name?" he asked. "I have given you mine."

He hadn't, not really, but: "Nirrim," I said.

"Nirrim," he repeated. "No last name?"

I was confused. "What is a last name?"

"True, they are not used in Ethin. But you seem different from other people here, so I thought maybe you were different in other ways, too."

I didn't want to ask how he found me different. I didn't like that he knew that I was. I had tried so hard, since what had happened to Helin, not to be different. I said, "I have never heard of a last name."

"In other places, in some countries, people have last names."

"What other places?"

"Do you want me to tell you about them?"

I felt ashamed that I knew so little of anything outside the Ward, and that a Middling knew so much more than I did of the world. He wasn't even High Kith. "No," I said.

"All right," he said easily. "Nirrim." His voice grew conspiratorial. "What did you *do* to be here?"

It was my turn to be silent. I remembered the militiaman falling to the pavement below. I remembered the exact cadence of his cry.

"Is it that bad?" Sid said.

"No," I said immediately. "It's not that bad."

"I believe you."

"I am not a bad person."

"Nirrim." There was surprise in Sid's voice. I had spoken loudly, with enough vehemence that I wanted to clap a hand over my mouth. Slowly, he said, "I never thought you were a bad person."

My good girl, Raven sometimes called me, and I was always so proud, and thought that maybe if I was good enough, she would adopt me as her true daughter.

Sid said, "Never mind, if you don't want to say."

"I stole a bird."

"A bird?" I couldn't see the expression on his face, but imagined his brows lifting.

"Not *stole*. Not really. I found it. I gave it back." I explained as best as I could.

"I'm not sure I understand," he said.

"You should. You're a thief yourself."

"I'm not."

"No?"

"No," he said. "I was *accused* of theft."

His tone made me doubt he was completely innocent. "What did you really do?"

"Are you easily shocked?"

"I don't know."

He was amused. "Will you tell me if I shock you?"

"Why would you care," I said, "if you shock a Half Kith?"

"It's important to me to know."

"Did you murder someone?"

"No! What kind of person do you think I am?"

I was quiet at that.

He said, "I took a lord's lady to bed."

"Oh."

"The husband came home. He got quite an eyeful. He wanted to punish me, and I can hardly blame him. It was quite obvious that she liked what I was doing far better than whatever he typically did for her. Now, he didn't want what I had done to be widely known. It would shame him, you see. How to solve his dilemma? Accuse me of theft, clap me in the local prison, and there I am punished and gotten well rid of."

"You didn't tell the militia the truth."

"I would never."

"To protect the lady's honor?"

"I am not interested in honor."

"Then why not?"

He thought about it. "I wanted to see what she would do."

"And she said nothing."

"Nothing at all."

"Did that hurt you?"

"No," he said, but I didn't quite believe him.

"Did you love her?"

"I am not interested in love. I did what I did with her because I wanted her and she wanted me." He seemed to mull it over. "I suppose I am disappointed. She could have told the truth. She didn't. I thought her more courageous than that. Oh, well."

"Oh, well?"

"So I *have* shocked you."

"You let yourself be thrown in *prison*."

"It's not so bad. I have you."

"I don't think you realize how serious your situation is."

"To tell the truth, I was tempted to see what prison was like."

Disbelief and anger knitted into a ball in my belly. "What was your sentence? Your tithe?"

"Tithe?"

"The fine."

"There was no fine."

I hadn't realized that only Half Kith had to pay for a crime. The ball in my belly hardened to stone.

He said, "I saw them take your blood."

"Of course."

"Of course," he repeated, drawing out the words, a question in his tone. "That's what you mean by a tithe."

"I was lucky."

"It could have been worse?"

"Much worse." I thought of the guard in my cell and perhaps Sid did, too, because he said, "I see. The law here is strange."

"It is as it is."

"You people always say that. Such an empty thing to say. What does it even mean, really?"

You people. And he was only Middling, not even High Kith. I was sick of the differences that ruled my life. I was sick of his arrogance, his curiosity, his light, fluid voice. I was sick of a world that would keep me in this cell, blood drained every day, when he would probably go free with everything that belonged to him still in his possession.

"Nirrim?"

Let him talk to himself, if he was so bored. He, who could insult a guard and get away with it. How could he do such a thing, even as a Middling?

He said, "I have offended you."

I didn't like how he could read me so easily without even seeing my face.

"I'm sorry," he said.

I backed into a corner of the cell. There was no pallet, only a bucket. It comforted me to think that he had nothing more than I did here. He, too, would have to relieve himself in a waste bucket and live with the stink.

Quietly, he said, "I *am* interested in honor. I just wish I weren't."

I did not care.

"Yes, the lady cared about her reputation. Yes, I stayed silent so that no one else would know about her and me. *She* led me to her bedroom, Nirrim. And then we were caught, and she was ashamed. Silent. I didn't love her. But yes, it hurt me."

I drew my arms around my knees. Surely he couldn't be surprised that the woman was embarrassed. She was married. And if he had been thrown into prison for it, well, maybe he would learn that he, too, shouldn't want what he couldn't have.

"I know that prison is different for you than for me," he said. "It was stupid of me to forget that, and act like that difference isn't important. Please forgive me."

The cold had spread through my body and had gone down to my bones. I missed my coat. I missed Raven. I thought of Annin and her hope for the bird, and what she would say if I told her what had happened. I thought of her sky-colored eyes widening, lighting up. I wished I were home. I wished I were safe. "I'm tired," I said.

"Sleep, then."

I shook my head, even though he couldn't see. "The guards might come back."

"They won't."

"Because they'll check the roster for your name?" I said it with sarcasm.

"Yes," he said simply.

"Who are you, that you think yourself so important?"

He was quiet. When he spoke, I thought he would remind me that if we were not in prison, I would be punished for speaking so rudely to an upper kith. But he said only, "I will wake you if they come back."

"You didn't answer my question."

"Go to sleep, Nirrim. I'll stay awake. They won't come back, and if they do they will do nothing to you. And I will wake you anyway, so that you'll see that they will do nothing to you."

"You will?"

"Yes."

My mind didn't believe him, but my body did, or at least it was so weary that it was already giving in to his promise. My head lowered to my folded arms. I dreamed, before I fell into true sleep, that I was still talking with Sid, but couldn't hear what we were saying even as we said it.

12

I WOKE SUCKING IN AIR, choking on it. I sat up from the stone floor in terror.

"Nirrim?"

I heard a rustle from Sid's cell and his steps as he approached his bars. The footfalls were light. They sounded as if they could be mine. He was likely close in size to me. I didn't know why, but that thought soothed me.

"Are you all right?" he said.

"Yes."

"Bad dream?"

I said, "I must have turned onto my side in my sleep."

I heard a soft, tapping sound: maybe his fingers rippling against the bars. "And that gives you nightmares, to sleep on your side?"

It had been that way ever since I had woken up next to Helin's body. "I try not to. Sometimes it happens anyway."

I thought he might press me to answer his question—he *was* pushy—but said only, "I was wondering whether to wake you."

"Did I talk in my sleep?"

"You *did* mention how attractive I am. How very handsome."

"Liar." I felt myself flush. "I can't even *see* you."

"Ah, but you know. Intuitively." Then there was a shifting, impatient sound, and he said, "Ignore me, please. Sometimes I can't help but tease, and you are very teasable. You said nothing. But you were . . . sad. The sounds you made."

I folded my arms around my knees. I couldn't remember the nightmare, but could guess at what it had been. Her cold cheek. Rigid flesh.

"Are you embarrassed?" he said. "Don't be. Think of me as the perfect stranger. You can say anything, do as you please. We are not likely to meet again outside this prison."

"Because you live beyond the wall and I live behind it."

"I suppose, yes, that is true. Also, I plan to leave this island before long."

"Really?"

"Don't get me wrong. I like it here. The city is beautiful. Glittery. As if a god skimmed a great hand over the bright sea to collect its colored reflections of the sun, then tossed it over Ethin. And the parties! So decadent. I especially love this silver-pink wine that makes you tell your true desires. I don't know what I like better: watching people drink it or drinking it myself."

I had never heard of such a wine. Was he making this up? Not wanting to reveal my ignorance about life beyond the wall, I said, "You don't seem like someone who has a problem saying what's on your mind."

"Is that how I seem?"

"You talk a lot."

"I lie a lot, too. Fair warning."

"So why would you let yourself drink this wine at parties? Aren't you worried people will hear your truths?"

"Oh, I drink that wine only when I am alone."

"So you just get drunk and talk to yourself?"

"I am excellent company."

"If it's so nice here," I said, "why do you want to leave?"

"To sail the next ship. See the next land."

"Bed the next lady?"

"How do you know me so well after so brief a time?"

I rolled my eyes.

"Nirrim. Are you rolling your eyes at me in the darkness?"

Not wanting to give him the satisfaction of anything, I said, "I didn't know that Middlings could leave the country."

"I am no Middling."

My silence sounded loud.

"I have shocked you again." He was delighted.

"But your clothes."

"I want to see your face," he said, "the next time I shock you."

"Your clothes," I insisted, "are Middling."

"Do you realize how strange it is, that the country of Herrath has laws about who can wear what kind of clothes? That your kith and clothes must match? *Kith* is such an odd little word. It seems like people use it to mean *clan* or *neighbors* or *family* or *class*. The militia who arrested me called me Middling, too. Not *I*, I said. I just happen to like this jacket's style. They didn't believe me. Not at first."

"You're High Kith?" My voice squeaked on the last word.

"No."

He was enjoying himself so much that I almost wanted to tell him I had just killed a man and he might be next in line.

He said, "What do you think I am?"

I remembered how, earlier, he had used the word *next*. The *next* ship. The *next* land. "You . . . are a traveler?"

"I like how you say that word. It makes me sound so exotic."

"But there are no travelers." I had never even used that word before, I was sure of it. I knew it only from books.

"There are now," he said. "That is the unusual thing about Herrath. It's a small island, true, but my people have been seafarers for generations. Why was Herrath on no map? How is it that we discovered it only earlier this year? It is not even so far from the mainland."

"I don't know." I rubbed my arms. I felt shivery, not just from cold but from my own ignorance. I didn't know anything about a mainland. There was so much I had never seen. The rest of this city, beyond the wall. The beaches, the sugarcane fields. But other countries? A whole world? The vastness of all there was to know made me feel small.

"Some old maps *did* mark this area," Sid said, "but as a vanishing point. A place of shipwrecks, where sailors were lost."

"And you sailed here anyway."

"Impressed by my bravery?"

"Struck by your foolhardiness."

"There were rumors of an island. I wanted to know the truth. Maybe," he mused, "what made your island so hard to find is connected to what brings travelers here now."

"What do you mean?"

"This country has something that no other country does, not in the whole world, so far as we know."

I said, "What do we have?"

"Well, not *you*. Not the Half Kith."

Of course not. Frustrated misery made my throat close. If there was ever anything to have we would not have it. And of *course* Sid would say it so airily. I found myself hating him. I hated his blithe carelessness. I opened my mouth to tell him so when a door down the hall opened with a metallic bark.

It was a soldier, a blood vial in his hand, its thin tubing wrapped around his wrist. He came to my cell. "Arm," he ordered. When I approached the bars, I could not see Sid beyond the soldier's body, and was grateful that this must mean Sid did not have the satisfaction of seeing me. I slipped the arm that hadn't been pricked yesterday through the bars. The soldier was not fastidious in finding a vein. He jabbed away, muttering to himself as I flinched, until the needle slid in properly. I couldn't see the blood flow through the tubing, not in that dim light, but I felt it leave me.

After the soldier had left, I sat in silence. My hand twitched lightly against my knee: a sign of oncoming sleep. I had a near dream: an illusion of a glowing creature the shape of a person but far larger. It had many small hands all over its body, opening and closing in panic.

"Nirrim, are you all right?"

I shook away the illusion. "Just sleepy."

"How much blood did they take from you?"

"A vial."

There was a moment of silence. "That should not be enough to make you sleepy."

"It is as it is."

"I would like never to hear you say that again."

Surprise at his anger cut through my drowsiness, but before I could say anything he said, "*Why* are there kiths? *Why* are some people made to live behind a wall?"

I hunted in my mind for the answer, but hit only blank resistance, as smooth and blind as stone. "I don't know."

"It's strange that you don't know."

"It is?"

"Yes. You should know your own country's history."

"You know yours?"

"All too well," he said. "Don't you *want* to understand why you live the way you do?"

Did I? Sid's questions stirred a sheer, shallow fear within me. I thought about moments when I made a passport for someone else and contemplated making mine. I thought about when I had decided to return the Elysium. Each time, it felt like I might turn into smoke. Like if I took a step that I could not take back, the person I knew myself to be would evaporate. I would no longer recognize myself.

"Never mind." Sid sighed. "Close your eyes."

"Wait," I said, though I was near sleep. "What is it, that Herrath has? That travelers have come here for?"

"Magic," he said.

13

WHEN I WOKE, I THOUGHT maybe I had dreamed the last thing he had said. "Sid?" I whispered, in case he had fallen asleep.

"Here," he said cheerfully. "Still locked up nice and tight."

"Have you slept at all?"

"Grumpy, Nirrim? No need to be."

"You haven't." I *did* sound accusing.

"Not since you arrived, no."

"How is that possible?"

"A Valorian trick."

"Valorian?"

"Yes, from the old Empire." When I stayed silent, he said, "The Empire used to encompass much of the known world through a series of conquests, save the eastern kingdom of Dacra. Twenty-so years ago there was a war. The Empire crumbled. Valoria still exists as a country, but it is greatly reduced."

"Are you from there?"

"No."

"Sid—"

"You have a pretty voice, did you know that? Soft but earnest. Warm, too. Like a steady candle flame."

I ignored the flirtation. He would have flirted with the bars of his cell if I weren't a slightly better option. "You said this city has *magic*."

"I did."

"Like in stories."

"Yes."

"What kind of magic?"

"As far as I can tell, magic that allows you to create fabulous things, like pocket watches that don't tell the time but rather tell you the emotions of the people standing around you. Had I one now, you would be at about the midday point of my pocket watch, and the glowing color at that marking would tell me that you were experiencing a slow but serious and completely understandable attraction to my very self. Of course," he continued over my annoyed sputter, "it is hard to know what magic here *could* do. The focus here is on the production of toys and giddy experiences. I love it."

"And that's why you're here."

"Yes."

"You're a pleasure seeker."

"Such disdain! You make pleasure sound so wrong."

They say that there was magic in this city when the gods still walked among us, that some people were god-touched. They had the favor of those beings, and a shadow of their power. These were vague stories, with the quality of a dream that begins to escape you the moment you describe it. I didn't know how much to trust Sid's words.

But if I had such power, I wouldn't squander it on pocket watches.

It was as if he had read my mind. "Maybe magic could be harnessed to do more worthy things," he said. "Hard to tell. Despite all my winsome sleuthing, I have as of yet been unable to tell how magic works here. Even *who* does it seems a carefully guarded secret."

"And it really exists nowhere else in the world?" Though I shouldn't have been surprised. After all, magic didn't exist behind the wall.

"It does not." Then he paused, considering. "Well. There have been rumors." He dismissed whatever he had been thinking. "Nothing proven. Nothing I've seen. What would you do, Nirrim, with a special gift?"

"I don't know." It can be hard to imagine things beyond your reach. It feels like you will be punished just for wanting what you'll never have.

"You could go beyond your wall."

I could do that already. As far as I knew, none of the documents I had forged, with Aden's heliographs, had ever been rejected by the authorities. I could make one for myself. For years, I had turned the possibility over in my mind.

"You could leave the city," he said. "This island. See the world. You could go to the eastern kingdom of Dacra and float down the canals that flow through its city like silver veins."

Longing bloomed within me like a thin-petaled flower. But I was also afraid.

I told myself to ignore both the longing and the fear. Regardless of how I felt, whether I wanted to leave or feared to leave, I couldn't. If I left, who would forge the documents? I thought of the wide-eyed child whose face was captured on one of the heliographs I had hidden in the rooftop cistern. Who would help her escape beyond the wall, and find a different kind of life where she wouldn't be stolen from her bed in the night?

"No," I said.

There was a silence. "You can't tell me that you like your lot. You've never seen anything beyond your Ward but this prison where your blood is sapped daily because you did a careless lady a good deed by returning her lost pet."

"I just want to go home."

"You mean the Ward."

"Yes."

"The Ward is as large as a small city," he said.

"Yes." I didn't see what its size had to do with anything.

"Is home a home if you can never leave it? You think you're in prison now, but you have been in prison your whole life. It's just big enough that you're able to forget what it really is. Don't you want to see more?"

"I don't want to leave."

This time his silence sounded disappointed. I got the sense that he had thought better of me, and now had no choice but to consider me a coward.

But what did it matter what he thought?

"I like leaving," he said. "It feels wonderful. The newness of what will come next. Like fresh, cool skin beneath my fingertips. Waking upon my last day somewhere, eating my favorite foods, burying my face in my favorite scents. Honeyed half-moons. A bay papered with ships. A song sung in my language. I love everything more when I leave it. Maybe, then, it's the most I'll ever love it."

"What's a language?"

"Pardon me?"

"A language."

There was a pause. "It's what we're speaking now. The words we're using. I'm speaking in your language, Herrath. There are many others in this wide world. I have a gift for learning them. Yours is especially easy for me because it so closely resembles Herrani. Your language . . . seems like an ancient version of mine."

"Say something in Herrani."

He murmured a stream of sounds that were soft but gently pointed in places, like meringue. "What did you say?" I asked.

"Tadpoles become tadfrogs."

"Tadfrogs?"

"It's what I called frogs, when I was little. My mother still teases me about it."

"A mother." It was good, probably, that I would never see Sid again, since every minute in his company only confirmed my impression of him as wholly different from myself: a young man from nowhere I'd ever seen, who knew things I didn't, who had a mother. "What is she like?"

"The worst! Always in my business, always telling me what to do."

I thought of Raven. "I have someone like a mother."

"I'm glad. I don't like to think of you alone in the world. It's good to have a mother to resent."

I chafed my bare arms. What would I do with a mother? I found myself longing to be asked to do a chore. To bring a glass of water. I imagined myself as a toddler and placing a hand on her knee, balancing the way I had seen children do, fingers curling for support. I could not envision her face.

"Nirrim?"

"I wish the ice wind would break." I didn't want to talk about mothers. "The guards stole my coat."

"Take mine."

"Then you'll be cold."

"I am made of stern stuff. Very strong. Stoic. What need have I of warmth?"

"Or sleep."

"Exactly."

"You can do without all pleasures and comforts of life, I'm sure."

"Well, not *all* pleasures."

"Let me guess which kind."

"Oh, we both know. Nirrim, come take my coat."

By the light of the lantern, I saw the shadow of his coat pushed through the bars. His face was still in darkness, but I could see his long, slender fingers dangling the dark coat.

"No, thank you."

"So proud," he said, "and so cold."

Well, and what could he take from me? I'd snatch the coat from him. He'd never see it again, and I'd be warm.

As soon as I approached the bars, however, I drew my reaching hand back, startled. He was still cast in shadow, the lines of his face blurred like pencil beneath my smudging thumb. Yet the orange glow of the corridor's lamp showed that he was not a liar in at least one respect. He *was* handsome. A quirked smile on his lips said that he knew I had seen it. Dark eyes that tipped up at the corners. A smooth sweep of his cheek. Mouth twisted with mirth. He was taller than me, though not greatly, and narrower than I had expected. It was easy to forget he was behind bars. It was easy to believe he could tempt a married woman into bed. Any woman.

I grabbed the coat. "Happy with yourself?"

"Always."

I shrugged into the coat. It was only a little too big, and warm. It was a color Middlings were allowed to wear, cobalt blue. If the blue were any brighter, only a High Kith could wear it.

"You smell like bread and sweat. And something green," he said musingly. "Like crushed grass. What have you been up to?"

I didn't want to think about clinging to the flowering indi vine while the soldier fell. I buttoned the coat. A fine perfume lingered in its fabric. "Well, *you* smell like a woman."

"Hardly surprising."

I tried to imagine the woman he had been caught with. Frail features. Long auburn hair. Exquisitely pretty. Yes, he would enjoy someone like that. I thumbed the coat's last button into its hole.

"Ah, better," he said.

I lifted my head, shaking hair out of my eyes. "What is?"

"My view of you."

I looked at him through the murk of the prison corridor. He smiled halfway. He said, "You are almost exactly as I believed."

"Almost?"

"I'll tell you how sometime."

"Why not now?"

"You are too far away. This is something better whispered."

"It is a good thing," I said, "that you are behind bars."

He laughed. "You look so serious."

I pulled away from the bars and out of the corridor's wan lamplight.

"I like it," he said.

I could smell the scent of his skin on the coat beneath the woman's perfume. I had seen the flash of his bare arms in the darkness. "You must be cold," I said. "I'm glad."

"Are you smiling when you say this?"

It was as if nothing I could say would bother him, as if he were coated with glass. Everything would slide right off him. I realized, with an unhappy spike in my belly, that I had wanted him to have been as arrested by my face as I was by his.

I had wanted to keep staring.

I wanted to reach the lamp and add oil, make the flame burn higher so that I could see if his eyes were truly dark or only looked dark in the darkness. Maybe, if I saw him better, I would understand why he fascinated me.

He said, "I would like to see you smile."

I said nothing, and he fell quiet, too, until I heard a rustle and what sounded like a suppressed yawn.

I said, "I heard that."

"You heard nothing! I am never tired!"

"Liar."

"Tell me a bedtime story, then."

"I am no storyteller."

"Tell me something about you."

I folded my arms around me. The coat was nicely made. Its warmth made me relax a little, despite my surroundings, despite the disquieting prisoner across the hall. "I am a baker." I heard how small that sounded, how insignificant I must seem.

"Tell me more."

I am a forger, I thought, but said nothing.

"Tell me something you like," he said.

"Sweet things," I said. "Apples."

"Tell me why you like them."

I was quiet.

"Nirrim, I am very tired and so, so cold. I want to fall asleep listening to your lovely voice. It would comfort me. Are you so unkind as to withhold comfort from a fellow prisoner? Your well-wisher? Your provider of coats?"

"Apples remind me of a friend," I said. "I miss her."

"Tell me about her," he said, "so that I may miss her, too."

14

THE BEDS FILED DOWN THE sleeping hall of the orphanage like neat, straight bones. Each night the girls washed their faces and hands and walked silently into the hall, hair braided into a scrawny rope that fell over the left shoulder, identical nightgowns made from stiff twill donated by a generous High-Kith lord and sewn by us. The babies, I told Sid, had crib mates. Sometimes I would pass the infants' wing and see them heaped together like skinny puppies. I longed for it. I could remember when I, too, had slept like that. I know it seems astonishing that I could remember being so tiny, but I did. I remembered how the play of shadow and light from the slats of the crib fell on the nameless baby who breathed shallowly next to me, who would never be named. A shadow fluttered over her chest. A dark moth, I thought, though I had no word for *moth*. Surely it would fly away. I nuzzled closer to her, closed my questing hand around her socked foot.

But one morning when I woke she was gone. A different baby lay in her place, less sickly. She could pull herself to her feet and bite the wooden rail of the crib and howl. This one lived. We slept together until we were four, and separated as they always separate toddlers. We were put into different beds far away from each other. In that first year of separation, I would try to catch up to her during our chores. I'd trip over my learning feet. None of us learned to walk quickly. We had spent too much of our first years in cribs.

Fourth years learned to clean. Easy tasks. I washed tin plateware in tepid water. *Cup* was my first word. I swept corners of rooms and never cried at spiders. I rarely received corrections. Even when I did, the slaps were never cruel.

I would call to my second crib mate. Her name was hard for me to pronounce and I had no words for what I wanted to say, like *friend* or *sister* or *love*. She did not recognize me. Unless she did, and ignored me. People say that they forget faces, but I never do. How can you forget a face? I understood, soon enough, that the first baby in my crib had died, because I never saw her face again, and I had looked.

I don't want you to think that I was lonely. I was surrounded all the time by people. I was busy, because our work required more attention when we became fifth years, then sixth, and seventh. We carved shells into buttons and learned to operate machines that punched holes through the blank disks. It was only later that I didn't like the work we were made to do in the orphanage. When I was much older we had to prepare tortoiseshell. This meant holding the live tortoise while prying the scutes from its back with a hot knife. I often lost my grip on the animal because of the blood. The tortoises gasped and squirmed. I remember things too well. I always have. I remember doing double work beside Helin because she couldn't bear what we had to do and I could.

The tortoiseshell, after it was boiled in salt water and pressed flat with a hot iron, was beautiful. Its mottled brown glinted with gold. The flakes were carved into combs or buttons or decoratively set in furniture. We were told to be proud of what we did. It was for the High Kith.

But we are the tortoises, I said to Helin under my breath.

Our mistress lashed Helin's palm for it. I protested. She did nothing wrong, I said. It was me. I was the one who whispered.

But she listened, the mistress said.

The more I tried to argue that I should receive the punishment, the more the mistress punished Helin.

You think it is unfair that she is punished for what you did? the mistress asked me once she stopped and sent Helin back to work. She said, This is how the world is. The sooner you know it, the better.

Her eyes had a hard polish to them. She was Half Kith like the rest of us.

This is sometimes how I see Helin in my mind, I told Sid. Her left palm lifted to the level of her face, head bowed, thin shoulders twitching at the fall of the slender baton in the mistress's hand.

It was because I let you do my work, she later said to me, wrapped hand cradled to her chest. The mistress saw me let you.

I think Helin meant to comfort me, to take blame when I believed she bore none, but I felt all the more guilty. I could tell, from her tight face and skittish eyes, that she felt guilty, too. Maybe this was what the mistress had meant: that there is no possible way to understand fairness and guilt when your world has already determined a set of rules that don't make sense.

Helin said she liked that I saw things no one else did, but this was no great asset of mine, and I did not share the fact of them with Sid. The visions were something I had learned to ignore: a shimmer of a fountain in the orphanage's bare brick courtyard. As a young child, I'd go to the fountain and open my mouth to taste. My tongue touched only air. I'd look again. Nothing. No fountain. No curved jets of fresh water flowing from marble fingertips, gathering in a pool at the sculpture's marble feet, a mosaic puzzle of colored tiles below the surface.

I'd realize that all the other girls were staring. They avoided me. Of course they did. The orphanage, while plain, with whitewashed interior walls, was a vast structure amply able to hold us all, with space enough for us to avoid one another if we wished.

For Helin, though, the things I saw were a source of pleasure. Like books, I suppose. Or theater, for the High Kith. To her it was an appealing strangeness. A difference from the daily work and fatigue and bland, wholesome food. Harmless, she said, and I came to believe this because I trusted her. They are dreams, she said, except that you have them while you are awake. I will tell you what's real.

She always did. She never laughed.

A wasting sickness came to the orphanage, I told Sid. Purple shadows under the eyes were the first sign, then a rash all over the body, rough red dots on the face. The signs were obvious. We all soon knew the symptoms and what came next. Dizziness. Lack of appetite. Dry, cracked lips. Oozing eyes. Many girls died, especially at first, and although no Middling or High-Kith doctors would enter the orphanage for fear of contagion, medicine was delivered that eased and sometimes cured the plague.

One night, at dinner, I glimpsed red speckles on the pale underside of Helin's light brown arm. It's nothing, Helin said, and shifted her arm away.

After we were supposed to be asleep in our own narrow beds, I went to hers. I touched her cheek. You're warm, I said.

I'm not, she said.

I will get the nurse, I said.

No, she told me. I'm just tired. I want you to lie next to me.

She shifted over to make room. We were both small enough to fit together in the bed. It was wrong, what we were doing. If we were caught there would be trouble. Girls are not meant to sleep with girls, we had been told. Boys do not sleep with boys.

Yet I was a child, and I remembered the comfort of a crib mate. I longed for it. Her skin was fiery with fever. When I told her so, she told me that wasn't true. She told me that I was imagining things. She had promised to explain always what was real and what wasn't, and I shouldn't worry, she insisted. Stay with me, she said. I just want to sleep, she said, and it felt so nice, so comforting to hold her, that I fell asleep even before she did.

When I woke up, she was cold and hard. A balloon of fear rose from my belly to my mouth.

She was gone. That was what the mistress said when she came running in response to my cry. She pulled me from the bed. The sheet tangled in my legs. Was she feverish? the mistress demanded. I don't know, I said. Why didn't you call to someone during the night? she said. I don't know, I answered, but I did know. It was because I was incapable of seeing something for what it truly was.

The mistress was not unkind. I wasn't punished for sleeping in Helin's bed.

I had to be sequestered, of course, out of fear that I too would come down with the wasting sickness. But I never fell sick.

This much I told Sid, but I didn't tell him about the grief clenched tight in my chest. How loneliness was a bone caught in my throat. How sometimes I remembered Helin's shallow breath on my face. I wondered what I had been dreaming, in my unforgivable sleep, when she breathed her last breath.

But I could not have been dreaming. If I had, I would remember the dream like I remember everything else, like I remember her.

15

I HAD NEVER TOLD ANYONE about Helin. I told Sid because I would never see him again, and because missing her felt like a full, heavy bowl I carried inside me. Usually I feared that speaking about her would be a way of spilling the bowl's contents, and I did not want to. I wanted to keep what I had of her.

But it was tempting, listening to Sid's lightheartedness, knowing that he was lucky. Life had treated him gently. His hands, surely, would be as smooth as his voice.

What would it be, to feel a little lighter? To be like him?

So I told him, and discovered that as soon as I poured the bowl out, it filled right back up.

There was silence for a long time after I spoke. I assumed he had fallen asleep.

I felt a mix of resentment and relief. Maybe it was best that he hadn't heard me, or hadn't heard the whole story. I huddled in his coat and imagined his closed eyes, head back against his stone wall, the way sleep might soften his mouth.

He said, "I'm sorry."

"Oh. I thought you were sleeping."

"Nirrim." He sounded startled. "I would never."

"Well, you are tired."

"Do I seem that callous?"

"Not *callous*."

"What, then?"

I thought about his desire to leave places. How he disliked his mother for interfering. His flirtation, which had the ease of long habit. "You seem hard to hold, I guess. Your attention."

He took a moment to reply. "That might be true, usually. But you hold mine."

Though he wouldn't see the gesture from where he sat, I swept a palm to indicate my cell and his. "You *are* a captive audience."

"Nothing is making me talk with you, or listen to you, beyond the fact that I want to."

I ducked my chin into his overlarge coat and felt the collar rub against my mouth.

He said, "Your friend sounds kind. Like you."

"But it was because of me."

"It was not because of you that she died. Have you been holding on to that idea ever since? It's not true."

"I should have known better."

"You were a child."

"I shouldn't have trusted her when she said that she was all right."

He was frustrated. "You trusted her because she was your friend and we believe what friends tell us. Trust *me*, Nirrim."

I couldn't expect him to understand. I hadn't told him about my visions.

"I'm sorry you lost your friend," he said. "I'm sorry you miss her. But I want you to trust me when I tell you that you did nothing wrong."

"You warned me that you're a liar," I reminded him.

"Not about this."

I didn't believe him. It was such a relief, though, to imagine the possibility that I *could*, so I said nothing to contradict him. I said nothing about the signatures I had forged, the legitimate documents whose words I made fade, then overwrote with new names, new physical descriptions. I said nothing about hearing the body's fall, or how blood leaked from it like thick red ink. It was so nice to accept, even if only for the moment, Sid's impression of me. Kind. Blameless. I liked his image of me so much I wanted to let it grow like a small fire.

He said, "May I tell you a secret?"

"What if I say no?"

"Unacceptable. I hate the thought of you saying no to me."

There were no windows to the outside. I had no idea whether it was night or day, or what the weather was like beyond cold. But his lowered voice made me imagine snow falling outside the prison, dusting lightly over stone. I imagined sitting beside him, my shoulder brushing his.

"It's not allowed, you see," he said. "You must always say yes."

He talked the way I bet Aden wanted to talk, but Aden would mean it and Sid didn't. Sid spoke lightly, as though he wanted his words to be easy for me to shrug away if I didn't like them.

Sid was entitled and nosy. And kind. Ready to laugh, even at himself. I didn't like everything that he said, but I liked him.

"What if," he said, "you agree to say yes to me three times only. A mere three times! In return, I shall do something for you."

Warily, I said, "What?"

"A favor."

"A favor?"

"I give very good favors."

Since I wouldn't see him again outside of this prison and there was little I could say yes to inside of it that I would regret, I said, "Yes, I agree to your bargain, which is already one time, and yes, I agree that you can tell me your secret, which makes twice."

He made an amused sound. "I had better cherish my last yes. I had better use it wisely."

"Go on, tell me your secret."

"I ran away from home."

"Why?"

"I suffered terribly there."

"Suffered! You *are* a liar." He hadn't suffered a day in his life.

"You have no idea," he said, "what a delight it is to annoy you. I could annoy you all day."

"*That* I believe."

"You see," he said, "my parents thought it was time that I should marry. They said, *When will you be serious?*"

"My guess is never."

"Exactly. *When will you grow up? Also never.*"

"Do they have someone in mind?"

"Oh yes."

"Someone you like?"

"Oh no."

"Someone you despise?"

"I don't despise anybody. I am simply not made for marrying."

I almost asked that he describe the woman his parents wanted for him, but a small, ugly feeling stopped me. I became aware again of the perfume on his coat. "You would seduce women anyway, even if you were married."

He sighed. "It wouldn't be the same."

"Does your family know where you are?"

"Not yet. I hope to keep it that way."

"Maybe you should just marry," I said. "Make them happy."

"But I can't." He sounded perplexed. "You must understand why I can't."

"I would make my parents happy, if I had parents."

"You would marry a man your parents had chosen? Someone you didn't love, and never could?"

I shrugged. "Yes."

"I thought—"

"What?"

"I thought you and I had more in common than we do."

"We have nothing in common."

"All right," he said. "If you say so."

"Honestly, your dislike of marriage is an excuse."

"Really." For the first time he sounded prickly. "In what way, pray tell?"

"Everything to you is an adventure. Being *in prison* is one. You wanted an excuse to run away."

He started to speak, but the gated door at the end of the hall clanked and creaked. Sid said something swift and angry under his breath in his language, but kept silent when the guard came to collect my blood. Swiftly, I took off Sid's coat so that the guard wouldn't notice I was wearing something beyond my kith. I offered my arm through the bars. The needle went right into the bruise that had already formed on my inner right elbow.

"Leeches," Sid muttered after the guard left with a vial of my blood. "And now you'll sleep, and I won't be able to argue with you."

It was true; I was instantly drowsy. Shivering, I tucked myself back into Sid's coat. "My sentence is for a month. Maybe yours is, too, and we can argue until we are released."

"A month? They are going to drain your blood every day for a *month?*"

"I hope so. Sometimes they keep prisoners longer than they say they will. Some people never come out of prison."

His silence seemed stunned. I closed my eyes. I curled into his coat and drifted toward sleep.

"I want you to think that what my parents would force me to do is wrong," I heard him say.

We are all forced to do things, I almost told him, but I felt too tired.

It occurred to me, belatedly, that Sid had sensed that sturdy bowl of grief inside me when I told him about Helin. Maybe everything that came after—the flirtation, the silly bargain, the secret—had been to distract me when he saw that he couldn't take away my sadness.

I thought I heard him call to the guard.

"It *is* wrong," I murmured to Sid. I didn't mean it. I would do anything for a mother, a father. But I said it again, deciding that I *would* believe it was wrong, for his sake.

16

"NIRRIM, WAKE UP."

There was urgency in Sid's voice. I heard footfalls coming down the hall. I got to my feet. "What is it? What's happening?"

"We're leaving," he said.

I was confused. "To go where? A different part of the prison?" Fear rose within me. "Why? What will they do?"

"Nothing. Don't be afraid. They are letting us go."

The footfalls came closer.

"That's not right." I began to doubt whether I was awake or had somehow slept for nearly a month. "How long have I been here?"

"Three days."

"Then my sentence isn't over."

"Now it is. I promised you a favor."

A pair of guards unlocked our cells and we were led through the prison's maze to a dimly lit office that seemed out of place: the size of a large cell, but with a thick rug on the floor, its pattern like interlaced fingers of many colors, and a tiny man behind a desk with a sputtering oil lamp. I wasn't sure where to rest my eyes. I could feel Sid beside me, taut with energy. Behind the tiny man at the desk, a window glowed silver. It was the moonlight. It was like mercury. It was so strong that I finally believed Sid: it had truly been only three days since the full moon and the festival celebrating its god, one of the few gods this city remembered.

The man at the desk looked through my passport and stamped one of the booklet's pages with a *T* for Tybir, the name of the prison. Sid had no documents, which was strange to see. I had never met anyone with no documents. There was, however, a letter that the man behind the desk read several times, looking up occasionally at Sid. Finally, the man scrawled something at the bottom of the page but did not stamp it. He folded the single page along its already creased lines and rose from his seat to hand it carefully to Sid. The man said, "Your—"

"None of that," Sid said. "My stay here was delightful, I assure you."

The man seemed flustered. Belatedly, I realized I was wearing Sid's coat. Worried I would be punished, my gaze darted between the man behind the desk and the guards, but they paid no attention to me. They stared at Sid. The air prickled with their fascination.

Sid strode past the desk to the door beyond it. He pulled it open. Warm night air wafted in, fragrant with flowers. The ice wind had broken. "After you, Nirrim."

"Really? We're leaving?"

"Yes. I've had enough."

The prison door shut behind us. The night was still. The moon was a large mirror, its light so bright that when I pushed up the sleeve of my—Sid's—coat, I could see the bruises on my inner arm. The wall was as white as polished marble in this light, though I knew by day it was pocked gray granite. A gate in the wall was flanked by guards, but I was already in the Ward. It was Sid who would pass through the gate to the rest of the city. "What did you do," I asked him, "to get them to release me early?"

"Isn't it more fun to guess than to know?" he said, and I finally turned to look at him.

I could see Sid more clearly now. I saw the mistake I had made.

Sid's face was even more striking in the moonlight: severe cheek-bones set in an unexpectedly soft face with a softly lined mouth, and eyes so dark they must be black. Short fair hair, which I had never seen before—no Herrath had light hair. Sid was a little taller than me, but not if I were to stand on tiptoe. I was struck, as I had been before, by Sid's beauty, but it wasn't that which stole my breath. It was the tunic Sid wore: sleeveless, as I had noticed before in the prison, showing bare, slender arms. What I had not seen then, and could see now, was that the tunic was tight enough that it showed the curve of her breasts.

"Oh," I said.

She lifted her brows.

My mind scurried back through our conversations. "I thought you . . ." I couldn't finish my sentence.

"You thought what?" She frowned, studying my face. Then her expression eased—not in a relaxed way, but rather into tired lines. "I see," she said. "Well, that's no fault of mine."

"I didn't say—"

"I can't help what you assumed. Did I say I was a man?"

"No." My face grew hot as I newly understood things she *had* said.

"Disappointed?"

"No," I said hastily. "Why would I be?"

"Indeed, why." Her shrug was extravagant, her long hands unfurling as if flicking away water after washing. Her black eyes strayed from mine to the wall. I had the impression that I had vanished, or diminished. I felt the impulse to apologize but sensed that the apology might grate more than the mistake, which seemed less to offend than to disappoint her, as though I had become suddenly far less intriguing. There was a pain in my chest, small and sharp as the snap of fingers.

It wasn't normal to feel pain at any of this.

It wasn't normal to feel drawn to her—not in the way I now knew I had been.

I started to shrug out of her coat. "Here," I said. "Thank you."

"Keep it. I don't need it now."

The warm night air was as soft as suede, salty from the harbor I had never seen.

"The ice wind might come again," I said.

"I'll be gone before it does." Then, with a twist of her mouth that seemed decided to be amused, she brushed my shoulders and tugged at the hem of the coat to straighten any wrinkles. The gesture felt at once affectionate and dismissive. "It suits you. Even if it's a little big." She placed a palm against my cheek. I started at her touch. She dropped her hand.

Later, I wished that I had called to her, that I had said I missed her as soon as she turned to walk away. I wished she had seen how I brought my hand to my cheek. Her touch shivered down my back.

It lingered long after she passed through the wall's gate.

17

THE INSIDE OF THE TAVERN was darker than the moonlit night. It took a moment for my eyes to adjust, and when I did I saw Annin asleep at a table, hair spilling over her arm. I was surprised to find her there, and wondered if she had been too tired from work that night to return to her room. I tried to shut the door quietly behind me, but the iron bolt was heavy. It thunked into place.

Annin stirred. She lifted her head from the table, rubbing her mouth. Then she saw me and stared. "Nirrim? Is that really you?"

"Shh," I said, but she bounded from the table to pull me into her arms.

"We were so worried." She pressed her hands to my cheeks, searching my face. "Are you all right?"

"Yes." When she hugged me again, her face brushing mine was wet with tears. Was it wrong to feel a small pleasure? I hadn't known she cared so much.

"What did they take?"

"Just my blood. You must be quiet. You will wake—"

"You're here, you're safe! They will want to know." She called for Raven and Morah. There came the sound of stumbling, the thin complaint of wooden doors. A nimbus of lamplight floated down the stairs before I saw any feet. Morah's first—bare, like Annin's—then Raven's slippers.

Morah stared when she saw me. "Three days only? Your face . . . where did you pay?" She looked ready to open my coat, to rummage over my body until she found the damage she was sure they must have left.

Raven approached me, her slippered tread heavy.

I thought of you, I wanted to tell her, when I was in prison. I thought of how afraid you must be.

But I would never betray you. I would never tell anyone what we do. How you find people who want help, and I forge their freedom.

You can always trust me.

She lifted the oil lamp to my face. "Not a mark," she said.

"No. I—"

"That coat." She gestured with the lamp at Sid's jacket, which I had not removed despite the heat. "You stole a Middling coat? You broke the sumptuary law? You fool."

"I didn't, I—"

She swung the oil lamp. It smashed against my cheek. I felt a lick of hot pain. I heard cries. I clapped a hand to my blazing cheek.

"How dare you," Raven said. "After all these years, after all the care I put into you."

I shrank back from her, glass cracking under my sandals. "The coat has nothing to do with it. Please, listen to me." I babbled the story of what had happened.

"You caught the bird?" Annin's voice was filled with wonder.

Raven turned to look at her and Morah. "Go to your rooms."

"But Nirrim," Annin said. "You have burned her!"

"Now," Raven said.

Annin protested, wide-eyed, but Morah took her by the hand and tugged her up the stairs.

"Oh, my girl," Raven said once we were alone. Her shoulders sagged. Her gentle face was lined with misery. "I am so sorry." She reached to touch my burned cheek. I flinched, I couldn't help it, and when I saw her eyes shine with sudden tears I felt guilty. I stooped to gather the shards of the lamp. She stopped my shaking hands. "Leave it," she said, and sounded so heartbroken that I began to cry, I said I was the one who was sorry, could she forgive me.

"Yes, of course," she said. "Come, sit. I will help you, and you will tell me everything." She fetched salve and a clean rag and a bowl of cool water. "Ah, no glass in the skin. That's good." She stroked the dripping cloth over my hot cheek. Water dribbled into my hair. "There. With any luck, you won't even scar." She smoothed the tingling salve over the burn. I gasped with relief. "You said nothing about the documents?"

"Never," I said. "I swear."

"Do you swear upon the gods?"

"Yes."

"Who was this person? That girl."

It felt strange to hear Sid referred to as a girl. I hadn't mentioned to Raven and the others that I ever thought her anything else.

It had been a mistake. I make them all the time.

Usually I see things that are not there. This time, I had not seen something that was.

But she had known what *I* was. She had been flirting with me.

And I had liked it. A flush in my cheek burned beneath the lamp-oil burn. A confused, private feeling bundled itself up inside me. It curled around the idea of her.

"She is no one," I said. "A stranger."

Raven smoothed my damp hair behind my ears so gently that I felt tired, ready to lay my head in her lap, if I dared, and sleep.

"You said the bird came to you," she said slowly.

"Yes," I said, and she was silent. Then she said, "Let's keep the matter of the Elysium to ourselves."

Of course. It would only bring unwanted attention.

"Sweet child," she said. "I was so frightened. Do you understand why I reacted the way I did? I had thought I'd lost you."

"It's all right."

"I love you," she said.

She had never said this to me before. Her words made me yearn for her love even though she had just offered it, as if my feelings were late, too slow to believe what she had said, or as if it was only now that I had her love that I could let myself actually feel the need for it. I have someone like a mother, I had told Sid. I hadn't been sure of my claim's truth. But it was true. I was so grateful.

I told her I loved her, too. She guided me upstairs as though I were half my age. She tucked me into my bed, just like a real mother, and tsked when she lightly touched my throbbing cheek. "You must see to that in the morning," she said. When she lost her temper, and hurt me, she was always so tender afterward, as though I were her treasure. It felt so good that it was almost worth being punished. And didn't parents correct their children, so that they would learn?

She stood in the moonlight, ready to leave, Sid's coat tucked in the crook of her arm.

"Wait," I said. "The coat. May I keep the coat?"

A flicker of annoyance crossed her face.

"Please," I said.

"What's the use? You can never wear it."

"I like it. Maybe," I stammered, "maybe Annin could help me alter it. Dye it."

"Well, you know, you did lose *my* coat. This one is just my kith." She must have seen the distress in my face. "Oh, very well." She returned to lay the coat across the foot of my bed. "You'll have quite a job making it look fit for a Half-Kith woman. But if it's what you want."

"Yes," I said gratefully.

She kissed my brow. "I would do anything for you."

After she left, I shifted into a sitting position in my bed, though moving at all made my cheek pound. I slipped my fingers into the inner pocket of Sid's coat and withdrew the crimson-and-pink Elysium feather that had fallen three days ago when I was on the roof, and that I had plucked from the gutter after leaving the prison. I had climbed back to the roof in the moonlight. I had collected the wet heliographs from the cistern, slipping the tin squares into my pocket.

The feather seemed to glow. Its quill was opalescent. I tucked it into my shirt, right above my heart. It tingled against my skin.

I lay back down and drew Sid's coat over my chest like a blanket. I wondered where she was. I tried to picture what she was doing beyond the wall, and couldn't. I remembered her voice and her face and her scent, though the coat didn't smell like her, not anymore.

~ 18 ~

"THAT *WILL* LEAVE A SCAR," Morah said in the morning when she dressed the burn.

"It's not so bad." I could feel it. The hot oil had left a thin streak down the hollow of my cheek.

She shook her head. "You can't see how it looks." We didn't really have mirrors in the Ward, except when we stole a glance in a polished steel plate or visited Terrin, who made lavish mirrors to sell beyond the wall. Some were so large they looked like sheets of still water. It was unsettling to visit Terrin's shop, to see myself refracted. I didn't like being surrounded by myself. Raven had little business with her, so I had been sent there only once to barter for a handheld dressing mirror, which was Raven's right as Middling to own. I offered what Raven had suggested: four blue duck eggs, which seemed too small a price to me. I could see, reflected all around me, embarrassment creeping pink into my cheeks. Terrin didn't even let me finish. Of course, she said, and gave me the palm-sized mirror backed with green velvet. She refused to take anything for it. What Raven wants, she gets, Terrin said, and

I flushed again, this time with pride, to see how much someone admired and loved my mistress.

Morah said, "There is a red stripe from your cheekbone to your jaw. You will have it forever."

"It will fade." I didn't like Morah's hard look. She respected Raven and obeyed her, but she didn't care for her. Morah didn't know, any more than Annin did, that Raven and I forged documents to help Half Kith leave the Ward, so I couldn't expect her to understand Raven's reaction.

I touched my chest above my heart, where the Elysium feather lay hidden beneath my shirt. The feather seemed to thrill beneath my touch. "Morah, why does a Lord Protector rule Herrath?"

She capped the pot of salve. "What do you mean, why?"

"How did that come to be?"

She looked at me strangely. "We have always had a Lord Protector."

"But not the same one."

"Of course not. When one dies, he is replaced."

"By the Council."

"Yes. You know this. Nirrim, you are worrying me. What happened to you in prison?"

I thought of Sid's questions, her frustration with *It is as it is.* "I am just thinking. There must have been a *first* Lord Protector. How was he chosen? And why *Protector*? To protect us against what? The rest of the world?"

Confusion crossed her face. "There is only Herrath. There is the Ward and the city and the island and the sea."

"That is not true. There are other countries across the sea. There have been wars."

"War." Morah said the word as if she didn't understand it. "There is no war. There has never been a war. You are making my head hurt."

"But—"

The door to the tavern opened, dumping sunshine across the floor. "Finally up, I see." Raven smiled, a heavy basket slung over each arm. She must have gone to the morning market, which was usually my task. "Little slugabed," she said.

I got to my feet to help her. "I'm sorry."

"Not at all! You needed your rest. Morah." Raven looked at her. Morah hadn't moved from the table where we had sat. Displeasure played along Raven's mouth, but she said only, "No need to rush to help your old mistress. Run to the kitchens. Annin will need help with the day's bread." Once we were alone, she said to me, "Since you've been gone, we've fallen behind on fulfilling our requests. Go to the printer's. He has agreed to loan you his press for a few hours." She slipped a folded piece of paper into my pocket. "Here are the instructions." Her eyes scanned my face. "Are you well enough? I hate to ask you, but we must make haste."

"I want to go." I was eager to feel useful. It was always good to hold the finished documents in my hands. "I want to be outside." That was true, too. Fresh air had crept into the tavern with Raven like the delicate green tendrils of a vine.

Raven smiled and she tipped my chin up. "That burn is coming along very nicely indeed. Soon you won't even know it was ever there."

"Are you sure I should go to the printer's?"

Raven's head reared back. She stared. I had never questioned her before.

"I mean," I said quickly, "it is so soon after my arrest. What if the militia is watching?" I didn't think that the soldier's death would be traced back to me, but I worried.

Her lips thinned. "Are you afraid? Remember: there are people who need our help."

"I know." I felt haunted by the heliographs I had dropped into the cistern the night of the Elysium and later retrieved. I had given them to Raven, but I kept seeing the faces, especially those of the children. I wanted them to have the chance to grow up beyond the wall.

"Risk is part of what we do," Raven said.

I nodded. When I stepped outside into the breezy sunshine, however, a voice in my head whispered, She takes no risks. You are the one risking everything.

But it was not my voice. It was Sid's.

Harvers, the printer, had an arrangement with Raven that went like this: I would exchange a few hours of simple labor for the use of his materials and press. He always praised my work. "So swift," he would say as I assembled the tiny metal letters in the frame of the press. So long as no one had changed the organization of the letters in the type box, I could pluck each letter from the box without even looking, and needed to glance only once at whatever manuscript or typeset page Harvers asked me to print.

It was like Aden's heliographs. The image of each page had been burned in my mind.

The workshop smelled of leather, ink, and ammonia. So did Harvers, whose back was perpetually slumped and his hands gnarled. He was not old, but a malady had taken over his body, causing his hands to shake. Still, he could make the most gorgeous books. I loved to see them lined up on shelves: jewel-toned leather bindings, golden clasps, the titles blind embossed. Inside were illuminated pages and words stamped in gold foil. He never minded me looking, or even reading, although these books were meant to be sold to Middlings, who could not keep them, either, but would sell them to the High Kith at a profit.

That day he asked me to print a book of poetry, one whose first edition was centuries old, he said, and written by a woman. Each poem was a fragment as brief as a breath. "A dirty book," Harvers said with a wink.

Harvers napped in an unvarnished chair in the sun as I assembled the lines of type. I didn't read as I worked. I arranged the words as though they were mere designs with no meaning, and stamped the pages. *Dirty*, Harvers had said, but I ignored the temptation to peek. That would only slow my work.

When I was done with that, I did what I had truly come here to do, and to which Harvers always turned a blind eye. He slept on— or pretended to—while I printed official-looking pages for the travel documents Raven needed me to forge. It was quickly done. I cast sand across the pages to help them dry. It would take some time before I could leave the workshop with the folded documents without fear of the ink smudging.

The poet's book hung in pages like flags from lines strung about the workshop. The tang of ink was sharp and strong. I could tell there were no pictures. This surprised me, given the kind of book Harvers had said it was. The surprise was like a fish hook beneath my ribs, drawing me closer.

There was no harm, I thought. No one was watching me.

I had already broken so many serious laws. I had illegally forged documents. I had killed a man. Reading beyond my kith was nothing in comparison.

And I was surely immune, anyway, to whatever the poet's words said. I had already done what there was to do with Aden.

I stepped close to the ink-wet pages.

Light from the window caught floating dust motes as I moved among the poems, which were about love. The poet's voice was pained, raw with longing. But I couldn't see why Harvers would say the book was dirty, unless he was joking.

Then I realized it was because the love poems were written about a woman.

In my mind I saw the poet and the woman she loved, mouths damp from kissing, limbs tangled together. A flush crept into my cheeks.

It wasn't allowed for a woman to love a woman, at least not in the Ward. It was a shameful thing. I couldn't even guess the tithe.

The Council encouraged Half Kith to marry. Babies are a blessing, we were told. Larger homes were allocated for growing families. Special Council-funded rations were awarded for births. I wasn't sure what a woman did with a woman in bed, but I knew that it didn't make children.

I started to turn from the poems, then paused before a page almost entirely white, with only a few bare black words.

Gold-sandaled dawn
Fell like a thief
Upon me

I wondered what kind of night was so precious that when morning came it felt as if you had been robbed, as if what you wanted most had been cut from you like a bloody tithe.

I had never had a night worth stealing.

I thought about how the poems would be sewn together and bound between leather and sold to a High Kith.

I saw Sid's hand turning the pages.

I saw her coat hanging in my wardrobe.

I remembered the pattern of colored lights I had seen in the city beyond the wall, and Sid's story about a pocket watch that could tell someone's emotions instead of the time. If such a pocket watch could read what I felt then, it would have shown danger.

I wanted to see the rest of the city.

I wanted to see Sid.

I went back to the printing press and finally, after so many years of wondering whether I would ever dare, I began to forge a document for myself.

19

I WAITED UNTIL EVERYONE WAS long asleep. I shrugged into Sid's coat. A reflection of me glowed in the lamplight on my bedroom window, hands moving up the coat as I buttoned it despite the heat. My heart stammered beneath my fingers. The face of my reflection was a black shadow, hair falling forward. I tucked my hair behind my ears and then untucked it, remembering the burn on my cheek.

A passport rested in the coat's inside breast pocket. After printing pages that described false personal details, such as my name and parentage, but my true physical details, I had stitched them into a thin, small booklet using dark blue Middling thread that I had taken from Raven's supplies, which were hidden below a floor tile in the kitchen that sprung gently open when you pressed its edge. The tile was white, but sometimes I thought I saw a shadow of something beneath the glaze, a figure or face. When I said that to Raven the first time she showed me this hiding place, she frowned and said that the tile was pure white and had always been white.

Using a finely pointed pen, I signed the name of a clerk for the

Council, slanting his *L*s and dotting his lowercase double *l*s with short, punctuated flecks that were more dashes than dots. He liked to sweep a complicated filigree below his name, and I remembered perfectly the true signature Raven had shown me, which I had replicated many times for other documents. I traced it on the paper. I glued the heliograph that Aden had made for me into a cardstock frame, which prefaced the pages that would show when and how many times I had passed through the wall's gate, or had left the city. I stamped a handful of dates on those pages for over the past few years, using watered-down blue ink for the older dates, and strong blue for the newer ones. The stamp had been obtained by Raven, as were all the others among her supplies. I didn't know how she managed to get them, whether through theft, money under the table, or favors owed.

Finally, I embossed the thin leather cover with a raised stamp. The pages looked and smelled too new, so I ran a whisk over each page— gently, to soften the paper—and buried the booklet in a bowl of sand to absorb the smell of ink. I kept the bowl under my bed, worried throughout the whole day it sat there that Morah or Annin—or, worse, Raven—would find it.

Raven would be hurt if she discovered what I was doing. I imagined her wounded eyes as she opened my passport. Was I not enough, she would say. What did I do, to make you want to leave?

I don't want to, I would say.

All I wanted was one night.

Just to see.

I will always come back.

Her eyes, however, would glisten. Her sadness would rush through me like storm rain in a gutter. Eventually, her sadness would thicken into anger. I would understand. After all, I had betrayed her. But . . .

One night.

She would never know.

I took the passport from the bowl, shook off the sand, and slid it into the coat pocket. It was rigid and felt heavier than it was, and somehow fragile, as though it were a pane of glass. Anxiety sizzled in my belly. I remembered Sid's words: You've been in prison your whole life.

I buttoned the last button. The coat would cover some of my drab Half Kith clothes, and with any luck the guards at the gate wouldn't discern the color of my trousers in the dark. My body was taut with fear.

I imagined saying to Sid, I bet that you are never afraid.

You left your home.

You sailed to a region marked on a map as dangerous waters.

You let yourself be sent to prison without protest.

Do you know what this feels like? What I feel like?

Come find me, she said in my mind. Ask me for real.

I blew out the lamp. Darkness doused the room. My reflection in the window vanished into black glass.

"Name?"

I kept my eyes down. The guard at the gate wore boots and crease-free trousers, the fabric crisp and red and with blue piping. "Laren." I had chosen a name with a common ending for a Middling woman.

"Occupation?"

"Merchant."

"Wares?"

I brought Annin's empty embroidered bag, the one I had used to capture the Elysium, from my pocket. "It's just a sample. I hope to interest someone in ordering more."

"That's a man's coat."

"My brother's," I said. "I always forget how the temperature drops at night. He loaned me his."

"Look at me."

I brought my gaze up. In the lamplight, the young man's expression was hardened into irritated boredom. "Green," he said disapprovingly.

"Excuse me?"

"This passport says your eyes are hazel. They are not. They are green."

Nervousness bubbled in my stomach. I had never thought of my eyes as green. I had glanced at them briefly, once, in Raven's handheld mirror. The color looked murky and unstable: not quite brown but nothing else easily named. "Hazel," Morah said when I asked.

I touched my chest, where the Elysium feather rested beneath the coat and my shirt. "It's just a trick of the light."

Perhaps the myths about Elysium feathers were true, because his expression softened as he lifted the lamplight to look more deeply into my face. "Pretty eyes," he said. "What's this?" He touched the burn on my cheek. I flinched in pain. "It's not on your heliograph."

"The burn is recent. It happened the other day."

"It *is* fresh." He kept his hand beneath my chin. His face was changing as he stared at me. I resisted pulling away. He said, "How did that happen?"

My mind raced through possibilities. "I was curling my hair." The laws stipulated that only Middling and High-Kith women could have waves or curls in their hair. Usually I straightened mine as best I could, but tonight I had run water through my hair to bring out its natural wave. "The hot tongs slipped."

He brushed a hand through my hair. Was this normal? Did all guards at the gates do this, even to Middlings?

The back of my neck prickled.

A Half Kith would let him touch her. Would a Middling object?

Could she?

I didn't know, so I pretended I enjoyed his touch. I smiled.

"A pity," he said, and his hand fell. He stamped my passport, returned it, and waved me through the gate.

A night market.

A sea of tents and stands clustered together in a labyrinth just beyond the gate. I felt small and easily lost, like a bead dropped to a cluttered floor. Lamps with stained glass in Middling shades of blue swung from ropes that zigzagged overhead. Middlings cried their wares.

Tables were heaped with fruit whose names I did not know. I had never seen their shapes. A woman near me, wearing a dress with a bit of embroidery on the sleeves that marked her as Middling, touched a yellow fruit and smelled it, so I dared to do the same to one with a satiny purple surface that dented beneath my thumb. It smelled dusky and tangy.

"Mind your kith," the fruit seller said.

I quickly set the fruit down.

"Perrins are not for the likes of you," he said. "You know as well as I do that no Middling can eat these. Unless you work for a family in the High quarter and have a writ to prove you're shopping for their kitchens, you have no business even touching this fruit."

"I'm sorry. Please—"

"Ah, child." He smiled a little. "I don't blame you for being curious. I can't eat a perrin, either. Now, *these* are perfectly ripe and just your kith." He gestured at the pile of yellow, oblong fruits that the Middling woman in the embroidered dress had been examining, but I darted away.

There were bolts of cloth whose shades I had never seen, piles of rugs whose intricate patterns overwhelmed my sight. I felt dizzy, like I might lose my way looking at the twists and turns of the woven designs.

I recognized Ward-made wares. I was astonished to pass by a stall laden with children's wooden toys and to see their labeled price. I knew the woman in the Ward who made those. She likely received no more than the barest fraction of the marked price.

At first I worried that someone would look closely and question the coat I wore, or would somehow be able to guess I wasn't the right kith. But everyone was preoccupied with selling and buying. The streets here, I could tell, were newer than in the Ward. The cobblestones were not as worn as behind the wall. At the outskirts of the market square I saw a rank of buildings, higher than anything in the Ward, with diamond-paned windows, flower-twisted balconies, and peaked roofs shingled in dusty red ceramic tiles. My nerves settled somewhat as I walked, and I gave myself over to fascination. If this was how the Middling quarter looked, what would it be like where the High Kith lived?

The city rippled up over the gentle hills around me, a dense patchwork of stone and brick and green vines and, far away, in the High quarter, kaleidoscopic colored glass and the gloss of marble shining in light cast by pink lanterns.

Ethin was vast.

I realized, in the crush of people, that it had been foolish even to hope that I might find Sid. Still, I retraced my steps to the fruit seller, who had seemed kind.

"Oh, you again," he said, friendly enough. "The shy girl in the boy's coat. I thought I had scared you off."

"I wonder," I said, "if you can help me. I'm looking for someone."

He lifted his brows. "A merchant?"

"No," I said, "I don't think so."

"Your sweetheart?"

I flushed. "No."

His smile became wise. "I know that look on your face. Go on. Describe him."

"Her." When he seemed surprised, I added, "She's a friend," though the word felt like it didn't fit. "She's my age, I think."

His brow crinkled. "She's your friend, and you don't know her age?"

"About my height, but a little taller. Large, black eyes. Her hair is short, cut like a boy's, light brown, maybe, or dark gold."

"No one looks like that."

"She's a traveler."

He shook his head. "Those are just rumors. There are no travelers. There is nothing beyond the sea."

I started to argue with him, but a Middling woman in dark green trousers and a green tunic edged with a finger's-width of lace approached and produced a writ fragrant with perfume and latticed with elegant handwriting. The purse that dangled from her wrist was heavy. He immediately turned his attention to her. I left the stand, and wandered.

"Dreams!" someone called. "Dreams for sale!"

I traced the cry to a booth densely surrounded by people.

"Your most deeply held desire! Or a dream of flight? A sweet cat-nap for the timid! A nightmare for the brave! One vial of dream vial for one hundred god-crowns."

"Who would buy a nightmare?" I murmured to myself.

"*They* would," said a voice behind me.

I turned to see a boy, a Middling child whose dark head barely reached my shoulder. His light eyes looked up into mine, then flicked left. I followed his gaze to see two young men approaching the stall.

High Kith. One wore close-fitting trousers in Elysium crimson; the other's hand flashed with a large emerald ring. Though I was far away, I could tell that his ear glinted with more jewels, and his black hair gleamed with intricate braids. Even if the men's dress hadn't marked their kith, their expressions would have made it obvious: the dreamy disdain as they made their way through the Middling crowd, the manner in which people stepped to the side to let them pass, as though each person in the crowd were a pleat on a fan rapidly folded. Faded amusement floated across the expressions of the High-Kith men.

"You're staring." The boy laughed.

"They would never buy a nightmare."

"Of course they would. When your life is filled with pleasure, a brush with danger is fun."

I thought about Sid treating imprisonment as a fascinating adventure. "Maybe you're right. What would you buy?"

He squinted one eye. "Middlings can't buy magic."

"But if you could." I said it quickly, so that he wouldn't think I didn't already know that.

He shrugged. "It is as it is." But his face was hard with dissatisfaction.

"I'm looking for someone," I said, and described Sid.

He rubbed his chin, a little exaggerated in the gesture. He probably knew full well that acting like an old man was charming in one so young. "And what kind of dream would *she* buy?"

I huffed. "Her most deeply held desire." Then I thought again. "Actually, I wouldn't put it past her to drink a nightmare and desire at the same time."

"Why do you want to find someone like that?"

I bristled. "You're a little young to be so nosy. Shouldn't you be in bed at this hour?"

"Shouldn't *you* be behind the wall?"

My breath caught in my throat. I felt as light as paper.

"Don't worry," he said. "I won't tell."

But I couldn't speak.

"I promise," he said.

When I remained silent, he said, "Me, I want a way up quarter, same as you. A way out. I want what they've got." He nodded at the High-Kith young men, who had purchased several dream vials, pocketing all but one. That vial they uncorked, and stood sniffing at the contents. "Why don't you ask them about your friend?" he said. "You don't make *such* a bad Middling. I just have a savvy eye."

"How," I said, "did you know?"

"Next time, pretend like you belong. Lie to yourself until you believe it."

Could I do that?

"It's a midnight lie," he said reassuringly. "High Kith are easier to fool than Middlings, since we mix around the city a lot and see all sorts of people."

One of the men touched a finger to the contents of a vial and then to his tongue. His eyes widened. Then he schooled his expression back into boredom.

"Go on," the boy said. "Ask them."

"I don't know."

"Well, do you want to find your friend or not," he said, and turned, ducking into the crowd of people behind him.

It *was* true that of anybody in this market, the two High-Kith men were the likeliest to know Sid. The deference that the warden of the jail, a Middling, had shown to her had made it clear that even if she came from a place with no kiths, here she was thought of as High—or at least she could play the part convincingly.

I thought about how I had believed Sid to be a boy simply because of her hair and clothes and that it was dark.

Well, and how she spoke about women.

How she spoke about me.

My cheeks grew hot. The burn on my cheek pulsed with pain.

Maybe, yes, I felt confident enough that the Middling boy was right, that most people don't think beyond what they believe they know to be true. But it wasn't confidence that pushed me toward the High-Kith men. It wasn't daring.

It was the need to escape my own blush.

I ignored it and marched up to them. "Excuse me," I said.

The one dressed in Elysium crimson dropped the vial he was holding. It smashed at his feet. A violet vapor rose from the shards and twined about his ankles.

"My dream of power," he said.

"*Ours*," his companion said. "You broke it."

"*It* broke it."

"I'm sorry," I said, "but—"

"It keeps speaking."

"I'm looking for—"

"Astonishing."

"Did we drink the dream already? Did I dream that the vial I purchased for one hundred gold god-crowns broke at my very feet?"

"No, fool," said the man in crimson. "Why would a dream of power be about an upstart Middling girl? It is not even a pretty one. Look at that nasty burn."

"Perhaps we are to make it do what we want. Perhaps *that* is the dream."

I thought about how easily Sid would turn this situation into what she wanted it to be. "This *is* your dream," I said. "The most powerful people are benevolent. I need your help finding someone. If you are truly powerful, you will help me."

"It is lying, brother," said the man in crimson. "But it *is* funny. *Help* it? Hilarious!"

"Pick this up." The man with black braids tapped his jeweled sandal near the broken glass.

As I knelt to gather the shards, I began to describe Sid.

"Shut up. So chattery," said the black-haired man. "Buzz buzz, maggoty fly. And stupid. I told you: pick this up!"

"I am picking it up," I said evenly. "Sid is a traveler, a friend of mine—"

He dissolved into laughter. "Absurd! Unbelievable!"

"She likes to go to High-Kith parties—"

"I told you to pick *this* up. *This* shard. The *biggest* one."

I let the small shards in my hand tinkle to the ground, and reached to collect the longest one, by his foot.

"Yes. *That* one. It is truly brainless, is it not, brother, even for a Middling? Now, fly. Cut yourself."

I froze, the shard in my hand. "What?"

"Cut yourself, I said. Your finger, your hand, I do not care. This is my dream. You will do as I say."

"I don't—"

"I want to taste it."

"Brother." The crimson man rolled his eyes. "You know that Middling blood is useless."

The other wagged his finger. "We do *not* know. This is a dream. The rules might be different. Three drops, little fly. Right on my tongue. And then"—his chin lifted proudly—"I will help you."

Hope lifted into my throat. Three drops of blood was an easy price to pay. If this had been a tithe, it would have been one of the gentlest, the kind taken from children. The man stood, head tilted back, mouth wide-open.

"I wish you could see yourself, brother." The crimson man giggled.

I pricked my finger. Blood welled. I squeezed three quivering drops into the High-Kith's mouth. He swallowed.

I said, "Now will you tell me where I can find her?"

"No!" He bent over with laughter. "Of course not! Stupid fly! Did you see, brother, how I tricked it? *Help* it! Oh, I want another dream. Give me another. You have all the vials. Quickly, quickly."

Shaking his head in amusement, the crimson man reached into his pockets, then frowned.

He removed his hands. He patted his clothes. "Brother . . ."

But his brother was not paying attention. He had straightened, laughter dying on his lips. He was staring at nothing that I could see, his face locked into a rigid expression.

"A thief!" The crimson man whirled around, pivoting to find who had emptied his pockets.

We saw a small shadow dart through the crowd and down an alleyway.

"Thief!" The High-Kith man shouted more loudly this time. "Catch him!" he cried, and ran toward where the boy had vanished.

His brother remained where he was—oblivious, it seemed, to anything around him.

I had been twice tricked. Once by him, and once by the boy, who had sent me on a fool's errand to use me as a distraction.

I sighed, lifting my eyes to the sky, which was when I noticed that it had grayed with light from the coming morning.

My stomach jolted. I had to get back. Soon, everyone in the tavern would be awake.

I rushed toward the wall, weaving through the diminishing crowd. The night buyers, weary, were heading home, too. I cast a glance over my shoulder. Behind me, the High-Kith man stood, stock-still, where I had left him. He disappeared behind me as I raced toward the gate.

Then invisible fingers tugged at the elbow of my coat. I yelped.

"Shh," said the boy, who pulled me into the alley where he had been hiding.

"You," I said.

"Don't be mad. You were great. Here, take one." He opened his hands. Eight vials rested on his palms.

"I don't want one." I had enough trouble telling what was real. "I don't need dreams."

"Boring! Go on."

"You probably kept the best one for yourself."

"You are a *smart* fly," he said cheerfully.

I looked at the labels on the vials. *Dream of demons. Dream of saviors. Dream of purple donkeys. Dream of kisses* . . . I stopped reading. I did not want kisses. I already knew what they were like.

The vials rocked gently on the boy's palms.

Dream of now, said one label, and I paused, then saw that the writing was scribbled. I had misread it.

Dream of new.

"That one." Why had I risked going beyond the wall, if not in search of some kind of beginning?

He handed it to me. "See, I was right," he said. "About those High men, how they like bad even better than good."

I wasn't thinking anymore about the vial in my hand. I was remembering how the man had frozen, staring. "My blood did something to him."

The boy shrugged, stowing the other vials into his pockets. "Nah. Those two were foxed."

"Foxed?"

"Drunk. Drugged. Or both. They definitely drank or ate something weird long before they began roaming the night market. The High Kith have got all sorts of stuff to addle their brains."

"Magic," I said.

"Hallucinations," he corrected. "Clever tricks to make the High Kith spend more money. The things people call 'magic' don't last. A flower that sings as it opens its petals? Withered and dead within a day. A tiny key that melts on your tongue and makes you the smartest person in the room? You're back to your old self after a few hours, with a headache to boot."

"That doesn't mean it's not magic."

"You *want* to believe that, just like everyone else. I get it. Makes life more exciting. And maybe you're right. But whatever it is, it's no good to me if it can't be kept."

I understood. Something that disappears isn't worth having unless you already have a lot of everything else.

But then I thought about sugar. I thought about this night, which was precious to me even if I hadn't found what I was seeking, even if—I glanced at the brightening sky—the night was almost over and I might never have another one like it.

"I've got to go," I said.

"Hey. Your friend. What's so important about finding her?"

Maybe she had already left the city. She *had* said we would never see each other again.

"Nothing," I said. "Not really. I just needed an excuse to screw up my courage to go beyond the wall."

I think I believed that, at the time.

⌒

Dawn was seeping through my window when I snuck into my room. Brilliant pink and syrupy orange. High-Kith colors.

I fumbled out of my clothes. I slipped my passport into a wide crack in one of the beams where it supported the ceiling. The dream vial I tucked among the dull clothes in my wardrobe, having no better place to hide it.

One hour, maybe, of sleep. Then work.

Work as always, days of sameness.

Except that *I* was different. I felt the difference shimmering all over my skin.

I returned to the wardrobe. I slid the *dream of new* vial from its hiding place. A splash of golden liquid sloshed at its bottom. The thin, curved glass was cool beneath my nervous fingers. I carried the vial with me into bed.

I uncorked the vial. Its liquid smelled like lemons and fizzed. Popping bubbles tickled my nose. This seemed somehow so friendly, so teasing, that I was reminded of Sid. I tipped the vial and drank.

The liquid burned, pleasingly, all the way down.

The pillow beneath my cheek felt as smooth as milk.

I dropped like a stone into sleep.

20

I WAS IN THE AGORA. I recognized it by its black-and-white diamond pavement, but it looked so astonishingly different from the agora I passed through every day that I didn't pay attention, at first, to the cluster of people at its sunny center.

The walls of the buildings that surrounded the agora had been white all my life. But in my dream the walls rioted with color. I was too far away to see the patterns, though the slight geometry to the lines and shapes suggested that the images were made by tiny mosaic tiles.

No gaping holes marked the pavement such as the hole where children had ice-skated during the ice wind. Instead, statues of marble and colored glass towered high: a girl with flowers cascading from her mouth; a man whose eyes changed from blue to lavender with the shift of light. He held aloft a twisting snake carved from green travertine. A leaping fawn bore the face of a human child.

There were too many statues for me to count. Some gleamed with jets of water: half statue, half fountain.

A cry rose from the crowd. Curious, I turned toward the seething knot of people.

Not yet, said a small voice behind me.

I turned.

A little girl stood there, rich black hair flowing past her shoulders, her oval-shaped face somber and quiet, her mouth finely shaped, as though painted by a delicate brush, yet firmly pressed in worry. Her eyes were grass green in the sunlight.

Oh, I thought, My eyes *are* green.

Which was when I realized who stood before me.

You're me, I told her. But I don't understand. This is a dream of what is new. You are old.

She shook her head. *You* are old, she said. *I* am a child.

No, I mean . . . you have already happened.

She shrugged.

Am I in the past? I asked.

Yes, she said, but something new is about to happen.

I took a step toward the crowd, whose shouts grew louder. I glimpsed a glowing knife.

The black-haired girl caught my hand. You can't, she said. You can't let him see you.

Who?

The god.

I nearly told her that there were no gods, but this was a dream, and she was my younger self, so it seemed pointless and even rude to insist on reality.

Her hand tightened around mine. He cannot see you, she said. If he sees you, he will *know* you. He will take you.

Before I could ask her what she meant, she pulled me behind a statue. Wait, she said, until it is over.

What is? What is happening over there?

Murder.

A scream split the air. I wrenched free of the girl and out of our hiding place.

Many people in the crowd had glowing knives now. Their hands lifted and plunged. Little fires danced off the blades. I could see now, through the roiling mob of people, a creature at the center.

It had a vaguely human shape, but hands all over its naked body. They stretched open in pain. It was the same creature I had dreamed about when I was in the prison with Sid.

It screamed. It tried to snatch at people surrounding it, but the crowd lopped off the many hands and struck at the creature's throat. Bright red spilled from its mouth and wounds, but it was not normal blood. It flowed like liquid flame, striped with pink, edged with orange.

The god's blood poured onto the black-and-white pavement, and the creature's screams faded to a whimper.

No one, said the girl by my side, has ever killed a god before.

When the fire-blood slowed to a trickle and then stopped, the crowd fled. The agora was empty now, save for the enormous mutilated carcass.

No one except the girl and I was there to see a duskwing, its cool gray feathers stammering at its sides, dip its beak in the blood.

It shifted before our eyes, wings painted with sudden scarlet. Its stubby, thin tail bloomed into long, soft, curling pink feathers. Its eyes winked like bright emerald chips.

That is the Elysium, I said.

She nodded. The gods' bird, she said, and fell silent as it took flight, its scalloped-edged wings illuminated by the sun. It ribboned through the sky, dipping and weaving through the hot blue.

Tell me, the girl said. Do I grow up happy?

It seemed wrong to lie and cruel to tell the truth. I said, Not everyone needs to be happy.

Her firm mouth flattened to a line. She said, Yes, they do.

I was going to say that she was a child and so could not possibly understand how the world gets in the way of happiness. I was going to say that hoping to be happy is a kind of greed. It should be enough to feel safe.

But as I started to speak, I realized that I no longer believed this.

It did not matter, however, what I thought or wanted to say, because I was pulled abruptly from the dream.

A hand yanked me awake, ripping the hair from my head.

21

I CRIED OUT, REACHING UP to grab a strong wrist and firm fingers, trying to slacken the hold on my hair.

"Finally awake, are you." Raven released me.

"I'm so sorry," I gasped. I felt sick with guilt. I had been caught. She had seen me somehow, going through the wall's gate. She knew—

"Where is it?"

My trembling hands tried to smooth my hair. I glanced up at the ceiling where my passport nestled in the crack alongside a beam. "I— I—" I tried to scrape together the right words to tell Raven the truth but in a way she would accept. Of course she was upset. I had betrayed her, I had touched her things without asking . . .

"Speak, damn the gods." Strands of my black hair trailed from her lifted hand. "Where is the heliograph?"

All the words I had been trying to find floated away. "Do you mean . . . my heliograph?"

"*My* heliograph, you stupid girl."

I blinked back sudden, hot tears. She had never called me that.

"The picture of you? With the ones I hid in the cistern the night of the Elysium? I got them back. I gave them to you."

"No. You gave me a stack of heliographs that I did not count and did not even *look* at until now, because I trusted you."

Dread swelled inside me. "It's lost?"

"*You* lost it."

"It can be replaced." I was shaken by her fury, unsure why this mistake was unforgivable. I wasn't thinking straight. I couldn't see the true problem. "We can make another one."

"Don't you think I know that? I'm not worried about it being lost. I'm worried about it being *found*."

There was a horrible silence as we both thought about what would happen if the militia discovered a heliograph in the Ward the exact shape and size of a passport image. They would find the face that matched the image. They would ask questions. Tithes would be taken.

"I must have missed it when I searched the cistern," I said, hoping it was true. "It must still be there."

Raven lowered her hand, shaking it free of the strands of my hair. "Get it. Make this right."

⌒

But it wasn't there.

This time I didn't even notice my fear of heights, I was already so afraid. I plunged my hands again and again into the cistern, swiping my fingers along the slimy bottom, the water up to my shoulders, splashing my chin. I had scoured the ground below, ignoring the curiosity of passersby, some of whom stopped to gape when I began to climb the gutter pipe. I had peered carefully through the greenery of indi vines as I climbed. I had paced the entire roof, staring down at its plastered surface. I had dug dead vegetation crisped by the sun out of the gutter.

Nothing.

I stared out at the vast city. At its edges twinkled the green-blue sea. Sunshine poured down on my hot head and jeweled the water dripping from me.

Maybe the heliograph had snagged somehow on the coat I had been wearing. Maybe it was still embedded its collar.

Raven's coat.

Which had been taken from me by the militiamen.

I placed a wet palm on my face.

If I had bothered to look, *really* look at the heliographs when I collected them from the cistern, I would have known right away that one was missing. I would have known exactly which one.

How could I have been so careless? The heliograph was gone. Raven would be so angry.

What do you do when you can't make something right?

When you know you won't be forgiven?

You lie.

⌒

"*This* is why you're here?" Aden's brow wrinkled with unmistakable hurt and offense. I quickly saw the need to repair the situation, but before I could speak he stated what I should have realized before I brought my problem to him. "I was sick with worry," he said. "You disappeared. Then I hear that you were released from prison and back at the tavern for *two* days. You didn't even spare a thought for me, did you? I began to think you'd never come by."

I felt a prickle of irritation. *He* could have come to *me*.

I wouldn't have had such a thought even a few days ago. Instead I would have felt rightly accused. I would have felt the truth of it: I *hadn't* thought about him, not at all, and he was so sincerely wounded that I would have assumed this must mean I *had* done something wrong. I would have rushed to apologize.

Which is in fact what I decided to do, because I would get nowhere with him otherwise.

"You're right," I said. "I'm sorry."

He softened. "I shouldn't have waited," he said. "I should have come to the tavern. I guess I was too proud."

This threw me off-balance. His accusation had vanished so quickly once I had said what he wanted to hear. Did that mean that my annoyance had been unfair?

"I wanted you to want to see me," he said, "first, before anyone else. I wish that you hadn't come only because you needed my help." He rubbed his mouth as though he had tasted something bitter. Once, his hand on my naked shoulder, gathering me to him as I lay with my head on his loud heart, he had told me that his mother had ruffled his hair when he saw her for the last time, her voice blithe, giving no clue that she planned to abandon him. She could have said good-bye, he said. It would have meant something to me.

Maybe she didn't want you to guess or worry, I said, and didn't take you because she didn't want to risk your life with hers.

Maybe, he said.

"Aden," I said now, "I'm glad to see you." It wasn't even a midnight lie. It became true the moment I said it. You understand me, he had once said, like no one does.

It is a pleasure to be told you understand someone best. It is as if you are the only one in the world who matters, as though you have a power that escapes everyone else. I was special—not because I was different, but because I was like him. I, too, longed for a mother.

He smiled a little. "I can't make a new heliograph without Raven knowing," he said. "She would have to sit for it. You know that the images of people's faces must be clear and are regulated. The ears must be shown. The person must look directly forward. There is no way I could secretly capture her image, and the moment I ask her to sit for a portrait, no matter what excuse I give, she will guess that it is for you. She is too clever."

I felt a sick disappointment.

"But"—his smiled widened—"I happen to have an extra passport heliograph of her. I took two images when she asked for one a while ago. I thought it might be useful someday, though I wasn't sure how. It felt like a bit of insurance against her."

"*Against* her?"

His light eyes blinked in surprise. He spoke as if he were saying something everyone knew. "She can be ruthless."

"But she does so much good for the Ward."

"Yes," he said, "in her way."

"She is good to me."

His gaze roamed over my face. He seemed to consider a response and then abandon it to say, "Well, she *would* be good to you."

I started to ask him what exactly that meant, when he brushed loose hair out of my eyes and tucked it fondly behind my ear. "It's easy to be good to you." His hand trailed down my neck and brushed over my collarbone, not quite touching my breast, but almost. "But you must be careful around Raven."

It was true: she was easily angered by me. But didn't I deserve it? Look how careless I'd been with the heliograph.

"Ask Morah," Aden said. "She knows better than anyone."

"Morah has never liked her."

"Of course she doesn't." Holding up a flat hand that asked me to stay where I was, Aden left the room. I heard rummaging sounds and then his heavy, approaching tread as he returned. He offered a small tin square. "It's not exactly the same as the one I gave you a few days ago, but she won't know the difference, will she, since she never saw the one you lost?"

I was awash with dizzying gratitude. I took the heliograph. Its sharp edges felt like salvation.

Aden took my hand and gently pulled me close. My gaze was level with his tanned neck. I saw him swallow. His breath brushed my brow as he said, "I have missed you."

His hands slid down my back.

I knew what he wanted, though he didn't ask for it, and it seemed like something he deserved, so I gave it to him.

On the walk home through the Ward, I kept my hand in my pocket, my fingers on Raven's image, tracing the sharp-edged square. Though I had rinsed my face and mouth and hands, I felt coated with something sticky. Sometimes people want things so badly you feel like it's your obligation to give it. I knew that was wrong, yet I had gone to bed with Aden anyway, as if I had built my own trap. Now he would expect more from me. A sick, worried feeling settled in my stomach. I blamed Aden. I blamed myself. I wasn't sure who really was to blame.

A snake spun itself out of a crack in the pavement. Viridian green, it looked as though woven from grass, it was aware of me, but it was the kind of snake that hides, not bites, and it trickled quickly away. I envied it. A snake will not stay to please you. It will do nothing it does not want to do.

I pity who I was then: a girl riven by her mistake, beholden to the needs of others, and trained to diminish her own. I was a snake that had not yet learned to strike.

Yet Raven merely nodded when I gave her the heliograph. "It's a good thing you found it," she said.

It worried me, how secrets were beginning to pile up. The heliograph. That I didn't share Aden's feelings. The dead militiaman. My passport. Going beyond the wall. Sid.

Surely, at some point, one of these secrets would slip into full view. It would be seen.

I would be seen.

But Raven barely glanced at the heliograph, and accepted without question that I had overlooked it the night I had retrieved the others from the cistern.

I touched the red Elysium feather hidden below my shirt. I was safe for now.

"Go to the kitchen," Raven said. "You're late for the bread. Annin had to start the rising without you *and* serve an early customer, an important one at that. I need to be able to rely on you, Nirrim."

I felt ashamed that I had just tricked her and strangely grateful that she was still not pleased with me. If she had shown me kindness I would have felt worse in my deceit. I promised myself that I wouldn't let her down again.

In the kitchen, Annin's eyes widened into blue mirrors when she saw me. "Someone came to be served breakfast. And so early!"

"Yes, I know. I'm—"

"I have never served someone like this. I was so nervous."

Annin was easily made nervous, especially under Raven's watchful eye, so I didn't think anything of this. Then Annin said, "She was *High*."

"Really?" My pulse fluttered in my throat. "Who was she?"

"Raven tried to act unfazed, but even *she* was impressed, I could tell. High Kith almost *never* come into the Ward. Of course you know that. You know how they are: too good for us. But this one was nice. I spilled the tea, and she didn't reprimand me but"—her voice dropped to an astonished whisper—"*helped me clean it up.* Can you believe it? Thank the gods Raven didn't see."

I hated to feel so hopeful, yet I was. "What did she look like?"

"You must know." Annin's expression turned conspiratorial and inquisitive. "She asked for you."

"She did?"

"How do you know her? Did you sell something to her? Do you think she might hire you to be a lady's maid? Maybe you will receive a special writ to work in the upper quarters. Is that possible? Maybe so. Maybe she is connected to someone on the Council. I wouldn't doubt it. She was so self-assured. Her clothes were so rich! Garnet silk and jeweled sandals and a pocket watch like a little sun. Nirrim, you could leave the tavern. You could go beyond the wall! Will you leave us altogether?"

"Please, you're going too fast. You're not answering my question."

She withdrew a folded note from her gray skirts. It had a black seal stamped with an insignia I didn't recognize: a pair of closed eyes with a little round mark where its forehead would be.

"I said, why don't you give this to my mistress to give to Nirrim, but she seemed not to like that idea. She said she trusted me, and that it was our secret."

With eager fingers, I cracked the note open along its seal. My darting eyes fell upon the first line of writing.

I hear you are looking for me, it said.

22

THE HONEY-STRIPED WOOD of the railing glided smoothly beneath my cold hand. Sconces lit my way up the winding stone stairs, and I could see parts of the Middling quarter through the diamond-paned windows that appeared at every floor.

The patched-quilt colors of the night-market tents.

A garden behind the wall of someone's home, bushes and trees blurred together in the darkness, warped by a defect in the window's glass.

The nearly uniform shapes of houses, the same rust-colored ceramic tiles, doors painted the same sage green as the door at the address Sid had given me.

It had taken me forever to find the house. She had included no map and no instructions. I had spent much of the night wandering, looking for street signs, not daring to ask anyone the way. *I assume that if you were able to get into the Middling quarter once you can do so again*, the note read. No one had answered my knock at the door of the tall Middling house, which even in the dark looked intimidating in its newness—rich red brick with an undertone of blue, shiny-painted shutters, carefully groomed flowers waving from their window boxes, petals sulfur yellow and soapy white. Flickering light from the oil-lit street lantern behind me wavered over the door. I knocked again. When no one answered, I tried opening the door, my pulse thudding. It unlatched easily, opening with the soft sigh of well-oiled hinges.

A warm breeze pushed me from behind, tunneling into the house, stirring my brown skirts. The empty room I entered glowed with the light of small lanterns that showed powder-blue painted walls, a soap-stone mantelpiece that bore a brass bell fit for one's hand. Old ashes lay in the grate, a sign that whoever lived here—was it Sid?—had had the comfort of a fire during the ice wind. A window was open. I could hear the muted cry of far-off seagulls. An uncorked bottle of wine and two delicate glasses sat at a little oval table. One glass was stained red at its bottom. A pink-striped chair looked dented in its upholstery, as if someone had recently sat there. I touched the silk. It was faintly warm.

A muffled thump, weirdly musical, came through the door at the other end of the room. I followed the sound.

Sid was lying on the floor under the belly of a piano, prying with a small knife at something I couldn't see.

The floorboard creaked beneath my step, so she must have known I was there, but she continued at her task. I saw her face only in profile, brows furrowed, chin tipped up, lips bitten in concentration.

"You're late," she said.

"*You're* rude. You didn't even answer the door."

"I was busy."

"What are you doing?"

"Getting started without you." She slid out from under the piano and stood, brushing herself off. She was dressed in Middling clothes, though without regard for how she would dress if she were in fact a

Middling woman. The trousers were a tight fit, made for a man, and although the dark blue tunic had a feminine cut that nipped in at the waist, it was free of the simple embroidery that a Middling would normally flaunt as a sign of minor status. In the buttery yellow lamplight, I could see details that I hadn't in the moonlight outside the prison: the fullness of her mouth; a freckle beneath her eye; her proud posture; the skin that was a few shades lighter than mine; the eyelashes surprisingly thick and black, a contrast to her fair hair. I could see that even in good light, it would have been easy to make the same mistake I had in the darkness. It would be easy to think she were a boy, if I only glanced once. But I couldn't believe that anyone would glance at her only once.

She smirked. "You're staring."

This was different from her friendly arrogance in the prison. There was an anger to her that seemed directed at me even though I had done nothing to deserve it.

She slid her long hand inside the open mouth of the piano, feeling around inside. The strings hummed and twanged.

"Do you play?" I asked. In the Ward we were allowed only little wooden flutes that played simple melodies. I knew what a piano was only because I had read about them in books at Harvers's printing shop.

Sid shuddered. "Not on your life." She roughed up her short golden hair, frowning into the instrument.

"I suppose you're no good at it," I said, "and don't enjoy something where you have no opportunity to show off."

Her gaze snapped up. Her black eyes narrowed.

"I didn't come here to be ignored." I wasn't sure what allowed me to give voice to the resentment brewing in my chest. Normally I wouldn't, to anyone. "I risked punishment going through the wall to meet you. I wandered for hours trying to find this place because you left no directions. So tell me why I'm here and what you're doing or I will leave."

Her expression changed, screwing up with rue. She scrunched her eyes shut and covered her face with her hand. "Directions," she groaned. "I didn't give you directions?"

"None."

"I thought you would recognize the address. I thought you must come to the Middling quarter all the time."

"The last time was my first time."

"I am such an idiot."

"You are," I agreed.

Her hand slid away from her face. "I'm sorry. I waited for a long time. I assumed you weren't coming. It bothered me." She said her last words slowly, seeming to consider them as she said them.

"Everything is safer for you than it is for me."

"You're right. I should have been thinking about that. I was thinking too much about me. About how I was feeling." She looked down at the piano.

My curiosity got the better of my fading anger. "What are you looking for?"

"A prayer book."

"There is no such thing as a prayer book." I studied her to see if she was joking or making this up. "No one worships the gods. They're not real."

"There *used* to be such books. It's an old book. And hidden, I've been told, in this piano."

"So this is not your piano."

"No."

"Is this your house?"

"No."

"Do you even have the right to be here?"

"No," she said cheerfully, "which is why I must hurry. I will understand if you wish to leave. I'll stay here until I find the book."

But I didn't want to leave. I planted my hands on my hips. "So you *are* a thief."

"I am many things. But for the moment, yes, you're right. Nirrim . . . will you be thieves with me?" She went back to inspecting the piano, knocking along its black lacquered wood.

"Have you tried *playing* the piano?"

She shot me a flat look of mock outrage. "We have already discussed my ability to play—or lack thereof."

"I mean: Have you struck each key? If a book is hidden inside, maybe it obstructs some part of the piano from playing. See if a note or notes won't work."

"Ooh, yes." She trickled her fingers up the keys, moving from the rumbling low notes.

"Why do you want a prayer book?"

"Information. Do you realize that although your city has libraries in the upper quarters, there are no history books? Why are there no history books?" She danced out the middle notes, shifting her hand so that she struck the notes only with her thumb and little finger, hand stretched. "And there are no books about the gods, even though people refer vaguely to them as having existed, even though there are statues of them in the High quarter." She hit a key that thudded instead of rang. The note was dead. She smiled at me. "Clever Nirrim." She reached inside the piano's body and fiddled with the tuning pins, then seemed to find something. She wrenched at the flat board that held the pins.

"You are going to ruin the instrument."

"It deserves it," she said. "It's in the way of what I want."

The board popped up. Strings squealed. Tuning pegs broke off, one sailing to the floor, the others dropping into the piano. Sid reached around inside, then slid out a small red leather-bound book, the edges of its pages bright with gold. She made a satisfied noise.

"What's so special about that book?" I asked.

"I want to know if Herrath's gods are the same ones my people worship. What they're like. Their supposed powers."

I thought about how she had phrased her words. "*Your people* worship them. Do you?"

"Pfft. Mere superstition. Fanciful tales. At least"—she closed the book—"so I always thought. But something is happening in this city, and I want to understand it. I'd like for you to help me."

"Me?"

"I have a proposition. Help me find the source of magic—or whatever trick is making things *look* like magic—and I will help you leave this island."

"But I don't want to leave. This is my home."

Sid exhaled impatiently. "If you like the trap you're in, I guess I can't make you leave it. What *do* you want, Nirrim? Why were you looking for me?"

I just wanted to see you, I thought, but that seemed childish to say. "Which one told you I was looking for you? The fruit seller, the boy, or the High-Kith brothers?"

She grinned. "Who is to say *all* of them didn't? I have many friends. Many admirers. You are hardly the first."

I huffed with irritation, though I was relieved that she had returned to the teasing tone she'd used so often in the prison, that empty flirtation that seemed like second nature to her. "Why do you want so badly to find the source of magic?" I thought of the dream vials. "Do you want to bring magic goods back to your country?"

"Not quite. I want leverage. Let's say this magic or trick can be bottled up. Its source discovered. Then I can bring it home—or bring the secret to it home. I could bargain with my parents. Marriage for a woman means the same thing where I come from as it does here: life with a man. Sleeping in his bed. I won't do it. I have tried to explain to my parents, but they don't want to listen. They never even let me finish. They have too much to gain by selling me off. So I can't ever go home . . . unless maybe I can offer them something valuable enough to secure my freedom. Something to offset the cost they'll bear if I don't marry."

I heard the muffled click of the front door latch. A gust of wind whooshed into the room.

"Why is the door unlocked?" someone said from the other room.

Sid shoved the small book into her back trouser pocket. She seized my hand. "Quickly." She tugged me toward glass doors and pushed through them to a balcony that overlooked a sweet-smelling, dark garden. Wind tore through the trees. "We have to jump," Sid hissed. I looked down into the garden and felt a sick twist in my stomach. "It's not so far down," she whispered.

I heard a cry of discovery from inside the room we had just left.

"Come on," Sid said.

My pulse pounded against Sid's hot hand. I touched my shirt and thought of the Elysium feather hidden beneath it. We jumped.

I tumbled into bushes, felt twigs scratch my face.

Sid tugged my hand. I heard shouts from the balcony as she pulled me through the garden and to the door in its wall. The knob didn't budge when she twisted it. She dropped to one knee and, in the darkness, used her little knife, working at the lock while my pulse filled my chest and throat. The lock clicked. She pushed us through, and we ran.

It was only when we reached the night market and dipped into the crowd of people that we slowed, and she turned to me with bright black eyes, mouth parted in exhilaration.

"You like danger too much," I told her.

She tipped her head slightly in acknowledgment. The lamplight caught the gold in her hair. "I know. It's a flaw."

I wondered, just for a moment, whether her short hair would feel like velvet at the nape of her neck.

I imagined it brushing my cheek.

I thought about drinking the dream of new, the way the liquid had fizzed on my tongue. Although the dream had been no more real than any other, and was filled as all dreams are with impossibilities, it had felt so vivid. I remembered the duskwing drinking the god's blood and transforming into the Elysium bird, and for the first time, as I looked at Sid's excited mouth, I felt a tickle of uncertain exploration, a wondering . . . *was* the bird special? Was it the gods' bird?

Did the feather hidden beneath my shirt lend me some power that made Sid look at me the way she was looking at me?

Like I was captivating.

"About our bargain," she said. "Will you help me?"

"Yes," I said.

"Good. What do you want in exchange?"

"I don't know."

She made an amused sound. "When you figure it out, tell me."

"What if you can't give it to me?"

She smiled widely. "Do I look like someone who would disappoint?"

"Not if it's something easy to give."

"That sounds like a challenge. And a criticism! You think I can't handle something hard? What do you believe I'd do then?"

"Run away."

"Me?"

"You."

"True! Luckily for both of us, I know already what you want."

"Oh, really," I said. "Do you."

"You just want to want *something*. You want the feeling of wanting."

I didn't like that. It made me feel too seen. "Maybe I want money."

"I can give you that. Though, honestly: *boring*."

"Or to live among the High Kith."

She waved a languid hand. "Done. If that's what you really choose."

A tree sighed above us in the dark. Sid caught me glancing up into the rush of its leaves and asked, "What is it? Why do you look so startled?"

"It's my first tree," I said. The tree rubbed against the gray sky. "I have never seen one before, not this close. There are no trees in the Ward."

"Why?"

"I don't know."

"We should find out." Slowly, she said, "I don't like that you have never seen a tree. It's like saying you have never seen the sky, or sun."

I looked away from the leaves and into Sid's black eyes. Then her gaze lowered. She was looking at the burn on my cheek. I immediately covered it.

"It was an accident," I told her. "It's ugly, I know."

She opened her mouth, then closed it, lips tightening. "It looks like it hurts."

"No," I said, although it did. Embarrassed by her disbelieving gaze, I said I had to leave. The sun would rise soon.

I thought maybe she was disappointed, and I couldn't tell whether it was because she knew I was lying about the burn and didn't like it, or because she believed me and wondered how I could be so clumsy.

Maybe she was second-guessing our bargain.

But she said, "Meet me here tomorrow night. Think about what you want from me. In the meantime, I can give you what you came looking for in the night market the other night."

I folded my arms across my chest. "And what is that?"

"Adventure."

23

IT WAS SO HOT THE FOLLOWING DAY that the silver ants came out, zipping up and down the white walls of the Ward in glittering lines like tinsel. They bite. You don't want to get in their path.

"So long as the windows are shuttered and we stay indoors, the heat should be tolerable," Raven said when she walked into the kitchen. The walls of the Ward buildings are thick, slabs of stone cut from a quarry I had never seen. They hold the chill of the night.

I was kneading the morning bread, sweat dampening the hair at the nape of my neck. It felt good to work the dough. It helped me not think too much about last night.

And what might happen later, this night, after everyone in the tavern was asleep and I snuck into the Middling quarter.

I punched the bread dough back down. I rolled it under the heel of my hand. The rhythm of this kept away my nervousness.

Or was it excitement?

"By noon, not a soul will be stirring in the Ward," Raven said. I had almost forgotten she was in the room.

Annin cut sun melon into thin, papery orange slices and dropped them into a bowl of pale wine. With a sigh, she said, "It will be so dull with no customers."

Morah said nothing. She cracked eggs into a bowl one-handed. Each tap of an egg against the rim of the bowl was precise and surprisingly loud. She watched Raven as she did it. She watched her the way you watch the silver ants, to see which direction they want to go in, so you can get out of their way.

"Now, girls," Raven said brightly, "it is never possible to be bored when there are things to do. There are errands to run in the Ward."

"I thought you said we should stay indoors," said Morah.

"And so you should! I can't even imagine setting one foot into that sun, particularly when I have been feeling so poorly."

"Nirrim, too," Annin said.

I lifted my gaze from my work in surprise.

"Just look at her," Annin said. "Those shadows under her eyes! They look like they've been smudged with that kohl the High ladies use."

Two nights of lost sleep were catching up with me. I hadn't realized that Annin had noticed.

Raven came close, tipping her head up. In the last two years, I had grown past her height. She tucked a lock of damp hair behind my ear. It was so reassuring to feel her tenderness. She could easily lose her temper, it was true, but who among us is in perfect control of our feelings all the time? And she always became kind again.

"My lamb," she said, "have you been sleeping badly?"

"No." From the look on her face I could tell she was remembering when I had first come to the tavern from the orphanage, and had woken, weeping, in the night, babbling about things that she assured me were not real—except Helin's death, which sometimes I would hope was one of the lies I had believed. "It's not like that," I said.

She smiled in evident relief. When you see relief on the face of someone you love you also see the worry that had been hidden. Her worry made me feel beloved. I was her girl. Her lamb. "I feel fine," I promised.

"Annin, she is fresh as a flower. Except . . ." She touched my hair again, but this time let her fingers slide free, and rubbed the fingertips as she grimaced. "Very hot. My dear, you are so sweaty!"

Morah cracked another egg. The yellow globe of the yolk and its slick transparent white spilled from the shell in her hand into the bowl. She gave me a hard look I didn't understand.

"I'll run those errands myself," Raven said. "Now, what did I come down here for? Oh, yes. A basket."

"I'll go," I said. "I don't mind. I'm already hot."

"We are *all* hot," Morah said.

"Oh, would you?" Raven said to me. "I bet you won't feel the heat a bit if I loan you my parasol."

"Parasols are Middling," Morah said. "She can't use one."

"That's right. I forgot. Maybe you shouldn't go after all, my dear."

"I want to," I insisted. "The dough can have its second rise while I'm gone." I untied my apron.

"Are you sure?"

If I had a mother, would I let her go out into this heat, especially when she was feeling ill? "Of course I'm sure."

As I left the kitchen, the basket on my arm and instructions on a slip of paper, I heard Morah say to Raven, "I don't know why you make her do everything."

I felt a twist of doubt.

But Raven *hadn't* made me. I had offered.

I shook away my discomfort and went out into the steely sun. The Ward was bright white, the walls shining like glaze on a cake.

"That's enough," Rinah called from the shadow of her home.

I glanced up from my weeding. I wiped sweat from my mouth. "But I'm not finished."

"You don't even have a hat on your head, child. You'll drop dead from heatstroke. What will your mistress do then? She has no use for your corpse, believe me. Come inside, drink some water, and take what you've come for."

I tucked my gardening knife into my pocket and followed her inside. The sudden cool darkness felt like a plunge into a well. I felt dizzy. I was more tired than I had realized. I gratefully accepted the tin cup of water Rinah offered with one hand, the other hand resting on her pregnant belly. Then she took my basket and filled it with enormous vegetables from her garden. Anything she planted always flourished. "Here is something extra," she said, and slid in a roll of tanned leather. "We slaughtered one of the goats." Rinah and her family had one of the rare homes with a plot of land. She had a coop and a few goats: rewards from the Council for bearing so many children. "I know Raven needs the leather," she added. I would dye the leather Middling blue and cut it to coded size for new passports.

"Careful in the Ward," she said, which is what Half Kith say to warn others against the militia.

"Why?"

"A soldier died the night of the festival. He fell from the rooftops."

I felt suddenly cold despite the heat. As nonchalantly as possible, I said, "He must have been chasing the bird."

"Well, yes, that is what everyone thought at first, but the militia said they found strands of black hair stuck in fresh paint on the walls near where he fell. The hair didn't match his. The militia think maybe it wasn't an accident. Soldiers have been poking around, asking questions."

I felt queasy but thought about how Sid would act in this situation. "Good luck to them." I forced myself to shrug. "Lots of people in the Ward have black hair. *I* do."

"So you do," she agreed, but absently. Her face scrunched in sudden discomfort. She rubbed a hand over her taut belly, which showed the little bulge of a kicking foot. "*Another* baby. My gods. And here I am with five children already. I keep having one right after the other, just like the Council wants." It was strange, perhaps, that the City Council encouraged the Half Kith to bear many children when overcrowding in the Ward might be a concern. Then again, the Council had ways of keeping the population in check. There were the vanishings. And arrests. Since so many people who went into the prison never returned, we could only assume they were dead or had become Un-Kith.

Rinah must have been thinking of similar things. Her discomfort and frustration slipped into worry.

"Do you not want the baby?" I asked, then felt horrible for asking a question that might have no good answer.

I remembered waking up inside the ventilated box outside the orphanage for unwanted babies. It was black with pinpricks of light. The box was cold. Maybe there had been an ice wind. I think there must have been, but I can't know for sure because I had been placed in the box while asleep and so had seen nothing of the outside world or the person who had taken me to the orphanage. I was newly born. I had known only the warmth of arms and the human-scented stillness of the indoors. The cold was new and frightening. I had been swaddled in a blanket, but my legs had kicked it undone. I wailed. I flung my hands out for the softness that I loved, the familiar scent, her voice. But there was nothing to touch. Her face was fuzzy in my mind. For years after that moment in the box I would wonder why I couldn't remember my mother's face well, until I learned that babies are not able to see clearly. But as I cried in the box I thought about her vague face, her floating ribbons of black hair, her thin sweet milk, a golden necklace dangling a crescent moon that swung gently when she leaned over to take me in her arms. The box smelled. Urine soaked my legs—hot, then clammily cold.

Rinah's expression grew tender and sad. "Yes," she said, "I want the baby."

I wondered briefly why she didn't ask Raven for a passport, but it was evident why: her family was large. It took a great deal of time and effort to produce even one passport made from authentic (or authentic-seeming) elements. Raven either bartered for the necessary items, like the leather, or shouldered the cost of them. And of course it was much riskier for a larger number of people to try to leave the Ward at once. "If even one of them is caught with a false document, *we* might be caught," Raven had said. "And if we are caught, who will help others?"

"I must return to the tavern," I said. "Raven might need me."

"She's lucky to have you."

This compliment made me feel good as I walked through the stunning heat. If not for Raven, I might have never known a mother's care. My own mother hadn't wanted me.

The Ward's walls were sunny mirrors with no reflections. I wondered what Sid was doing. Was she sleeping through the heat? I pictured her curled up like a cat. I felt a rush of eagerness. I couldn't wait for night to fall. I couldn't wait to see the cool dark pool into the sky.

You mean you can't wait to see *me*, Sid's voice said slyly.

But there was nothing wrong with that. It made sense, didn't it?

Everything about her was new. New things are exciting. Everyone knows that.

The word *new* clung to my mind. I thought about the dream of new I had drunk from the vial.

My pace slowed.

I thought about Rinah, who wanted her baby.

I thought about my newborn self, squalling inside the orphanage box.

I glanced around the quiet, white, deserted streets, remembering in my dream, the walls were lushly painted with colors.

It was just a dream, of course. But as my steps slowed to a halt and sweat oozed down my back, I considered how Sid made me question what I believed I knew.

It occurred to me that although for years I had believed my mother didn't want me, I couldn't know that for certain. Maybe something—or someone—had *made* her abandon me.

It occurred to me that I had never questioned why, every year for the moon festival, the men painted the walls freshly white.

How many coats of paint lay thick on the walls?

Had the walls always been white?

What if my dream had been somehow real?

Normally this last thought would have sent me scurrying home, shoving the idea away, because it was the sort of thought that had always meant confusion and grief. It had been so hard when I was younger to tell illusion from truth. I should have grown out of it by now.

I needed Helin to tell me what was real. I needed Raven.

Or, Sid said, you could always find out for yourself what is real.

I looked around me. The air was heavy with heat. There was no one. Nothing moved except the marching silver ants.

I slid the gardening knife from my pocket and opened it. I approached the nearest wall and its smooth expanse of white limewash.

I scraped at the paint with the knife. White flakes peeled away, sticking to my knife, my sweaty skin. Silver ants came to see what I was doing. They walked up my knife and over my wrist, biting me as I swatted them off.

I'm not sure how long I carved away at the years of paint until finally, just when I thought I had gone crazy again, like when I was little, when I was seduced into believing impossible things no one else saw, my knife stripped away one last layer. Beneath the white lay a bloody red paint.

<hr />

I can only imagine how I must have looked when I walked into the tavern. Garden dirt smeared on my face. Sleepless hollows beneath my eyes. Sweaty clothes, sweaty hair. Ant bites in a lurid string of red bumps up my arm, even some on my neck and face. Dirt and white paint under my nails. A startled expression on my face that probably grew even more bewildered when I saw who was waiting at a table inside the tavern.

Sid looked up from her plate of sun melon slices. She saw me and laughed. Her skin was clean and pure, her thin, pomegranate-colored silk dress falling in elegant folds.

Annin, who had frozen in the act of pouring Sid iced lemon water, stared at me. "Nirrim! You look *awful*!"

"You really do," Sid said. "What have you been doing? Rolling around in a rosebush? What are all those red marks? Tell me."

A blush burned in my cheeks. "No, I don't think I will."

"Oh, come on."

"You said I look awful."

"No, *she* did." Sid unfurled a lazy hand in the direction of Annin, who was glancing between us. "I merely agreed. Did you . . . tussle with squirrels? Dirty squirrels? Vengeful ones?"

"Shut up."

Annin gasped. "Nirrim! She is *High*."

"What are you doing here?" I demanded.

Sid's laughter melted into a slow smile. "I got tired of waiting for you."

～ 24 ～

RAVEN BUSTLED INTO THE ROOM, carrying a tray laden with all the delicacies we could offer: a small sugar loaf made by me, ice cherry preserves richly purple in a tiny glass jar, chilled indi flower tea, and goat milk custard glazed with amber caramel. She had eyes only for Sid. "My lady, we are so honored! You will not want for anything here in my home, I assure you. I shall serve you myself. Annin, why are you staring?" Raven, who clearly hadn't noticed my arrival, finally glanced in my direction. Her eyes widened and her mouth firmed. "*Nirrim.* Your appearance is disgraceful. How dare you embarrass me in front of our guest."

"I didn't know she would be here," I said.

"That is no excuse!"

"Why not?" Sid said mildly. "It looks like she was doing work in the heat. I'm not surprised by how she looks, only by the fact that someone let her—what, garden?—in the sun on a day like this."

"She insisted," Raven said. "I tried to stop her. Nirrim, you stupid girl. Shut the door. You are letting the heat in."

Sid's smile hardened. When I shut the door, her face was thrown into sudden shadow. Her eyes glinted. "Apologize," she told Raven.

"Of course, my lady. I had no idea that one of my servants was capable of such bad manners. Forgive me, please. It won't happen again."

"Apologize," Sid said, "to *her*."

I could tell that Raven at first had no idea what Sid meant, but then she blinked. "Nirrim, dear girl, why don't you have a cool bath. Help yourself to one of my soaps. You poor thing, you look exhausted."

Sid said, "That is not an apology."

Raven cut a startled look in Sid's direction before glancing again at me. "Nirrim, I'm sorry. You know I am always sorry when I lose my temper."

It had hurt the first time she had called me "stupid," when she had discovered the lost heliograph. This time it hurt even more, because I had believed that she would never do it again, and now she had just done so in front of someone I wanted to think well of me. I swallowed and said, "It's all right. I shouldn't have left the door open."

Raven nodded in satisfaction. Sid looked unaccountably angrier.

But Raven didn't actually think I was stupid. I had done a stupid thing. I had humiliated her in front of an important guest. Her reaction, I felt, was understandable.

"You were dazed by the heat," she told me, kind. The wobbly feeling inside me steadied. "And I was so hot and irritable! I was not myself—"

"I will be staying here for three nights," Sid said, cutting through the tail end of Raven's words—rudely, as though she would have preferred to clamp a hand over Raven's mouth. "I require a maid to attend me. I will pay extra for the service, of course."

Raven said, "Annin—"

"I want Nirrim."

Raven studied Sid. Her expression wasn't suspicious, exactly, but her curiosity was growing.

"She will also serve as my guide to the Ward," Sid said. "I am a traveler from afar."

"There are no travelers."

"There is one now." She ignored Raven's stare and Annin's. "We have nothing like the Ward where I come from. I would like to see more of it before I leave this island." Sid opened her purse and withdrew a handful of gold coins. She let them slide from her palm onto the table.

"Nirrim will do whatever you need," Raven said. "Won't you, my girl?"

⌒

"How do you know her?" Annin said in a hushed voice as she walked with me toward the kitchen, where a bath lay in an adjoining room.

"Know who?" Morah glanced up from her mortar and pestle as she continued to grind spices.

"The *lady*."

"Why is she here?" Morah said. "High Kith never come to the Ward."

"But she is not *really* High," Annin said, then scrambled as if she had said something offensive for which she could get in trouble. "I mean, she is different. But in her country she must be whatever they call High."

"Maybe she's faking," Morah said. "How do we *know* she is High where she comes from? Just because she acts like it doesn't mean she is. How do we even know she is a traveler? There have been only Herrath people on the island of Herrath. Travelers only exist in stories."

"She doesn't look Herrath," Annin said. "She looks like no one I have ever seen."

Morah sniffed. "That much is true."

"She is so elegant. Did you see her dress? I would die to wear something like that. She is beautiful."

"She would be," Morah agreed, "if her hair weren't so short."

"I suppose that's the fashion where she comes from, but it is a pity. Such a pretty color!"

"What's wrong with short hair?" I said. "*I* have short hair."

"Not that short," Annin said.

"You would grow yours if Raven let you," Morah said.

"It looks like she paid a tithe!" Annin said.

"It looks like a boy's," Morah said.

"I like it," I said. They looked at me in surprise. I gathered a large towel and a bar of soap from Raven's store. My chest buzzed with annoyance. Ever since Annin had said *beautiful*, something had been pinching at my heart. I didn't know who deserved my anger more: Annin and Morah for making such a fuss over something that had nothing to do with them, or me for being so affected by a simple word.

Annin and Morah seemed to feel my annoyance. They fell silent, but their silence was annoyed, too, because they could see no reason for me to be angry.

But I could see a reason, and was relieved that they didn't.

⌒

"What are you doing here?" I demanded as soon as I shut the door to Sid's room behind me. Her back was to me. She sat at a small table, writing what was perhaps a letter in her language. The page was covered with unfamiliar script. "We were supposed to meet in the Middling quarter."

She set aside her pen but didn't turn around. "This is better."

"Why?"

"I wanted to see where you come from." She turned around. Her gaze flickered over me. "You're dripping," she said, "from the bath."

I ignored this. "I don't know where I come from."

Her attention, which seemed to have drifted, returned. "What do you mean?"

"I was newly born when I was left outside the orphanage in the baby box. I don't know who left me there."

"Baby box?"

"Yes, the metal box for unwanted ones. There are two boxes, actually, one on either side of the wall, so that anyone of any kith can leave a baby there."

Her face was fierce in the lamplight, her black eyes almost feral. "That is barbaric."

"Don't worry. There are holes for a baby to breathe, and a matron checks the box every hour, except at night."

"How comforting."

"The Council says it is the best way to protect unwanted babies."

"If the Council says so, I suppose it must be true."

I thought her sarcasm was unfair. "If parents had no way to abandon babies in secret, they might murder them."

"So you were raised thinking that if you hadn't been left in a metal box, your mother would have murdered you? That if Raven hadn't taken you in, you would have lived in the orphanage forever?"

"Not forever. When I turned eighteen, if I didn't show promise as an artisan, and wasn't apprenticed to a shopkeeper, I would have become Un-Kith and taken outside the city."

Sid's mouth was flat. "You say this as if it is nothing to you."

"I am lucky. I owe so much to Raven."

She stared at me. Then she shook her head in helpless dislike—which

bothered me, since I had done nothing to earn it. I said, "Are you thinking that I am even farther beneath you than you'd assumed?"

"I am thinking that your life has been very different from mine," she
said, which was a politer way of saying *yes*. Then she said, "I could help
you find out where you come from."

I shook my head. "Impossible."

"I'm good at finding things out. I want to do something for you. Tell
me what I can do."

I didn't want to tell her. I didn't want to choose yet how she would
reward me for helping her. I had lived with so little choice behind the
wall that it was as if I had never left the baby box. I liked that there was
something undecided. I liked that Sid hadn't yet made me decide.

"Start by explaining what a ladies' maid is supposed to do," I said.
"I have no idea."

She cocked a flirtatious brow. "You could always help take off my
clothes."

I flinched, startled by her daring. But it was just a joke, one made
for the pleasure of seeing me squirm. She laughed. "I don't need you to
do anything. I asked for you to be my ladies' maid so that we could talk
in private. Though, to be honest, dresses *are* a pain. All those fastenings
in the back."

"I have never seen you in one before now. You don't look like yourself."

She glanced down at her deeply red dress. "Too much fabric. Too
flowy. But it's fine."

She didn't sound like it was fine. I said, "You don't like it."

She shrugged. "It's what people expect. But it reminds me of my
old life. It makes me look . . ."

I thought of Annin's word: *beautiful*. "Like a prize to be won?"

"Let's be honest, I *am*. Tomorrow will you show me the Ward?"

I thought about how it would be for the two of us to walk through the Ward. Everyone's eyes would be drawn to her. I would look drab by her side.

"What's wrong?" Though her back was still to me as she sat in her chair, her body had curved toward mine, her face tipped up, studying me. "Are you worried about your employer? She'll let you go. I paid her well." Sid's mouth curled in distaste. "She will do anything for money."

Defensively, I said, "Of course. She doesn't have much of it."

"I suppose that's true," Sid said slowly, maybe seeing my anger. She couldn't possibly understand Raven's life—or my own.

I said, "*I* don't have money."

"That has nothing to do with what I think about you. That's not why I don't like Raven. It's because she is not kind."

"Yes, she is."

"She insulted you."

"I left the door open."

"So what?"

"She was anxious to impress you."

"Why are you defending her?" Her eyes got narrow. "Wait. Is *this* the woman you mentioned in prison? The one you said was *something like a mother?*"

I didn't like the disgust in her voice. I felt like a child caught pretending that a rag doll was a princess. I hated even more the way Sid's expression was shifting into pity.

"There is no excuse for how she behaved toward you," Sid said. "I don't think you see things clearly."

Which had always been exactly my problem, although after finding streaks of color beneath the white paint on the walls of the Ward, I was starting to wonder whether my judgment was really as bad as I'd always thought. "My life is none of your concern," I said stiffly. "You and I have a bargain. I will help you, and when you have what you want you will leave. You won't even remember this conversation."

"Of course I will."

I shook my head. How many times had someone forgotten a conversation that I remembered perfectly?

"I will take you anywhere in the Ward you want to go," I said. "But there's something important I want to show you." I told her about the colored paint beneath the whitewashed walls. "I dreamed about it, after I drank a dream sold in the night market."

"Tell me about this dream," she said, so I did. I wanted to pull us away from the fact that she would leave here and go back to her old life. I didn't want to hear her insist again that somehow, in the midst of a life that I couldn't imagine, one far away from here, she would remember me. I told her everything about the dream, except that I had had a conversation with my younger self in it. That felt too personal—and too strange—to share.

She stood and reached for a gorgeously pink damask purse. Its lining was a shocking blue. When she reached inside the purse it looked like her hand was disappearing into a midday summer sky. She withdrew the prayer book of the gods and gave it to me. "Can you find the murdered creature from your dream?"

I sat at the edge of her bed and paged through the book. I'd had no idea that people had once believed in so many gods. The god of echoes. Of tunnels. Of unspoken words. Of lies. Of games. The wind. The lost.

There were illustrations, and when I found what I was looking for I paused, then continued through the book, glancing at each page only long enough to record the image of it in my mind.

"You read quickly." Sid came to join me at the edge of the bed. The bell of her sleeve brushed my bare arm. A shiver traveled up the back of my neck.

I edged away. "I'm not really reading." I returned the book to her. "It was the god of discovery."

If she was bothered by my shifting away from her, she didn't show it. She said, "I wonder what it takes to kill a god."

"There are no gods."

"What if there were, and they were all killed? Or what if there were, and they all fled?"

"I thought you didn't believe in them, either."

"I was raised to consider all possibilities."

"Because your parents believe in gods?"

Now she looked uncomfortable. "It has more to do with strategy."

"What do you mean?"

"People can refuse to see a possibility. Maybe they don't want it. Maybe it never occurs to them, or is even awful to them. But people make bad choices when they don't know the full range of choices. People come to wrong conclusions if they don't understand all the possible questions."

"Are your parents scholars?" I asked. Sid's eyes widened in amusement, so I tried again. "Merchants?"

"Well, they certainly wanted to sell *me*." Sid rubbed the back of her neck and tugged absently at the fastening at the back of her dress. "Don't take what I said about strategy too close to heart. Being open to all possibilities has a flaw, too."

"What flaw?"

"It can make you doubt what you know." Then she imitated someone else's voice, someone who spoke in a too-elegant way. "But how can you be *sure*, Sidarine, if you've never so much as looked at a man? How can you *know*, when you've never even kissed one?"

She said it steadily. Her face was unchanging, her expression perfectly even. Her long hands lay folded across her knee, the lines of her arms so poised, so ladylike, that I could see a different version of Sid than the one who had rummaged through the piano and made me jump off a balcony.

I said, "Sidarine is a pretty name."

She pinched her silk sleeve. "It's like this dress." Then she cut a mock-menacing look in my direction. "Don't ever use that name, or our friendship is over."

Friendship? Was that what this was? I felt a sudden, hard determination to be unfazed by Sid, who so clearly enjoyed fazing everyone. I want to see your face, she had said in the prison, the next time that I shock you.

"Turn around," I said.

Her black eyes widened. I saw her start to ask a question. Then, to my surprise, she did exactly what I had told her to do. She shifted her weight on the edge of the bed and turned so that I saw the back of her head, her neck and the perfect posture of her straight shoulders, the three hook-and-eye fastenings on the back of her dress. Steadily, I opened each one. "Since you have trouble doing it yourself," I said. "Since I'm supposed to be your maid."

She was quiet. The red silk of her dress lay open on her shoulders, exposing the skin of her back down to her waist. I had decided, resolutely, not to look at her bare skin. But a drop of water fell between her shoulder blades. For a moment I didn't understand where the water had come from. I thought it might be an illusion.

But it was from my hair. The water droplet had slipped from the ends of my hair, wet from the bath. I saw her skin twitch. The water slid down her spine. It disappeared into the silk at her waist.

I stood. I said good night. I closed the door behind me.

I don't think she knew my heart was twisting inside me like a blind animal.

I don't think she knew I had held my breath as I undid each fastening.

She couldn't have known how I went to my room and crawled into bed, worried about how bold I had been.

What I had done could easily have looked like nothing—no more than me performing my new job as her maid, for which she had paid handsomely.

But I knew what it really was.

I liked Sid too much. I liked the sight of her bare back. I had wanted to follow the water droplet with my fingertip.

In my bed in the dark I touched the Elysium feather where it burned against my breast. I wondered if the feather had made me want Sid. I wondered if it could make her want me.

25

MAYBE IF I HAD BEEN able to keep the Elysium bird, people in the Ward would have looked at me the way they did with Sid beside me: in disbelieving wonder. The heat was as bad as it had been the day before, but people came out into the streets when they heard the gossip about a High lady visiting the Ward. They saw the gold-embroidered indigo batiste of her simply cut dress, her easy yet perfect posture that made everyone else look like they were slouching, and how the sunlight caught her short hair. Sid refused to carry a parasol.

"You'll burn," I warned. Her skin was too pale.

"*You*, I notice, are not carrying a parasol."

"I'm darker than you. Anyway, I'm not allowed. It's not my kith."

She glanced at me as we walked. I liked having an excuse to meet her gaze.

"I want my hands free," she said. She made a face, as if a parasol in her hand would be a burden, and even the idea were an itchy cloth irritating her skin. She spoke as if she were a worker who used her hands all the time. It was true that her hands didn't look like a lady's hands. She wore no rings. Her nails were cut to the quick. Little scars marked the fingers. A long, narrow scar crossed the back of her right hand.

"Where did you get that?" I asked.

"This? Fighting a tiger."

"I'd like a real answer."

"A lovelorn girl who just couldn't let me go."

"Sid."

"A duel to the death. I won, of course."

"Is it possible for you to tell any story in which you're not the hero?"

"So you would like a *boring* lie?"

"I'd like the truth."

"No," she said cheerfully, "I don't think you actually do." She ran a hand along the white wall as we walked toward the artisan workshops. "So the whole Ward is painted white? Show me the spot you found, with the colored paint beneath."

I shook my head. "Later. I don't want anyone to see us do it. Everyone is staring at you."

She lifted her brows. "*And* you."

I had never before had so many eyes on me. I tried to do my usual trick of pretending everyone on the streets had forgotten me, but I found that I couldn't, maybe because I couldn't forget *myself*. I felt too aware of my body: the sun in my face; the narrow distance between Sid and me; the swish of her dress; the scuff of my sandals; the prickle down the back of my neck as I realized that it wasn't just that people were staring at Sid, at her strange beauty, or at me, the little shadow walking beside her. It was her *and* me, together, that captured their attention. Gazes darted from her face to mine.

I showed Sid the workshops of the makers in the Ward. She appreciatively examined each item, praising the maker, but I could tell from the slight furrow between her brows that she was disappointed, that the carved jewelry box with its cunning secret compartment held no real interest for her, that the pink blown-glass vase that she claimed was gorgeous was in fact useless. Although she flattered every artisan, who seemed to grow a little taller with Sid's expressed admiration, I knew she hadn't found what she'd hoped.

I worried that she wasn't easy to please, despite whatever words she might say to the contrary.

I worried that I was too attuned to what she wanted.

She shut a compact mirror. We were in Terrin's shop, the two of us reflected everywhere in the mirrors surrounding us like facets of an enormous, hollow jewel. I saw Sid's dissatisfaction.

"What is it?" I said. "What are you looking for?"

She tugged me gently in the direction of the door and the streets outside the shop. I saw her hand on mine from all the angles of all the mirrors as she drew me toward the door. Terrin's eyes widened at such an unexpected, even shocking, gesture between someone of Sid's kith and someone of mine. I wondered what my face showed as my fingers tightened around Sid's hand, the one with the long scar.

"Everything is just . . . normal," she said when we'd left the cool of the shop. A wind had picked up, but it was so hot it felt like the breath of a dog. "There are mirrors like that compact beyond the wall, but one half shows yourself and the other shows how you want to look. If you stare at that half long enough, your face will change to match what you see, at least for an hour or so. But there is nothing unusual about Terrin's mirrors, or any other goods in the Ward. The objects are inert. Dead. If there is magic, it isn't *here*."

Something dwindled inside me. "Does that mean you'll leave?"

But she didn't answer, because a man called my name. She dropped my hand.

It was Aden, striding toward us.

～ 26 ～

"NIRRIM, I NEED YOU," he said.

"*Need?*" Sid's mouth curled.

"Excuse us," he told her, just barely polite, with an expression that betrayed frustration that he needed to be polite with her. "Nirrim, now."

Sid's face showed disbelief but also a knowing look that I didn't understand and didn't like. "Just a moment," I told her, and pulled Aden across the street.

"What is wrong with you?" I demanded.

"With *me*? What are you doing with her?"

"I'm working."

"You're prancing around the Ward like you're that lady's pet." His blue eyes were bright with disgust. "Everyone's been talking."

"It's a job. I'm her escort."

"I don't care how she's dressed. She's not High. She's not even Herrath. A traveler, they say. Maybe so, maybe there *are* other countries across the sea, but if she is from one of them all that means is that she can tell whatever lies she likes and her countrymen aren't here to prove her wrong."

"She paid," I said. "In gold coins."

"So what? People fake their kith all the time. You know that. You *help* them do that. Gold coins and a fancy dress and a fancy attitude don't mean anything."

"Why are you so angry? This has nothing to do with you."

"I don't like how she looks."

"She can't help being born High Kith any more than we can help being born Half Kith."

He snorted. "If you don't see what I mean, then maybe it's for the best."

But I did see what he meant. He could have meant that she looked foreign, but there was another possible meaning to his words. I became uncomfortably aware of all the times Sid had mentioned being with women. I knew what she was. Did Aden somehow know, too?

Was it something you could see on a person's face?

I felt myself flush. "Did you come find me just because the Ward is gossiping and you wanted to yell at me about a bored foreigner with money to spend?"

"I came here for *you*. I came because I care about *you*." He took my shoulders in his large hands.

I stepped back.

"Nirrim, did you hunt the Elysium the night you were arrested?"

Raven had said we should keep what had happened with the Elysium secret. "No, of course not."

"A soldier died that night."

Dread crept through my belly. "So?"

"The militia think it wasn't an accident. They think it was murder."

I glanced across the street to where Sid waited, her right hand at her waist. I said, "That has nothing to do with me."

"*Except* that Annin said you caught the bird and turned it in."

"Why did you ask me a question you knew the answer to?"

"Why did you lie? You lied to *me*, Nirrim." His expression grew wounded. I felt instantly guilty but also angry, because he *wanted* me to feel guilty, and his question had never been a question. It had been a test.

He said, "My friend Darin saw a girl climbing to the roof to catch the bird. The soldier climbed after her."

I felt instantly cold despite the heat.

"He described her to me," Aden said. "He said it was you."

"She wasn't me," I whispered.

"She kicked the soldier to his death."

"I didn't."

"The militia found black hair stuck to the building's fresh paint. Like yours."

I remembered how, that night, a lock of my hair had gotten matted with paint. "Lots of people have black hair. It's common." But my voice trembled.

Aden touched my cheek. His hands fell to my shoulders again, and this time I allowed it. I had no choice. I let him pull me into his arms.

"You lied to me because you were afraid," he said.

I *was* afraid. I was afraid of him. He could so easily ruin my life.

"You don't need to be," he said. "I told Darin not to talk about what he saw. I'll protect you." I looked up at him. He brushed the hair from my face. "I love you," he said. He kissed my cold mouth.

"I love you, too," I said, because there was nothing else I could say.

He let me go then, reassured, the anxiety that had been sparking all around him soothed now into satisfaction. He glanced across the street at Sid with something like disdain, or disinterest, or pity, before he kissed me again, deeply, and left, promising to come to the tavern as soon as he could.

When I walked toward Sid, I saw that her hand was on the hilt of a large knife I had never noticed before. It seemed to be belted beneath her dress, hidden under the fabric, its hilt now showing through a slit in the side. Sid shifted her hand and the dagger disappeared again beneath the fabric. Her expression was neutral yet closed. Everything felt huge inside me. I wanted to explain everything that had happened with Aden. I wanted it to spill out like a confession, like milk from a broken jug. But then I remembered Aden suggesting that Sid was faking her kith, and even though I didn't care if she was faking it, not exactly, I became frighteningly aware of how little I knew about her.

Aden, at least, I knew. Aden, I could trust.

What would Sid think, if she knew I had killed someone?

What would she do?

"I suppose that's your sweetheart." Sid's voice was cool.

"No."

"Ah, Nirrim. It's never wise to lie when no one will believe you."

27

"WHY DON'T YOU LEAD ME to the red paint you found," Sid said, "beneath the coat of white." Her voice sounded friendly enough, but too perfectly calibrated to be truly friendly. She was like that the whole way to the building, commenting on the surprising charm of the Ward. "Not bad, for a prison," she said.

I glanced around. "It's so plain. You are surely used to better."

"It has been made to look plain."

We were passing through the agora. She said, "Do you see that temple?"

"It's not a temple. It is for storing grain."

"Look at the cornices along the top. It looks like decorations have been chiseled away. And there." She pointed to the holes in the agora's paved square. "What used to be there? Statues, maybe? The holes seem the right size for it."

I thought of the visions I had had of the agora. It felt dizzying to hear Sid suggest, without knowing it, that what I had seen was real. For so long I had thought of those visions as dangerous signs of my unsteady mind. It unnerved me to wonder if Sid was right—if *I* had been right, all these years. I wasn't sure what it would mean if she and I were both right.

I repeated what Morah had once said to me. "The agora has always been this way. It is as it is."

Sid shut her mouth. The sky darkened as we walked. Indi flowers growing along the walls nodded in the warm wind. Silver ants glinted as they disappeared into cracks along the walls. The heat would break soon.

I asked, "Why do you carry a weapon?"

"Oh, that."

"You looked like you would use it."

"I was worried about you," she said. "I didn't need to be."

"I've known Aden for years. He's harmless."

"If you say so."

"He would never hurt me."

Dryly, she said, "What a compelling reason to care for someone."

But it *was* a good reason, and if Sid could laugh at it, it was only because her life had been so easy. "As if you need a reason," I said. "As if you don't just tumble into any woman's bed."

"You wound me, Nirrim." She lay a hand on her heart. "Not just *any* woman. I have standards. They must be beautiful. Adoring." She ticked the criteria off with her fingers. "They must let me have my way. And never stay longer than one night."

"How romantic."

"Oh, yes. Just like your hero back there. Such broad shoulders! And his jaw. I loved his jaw. Why, you could shovel dirt with that jaw."

I didn't want to talk about Aden. It sounded like she was mocking him, but really she was mocking me. "You didn't answer my question about that knife."

"Dagger."

"Why do you wear it beneath your dress?"

"I always wear it."

"But why do you hide it?"

She brushed her hand through the air as if batting something away. As we walked, the wind grew. The sky turned the color of slate. "It's not the custom here to wear a weapon openly."

"But it *is* the custom where you come from?"

"For some people."

"Which people?"

"Nirrim, why are you interrogating me about my dagger?"

Frustrated, I said, "Because you're dodging my questions."

"No, I'm not. I've answered them all. How much farther to that wall of yours? Is that thunder?"

That faint rumble *was* thunder. It would rain, just as Sirah had said that it would. As always, she had been exactly right about when the rain would come. I was glad for the coming storm. The people of the Ward were going into their homes, which meant that Sid and I were the only ones left on the street.

I said, "I want a straight answer."

"Very well. I will give you a straight answer if *you* give *me* one."

"To what question?"

"So suspicious! All in good time," she said. "If you must know, I wear that dagger because it is Valorian, and that is what Valorians do."

"Valoria is the old Empire? The one that conquered so many countries?"

"The very same."

"You said you were Herrani."

"I am both. There was some intermarrying after the last war, the one that ended Valorian rule."

"Really? Even though the two people had been enemies?"

"Oh, yes. The king and queen of Herran are a mixed couple, and theirs is a love for the ages, celebrated in songs and stories. They became a model for their people. Intermarrying is . . . not common, but accepted. More or less."

"So your parents are like the king and queen."

"You could say that."

"Are there many people like you, where you come from?"

"There is no one like me," she said. "I am beyond compare."

"Sid."

Her pace slowed. I felt a drop of rain.

"What do you mean, exactly?" she asked. "Someone who is mixed, or a woman who likes women?"

It startled me, how easily she could mention something that, at least in the Ward, was scandalous. "Someone who is mixed."

"No," she said. "Not many. There are unkind words for people who are half-Herrani, half-Valorian."

"But you're High. No one would dare call you something unkind."

She widened her black eyes. "Of course they would."

"But if the king and queen—"

"People adore them, but that doesn't mean they adore *me*. I live in Herran, and most people there have very bad memories of what the Valorians did. The way I look reminds them of that. I look very Valorian."

Sid's mouth had twisted ruefully when she said *adore*. I asked, "Do you not like the Herrani rulers?"

She shrugged. "They are a problem. They had a chance to remake the world. All they did was reestablish the Herrani monarchy with themselves as the rulers."

"What are they like?"

"Oh, I don't really know them." Thunder rumbled again, louder this time. She looked up and seemed to speak her words toward the sky. "They're smart. Scary. Benevolent, I guess. Kind to their people. But you definitely don't want to cross them."

"It sounds as if you *do* know them."

"Well," she said reluctantly, "I worked for the queen."

"Really? What did you do?"

"A little bit of this, a little bit of that."

"Straight answers, Sid."

"I ran her errands."

"You don't seem like a runner of errands."

"And yet it was so," Sid said. "The queen's wish was my command."

"Did you enjoy working for her?"

"It was interesting work. A good position for someone like me." But there was a stiffness to the way Sid said it.

"Was it," I guessed, "something your parents made you do?"

"Yes." She smiled, a little sadly. "Exactly. Now it's my turn to question and yours to answer. Tell me, have you told that young man of yours yet that you love him?"

I paused on the cobblestones.

"Why have you stopped?" she asked.

"We're here." I crouched by the white wall I had scratched at yesterday. I couldn't see the red paint anymore.

"A straight answer, Nirrim. As we agreed."

I ran a hand over the wall. It was perfectly white and smooth. Had I imagined scraping paint off the wall? Had it even happened? I was so confused, and Sid was waiting for an answer that I didn't want to give. "It's complicated," I said.

"Yes or no."

I wanted to tell her that sometimes you can't explain one thing without explaining everything. Sometimes an answer is not as easy as yes or no. Sometimes the truth gets lost even as you tell the truth. "Yes," I said, "but—"

"That's what I thought."

Thunder cracked the sky. Rain darted down. It pelted my head, my shoulders. It dropped like pebbles. I knelt before the white wall. I forgot about Aden. Panic grew inside me as I searched for where I had scraped away the white paint. The scratched-off patch was gone.

"Nirrim, what are you doing?"

"It was here." My voice rose. "The red paint." I dug at the white wall with my wet nails.

"Stop that," Sid said. "You'll hurt yourself."

"I swear it was here." The rain fell harder, blurring my vision. "I'm not making it up."

"I believe you."

"Lend me your dagger. I'll show you. The red paint is there."

"You don't have to show me."

I looked up at her. Rain dripped from her eyelashes. It dripped from her full mouth. It had already soaked her thin dress, darkening its hue. I could see clearly the shape of her narrow body, the little dip of her navel, the rigid outline of the dagger and its leather belt beneath the wet silk. She pulled me to my feet. I was so unprepared for that—or maybe she had tugged harder than she intended—that I wobbled on my feet. I swayed too close to her, to her rain-wet mouth. My hand went to her shoulder. I didn't mean to do it. It was instinct, to steady myself. For a moment, she allowed the touch, then stepped back. My hand skidded down the sodden, rumpled silk of her arm and fell away.

I had regained my balance, but inside I was still unsteady. My fingers were alive, feeling strangely as though they had brushed against something rough that pricked my skin with splinters of pleasure. I tucked my fingers into my hand. The rain helped the feeling go away.

Her eyes narrowed in what looked like caution. She kept a clear distance between us. She wiped water from her face, and said, "If you say you saw it, it was there."

"You don't think I imagined it? *You* don't think I'm crazy?"

"No. I think the Ward is hiding something."

28

THE RAIN STOPPED AND THE sun came out again, but gently, so that the white wall glowed like a slick pearl. We retraced our steps to the tavern. Everything seemed new. The alleys smelled as fresh as clay. The sky was clear. Water dripped brightly from the fragrant indi flowers.

"Someone painted over the wall," Sid said. "Someone who doesn't want anyone here to know the Ward's past. When was the Ward built?"

"I don't know."

"I have seen all the quarters of Ethin. The Ward is its oldest section. It is the heart of the rest of the city, which has grown around it like rings around the core of a tree. Why was the wall built?"

I thought at least *that* answer was obvious. "To keep the Half Kith where we belong."

"But why?"

"It has always been so."

"There is no such thing," she said, "as *always*. But I suppose it doesn't matter." She shrugged. "Sometimes it's best to let people and cities keep their secrets. It takes so long to ferret them out."

This worried me. She sounded already bored, her voice distant and languid, and she had been in the Ward only one day.

We reached the tavern. I knew that as soon as we walked in there would be exclamations over our appearance. Sid was sunburnt and her dress ruined. She was barely looking at me, so I couldn't read any clue in her eyes as to how I looked, but I guessed that it couldn't be good, with my dress stuck to my skin, my sandaled feet dirty and damp.

Before I opened the tavern door, I said, "Will you need help? Getting out of your dress. Because it is wet." It shouldn't have felt like a brazen question. I shouldn't have stumbled over it. I had been employed as her maid and she had complained about a dress's fastenings, which I had already helped once to undo. I had been paid for a job. I was merely offering to do it.

Her face tightened. "No," she said, "I won't." She opened the door and stepped inside. The tavern's interior was a soft mouth of darkness against the crisp, pale sunshine. The shadows swallowed her whole.

Raven wasn't in the main hall of the tavern, where Annin was serving Middling merchants who had come into the Ward to trade with Half-Kith artisans and had been trapped inside by the rain. I sent myself to the kitchen anyway, since I knew Morah needed my help and Sid had an impenetrable politeness to her that made clear she didn't want my company.

"You're behind," Morah said, trussing a loin to be roasted. "Our mistress said to remind you that you're not to let the honor of being a ladies' maid for a few days go to your head. You are to do your chores as you always do, in addition to the new extra work, which means you had better get started on the bread and pies."

I had already lost so many hours of tavern work. My feet were heavy and sore from walking all over the Ward. If I was required to bake a batch of printed breads for Raven to sell beyond the wall, as well as to prepare desserts for the tavern, I would be awake late and exhausted the next morning. I had better get started. I stuffed my ragged, damp hair under a cap, tied on an apron, and washed my hands. I bustled into the pantry, fetching canisters of flour and yeast.

"Look at you," Morah said as I measured flour into a bowl.

"I know." I was embarrassed by my appearance, though not because Morah would care. I wished, for a moment, that I could look impressive the way Sid did, even when she was wearing a Middling man's clothes. Especially, somehow, then. I touched the Elysium feather above my heart. "I must looked like a drowned rat."

Morah snipped the twine. "I meant, look how eager you are to obey."

A too-large quantity of flour slid all at once into the bowl. A white cloud billowed up. Stiffly, I asked, "Do you think I should shirk my duties?"

"No."

"The High-Kith lady will leave in two days, and then my life will be exactly as it was before."

"I know."

I swallowed the tightness in my throat. "So in the meantime am I supposed to ignore what I need to do to help Raven earn the money that feeds us? Am I supposed to let you and Annin do twice the work to make up for what I neglect?"

Slowly, she said, "I know you love her."

My chest raged with sudden fear. I opened my mouth, ready to deny it. I didn't love Sid. I barely knew her. What had Morah seen, what *could* she have seen that would make her say that? It was an attraction, nothing more. Plus, it was understandable. Surely it was. Sid represented so much of what someone like me would long to have: wealth, comfort, status, confidence. It was *that* that drew me, I was sure of it. Not *love*. Love wasn't possible between women, and although I knew from the way Sid talked that other things were possible, they were not possible for me.

But when I saw how surprised Morah was by what must have been a vehemence in my expression, I realized what she had really meant. My fear flowed away. "Of course I love Raven. Of course I work hard for her. She works hard for us."

"Does she?" Morah tilted her head. "Where is she now?"

"Running errands, I suppose, beyond the wall."

"That's what she *says*."

"Then it must be true. She is not a liar."

"You don't launder her clothes," Morah said. "I do."

I didn't see what that had to do with anything. "So?"

"Sometimes her skirts twinkle with glitter after she goes beyond the wall. Her pockets have empty packets of pleasure dust."

"I don't know what pleasure dust is."

"You don't know *anything*." She thumped the trussed loin into a roasting pan. "Raven has kept you and Annin so innocent. She learned her lesson after what happened with me."

You must be careful around Raven, Aden had said. Ask Morah. She knows better than anyone.

"She has given you a home," I said to Morah. "She has been like a mother to us."

Morah wiped her meat-bloodied hands on her apron. Though the window to the kitchen was small, the sunlight coming through it was strong. It burned through the room. She said, "You think that only because you don't know what it means to be a mother."

"Why don't you like her?" The question burst from me. I heard how wounded it sounded.

"Nirrim, I hate her."

"Why?" As soon as I asked I wished I hadn't. I suddenly dreaded the answer.

"She took something from me."

"Well," I said, relieved that the reason was so small, "you should ask for it back. If she understands how much it means to you, she will return it. Then you will feel better."

"You don't understand."

"She probably didn't even know it was yours."

"There you go," Morah said, "always making excuses for her. Even when she smashes a lantern against your face and scars you for life."

"She didn't mean to hurt me."

"But she *did* hurt you." Morah's hands, still bloodied around the knuckles, clenched into fists. "She hurt *me*. She is a thief."

"She has given you so much. A home. Good work. Food. A family."

She shook her head. "I haven't wanted to say anything because I know how important all of that is to you. You looked so lost when you came here. You were thirteen but seemed so much younger. Your hands could never be empty. You always had to hold something, to cuddle it to your chest. You had a small rag. Do you remember?"

I did, but I didn't want to think about that. It had been a scrap of cloth from Helin's dress. In the orphanage, we had only two sets of clothes: a work dress and a nightdress. Helin's body had been taken away in her nightdress. In the night, I had found her other dress hanging beside mine in the wardrobe. My hands shaking, I had cut a thin ribbon from the hem. I would bundle it in my hand at night. It helped me sleep. She had been my only friend.

"Raven burned it," Morah said.

I remembered the raw pain in my throat when I couldn't find it. My cheeks wet. How I had sobbed and Raven had comforted me, saying that she would help me find it. Chin up, she said. It is just a dirty old rag, she said. What could I have wanted with it anyway?

"No," I said. "She looked everywhere for it."

"I saw her burn it, in this very stove."

I felt like I was groping for familiar things in an unfamiliar darkness. "Well," I said, "if she did it's because she didn't know what it was."

"She knew. *I* knew. It was a little strip of gray wincey."

"Then," I said, "she didn't understand what it meant to me."

"She did it *because* she understood what it meant to you. That was why she took my baby."

I remembered my illusion of a baby in Morah's arms. Of a child standing near her, growing older as the years passed until my eyes refused to see the little boy, before I became successful at banishing most of the strange visions that afflicted me.

Morah's face was wooden, her expression set as if pins held her features in place. "Nirrim, she tried the same things on me that she always uses on you. She told me it was for my own good. That she cared about me, that I was like a daughter to her. She was looking out for me, even if I couldn't see it. What good would it do to keep the child? The father was gone. He was so young. He had tried to climb over the wall. I had been so sick, early in the pregnancy. I couldn't stop vomiting. I hid my sickness from Raven, hid my growing belly. My sweetheart thought that surely there would be medicine in the Middling quarter for me. He tried to climb the wall during the night, and fell, and died. So I told Raven everything because, like you, I believed in her. I thought she cared about me. And at first, it seemed that way. She gave me the best foods. She held my hair when I vomited. She never let me rest from my work, but I believed her when she said it was for my own benefit, that work would distract me from my sickness and keep me fit for when the baby came. And when my baby came he was so sweet. His nose and mouth and fingers were so small, his hair so dark. I missed his father but thought I was strong enough to make a home for my baby, to raise him alone, because I was not truly alone. I had someone who loved me like a daughter. Someone who would love my child like a grandson. But she took him while I was sleeping."

An emotion swept over me like vertigo. I had no name for what I felt. The namelessness reminded me of when I was a baby and couldn't understand what people said, when their voices tumbled like thick gleaming oil, when sounds dropped from their mouths like rocks, like the whine of a draft through a window, when I didn't know what *oil* was, or *rock* or *window*.

But as Morah's eyes welled I understood the name for that sick chill creeping over my skin and seeping into my belly. It was loss. What I felt was not Morah's loss, though I could see that clear on her face.

It was my own.

"Why don't you want me to love her?" I asked. "You are jealous that I am her favorite. You tell me lies to come between us." But I had seen the ghost of that boy hovering near her. Haltingly, I said, "If it's true, then where is your child?"

She looked straight into the light of the window. The light must have hurt her eyes. I understood, now, this habit of hers, which I had seen her do so often before. It was a trick not to cry . . . or if tears were shed, for them to seem due to nothing more than strong light. "I don't know," she said. "Raven promised me that she found him a good home. She said it would do me no good to know where. I believed her because I was desperate to believe her. Now I believe what I refused to believe then: that she brought him to the boys' orphanage, where he starved or died or grew up to be Un-Kith or was apprenticed to someone in the Ward, and is almost grown out of being a child, is almost an early man. I look for him when I walk in the Ward. I used to hope I might find him. Now I know he is grown past recognition, and I would never recognize him even if I saw him."

"But if this is true, how could you continue to work for her? How could you not leave?"

She shrugged. "Raven is powerful in the Ward. You know this. No one would hire me if I left her. I would become Un-Kith."

"You want to hurt me. You want to take away the one person who cares for me."

She gripped my hand and pinned it to the table. She squeezed it. "*I* care for you."

My tears finally spilled over even as Morah's eyes stayed dry. "I don't believe you," I said, but I did. I had seen it with my own eyes: her cuddling a ghost baby, her keeping knives out of a ghost child's reach. "Maybe she meant what she said. You must have been so young. Maybe she was trying to help you."

"It was *my* child." Her hand was hard on mine. "She had no right."

"Why have you told me this? You want me to hate her."

"Yes. I do want you to hate her, for your own sake."

"I don't understand."

"You have a chance to leave. You must take it. You must not stay here, hoping that Raven will love you like a daughter. She never will."

"What chance?" I said, but I guessed already what she would say.

"The High lady. She has taken an interest in you."

"As her servant."

Morah shook her head. "Why did the orphanage mistress teach you to read? She didn't teach *me*. Why does Raven keep you so close? Why have you caught Aden's heart, when every girl in the Ward wants him? There is something special in you. A shine. When people see it, they want it. That High lady is no different. If she offers to take you from the Ward, you must go. Promise me."

But it did not matter what I would have promised Morah, because Annin entered the kitchen with the news that Lady Sidarine was leaving the Ward. She wanted Annin to pack her things, not me. When I asked Annin if I was needed I was told no, I wasn't. The lady had said so.

Sid was leaving the Ward even sooner than she had planned. It turned out that I had been right about her: she was easily fascinated by some new idea, a new city, a new person. Maybe, before, I had caught her attention. But I no longer held it. I had been right about her, just as I had been right about the ghost child I had seen at Morah's side, was right about the colored paint beneath the white walls, was right about the statues that had once stood in the agora . . . was right, I was suddenly sure, about all the visions I had ever had, the visions I had dismissed as unreal or as signs of an unsteady mind.

I had been right about everything, including that Sid would leave me behind.

29

I WAS NOT BOLD.

It simply wasn't my nature. You see that. You have guessed, perhaps, that at some point in the orphanage's baby box, after the hot urine that soaked my swaddling had chilled in the cold and then warmed again from the heat of my small body, that I came to like it in there. The ventilation holes became stars in the close dark. I stopped crying. My fist found my mouth. I sucked. I turned my face into the metal corner. Maybe you know already that I didn't cry again until someone opened the box, drowning me in light. Then I wailed. I didn't want the hands to take me out.

Maybe, because you pity me, you will say, But you climbed to a roof, though you were afraid to fall.

You didn't confess to a judge. You betrayed no one. You kept your secrets.

You went beyond the wall. Is that nothing?

They were exceptions.

At heart I was a coward.

At heart I took comfort in what I knew, the sure things of the world: stones, hot bread, old wood, and yes, the wall—how high it was, how small it made me feel, as though I were at the bottom of a great bowl. The wall kept me in, but it also kept the unknown out.

It was another me that told Annin to disobey Sid, and stay exactly where she was.

I think it was an infection in my blood. A need that rioted in my heart.

It was something that had crept inside without me knowing it: a parasite, a pale ribbon worm that must be pulled out little by little from a slit in the skin, so intent it was on remaining in my flesh, making me do things I normally would never do.

Like abandoning the task I had been assigned.

Like sneaking through the tavern, hoping Raven wouldn't see me.

Like knocking on Sid's door and—when she didn't answer—pushing my way in.

30

A TRUNK LAY OPEN ON THE FLOOR. Sid sat at the desk, writing. She didn't turn when I came in. The water-stained dress lay on the floor in a skinny, translucent trail of fabric like a snake's shed skin. She was wearing a Middling man's clothes: fitted tunic, thin black trousers. Her body looked sharp, pointed at the knees and elbows.

"Not you." She didn't turn around, didn't cease writing. "I asked for Annin."

"Take me with you," I said.

Her laugh was no more than a short breath. She set aside her pen then, and stood, and faced me. Her expression was closed and tight. Not quite cruel, but hard enough to make me remember that she must be armed with that dagger, though I could not see it. It occurred to me that the boredom I had seen earlier that day had been a mask for something more intense. "No," she said. "Now you may leave."

My heart kicked against my ribs. I wanted to demand again that she take me with her, but I was struggling to keep my breath even. I thought that if she said *no* again I would embarrass myself more than I already had, that I might cry. I made my hands into fists. "What were you writing?"

She gave me a slanted look. "A letter."

"To whom?"

"No one important."

"How will you send it? By ship?"

"I won't send it."

I frowned. "Why are you writing something you won't send?"

"I was right," she said, "when I first met you. You *are* persistent. Tenacious. But I suppose you would have to be, to be who you are in a place like this." She gave me a cool, appraising look. "I am writing a letter I will not send because it helps me to write it and it would be unwise for its recipient to read it. Now I have answered your question. Go tell Annin to pack my things."

"No."

"No?" She lifted her brows. "You have an obligation to obey your employer."

"You are being awful."

"I am awful, sometimes. You just haven't known me long enough to realize it."

"You are my *partner*."

"You mean that silly bargain we made to find magic?"

My eyes stung. "It is not silly."

"I was born in the year of the god of games."

"I don't understand what you mean."

"I like games." Sid drew her shoulders in tight and spread her hands, as though I had accused her of something and she was ready to defend herself. "I like to wear a man's clothes and I like that it startles people, and then even if I hate dresses I enjoy wearing one to show you that when you thought I was one thing and changed your mind you must now change it again. I like disappearing and showing up when I am least expected. I like pretending. Sometimes I forget myself, and fall for my own game."

She began to remove her clothes from the wardrobe and pack them in the trunk herself, neatly, with perfect folds. It made me wonder if what she had just said, her confessed love for pretense, meant exactly what Aden had suggested: that she had been faking her High-Kith status. After all, would a noble lady know how to fold her own clothes, let alone do it? I said, "I don't care what you are."

She laughed a little. "Oh, I know."

I said, "I don't care if you're pretending to be High." She paused in the act of folding and then resumed. I wasn't sure if her pause was because I had touched on the truth that she was not High Kith, or because she had thought I had meant something else entirely when I said I didn't care what she was. Before I could ask, she said, "*You* are my game, Nirrim. This city is my game. The Ward, too." She placed an airy scarf in the trunk. It wasn't made for warmth—few clothes in this city were. It was a lattice of pink lace. It looked like the decoration on a cake. It was hard to imagine Sid wearing it. She glanced at it in surprise, as though she had forgotten it belonged to her. The anger that had armored her, which I realized only then was anger, sizzled down into tiredness, or the appearance of it. "There is nothing here for me," she said. "I have just been avoiding going home."

"But you had a plan. You believe the city is hiding something. You said so."

"Everybody and everything is hiding something."

"But the white wall. The paint. The compact mirror in the High quarter that changes your face."

"Yes, yes." She waved a dismissive hand. "But the fact that this city has a secret is not proof of magic, and what looks like magic might be nothing more than some science we don't understand."

"Whether it's magic or science doesn't matter, so long as you find out how it *works*."

"And how long might that take to discover? Am I supposed to grow old and die here?"

"You've barely even tried. You . . ." I floundered for words. "You are giving up so *easily*."

Her eyes flashed, but she said nothing.

"It *is* magic," I said. "I know it is. I can prove it," I added, though I didn't fully believe what I had said.

"Even the word *magic* sounds childish," she said. "Unreal. It was a fool's errand to come here. I don't want to feel like a fool."

"Aren't you curious? Don't you want to know? Why would you give up now and go home without the leverage you wanted over your parents?"

"Oh, I'm not going home quite yet."

"Where are you going?"

She shrugged. "Somewhere else. I'm in this city on borrowed time anyway."

"What do you mean?"

"I pulled a few strings to get us out of that prison. Someone's going to collect on that favor eventually." She winced.

"Someone dangerous?"

"You could say that."

"So you're running away?"

"You make it sound like I gave you the impression that I was some-one who stuck around."

"You didn't," I said, exasperated. "But I thought——"

"Yes?" She straightened, and looked directly at me. "What did you think?"

I blurted, "That when you wanted something, you wouldn't rest until you got it."

"Only when we are talking about women, dear Nirrim."

Her words made me hot with shame, because I realized that if she wanted me, she would have had me. It must not have been on her mind.

But it was on mine.

I said, "Aren't you going to ask me why I want to go with you?"

She stepped closer. She looked down at me, black eyes roving over my face. I could smell her perfume. It smelled like citrus kept in a cold metal cup and then poured over burning wood. "Why," she said, "do you want to go with me?"

"I am special." I cringed as the words came out of my mouth. They sounded like the worst kind of lie: the kind that people laugh at.

Yet she didn't laugh. She said, "I know."

"I have magic."

Her brow crinkled. "What do you mean?"

"I see things that no one else does. Things that are true. Things about the past."

"Like what?"

"Like that dream about people in the Ward killing the god of discovery long ago."

"How do you know that's true?"

"I found the colored paint beneath the white. If *that* is true, then maybe the rest of the dream was true, too."

"That's not exactly sound logic. And the colored paint *wasn't* there."

"You said you believed me that it was. That it was painted over."

Slowly, she said, "I do. But you drank a strange substance. A drug, probably. You can't trust that everything you dreamed is true just because one part is. As for the colored paint, maybe you heard or read that the Ward had brightly colored walls. Then you forgot that you knew it, and when you slept, the dream—or drug—returned your memory to you."

"But Morah." I described what I had learned in the kitchen.

Sid hesitated, but said, "Again, you might have heard a rumor years ago. Maybe even just the fragment of a rumor. Part of you understood it, and you imagined the vision of a baby, and forgot the source that made you think it. Memory works in peculiar ways."

"I never forget anything."

"Everybody forgets things."

"No," I said. "Not me. I remember the day I was born. I remember the pressure. My whole body was squeezed. My head felt like it would burst. The world tore open. It was so cold. Air scraped my lungs. I didn't even know what it was, then: air."

"Have you seen a baby being born?"

"Yes, but—"

She opened her hand, the gesture smooth, her hand moving as if scooping something invisible and then turning upward, unfurled, to release it to the sky. "There you go. You saw a birth. You imagined your own. The imagination now acts as 'memory.'"

Sid was talking the way Helin had in the orphanage, finding reasonable explanations that made me seem ordinary, but while Helin's words had comforted me, Sid's unleashed desperation. I *did* feel that I was inventing something. I felt as though I was begging her to believe what I didn't fully believe myself.

Who was I, to claim that my strangeness was *magic*?

An orphan.

A baker.

A criminal.

No one.

But I looked up into Sid's dark eyes, black like ink, the sunburn from earlier that day pink on her cheeks, as if she were blushing, though I couldn't imagine her ever blushing. I couldn't imagine her embarrassed, or afraid to claim what was hers—or even what wasn't.

I knew that if she left the tavern I would never see her again. "My memory is perfect," I said. "I can prove it. Where is that stolen prayer book?"

Wordlessly, she drew it from her trouser pocket and held it aloft between two fingers.

"You saw me read it," I said.

"I saw you look at each page," she corrected.

"Ask me about any god."

"All right." She flipped the book open to a page only she could see. "Tell me about the god of sloth."

So I told her about how ivy grew on the god of sloth, so loath was he to move; the only way to anger him was to wake him, and he would swallow whoever did, too lazy to chew. She asked me about the god of desire, and I recited the page I had read, the prayer to the god, and kept my gaze fixed on Sid's collarbone, unable to look at her face, my blood hot in my cheeks. I almost hated Sid for choosing that one. She must have known. She must have been toying with me, amused to hear words on my tongue that I would never dare say on my own.

"The god of games," Sid said.

The god of games: never spiteful, never faithful, slippery and cunning and sweet, with a liar's heart and a knack for knowing exactly what you want and are willing to lose, so that she can take it all from you. The god who never loses a wager, who as good as steals, who won the moon from the sky and the god of ghosts' mirror and the god of war's heart.

Sid closed the book. I stopped reciting. "I can recite the whole book," I said, "from beginning to end."

"I believe you can," Sid said. "Had you read this book before I took it from the piano?"

"No."

"Maybe you already knew about the gods, far more than you pretended."

"No."

"Maybe you are lying to me."

"*No*," I said. "Give me your letter."

"My letter?"

"The one you just wrote."

"It is in my language. You won't be able to understand it."

"That doesn't matter."

Looking reluctant, she lifted the letter from the desk. It was a single sheet of paper, barely a letter at all, more like a note. It floated in her hand, a white bird's wing, as she returned to me. I took it from her, though her fingers held the page tightly. I glanced at it, then folded it shut. Looking at the image of the page in my mind, I pronounced as best I could the foreign words, grateful that the script of her language looked almost like mine. The syllables I spoke were melodic. Sound cascaded from my lips. I understood none of it.

She winced.

I stopped, and said, "What?"

"You're pronouncing it all wrong."

"Oh. Sorry," I said, and was silent.

She tugged a hand roughly through her short hair. "No, I'm sorry. I shouldn't have said that. I'm acting like pronunciation is why I don't like to hear you speak the words I wrote. That's not fair. You *do* remember all the words. You remember their exact order. You remember where to breathe, and for just how long, where the punctuation is. But that letter was never meant to be read."

"I don't understand its meaning."

"I know. It's just—" She winced again. "It's hard to hear you say it."

"But you see."

"Yes, Nirrim, I see. Your memory is perfect. But I have heard of this before: people who can remember the page of a book as though it were imprinted on the mind."

My hand that held the folded page lowered.

"Nirrim, what exactly do you want me to do with you?"

The question hung in the air, soft and dense and dangerous.

I swallowed. Does a coward always have to be a coward? Was it so wrong to want something, whether I deserved it or not? I said, "I want you to stay in the city for a month."

"Why?"

Because I would miss you. Because I am not ready to let you go.

"Because I think you are giving up too easily," I said.

"A month," she repeated. "That's a terrible idea for me."

"I want you to hire me as your Middling maid for that month. I want you to take me into the High quarter. Maybe I'm not magic, but I can be useful. I have a skill you don't, and even if you are right—that everything I remember about the past has a reasonable explanation—those memories might help you. I might remember more. You said yourself that there is no magic in the Ward. It's all beyond the wall, and concentrated in the High quarter. So take me there, and I'll help you find what you need, like we agreed before."

"And then what?"

"You go home with your leverage. Just as you planned."

She tapped a finger against her lips, considering. "And you?"

"I will come home, too."

"Home," she repeated.

"Here," I said.

She made a face. "So you want . . . a month's vacation in the High quarter."

"An adventure," I reminded her.

"And then you'll come right back here and bake for your mistress and kiss that very tall man you love." She sounded mocking. "Like nothing ever happened, no matter what happens."

"It's just a month," I said defensively, unsure of what else to say. "This is what I want."

"Why do you want this?"

The answer was too big and frightening to explain, even to myself. "I just do."

"Well," she said, "I *do* like giving women what they want."

"Is that a yes?"

She let out a sigh through her teeth. "Yes, that's a yes. Gods help me."

"Thank you," I said, and she laughed. "So prim," she said, "for someone so demanding. Now. I'll have that back." She reached for the letter.

I pulled it away. "It's mine now."

"Oh no." She wagged a finger at me. "No, no, no."

"You said you wouldn't send the letter anyway. And I don't understand its language. You should have no problem giving it to me."

She scrunched up her brow. "Why do you want a letter you can't read?"

Because it's written in your hand, I wanted to say. Because it will be a piece of you I can keep when you eventually *do* leave. "Because you were rude to me, and I claim it as payment."

"Rude?" She grimaced. "I was *horrible*."

"The worst."

"I was the worst!"

"Like a nasty, cold queen."

"King, dear Nirrim."

"I'm not going to forgive you."

She caught my empty hand. "Please." She was serious now. "Forgive me. I was angry."

She held my hand a little too hard, but I liked it. I curled my fingers around hers. And that was all right. A woman could hold a woman's hand. Friends did that in the Ward all the time, and no one looked at them with reproach. Sid's skin was soft, her hand warmer than mine. Looking at my fingers entwined with hers, I asked, "Why were you angry?"

"I was angry at myself."

"That's not an answer."

"It's all the answer you'll get." She opened my hand and studied the well of my palm. She ran a thumb over it. I felt the echo of her touch travel up my back. She brought my hand to her mouth. She kissed my palm, then closed my hand around the ghost of her kiss, which sang into my closed fingers. Pleasure poured down my wrist.

She dropped my hand.

"That's a custom," she said breezily, "in my country. It's a way of saying thank you for being forgiven."

It sounded believable. What did I know, anyway, of her country, except what she had told me? But something made me say, "Is that a lie?"

"Maybe," she said. "Will you help me pack?"

So I did. Together we settled her gorgeous clothes into the trunk as though putting them to bed, tucking them in gently. I was glad to busy my hands. I needed to ignore my singing skin, to ignore that kiss, which had no meaning, or only the meaning that Sid gave it.

But:

She was staying in the city.

She was taking me up quarter, even if it was only because of what she thought I could do for her.

31

"YOU WANT TO LEAVE ME?" Tears welled in Raven's eyes.

"No," I said, "of course not. It is only for a month. Then I will come home."

"Don't you love me? How can you leave me alone?"

I knelt beside her chair. Sid, who had insisted on being present when I told Raven, looked on, her expression closed. I took Raven's hands, which were folded limply in her lap. I pressed them to my cheek. A thick sludge of guilt bubbled up. I remembered what Morah had told me about her baby, but maybe Morah didn't understand Raven like I did, how much emotion the older woman had within her, how important it was to hold her three girls close, as she would any children. She made mistakes, but no one could doubt her affection, not when tears were slipping down her face and loneliness aged her face. "I love you so much," I told her. "You won't be alone. You have Morah and Annin."

"They are not *you*."

Her words glowed within me. It was selfish, I knew, to be so happy to be her favorite. And it was wrong (I knew this, too), but I couldn't help thinking that what had happened with Morah could never happen with me. I was Raven's special girl. When I gazed upon her, I saw the worn face that I loved and the glint of a golden chain at her throat, half hidden by her dress, that reminded me of the moon necklace my mother had worn. Sometimes I would catch a glimpse of Raven's delicate chain, and I would pretend that if only she untucked the necklace from her dress I would see the crescent-moon pendant dangling from it. I would pretend that she was my mother. Raven had always promised to protect me, to care for me, to make certain I wanted for nothing. "I will be back, Ama," I said, using the word for *mother*, "I promise."

Raven's hand tightened hard on my chin. She forced my face up so that she could stare into my eyes. It hurt my neck and my jaw ached beneath her thumb, but I said nothing because Raven did this only because she cared so much and was scared to lose me. "You call me *Ama*, but you don't mean it. How can you mean it, when you can leave me so easily?"

I heard the scrape of Sid's boot. "Let go of her," Sid said. "You are hurting her."

Raven released me, her blue eyes bright with sadness and anger. "What about our project?" she asked me, with a cautious eye on Sid. My heart sank as Raven carefully chose her words to screen their true meaning from Sid. "Even if you care nothing for me, how can you abandon everyone who depends on you?"

It was true. Without me, Raven wouldn't dare forge passports. She could trace officials' signatures, perhaps, but she couldn't remember the tricks of their various and different handwriting the way that I did, the quirks and squiggles that would occur in the longer textual portions of a passport, the sections that described the bearer's family, background, and appearance.

"You know as well as I do," Raven said, "that if you leave, lives will be ruined."

"Lives will be *ruined*?" Sid's voice was cool and incredulous. "Because she leaves the Ward for a month? What *do* you put in your breads and cakes, Nirrim, that the fate and happiness of so many will hang in the balance without them?"

Raven gave me a hard, warning look. Her hand twitched. I swallowed. "When I return," I said carefully, "I will bake twice as many."

"Three times," Raven said, "to make up for lost time."

"So you'll let me leave?"

"I didn't say that. Leave me? Oh, my girl." Raven's tears returned. She wiped them from her cheeks with the hem of her apron. "You are cruel."

"Nonsense." Sid's voice was crisp. "Nothing can be so dire that a baker can't leave her place of employment for a month without people languishing."

"You don't understand," I told Sid.

Raven gave me a satisfied smile. Her smile warmed me. It made me feel less nervous. I was still capable of winning her approval, even if I was selfish enough to leave her alone with the task of helping the Half Kith who needed to leave the Ward. "Yes," she told Sid, "you don't know what it's like to scrape by. To make do with so little. You don't know what it is like to have a business to run, how hard I work for my girls. These hands." She lifted one. It was gnarled and soft. "I work them to the very bone. With my best girl gone, what will I do?"

Sid rolled her eyes.

Her contempt made me angry. Whatever her life had been like, she had been so *spoiled*. A mother, a father, a trunk of luxurious clothes, a seemingly endless supply of gold. She couldn't even begin to comprehend Raven's situation. "Give Raven my earnings," I told her.

Sid didn't like that. "We didn't discuss payment."

"Well, now I come at a price."

"Fine," Sid said. "Service rendered deserves fair pay. But I have hired *you*, not your mistress."

"It's one and the same. I would give everything to Raven anyway."

Raven gave me a tiny, proud smile. Sid looked furious. Her eyes were black fire. She reached inside her jacket, pulled a small leather purse from an inner pocket, and handed it to Raven. I could see the rich luster of gold peeking from the purse when Raven opened it. Her face grew peaceful for a moment, then almost instantly tight and worried again. "That's all?" she said. "For a whole month?"

"I'll give you twice that," Sid said. "You'll receive the second half upon her return to the tavern."

"Oh, I know how it will be," Raven muttered to me. "She will turn you against me. You will never come home. I know this woman's ways. I see what she wants. She will keep you for herself."

"I will do no such thing." Sid sounded disgusted.

"One day I will be gone," Raven said to me, "and you will remember this. You never forget anything. You will remember how I begged and you abandoned me."

"Oh, please," Sid said.

"You're heartless," I told her.

"Thank the gods I am." She offered more gold. "Here. For your pains."

Raven took the money and folded her hand quickly around it, probably because the offer shamed her even though she needed it. "Well." Raven gave me a brave little smile. "I suppose I don't have a choice, do I?"

"It's only for a little while," I promised.

Raven nodded slowly to herself, but she looked so much older, with a quiver to her chin. She got to her feet unsteadily, patted my cheek, and shuffled from the room. When she had gone, Sid took one look at my face and said impatiently, "For gods' sake. It's not like she is going to die without you."

"It's hard for her to give me up. She loves me."

"She *sold* you," Sid snapped. I said nothing in reply, because it was clear that she didn't understand, and didn't want to.

"I am so jealous," Annin said. She had burst into my room telling me that she wanted to help me pack, then looked at my clothes and told me that if I took them with me she would kill me, they were so impoverished of any beauty, any joy, any *life*.

"I wear them every day," I said.

"Not one day more! You can't wear *this* in the High quarter. You would look like a stillborn mouse. Like a sick wren. Like an old woman! Like Sirah the rain-sayer. Please, Nirrim. For my sake. Promise that you will wear gorgeous clothes and think of me. Your mistress will give them to you. She is so kind."

"Is she?" I wondered out loud, remembering how cold she had been to Raven.

"Of course! Look." From her pocket Annin pulled the pink lace scarf I had seen earlier in Sid's trunk.

"Oh," I said.

"Don't you think it's beautiful?"

Sid barely knew Annin, yet she had given a gift perfectly suited to please her. I felt an unpleasant, jealous twinge. I looked into Annin's eager, pretty face. "You can't wear it," I told her. "It's High."

Her face fell a little, but she just stroked the scarf and said, "I can wear it in my room."

"What's the point if no one will see you?"

"*I* will see."

"You don't have a mirror."

"I will *know* I am wearing it," she insisted, clutching the scarf, and it reminded me of the rag I had cherished once, the one from Helin's dress. I brushed a loose tendril out of Annin's face. "You're right," I said. "Of course you will. It's the perfect color for you."

She beamed. "Isn't it?"

I removed two dresses from my wardrobe, a sleeveless one for hot weather, and one for cooler weather, just in case an ice wind came. The dresses were made of good, sturdy cloth—a little rough, and in shades of taupe and dark brown, but I was used to them, and I didn't want to have to ask Sid for anything.

"Nirrim, *no*. They make you look like you've been molded out of clay!"

"They suit me." I folded them into a large satchel.

She blew out a wistful breath. "I wish *I* were going."

I looked up in surprise from my task, though I shouldn't have been surprised, because I had always believed that out of all of us who worked in the tavern, she wanted the impossible the most. Maybe what surprised me was that it had turned out that *I* was the one. I had wanted the impossible—to go into the High quarter—and I was getting it. And it wasn't the only impossible thing I wanted. Maybe what made me pause was the realization that wanting one impossible thing and achieving it is only a little satisfying, because then you are encouraged to want more. I touched the Elysium feather hidden above my heart. I remembered how I had wondered whether the feather drew me to Sid, or Sid to me.

"I want you to have something," I told Annin, and withdrew the feather from my dress.

She gasped. "Is that——?"

"Here." Held aloft in my fingers, the feather looked like a billowing flame.

"I can't. It's too beautiful. How can you even bear to touch it?"

I tucked it in her hair behind her ear. Annin reached up gingerly to touch it with her fingertips.

I said, "I don't want you to think that a stranger, just because she's High, can give you better gifts than a sister."

"A sister?" Her eyes widened. "Really?"

"Really."

"I will miss you," she said.

This made me feel guilty—not because I wouldn't miss her, but because she didn't know that I had given her the feather not so much as a gift, but to be rid of it. I *did* half believe that it had some power to pull Sid toward me. Why else had she agreed to my demand?

At the time, I believed I was giving Annin the feather so that, if it had any power, it would no longer affect me. It would no longer affect Sid. She would be my mistress and I would be her servant, and we would be partners in a strange quest. I would never long for anything more, without that burning feather above my heart.

Now I know that it was more complicated than that. I gave away the feather because I wanted to see if Sid would like me without it. I wanted her to want me for myself alone.

32

"READY?" SID SAID. HER ENORMOUS trunk sat inside the tavern, waiting for a pair of hired men to collect it and convey it through the wall. We stood outside the door on the unevenly paved street. The rain had washed away some of the heat, or at least the way heat sticks to the skin like a layer of grime. The sky was marbled with shining clouds. A cool breeze played with my hair. I tucked it behind my ears.

"Not quite," I said. "I have someone to see first."

Her mouth curled. "Someone special?"

"I can't leave without saying good-bye."

"I do it all the time."

"I'm not like you."

"Go then, and collect your kiss." Her tone was amused yet bored.

Disappointment puddled inside me. I knew enough of what I felt for Sid to understand that her indifference to Aden was a rejection of me.

"Explain to me," she said, "what is so appealing about a boy's kiss? Is it the rasp of stubble?"

I could have said: Sometimes it is comforting. I could have said: It used to be, at first, that kissing him felt like an important skill to learn. I liked to learn things. And part of having a good memory was remembering exactly how Aden liked to be kissed. What was so wrong in enjoying that I could do that? It used to be nice to kiss him. Warm and safe. I could have said: Kissing him is better than dealing with his hurt if I don't.

I could have said: I am afraid of his hurt.

I could have confessed that I had killed a man and explained that Aden knew, and maybe he would no longer protect me if he couldn't claim me as his.

He must believe that I am his, I could have said.

Instead I said, "I'll meet you at the wall."

"Don't keep me waiting long," Sid said, and walked away, whistling a tune I didn't recognize.

———

"I don't understand," Aden said when I pushed his hands away. His eyes had brightened when he saw me at his door. He had pulled me out of the sunny street and into the darkness of his home. "Why are you always so cold? All I want to do is show you how much I love you. I miss you when I don't see you."

"I came here to tell you something."

He started to draw me in the direction of his bedroom. "You can tell me later."

"No," I said. "I don't want to."

He abruptly let me go. He held up his hands dramatically, large fingers spread wide and empty, as though to show he had no weapon. "Gods, Nirrim. You're acting like I'm forcing you. It would be nice, you know," he added bitterly, "if for once it was *you* who wanted *me*."

I imagined lifting my mouth to Sid's. Heat rushed into my cheeks.

Aden touched my warm face. His anger relented into affection. "You're so pretty when you blush," he said. "I understand if you feel shy sometimes. I know that girls do. There are men who take advantage, but I never will."

But you *are*, I wanted to say. You are using what you know to keep me in place, right by your side. You don't even know you're doing it, and I am too afraid to say what you're doing, because of what you might do to me.

"I can't help wanting you," he said, "and I get carried away, yes, but it's only because I love you. Do you hear me? Nirrim, I want to marry you."

My body went very still. "You do?"

He smiled. "You don't believe me?"

Dread unspooled in my belly like black thread. "We're too young."

"You're nineteen! Half the Ward is engaged or married by then."

"I . . ." I searched for a reason that would make him not want me. "I don't want children."

"We don't have to have them right away. You already take the anys," he said, referring to the herb Raven gave me monthly to prevent pregnancy. It was illegal in the Ward, where the prevention or termination of pregnancy resulted in prison, but I couldn't imagine having a child, especially not when children could be snatched in the night.

"What if I never want one?" I said.

He waved a dismissive hand. "All women want children at some point. You'll make a wonderful mother. Our babies will have your beautiful green eyes."

"Aden, I came here to tell you that I'm leaving the Ward." I explained quickly, my voice rising as though I were trying to talk over him, but he was silent, face growing stony with displeasure.

"A month," he repeated. "In the High quarter. With that foreign woman."

"It's the chance of a lifetime."

He shook his head, looking out a window at the wall. In the sun it looked as white as salt. "You already think you're too good for me."

"What is that supposed to mean?"

"I just asked you to marry me, and it's like I said nothing at all. Can you imagine how that feels? Gods, Nirrim, why don't you think about someone other than yourself for once?"

That felt unfair, but I couldn't explain why, especially when his accusation sounded reasonable. I felt a twinge of guilt. I knew what it was like to want someone who didn't want me back. I would feel so wounded, so small if I were him. "I'm sorry," I said, and meant it.

"Have you even rationally considered this? You will be completely at that woman's mercy."

"She's not a monster. She just needs a servant."

"And out of all the people in this city, she chooses you. Isn't that odd?"

I felt my jaw get tight and stubborn. "No."

"*Think*, Nirrim. She can cast you into prison with one word."

So can you, I thought.

Aden said, "What will happen when she tries to make you do something you don't want to do?"

"I don't know what you mean," I said, though I knew exactly what he meant.

"I saw how she looked at you."

My face flushed again, this time with shame for how much I wished he were right. "You're mistaken."

"The High Kith have no morals. All they care about is decadence.

Nothing matters except what they want. Wait and see. She will try to use you."

I want her to, I almost said. Then I saw, as clearly as a god's prophecy, everything that would happen after. His look of horror, maybe even hate. The disgusted words that would fall from his mouth. I saw how he would see me, which would be how other people would see me, too. It filled me with fear. I reached for him and kissed him hard and deep, my hands in his hair, his chest flat against mine. "Don't worry," I murmured into his mouth.

"Of course I worry." He stroked hair from my face. "You'll have no one to protect you in the High quarter. If you step out of line with that woman . . . Nirrim, even if it's something small—a ribbon crookedly tied, a disobedient look—she can have you punished in ways you can't even imagine."

She *could* have me thrown into prison with the slightest word. Sid, who hedged around questions like they might expose some enormous secret. Sid, who had already shown that she could be unkind, as she had been toward Raven. No soldier, no judge would believe a Half Kith over someone of her status. Cold worry seeped into me.

Aden must have seen it. His expression grew comforting. He touched my lips with one finger. "I have an idea." He left me and disappeared into another room. He returned with a small paper packet in his hand.

"What is that?" I asked.

"Poison."

The blood drained from my face. "I'm not going to use that on her."

"It's gentle. Whoever takes it will fall into a long sleep and never wake up."

"Aden, I don't want this. This isn't necessary. She is not a threat. You're acting like she is a villain in a story."

"And what about the rest of the High Kith? You think you will be safe among them? *All* of them? Take it, for my sake. So I know you have something to protect you when I can't be there."

Uneasily, I slipped the packet into my dress pocket.

"Maybe it will be good for you to disappear from the Ward for a month," he said. "If you're not here, the militia can't question you. They are still going door to door, asking about the night of the moon festival, and that soldier's murder." He saw me twitch at the word *murder*. "Don't worry, Nirrim. This will all blow over. There is no proof the man didn't just fall to his death."

"Except the testimony of your friend."

"Let me deal with him." He kissed me again. "Nirrim, I want you to miss me."

I took a breath. "I will miss you. And I'll return with enough money for us to start a life together."

His smile was broad. "Is that a yes? Are you saying yes, you will marry me?"

I swallowed hard. Sid would leave this city and I would stay. It was so easy to disappoint Raven. What if she tired of me? What home would I have then? Aden was ready to be with me always. "Yes," I said, and meant it.

Although all the other girls thought he was the best boy in the Ward, I knew he was the best I could do.

He picked me up and whirled me around the room.

～

As I approached Sid, who stood outside the gate to the Middling quarter, she made a show of taking a little gold watch out of her pocket. It was a man's watch, to match her man's clothes. She opened the watch and widened her eyes in comic disbelief at the time she saw there. She squinted at the watch, looked at me, looked back at her watch, letting her full mouth part in mock outrage.

"All right, all right," I said.

"Took your sweet time," she said.

"Let's go."

"And was it? Sweet, that is?" She flicked a lock of hair away from my neck and saw a mark that Aden's kisses had left. "Ah, I see it was."

I batted away her hand.

"Ooh, touchy," she said. She looked me over, noting the knapsack I carried. "That's it?"

"Not all of us need an entire wardrobe of women's and men's clothes."

"May I peek?" She reached for the knapsack.

"No." I pulled it out of reach.

"What's in there?"

Two dresses. A set of tools for forging. Sid's letter written in her language. And a little packet of poison.

"You don't want to say?" Sid said. "Keep your secrets then, dear Nirrim." She closed the pocket watch with a quick clasp of one hand, but not before I glimpsed that the watch's face looked bizarre, containing no numbers, but rather words. Though she closed the watch too quickly for me to read the words in that very moment, I could see the watch's face in my mind, and realized with wonder—and then, quickly, extreme embarrassment—that she had not lied in the prison. There *was* a watch that could read someone else's heart. Words for different emotions ringed the dial. The word that had glowed as the watch's hand pointed to me was *desire*.

"He must be very special to you," Sid said, and I didn't know how to correct her mistake without telling her the truth.

What if she guessed that what I felt for her grew stronger every day? That my desire was for her, not Aden?

She might laugh at me, like she did at everything else.

I strode ahead of her toward the gate. She tagged along at my heels, strolling with deliberate ease.

"Do you know the way?" she asked.

"To the gate right in front of our faces? Yes, I think so." I reached into my dress pocket for my passport.

"Hmm," she said. "Well, the gate *would* work, if you wanted to go to the Middling quarter."

I stopped midstride. "Don't you have to go through the Middling quarter to reach the High quarter?"

"Some people do."

"And other people?"

"Other people—let us say, *very important people*—get to take the shortcut. Why don't you let me go through the gate first?"

I swept an exaggerated hand in front of me to indicate that she should go ahead. When she did, she approached the guard and showed him a tiny gold key on the palm of her hand. He barely even glanced at my passport after that, but stepped aside and gestured at the blank stone wall behind him, the thick spine of the wall. As I watched in wonder, a glowing outline of a door appeared. The stone door slid aside, revealing a tunnel.

The wall, which looked so thick on the outside, was hollow inside.

The gate to the Middling quarter disguised another gate. There was the gate through the wall, and then the gate *into* the wall.

Sid looked over her shoulder at me and grinned.

"You're going to have to stop that," I said.

She made innocent eyes. "Stop what?"

"Being so smug."

"Why would I," she said, "when you love it?"

She disappeared into the tunnel, and I followed.

33

THOUGH AT FIRST THE TUNNEL appeared almost entirely dark, a greenish-blue fluid ahead of us glowed from the tunnel's floor, flowing like lovely sewage into the darkness.

"You have to walk through the river," Sid said. "Are you squeamish? Easily frightened? Maybe you should hold my hand."

I gave her a flat look and unstrapped my sandals, carrying them as I stepped toward the little river and then, defiantly, without testing it with a tentative toe, stepped right into the luminous sludge.

I nearly fell. As soon as my feet sank into the water—if it *was* water—cool pleasure traveled up my calves, creeping up under my dress. I heard Sid's laugh but didn't see her, because the river was already carrying me forward, though I took no further steps. Its current pulled me, the strong tide flowing around my ankles as thick as velvet.

"Do you like it?" I heard Sid beside me as the river carried us through the darkness. The liquid caressed my feet, tickling my toes. It smelled floral, though not like any flower I knew. "Don't drink the water," she said. "Some people do, and wander through the tunnel for days, drunk and giddy and singing."

I couldn't see Sid, but my hip brushed her side. I felt a warmth that had nothing to do with the river. I asked, "Have you tasted it?"

"Of course."

The tunnel slid past. The current grew stronger. Her fingers curled into mine. "I don't want to get separated," she said. The river grew loud with its rushing. I nearly lost my footing. I held more tightly on to Sid.

"Here," she said, and pulled me toward a door whose outline glowed up ahead on the right. She wrenched it open and spilled us into sunshine.

Then I did fall, blinded by the sudden brightness. Sid came down with me, her limbs tangled with mine, the weight of her on me, the hilt of her hidden dagger jabbing into my side. She slid to my side onto the grassy lawn beneath us, one leg still trapped between the sodden skirts of my dress, laughing, lying back on the lawn, her eyes closed against the sunlight but her face tilted up toward it, luxuriating in the light.

My pulse was jumpy, but I couldn't make myself pull away from her. I hated how easy everything was for her, how she could lie so close to me, her leg between mine, and show no sign that she was even aware of this—or of the people, I now realized, who were picnicking on blankets of vibrantly colored silk, their faces shadowed by lace parasols, crystal glasses of green sparkling liquid raised to their lips. Exquisitely tiny pastries adorned silver platters like jewels. The High Kith murmured, peering at us.

"They're staring." The High Kith were out of earshot, but I whispered anyway.

Sid opened her eyes. "Let them stare." She shifted onto her side to look at me better, propping herself up on her elbow. She studied me—waiting, maybe, for me to notice that her leg was still languidly between mine. When I said nothing, her expression got slow and searching.

"Won't we . . . get in trouble?" I asked.

"For what?"

I shifted my body away from hers.

"Oh," she said. "For *that*." She stood abruptly and offered a hand to help me up. Her touch was capable and brief. "You needn't worry. People get spat out of this gate all the time. It's entertaining to watch. The High Kith are staring because they are amused at our awkward tumble."

"That's all?"

"Well, and because of how you're dressed."

I glanced down at my earth-colored clothes.

"Many of them have never seen a Half Kith before," Sid said. "I doubt they even believe you *are* one. They probably think you are disguised as one for fun. Sometimes that happens here."

"Why would anyone look poor for fun?"

Sid shrugged. "They get bored with being rich."

I shook my head. It wasn't that Sid was wrong, but that what she had said made me realize a more complete answer. "Dressing up as someone like me makes them feel even richer," I said, "because they are *not* me."

Birdsong floated across the lawn. Crystal glasses tinkled. Someone giggled, the sound softened by the wind. Trees were everywhere: immense clouds of pink flowers, green-and-yellow-striped blades, branches lush with leaves and trailing white veils of creeping flowering ivy. I knew that trees were quiet things. But I had seen only one before, and the sight of so many was overwhelming. They clamored for my attention. They were a gorgeous roar of color.

I looked behind me for the white familiarity of the wall. It steadied me. Its height comforted, its stony length. The wall held my home. I fought the impulse to reach for it, to lay a palm against its solid warmth. It would be hot in the sunshine. But I was afraid that Sid would tease me . . . or worse, pity me.

I turned back toward the park and its host of lords and ladies. A child played, pulling at the grass, her fanned skirts lavender tulle, her dark hair curled into long, bouncing coils.

No one was watching us anymore.

Sid tipped her chin in the direction of the hill. "Come on. I want you to see something before I take you to my place."

"I meant something else." Nervousness raced through my chest. "When I asked whether we would get in trouble."

"Oh?" She lifted her brows in pretend surprise. "Were you worried that we looked . . . inappropriate?"

"I would have gotten in trouble, in the Ward. I might have been tithed."

She stopped looking amused.

"It's against the law," I said.

"I see," she said slowly. "Why?"

"Because it's wrong."

She blinked. "Is it?"

"*I* don't think it is."

"Such a relief," she said dryly. "It'd be a little late for you to decide I'm immoral. Are we done talking about me? Because I want to show you something."

"But I need to know the rules."

"Rules?" She widened her eyes. Laughing, she said, "Are you asking for a handbook on the seduction of women? It is an art, Nirrim, not a science. Oh, you didn't like *that*. Such a scowl! Are you going to stamp your foot?"

"You make light of everything."

"I make nothing too heavy to bear."

"I am not asking how you make women love you."

"Who said anything about love?"

"I need to know the rules here in the High quarter. If they're different from what I grew up with. All the rules."

"Well, *all* the rules is quite a tall order. Let's start with the one you keep tiptoeing around so delicately, like you're going to offend me, which you won't, probably, unless you *do* decide I am a deviant monster, which some people do, but none whose company I care to keep. It is not against the law in the High quarter for a woman to be with a woman or for a man to be with a man. No one is going to prison for it. I'm not sure why it's different in the Ward, except that the Council wants the Half Kith to make babies. To build up the workforce, I imagine. *Here*, beyond your wall, the High Kith are concerned with concentrating wealth within families, which means having one or—at most—two children. And the High Kith care most about pleasure, so they don't mind others seeking it. Are there some who might look at me with dislike? Yes. Will they get in my way? They had better not. Even that lord who had me arrested for thievery probably cared less that I was a woman than that his wife had played him for a fool. Now. Are the rules clear? Need we talk about people hating me?" Her tone was airy, but her dark eyes now had a hard, lacquered look to them. "We can do that if you want, but it's an ugly topic for a pretty day."

"No." It hurt to think of anyone hating her. "I want to see what you want to show me."

It was a tree, set apart from the others, smaller, wizened—and, oddly, with patches of gold on its trunk. I walked barefoot across the grass to it, sandals still dangling from my hand.

Grass. I scrunched my toes in it. It prickled against my heels. I had never seen so much grass—just stray pale strands creeping up from the dirt between the Ward's cobblestones. The lawn felt cool and plush. Its green looked deep and inevitable. It smelled like rain's sister. I wanted to bury my face in it.

The tree's leaves swam in the wind. The trunk's gold patches gleamed in the shifting light.

"This tree," Sid said, "will tell your fortune."

I looked into her face to see if she was joking, but her expression was serious. She was cast in roving leaf shadows, her skin honeyed in the dappled sunlight.

"So there *is* magic," I said. "Like in the tunnel."

"Not sure. That river is essentially a potent liqueur. The picnickers are drinking a version of it. It alters your perception. A magic river that carries you along without dragging you under?" She lifted one hand, palm up. "Or"—she lifted the other hand—"a conveyer belt operated by hidden machinery and shallowly covered with an intoxicating liquid that, even if you don't drink it, might nevertheless affect you? Take this tree. Maybe it's being tended to by an artist—horticulturist?—who writes fortunes on strips of bark and seals them back onto the tree. Do you want to have your fortune told by a tree? Tear a bit of bark away."

I hesitated. "Will I hurt it?"

She smiled a little. "Sweet Nirrim. Go ahead. It's just bark. The tree is healthy. Its leaves are thick. And as you see, a gardener has gilded the patches of missing bark. High Kith can't bear to see anything ugly and mangy, even a tree."

I stepped toward the tree, curiosity overcoming my hesitation. I found a split in the bark and peeled a narrow strip away. It came off in my hand, as thin as paper, and instantly curled up like a little snake. I uncurled it and looked at its inner skin. My stomach turned to stone.

"What is it?" Sid said. "Will you tell me?"

"Has it told your fortune?"

"Yes."

"Has it come true?"

"I don't know," she said, "yet."

"Tell me yours," I said, "and I'll tell you mine."

She wagged her finger *no*. "Secrets all around"—she smiled—"and truths for none."

She led the way out of the park, telling me we weren't far from the center of the High quarter and her lodgings. When she wasn't looking, I crushed the bark in my hand and let its flakes fall to the grass. I didn't need to look at the fortune again. It was written on my mind.

You will lose her, it said.

34

THE PARK LED TO TERRACED stairs chiseled into the hillside, which gave way to a path. A musician in Middling blue played an instrument that I had seen in Harvers's books, a many-stringed lute held on the man's lap. Soap bubbles from a source I couldn't see drifted past the man and seemed to swallow notes as he played them, their iridescent spheres suddenly silencing parts of the tune. I saw one float ahead of us to a man and woman walking arm in arm, her lace parasol as fine as spun sugar, her perfect face tipped up toward his, coral lips smiling as he reached to pop one of the silent bubbles. I could hear, faintly, as it burst into a few stolen strummed notes.

The path opened into an enormous agora. A few lavishly dressed people sat at the fountain's edge, its colored waters tumbling and crashing. A councilman passed, his red robe trailing. I had never seen a councilman before. I had been taught about them in the orphanage, their importance in decreeing and overseeing laws and advising the Lord Protector.

Sid followed my eyes. "We should steer clear of the Council," she said. "I don't think they'd appreciate my plan to swindle their country out of its magical secret and run off with it for my personal profit." Sid squinted at the glowing agora. "So flashy. Honestly, it hurts my eyes."

Instead of stones, the agora was paved with translucent glass tiles arranged in patterns of colors, pink and red and green—the colors of the Elysium bird—most dominant. I stared at the tiles. "I know who made these," I said. "An artisan in the Ward. I have seen them heaped in baskets in her glass-blowing workshop, but I never guessed they would be made to *walk upon*. It's so impractical. Don't people slip and fall?"

"No one here moves very quickly," Sid said. "They take really delicate steps. Or they are carried in palanquins by Middlings."

I stepped onto the tiles. They lit up beneath my weight. My skin was bathed in green light. Sid walked along beside me, different shades of light coloring her skin, shifting from one color to the next, her cheeks pink, her mouth green, her hands bright red. She sighed, glancing down at her crimson hands. "It's fun the first time."

I said, "What a surprise to learn that you are easily bored."

She paused, her face and neck a gold-sprinkled blue. "*Games* bore me, eventually. They are too easy to master, which is why I constantly need new ones. People are different. People always fascinate me. Or," she amended, "at least *you* do."

"Me?"

"I always want to know what you are thinking. What do you think"— she swept her hand at the agora—"of this?"

My heart felt hot and hard with resentment. "I think it must have cost a fortune. I think it's not fair that the High Kith should have so much beauty when we get so little."

"Sounds revolutionary of you, Nirrim."

"The tiles made in the Ward are pretty but . . . *ordinary*. They don't *glow*. I think someone is purchasing things cheaply from the Ward and . . . improving them somehow."

"An interesting idea. Worth investigating. But your thoughts are very different from mine. *I* am thinking that shade of green light suits you, but I prefer your beauty without it."

"You are not really thinking that."

"I am."

If someone stole her voice, she would still find a way to flirt, even silently, with whomever was nearest.

"I suppose I can't be believed even when I'm telling the truth," Sid said. "It's the liar's curse."

As much as she claimed she was a liar, I could not recall, now that I thought about it, an actual lie she had told—which meant she never had, at least not to me . . . or she *had* lied, and I didn't know it yet.

We left the colored lights of the agora, which narrowed to a path carpeted with pink and white petals. Tree branches laden with flowers arched overhead. As we walked, buds opened and bloomed in soft bursts, petals cascading down onto us, floating onto Sid's shoulders, catching in my hair. The branches instantly grew tight new buds. They, too, flowered open and shed their petals. My sandaled feet sank into the petals up to my ankles. Their fragrance wafted up. More petals came down like snow. "Why," I asked, "would I fascinate you?"

"I want to know," Sid said, "how someone who has so little can be so brave."

I thought about how much I liked the way she walked, her hands in her pockets yet never slouching, her shoulders straight. I thought about how I had liked her leg tangled between mine. Her light weight on me. I thought about how terrified I was of ever admitting any of this. "I am not brave."

"And yet you are here, with me—and with a forged Middling passport. Don't think I didn't notice. *Where* did you get *that?*"

She smiled at my silence.

It occurred to me that it was a special person, a gentle one, who allowed another to keep her secrets.

Or it was the sort of person who had secrets of her own.

Most of the homes in the High quarter looked like miniature palaces separated by swathes of lawn and low marble walls. But Sid led me to a hilltop square with an elegant yet skinny house much smaller than the rest. The eaves dripped with decorative trim that looked as fragile as icicles. Roseate windows had stained glass and the balconies had been wrought with gleaming green metal that curled like a living thing, with finials spiraling into themselves like new-sprung fiddlehead ferns I had seen in one of Harvers's botanical books. Twilight was gathering on the rooftop. Duskwings called, each with a different song. I instantly remembered each one's call, and as they swooped through the silky pink sky, the pattern of where each one was rearranged itself in my mind, their map of song constantly shifting.

Sid unlocked the door. "There are not many homes for rent, but this one suits my stature well enough. Plus, I like the view."

"What exactly *is* your stature?"

She pushed open the door. "Well, I'm not *the* most important person in Herran. Merely the most charming."

The inside of the house was dark and silent and smelled of roses. "Where are the servants?" I asked.

"There are no servants."

"Only *me?*" my voice squeaked. "You expect me to take care of an entire house on my own?"

"Nirrim, no." My eyes had adjusted to the darkness, and I could see from the fading light coming in from the windows that Sid was insulted. "You are not my servant. You are my partner."

"But"—I sputtered—"who will clean?"

"Me."

"Who cooks for you?"

"I do."

"I am confused," I said. "Everyone thinks you're a high-bred lady. What exactly *are* you?"

She shrugged. "Someone who likes to be self-sufficient."

"But you *hired* me."

"Oh." She waved her long hand. "All that business about paying for your services was just to get you out of that awful woman's clutches."

"She is not awful."

"You are too kind and too loyal to see it."

"She is the only one who has ever taken care of me."

Sid paused at that, and more quietly said, "I'm sorry. Maybe I'm wrong." She beckoned me toward the stairs. "Before the light fades."

She lit no lamps along the way, so the home was nothing but heaps of shadows around us. The stairs were soundless beneath my feet. I had never walked up stairs that didn't creak. At the top of the landing, she opened a door to a little bedroom that smelled like her—like her dusky perfume, her skin. And brine. The glass-paneled doors to the balcony were full of pink sky. Sid opened the balcony, and the scent of the sea rushed in.

I followed her out onto the balcony. The sea spread before me. It rumpled darkly against the coast. The sun was drowning on the water. I heard the muted calls of gulls. And nowhere could I see the wall.

I had never seen the sea.

I had never not seen the wall.

"Do you like it?" Sid asked.

"I don't think I believed the sea was real," I said. "I mean, I accepted that it was there even though I couldn't see it. But it's only now that I *do* see it that I realize that I didn't really know what it was. My belief was half pretend. But I didn't know, before now, that I was pretending."

She nodded. "I think I understand, though it's hard. The sea is one of my earliest memories. I grew up escaping to the harbor every chance I could get. The sailors would drag me home to my parents." She peered at me through the rosy light. She lifted her hand to stroke my hair.

I flinched in surprise.

"Just a petal," she said, pulling a white one from my hair. It curled like a thin shell in her fingers.

"Oh." I tried to ignore my stuttering heart. "Thank you."

Her nonchalance changed to amusement. "Well, yes, and you *should* thank me, for accomplishing such an arduous and unpleasant task as removing a stray petal from your hair."

"No," I said. "Thank you for everything. For *this*."

"I *am* a gift from the gods, but I confess that I didn't create the sea."

"Don't do that."

The light was dimming. Her eyes were shadows. "Do what?"

"Praise yourself."

She drew back a little. "Do you think me arrogant?"

"No," I said, though I *had* thought it, up until that very moment. "You sound like you're bragging, but really you're just making fun of yourself."

She opened her mouth, then closed it.

I said, "Why would you do that?"

"Maybe," she said slowly, "so that you won't make fun of me first."

"I would never."

"Then I won't do that," she said, "if it bothers you." She rubbed the petal between her finger and thumb. "Take this room. It has the best view. I'll be in the one next door."

"This is *your* room."

She looked at me.

"It smells like you," I said.

She winced. "Maybe I don't clean all that well. Since we've decided I'm to be more honest and not lay claim to skills and attributes I don't have. Do you want the other room? It might be less, ah, fragrant. It's unused, though maybe"—she cringed again—"a little dusty."

"I want this one." I hoped she wouldn't ask why.

She nodded. "There's a spare key to the house on the nightstand, so you can come and go as you please." She must have seen my surprise. "Did you think I would keep you prisoner here? You've had enough of living in a box."

She moved to leave the room, then paused, her hand on the door. "Don't thank me yet, Nirrim. I expect you to uphold your end of the bargain. Tomorrow night I plan for us to do a little investigative work at a party. That night will be as late as dawn, so get your rest."

I waited long after the door had shut to do what I wanted, which was to slip into the bed. I drew the sheet up over me, the fabric so fine it felt like air. The salty breeze pushed against the curtains. It was cool at night, this high up in the city.

I pressed my face against the pillow. It smelled like Sid.

She had taken the petal with her when she left the room. I had seen it, thin and white, between her fingers.

⌒

I couldn't fall asleep. I imagined Sid sleeping in this bed, which was softer than I knew beds could be. The bed felt like sleep itself, the best kind of sleep: plush and buoyant. But my body was fully awake. It was pretending to be under Sid's body. It was pretending to be that white petal between her fingers. It was as if my mind had nothing to do with this imagining, as if it weren't my brain conjuring images of her mouth on mine, or remembering the exact shape of her hands. It was my skin and my needy bones. It was my heart going too hard.

Think of something else.

Think of something that is not like her.

Something reliable. Safe.

I thought of the wall.

But the pillow smelled like her. The sheets smelled like her.

Thinking about the wall wasn't enough to soothe me. I needed to see.

I put on my sandals and took the key, and left the dark house.

The city was lively, windows blazing in every room of the enormous houses. People spilled, laughing, into shadowy gardens. In the agora, men and women shouted and ruined their finery in the fountains, drinking from crystal glasses they smashed on the glass tiles, whose colored light surged dizzyingly in the night. I kept to the shadows. I retraced my steps back toward the wall, following the map in my mind.

I would just look at the wall. Place my palm against it for a moment. It would steady me.

But that was not what I did, because I saw the fortune-telling tree first.

The missing patch of bark where I had torn away my fortune was already painted gold. I touched the slick, gilded surface. I touched the papery bark. I thought about my fortune, which was only what I had already known. *You will lose her.* And yet I hadn't fully known, until I saw those faint amber words, written as though with the sappy blood of the tree, how much I hoped they would never come true.

A tree is an astonishing thing. So much of it you will never see. Not its roots: a whole secret life spreading out in the blind earth, drinking from unknown sources. Not its core: the sapling it once was, clad by each successive year of growth.

Does a tree know how deep its roots go? Can it locate its original seed?

I thought about how all seeds are necessarily lost things, dropped and abandoned.

This tree, I thought, felt familiar. It felt like me.

It had been stripped like me, like anyone who had ever been tithed. The difference was that someone had taken care to gild the tree's wounds. I was luckier than so many in the Ward—I had lost only blood. But I didn't move through the world the way Sid did, as someone who fully owned her body. I had always been afraid. I never knew what would be taken from me or when, and although I didn't always think about it or fully feel that fear, it was as much a part of who I was as my light brown skin, my sturdy hands.

It was so tiring to be afraid all the time.

So I decided I wouldn't be. I wouldn't go to the wall and touch it the way children touch their mothers. I decided it didn't matter that I was afraid of heights. I chose not to be.

I began to climb the tree. I ignored how sweaty my hands got, how my breath rattled in my throat, how my mouth got dry. I didn't dare look down.

I went as high as I could, working my way up into the branches, then settled into a crook that was almost comfortable, though my rear ached and my leg eventually fell asleep.

The ground stretched below. The ground feels like such a safe thing . . . until you get too far above it.

But the leaves rushed and played around me. My breath calmed. I listened to the leaves. Their whispers almost made sense. I realized that was a strange thought, the kind that means sleep is coming, but as soon as I knew it was coming, it was already there.

I didn't know how much time passed before I woke in the darkness.

I heard the hush of someone walking over grass. The sound below grew closer, and then there was a musical glug and slosh of a large quantity of water flowing from a metallic bucket or can.

Someone was watering the tree.

Carefully, as soundlessly as I could, I shifted to peer down through the branches.

The man emptied his tin watering can. It thumped hollowly against his thigh as he walked away, the smell of wet earth strong in the air. His red robe trailed behind him.

It was a councilman.

35

"HMM," SID SAID THE NEXT DAY, dipping a thin, buttered slice
of toast into the soft yolk of an egg. She had knocked softly at my door
before bringing in a tray with breakfast for both of us: soft-boiled eggs
encased in pale blue shells, pink pastries clouded with cream piped
between wispy wafers, spongy pancakes dotted with holes and sopping
with butter, a dish of amethyst-colored jam, a lily-yellow pot filled to
the brim with steaming black liquid that scalded my tongue and made
my heart race. "A councilman." Sid squinted as she stared from our little
table on the balcony out over the bright sea. I had slept until midday.
The sun was high. It honeyed Sid's skin and made the freckle beneath
her eye stand out like a star. In this light, I could see other, fainter freckles on her cheekbones, and even one near her upper lip. She sipped the
hot black drink. The sun shone through her peacock-blue porcelain cup.

She caught me staring and held out her cup for me to drink from
it, even though my own full cup remained untouched after my first sip.
I refused. "You don't like it?" she said.

"So bitter."

"It's coffee, imported from the east. I always travel with my own supply. I adore it. Tea tastes like water to me, and coffee from anywhere else in the world is truly inferior. Here." She uncovered a little jar shaped like an Elysium bird nesting on golden eggs. The bird's back was a lid that revealed sugar molded into hearts. I had never seen so much sugar. I resisted the temptation to sneak the whole jar into my pocket. Sid dropped one sugar heart into her cup, then looked at me, considering, and dropped in two more. She offered the cup again. "You said you like sweet things."

I was surprised she remembered. I didn't think any amount of sugar could make me like the coffee, but I wanted to drink from Sid's cup. I wanted to put my mouth where hers had been. I tried the coffee again, and made a face.

"Still too bitter?" she said.

I handed the cup back, but she said, "Now it's too sweet for me," and chucked the cup's contents off the balcony. She laughed at my gasp.

"You can't just *do* that," I said. "You could have burned someone below."

"I heard no scream." She was impishly delighted by my moral outrage.

"Sid."

"We are above a garden. There is no one below. Anyway, the whole High quarter is still asleep. It's only just past noon."

"You *wasted* it."

"You didn't want it and neither did I." She tucked half her smile away when she saw me shake my head. "Very well, I won't do it again. Let's find something you *do* like. We need to nourish you. Since you slept in a tree. Try a pancake with jam."

"I didn't *sleep* in it. At least, not on purpose. I was—"

"Spying?"

She reached across the table to spread the purple jam on a pancake that she placed on my plate. I was too surprised to stop her. This entire breakfast was surreal. No one had ever served me anything before.

"I don't understand why a councilman would water a tree," she said. "Middlings with special scripts to serve the High Kith tend to gardens. And clean, and run errands, and generally do all the things no one really wants to do."

"That's why it is so interesting." I took a bite of the jammy pancake. The delicious goo of jam and the sunny taste of butter flooded my mouth. "What *is* this?"

"Perrin jam."

"Perrins." I lowered the next forkful. "I can't eat perrins. They're not my kith."

"Yes, you can."

I smiled. "You're right." I reached for more jam.

"Look at you, taking what you want. So very High of you."

I made an incredulous noise.

"What?" she said.

I remembered perfectly the last time I'd seen myself in a reflection, in one of Terrin's mirrors. I hadn't looked carefully, true, but even so I could see how faded my face was, the grim set of my mouth, the black messy blur of my hair. The idea that anything about me was High seemed like another one of Sid's jokes. I brushed past her question. "I think there was something in that councilman's watering can other than water," I said. "Something that he couldn't entrust to a Middling gardener. Something that makes that tree tell fortunes."

She considered this, nodding—not in immediate agreement, but in recognition of a valid interpretation.

"Will there be councilmen at tonight's party?" I asked.

"Doubtful. They serve the Lord Protector. They are too serious for parties. We should go anyway. I want to know what you make of the night's entertainment." Then she hesitated, her eyes roving over me. "Do you like what you're wearing?"

I glanced down at my pale brown dress with its frayed hem. "I don't know."

"How can you not know?" She seemed genuinely surprised, which I could understand, given how much she cared about what she wore. It was evident in the expertly fitted quality of her trousers and her sleeveless tunic with its short collar, the fabric thin enough for the heat and so exquisitely sewn that you could not see the seams. They were men's clothes, though far simpler than the embroidered, jewel-toned clothes that the High brothers in the market had worn. "Clothes are important," she said.

"To you."

"But not to you?"

I thought about it. "They're important to you because you have so many choices," I said finally, "and what you wear shows what you want. They hide your body, but they also show yourself. I don't have much choice. It doesn't really matter whether I wear beige or brown or gray. They are shades of the same thing. There is no meaning to whether I wear a dress or trousers, beyond whatever is most comfortable for work. It's different for me."

"It's not just about how I look. It's how I feel."

"Isn't how you look part of how you feel?"

She glanced at the sea. "Yes."

"I can't go to the party dressed like this, can I?"

"You can. You should wear whatever you want."

"I don't know what I want. Even if I did, I could die for wearing it. If I wear this and get caught as Half Kith, I'll be punished for having a forged document *and* going beyond the wall."

"As I said, people here think you're playing a game. That your clothes are a costume. A joke."

Her hesitancy, though, made me guess at something else. "But tonight it would be odd. They would stare."

"Yes."

"Would that embarrass you?"

"No."

"I have a Middling passport. I could dress as Middling, and go as your servant."

"You're not my servant."

"Aren't I?"

"No." Slowly, she said, "I don't like that option."

"I don't have any good options. I could wear a High dress, and if my passport is checked and I'm believed to be Middling, I'll be punished for breaking the sumptuary law. I don't know what would happen to a Middling for that. And if my passport doesn't pass muster and it's found to be forged, then we're right back where we were before, with me imprisoned and executed."

"No one checks passports at parties. It would spoil the mood."

"Then maybe it's best for me to wear High-Kith clothes, if you think I'd blend in."

She widened incredulous eyes.

"What?" I said.

"The idea of you blending in."

"You think my manners won't match how I'm dressed, and I'll be classed anyway?"

"No."

I was growing angry. "Or that nothing I wore could ever make me look as good as you?"

"*No.*" She was angry now, too.

"Then what is it?"

Her words came in a sudden rush. "You're hard to look away from. I can't look away from you. I don't know how anyone could."

This wasn't flirtation. The words had none of her usual ease. She sounded agitated. She sounded unlike herself.

I touched the burn on my cheek. It didn't hurt anymore, at least not on the skin. I pushed my ragged hair behind my ears. I felt hollowed out, like one of the pale blue eggs on Sid's plate. She saw the gesture, and frowned, and started to say something, but I spoke over her. "What do you think?"

She roughed up her hair. "I think this conversation makes me uncomfortable."

"I want to know what you think I should do."

"High clothes would be the safest choice for you. That doesn't mean it is the best one."

"I want to feel safe tonight."

She slid a card from a trouser pocket and passed it to me. The front showed a symbol I had already seen her display: the face of a man with closed eyes and a mark on his brow. The back of the card had a map drawn in Sid's hand. "If you go to the dressmaker's shop marked on that little map, Madame Mere will see to it that you're taken care of. Get whatever you like. This won't be the last function we attend, so you will need an entire wardrobe. While you are choosing what you want, I'll see if I can enter the Keepers Hall and find out why one of their members might be night gardening."

I gave the card back to her.

"But you need this," she said.

"I remember the map."

"You'll need this insignia." She placed a finger on the sleeping face. "So the dressmaker can be assured I will cover any costs."

"What *is* that image, exactly?"

Sid shifted uncomfortably. She glanced again at the sea. The harbor was in sight, its ships a cluster of toothpick masts and tiny scraps of sails. "I took the card from the queen of Herran."

"You *stole* it?"

"Sort of."

"Sid, are you looking at the harbor for your ship?"

"Maybe."

"Are you planning on running up high bills on a false line of credit associated with your country's queen and then setting sail as soon as the truth catches up with you?"

"No! I just like to look at my ship. I like to know that it's there. My crew better be, too, or there'll be hell to pay."

"I don't believe you."

"Oh, they would pay, trust me."

Exasperated at her deliberate misinterpretation of my words, I said, "Did you steal this house?"

"I am a thief only of hearts."

"We agreed. We agreed about the bragging."

"That wasn't bragging. That was true."

I took the yellow pot and poured all of its coffee out over the balcony.

"That was cruel, Nirrim."

"Answer at least *some* of my questions."

"Listen." She turned serious. "I always pay my debts. I have plenty of money. My family is swimming in it. That card . . . gets me some necessary respect. Should I have the card? Debatable. Should I use it? Definitely not, and doing so will definitely catch up with me. But money isn't enough here. You know that. Class matters. Gold isn't going to get us into that party tonight. Prestige will. My association with the queen will."

"You said you work for her."

"*Worked.*"

"What did you do?"

"If I tell you, will you trust me, and stop thinking that I'm a horrible person out to cheat people of their honest work?"

"How will I know you're telling the truth?"

"You will have to trust me."

"You are asking me to trust you in order to trust you."

"I am asking you to trust yourself. To believe in your instincts. Do you think I am a horrible person?"

I looked at Sid: her skin was amber in the sunlight, her few freckles stark, her eyes worried in a way I had never seen before. It meant something to her, I realized: what I thought of her. I looked at the breakfast, at all the sweet things she hadn't touched, which she had cooked or fetched while I was sleeping, and which must have been for me alone. "No," I said. "I think you have a good heart."

"Well, we don't have to go *that* far."

"Tell me what you did for her," I said, "and I'll believe you. For now."

"I thought I wanted you to trust me, but I confess that now I am enchanted by this new, suspicious side of you. It makes me feel like I had better live up to your expectations of me or I will be in really big trouble."

"Sid."

"Nirrim, I was her spy."

I stared.

"Why is that so surprising?" she said. "Kings and queens have spies. It is common knowledge. How else does one run a country?"

"I don't think spies admit they are spies."

"*Ex-spy.*"

"I don't think spies reveal the identity of their spymasters."

"Well, really, who else would it be? The king is too noble. The queen, however, is perfectly willing to get her hands dirty. Everyone knows she is the mastermind of the monarchy. It's an open secret. Really, the queen *wants* her people and foreign dignitaries to know exactly what she is. It makes them wary of her."

"You told me you ran her errands."

"Which in a way is very true. And it so happened that on one of those errands, I heard rumors about a magical island. I decided to do a bit of research in the archives. I found accounts dating back hundreds of years that described this region of the sea as notorious for the disappearance of ships. It seemed worth investigating."

"So you sailed to an area known for shipwrecks."

"Yes."

"After you quit working for the queen."

"To be honest, one does not exactly *quit* being her spy."

"And stole an insignia that represents her authority."

"Yes."

"I don't see how this is going to end well for you."

"What fun would it be," she said, "if you could?"

36

MADAME MERE WAS CLASSICALLY HIGH Herrath, her eyes
storm gray, her black hair woven into a mass of intertwined braids.
Streaks of pink locks dipped in and out of the black. She was perhaps twenty years older than me; her eyes delicately wrinkled at the
corners when she smiled. Her silk sapphire sheath was deceptively
simple—Annin would have wept over the beauty of its careful lines—
and served as a contrast for the elaborate, spangled wings made of
wire and tulle that arched from her back. Butterflies blinked their iridescent pink-spotted wings open and closed as they fluttered around
her and settled in her hair, on her shoulders. They exhaled a floral
perfume as they passed. I reached out. A butterfly flew right through
my fingers.

"An illusion." Madame Mere smiled at my astonishment. The wall
behind her was stacked with oblong bolts of wound fabric categorized
according to color and pattern. A glass pot of chilled pink tea sat behind
her on an ornate table made from ebony, a wood harvested by Un-Kith

in the tropics of this island, or so I had read in Harvers's books. "*Please tell me you are not going to the duchess's masked ball as a Half Kith,*" she said. "That is so last year."

I handed her Sid's card. The dressmaker's expression turned sly. "I see. And shall I be outfitting you for Lady Sidarine's pleasure?"

"What is that symbol on the card?"

"The insignia of the royal family of Herran."

I was relieved to learn that Sid had been telling the truth. "What is her connection to that family?"

"No one knows. Rumor has it that she is a minor Herrani aristocrat. Honestly, though, no one had even heard of Herran until she arrived. There have been a few travelers before, here and there, who have turned up on our shores, but no one like her. I think"—the woman's voice lowered conspiratorially—"she has capitalized wonderfully on the air of mystery surrounding her. Questions are so much more desirable than answers." She poured herself a cup of tea and sipped as she stood, the wafer-thin saucer on one palm, her gray eyes smiling at me over the glass cup's brim. "Watch out, dear."

"Why?" I felt heat rise to my cheeks. "What else is said about her?"

"That she is as bad as a boy."

She drew me in front of a tall, scalloped mirror that I recognized as having been made by Terrin in the Ward. Madame Mere positioned me in front of the mirror and stood slightly behind me, looking over my shoulder at the two of us in the reflection. At first, I was too distracted by Madame Mere's words to truly see myself. They warmed my skin. They reached deep inside me to tug at my heart.

And then I was distracted by the dressmaker's wings, how they arched behind both of us as if they belonged to me, too.

But finally, my eyes settled on myself in the mirror.

Large eyes. Careful mouth. Wild hair. A nearly healed burn that would probably never go away completely. My dress looked like a sack.

Madame Merle plucked at the cloth, rubbing it between forefinger and thumb. "I'm not sure who dressed you," she said, "but the look is impressively authentic."

My gaze shifted to her face, to see if she suspected. But her face looked placid . . . *too* placid. Perfectly lineless, even. I turned from the mirror to look directly at her. The wrinkles I had seen earlier on her face had somehow smoothed away.

"Tell me what you want," she said, "and I will make it happen."

I want my liar, I thought.

I want her mouth.

I want her perfume to rub off on my skin like bruised grass.

A bubble of longing rose into my throat. "I want to be beautiful."

"Of course," the woman said. "Don't we all?"

37

MIDDLING BOYS WERE LIGHTING THE streetlamps as I walked back to Sid's house, carrying a long pink box that held my party dress. The rest of my wardrobe would be sent later, Madame Mere said, though she insisted that I put on a vivid cyan crepe dress with short, ribboned sleeves before I left her shop, and had smoothed and curled my wild hair while I sipped her surprisingly tasteless pink tea. She tucked my hair into patterns, using pins the shimmery green of a scarab beetle. She rubbed cream into my cheeks. "I don't like for someone to leave my shop looking anything less than glamorous."

She did not like that I would be carrying my own dress box. "You are taking the Half-Kith act too far, my dear," she said. I was amazed at how people's assumptions overrode the obvious, though I was not one to cast judgment on anyone for not seeing things as they really were.

As I walked up the hilly street, the dress box beneath my arm, I thought about Helin and her gentle effort to shield me from my strangeness. How she had promised to be my guide, to tell me what was real and what wasn't. I still missed her. I still felt sad, but it was a softer sadness, because the crippling guilt had lessened. I hadn't understood how sick Helin was the night she died. I had believed her when she said she was fine, because I had trained myself to believe her and to mistrust myself.

But even if I hadn't been plagued by illusions I didn't understand, if I had been normal, I still could have made the same mistake. The inability to see clearly had felt like my problem, my curse. But maybe it was everyone's.

The lamplighters lifted their long poles, each as slender and black as a heron's leg, and touched flames to the lamps' wicks. The lamps glowed, one by one, against the lavender sky.

I glanced around the quiet street and wondered if I could make myself see the sort of vision I had always tried to ignore. The more I considered the images I had seen in the Ward, the more I wondered whether it was not simply that I had a perfect memory.

I could also see into the *city's* memory.

For years I had tried to harden myself against the illusions. It felt uncomfortable to invite them. But I imagined myself as tender and vulnerable: a downy chick out of its egg.

And for a moment, I saw not a lamplit street before me, but an empty, grassy hill, the wind shivering in the green.

I glanced behind me, toward the wall.

There was no wall. There was only the Ward—defenseless, surrounded by nothing but hills and sky.

"Hey there," said a voice.

I turned, and the vision vanished.

"You," I said. It was the brown-haired boy from the Middling quarter who had stolen the dream vials. A lamp-lighting pole rested against his shoulder.

He whistled. "You are looking awfully fancy. I almost didn't recognize you. Come up in the world, haven't you?"

I took a wary step back. "Are you planning to turn me in?"

"Me? No. Honor among thieves and all that."

"I'm not a thief."

He squinted one eye shut, peering at me. "Aren't you stealing a place in society that isn't yours? Believe me, I'm going to do the same, given half a chance."

"Then what do you want from me?"

"To give you a message. Your foreign friend says she'll be late, so you should meet her at the party." He handed me a scrap of paper with a map. "She says you are to use her card with the insignia to get in."

"It was *you* who told her I was looking for her in the Middling quarter."

"You've got no call to act so betrayed. It's not like you asked me *not* to tell her. If she gives me a bit of gold to bring her interesting tales, who am I to say no?"

Then he strolled away, carrying the pole lazily over his shoulder as if he were going fishing, the lamps glowing in the dark, the other Middling boys' roving shadows ahead, disappearing into the night.

～

The map led me to a house so overgrown with ivy and fist-sized flowers that I couldn't see the walls behind them. Hummingbirds darted in and out of the blossoms. Milling people waited in the courtyard to enter, their clothes extravagant, artfully constructed. Golden hoops around a waist trailed transparent lace that showed bare legs. Wire-and-satin petals bloomed around the green stem of a body. There was wild plumage. Slithering snake bracelets. The guests seemed inhuman, like strange creatures—part bird, part snake, part flower—or gods. Women had impossibly lush hair, left long in thick capes around their shoulders, or twisted into towering architectural wonders. A man blinked blue eyelashes fringed with lime-green petals at me.

Sid stood in the shadows of the courtyard. She was dressed in a man's fitted black dress jacket buttoned over a paper-white collared shirt, the chain of her watch trailing from her pocket, her golden hair slicked back. The corners of her tipped-up eyes crinkled as she smiled at something a lilac-haired woman whispered, her glittered lips a mere breath away from Sid's ear.

All my nervousness and wonder clumped into sick jealousy.

I walked quietly up to them. Sid's hands slipped into her trouser pockets. The woman touched Sid's white collar, then rested her hand on Sid's shoulder as if for balance. Sid's mouth quirked, and she said something that looked like an easy admission. Then she glanced up and saw me. Her face went still. She murmured something to the woman, who frowned as I came close.

Sid gave her a quick kiss on the cheek. "Do excuse me," Sid said to her. "My companion is here."

The lilac-haired woman swept haughtily away, the feathered trail of her dress singing as she went, notes of birdsong rising from her dress and then fading as she went into the flowering house.

"How surprising," I said, "that, for you, being late to a party actually means showing up on time to get a head start on luring a girl into bed."

Sid started to protest, then stopped, staring at me. "Nirrim, what did you do to your face?" She lifted her fingers to my cheek.

I resented the pleasure of it. "Don't touch me."

Her hand fell. She looked embarrassed. "I'm sorry. I didn't mean to. It's just . . . the burn on your cheek is gone."

I touched my cheek. Where the skin had been new and tender, it now felt perfectly smooth. "How?"

"You don't know?"

"Madame Mere rubbed cream into my face . . . maybe it's cosmetic. Or her mirror? Maybe it was magic." I remembered how I had looked at my own reflection. This is the pain of having a perfect memory: it was impossible to ignore how I had stared at every flaw, how I had felt filled with longing. "She shouldn't have done it." I was angry at the dressmaker for changing me without my permission, angry at Sid, angry at myself.

It was for nothing, the silver dress I wore, the fringe of whispering glass beads that drifted over my bare arms like tiny bubbles.

Sid was still frowning. "I am not going to sleep with Lillin."

"She clearly thought otherwise."

"Well, I *did* bed her once. But it was so long ago."

I made a sound of helpless disgust.

"Are you—?" Sid stopped herself. Slowly, she said, "I didn't think it would bother you if I talked with her."

"It doesn't."

"All right, it doesn't."

"You don't think it's wrong to lead her on?"

"Is that it? I was quite clear with her that I wasn't interested."

"You kissed her."

"Just a little bit."

"How does that show a lack of interest?"

"It was a sisterly kiss. A good-bye kiss."

"You are impossible."

"I could say the same about you."

The number of partygoers in the courtyard had dwindled. Almost everyone had gone inside.

Sid rubbed the nape of her neck, studying me. Then she stuffed her hands into her pockets, hunching her shoulders. Quietly, she said, "You are my favorite impossible person."

"Me," I said, uncertain.

"You are the only one I want to be with."

"Tonight." I didn't know what was worse: that she had seen my jealousy, that she was trying to soothe it, or that I knew—just as Lillin or any woman Sid had ever been with should have known—that nothing Sid said or did would last.

"Any night." She offered her arm like a man would. "Will you come inside with me?"

I took her arm. The fabric of her jacket brushed my skin. I wanted to turn in to her, to press my face against her neck. I said, "We'll look like a couple."

"Do you want that?"

Truth can demand so much bravery. I did not feel brave. I would not have been brave, if her question hadn't sounded a little hopeful. Yes, I wanted everyone to think she belonged with me, that I belonged with her. Yes, even if it was only for one night. My voice was small. "I do."

Her mouth twitched with surprise, then curled with inquisitive pleasure that I loved to see. Maybe this was a game to her, but it felt so good to be her game. "Nirrim," she said, "I am *really* sorry that I am not late. May I tell you all the things I will do to make you forgive me?"

I smiled as we went inside.

38

THE FOYER WAS OVERGROWN with branches. They twisted around oil lamps with green flames blazing in their glass cases. The ground was soft with dirt. I realized that the house wasn't covered with vegetation: the branches and flowers and leaves *were* the house. "Someone *grew* this?" I said. "Who?"

"No one knows. It grew overnight." We turned down a hallway paved with acorns. "It will wither and fade soon enough. The magic always does."

"So you *do* think it's magic."

"I think 'magic' is convenient shorthand for a mystery we haven't solved."

"Why were you not late to the party?"

"I couldn't get into the Keepers Hall. It was too heavily guarded and, somehow, my ample charms weren't working on anyone. So that didn't take as long as planned. But Lillin's brother is a councilman, and she thinks she can get me maps of the hall. You see why I had to be friendly with her."

"Do I?"

Sid smiled. "Not *too* friendly, of course."

We passed a room shaped like an enormous bird's nest, the kind mud larks make, spherical and entirely enclosed, with an oval entrance. I heard a joyful cry, accompanied by a crowd's roar. I peeked inside. The entire interior of the round room was felted with thousands of little woven twigs. A table made of hardened mud occupied the center of the room. A woman with her skin dyed in butterfly patterns was scraping a pile of gold toward her while the other people at the table slapped cards down in irritation. Onlookers cheered. "They're playing a card game," I told Sid.

"Oh?" she said, interested. She glanced inside. "Oh," she said again, her interest gone. "They're playing Pantheon. I already know that one."

"How do you play?"

"There are one hundred face cards, one for each god. Each face card has a value, with Death being the highest and the Seamstress the lowest, since she was mortal before Death made her a god. God of games reverses the order of play. God of thieves is wild. And then there are the blanks. I don't know what they represent. No one does, or if they do they won't tell me. The dealer decides how many blanks to shuffle into the deck. Blanks don't have value of their own but can augment the power of your hand or diminish your opponent's if you play one against him."

Sid continued, describing the best combinations of cards and the most effective lines of strategy.

"Do you want to play?" I asked.

She shook her head. "Too boring. I always win."

Gently, she guided me down the hall toward the ballroom where Middling musicians played and High Kith were already swirling across the floor in dancing pairs.

The ballroom was papered with birch bark. Tree frogs clinging to a bramble chandelier burbled along to the music. The ceiling above the chandelier was a gray mist. Two men stood close together in a corner of the ballroom. One stroked a finger across the other's mouth.

So easy.

No one was looking at them. No one cared. The only one staring was me.

Sid followed my gaze. She started to say something when a Middling servant gave me a crystal cup filled with sparkling liquid almost the same color as the mist, yet slightly pink. The servant hurried away before I could thank her. I lifted the cup to my lips.

Sid placed her palm over the glass.

"That's rude," I said.

"It's silver wine," she said. "It will make you tell the truth."

"Oh."

"I don't want you to say anything you don't mean to say."

"We could always share it," I dared her.

Sid gingerly took the glass by its rim, her fingers pinching it as if it contained something dangerous, and made an exaggerated play out of setting it down on a nearby birch-bark table and backing away slowly.

"So cautious," I said, "so protective of us both."

"I am a hero."

"And yet you have that pocket watch."

Sid looped a finger around its chain. "This?"

"Isn't that another version of the silver wine?"

"The watch doesn't work anymore. I wear it because I like the style. Look, it's still stuck on the same word from the last time I used it."

Desire.

There was a crack of thunder. I glanced up. The mist gathered at the ceiling had condensed into a dark fist of clouds. Lightning flashed. Thunder rumbled again. Rain showered down. The music stopped. Frogs shrilled. Dancers shrieked and laughed and ran from the room. Sid and I followed, since it was that or get trampled.

We pushed past dripping High Kith clumped together in the hall-way, some giggling, others complaining about their ruined clothes.

Sid's sooty eyelashes were spiky with rain. Her mouth was wet with it. Her soaked white shirt stuck to her skin. I could see the ridge of her collarbone pressing against the cloth.

"Your hair," she said distractedly, "curls when wet." She brushed away a lock of hair that was plastered to my face.

For one mad moment I leaned into her hand, which was warm and steady.

"Tired?" she asked, stroking her thumb across my cheekbone.

I shivered. "No."

Her eyes searched mine. "Lonely?"

I was lonely for her even though she was right in front of me. I worried that if I said no she would stop touching me, and that if I said yes she would pity me. "I'm cold," I said, which was true, but the sort of truth that acted as a lie.

Her hand fell. Her expression closed, and she nodded, not really in response to my midnight lie but as if to a thought in her head. She glanced up and down the hallway, which was emptying of people, and said, "Maybe there's a blanket of moss somewhere. Or, I don't know . . . a coat of feathers in a hollow tree wardrobe."

I missed her hand. I felt embarrassed that I missed it, that I had said the wrong thing. I shivered again, this time cold inside and out. I began to undo the tiny crystal buttons that ran down the front of my wet dress.

Sid's attention swiftly returned. "Are you . . . taking your clothes off? I hadn't thought we had reached that stage of our relationship."

"It's the whole point of the dress," I said, glad that she was teasing me again. "It is *many* dresses."

"But I like this one. You look like you're wrapped in starlight."

"It's wet." I shrugged out of the silver dress, revealing another one in pleated crimson faille.

"Ohh," Sid said, "I want to see the rest."

"You always want to rush everything."

"Actually, I think I show a lot of restraint around you."

"One more. This layer is damp, too."

"Wait. Stop there."

The dress was now a clingy emerald satin, simple and fluid. I paused in the act of undoing its ties.

"Please," she said.

"Is it your favorite?"

"Your eyes," she said, low. Then her voice firmed. "I want this one, and you owe me a yes."

"Unfairly extracted from me when we were in prison."

"As I recall, you cleverly wriggled out of two other yesses, so I think one is perfectly reasonable."

"You would waste it on a dress?"

"On you in this dress? Worth it."

I felt warm again. "Keep your yes. I'll owe it to you another time. I want to wear this dress, if you like it best." I glanced at the gold chain of her pocket watch. "There's something else I want."

"Name it."

"To play you at Pantheon."

"Bad idea."

"Afraid?"

"Yes, of you after I beat you."

"Is everyone from your country all talk and no action?"

"Don't say I didn't warn you," she said.

39

WE JOINED THE MUD TABLE in the bird's nest, where several High Kith were already playing, some dipping fingers into tortoiseshell bowls full of glittery gray powder that they brought to their lips between rounds. "Pleasure dust," Sid murmured in my ear. "Those players will do better than they should at first, but not for long."

There was a pile of gold and silver on the table, but random things, too, like mother-of-pearl earrings, an open enameled box with a tiny meowing clockwork cat inside, and a little metal stoppered vial. I pulled a green comb from my hair and added it to the pile as ante. Sid tossed in a coin.

As we played, Sid was quieter than usual, eerily serene, producing winning hand after winning hand. Several players dropped out. I added more green combs to the pile and lost them. I was not playing to win, at first, but to observe when Sid bluffed and when she didn't, which was easy enough to tell, not from any change in her demeanor, but from the simple fact that I remembered where every single card went, and who had what. Even if I didn't know each exact card in her hand of five, because the entire deck of one hundred plus four blanks hadn't yet been dealt, I more or less knew what Sid had when she folded, her cards facedown, showing only their gleaming black-and-gold backs.

Then, steadily, I began to win, which became easier as the deck played down. The first time it happened, Sid sweetly congratulated me. The third time, she cocked a wary brow. It was surprising to me how easy it was for people to forget what they knew, since it didn't seem to occur to Sid that I had memorized the distribution of the deck, so intent was she on winning—and so confident, probably, with her history of dominating the game.

Soon, everyone had dropped out but us. I had an enormous pile of winnings. Sid dealt the remainder of the deck.

I glanced at my cards and knew instantly what she held. I pushed my winnings forward. "I bet it all."

"Oh, don't do *that*," Sid said, and it wasn't bad advice, since she held the god of Death.

"Match me," I said. When she sighed and reached into her jacket for gold I said, "No. I want the pocket watch."

She slipped a finger around its chain. Thoughtfully, she slid the watch from her pocket and weighed it on her palm. "*This?*" she said. "Why?"

A flush crept into my cheeks. In a way, I had already showed my hand. "Do you fold?"

She turned the watch over in her fingers, inspecting it, yet did not open it. Understanding flashed across her face. "It's not broken, is it?" she said. "In fact"—she tossed it onto the pile—"I believe it works perfectly well." She turned over her cards and grinned.

I turned over mine. I had mostly nothing . . . except the god of thieves and a blank, which was as good as two Deaths.

"Ohhh." Sid planted her face in her hand. She groaned again into her palm. When she lifted her face I saw that she had realized what she should have known about me for the entire game. She leaned across the table to put the watch in my hand. Her soft cheek brushed mine. "You cheated," she said in a delighted whisper.

"I won," I corrected, and dropped the watch to the ground to crush it beneath my heel.

We had scooped my winnings into one of my damp dresses, twisting the cloth to form an impromptu sack, and were walking down the acorn hall when a fight broke out. A man drinking silver wine threw the contents of his glass in the face of his friend, who punched back, dropping his own glass. In the tussle, one shoved the other against the dirt wall, which exploded into a brown spray that completely covered a nearby woman.

The men fell through the wall. The woman, her face a mask of dirt, screamed at them. Their fight, accompanied by thumps and shouts, got farther away.

The dirt-covered woman looked down at her filthy dress and burst into tears.

"You are being silly," a woman with wire wings told her.

"I loved this dress!"

"Who cares? No one wears the same thing twice anyway."

All of my glee at winning Pantheon slid out of me. I looked at the High Kith in the hallway and the atrium ahead, at their colored eyelashes and heaps of hair, and realized that even I, who remembered everything, was capable of ignoring what I knew.

The hair and lashes were false. They were tithes. They had been taken from the Half Kith.

The tortoiseshell bowl filled with pleasure dust had been made by orphans.

The woman's wings were not, like Madame Mere's, made from silk, but from skin. I shuddered.

"What's wrong?" Sid said.

"It's not fair." I felt near tears.

"What isn't? Tell me."

I thought of the men who leaned into each other in the ballroom, how I had been jealous and yet still afraid for them, tensing for some blow that might fall, because no one in the Ward could do what they did.

I thought of Annin, who was starving for just a little bit of beauty.

I thought of Morah, who hadn't even been able to keep her own child, and Raven, who had to live with the guilt of taking Morah's baby from her because she had thought it was for the best, because the Ward was no place to raise a child.

I thought of everyone who went to prison and never came back. Of all the parents whose children had vanished.

Of me, so used to being trapped that I was afraid of being free.

Of me, laughing in my dress that was many dresses, enchanted by everything that I had never had.

"Do you want to leave?" Sid's voice was anxious.

I nodded.

We pushed our way out into the courtyard. The stars were fading. Dawn was creeping into the sky.

"You are worrying me," Sid said. "Please talk to me."

"They have everything."

Her face grew quiet. "Yes," she said.

"I want to take it from them."

"Of course you do."

"I *will*. Promise me you will help."

Sid paused. "We don't know what *it* is."

"I don't care if it's magic or science. You said that if I helped you find its secret, you would give me what I want. I want you to help me take it from the High Kith and give it to the Ward. Will you?"

"Yes."

"Promise me."

"I swear by the gods."

"You don't believe in the gods."

"I believe it means something to swear by them."

"That's not good enough."

"What is?"

"Swear by your parents. Swear on their lives."

Sid's face got tight. She shook her head. "I swear on my own."

40

A COOL MORNING BEFORE A hot day holds a sweet freshness. The gray dawn gave in to the coming sun as we walked home, the wind gentle in my hair, slipping over my skin like water. Pink heated the sky. I could feel the promise of a blazing day, and the breeze, like a friend, giving me what it could.

I was so tired. My feet were sore. I leaned into Sid as we walked, my head on her shoulder, half asleep. I felt, through my sleepiness, that she was wide awake. Whatever she was thinking seemed to whir inside her. I let myself feel safe, not caring if I'd discover, later, that the feeling had been a mistake. The skin of her throat felt too soft against my cheek, and her arm around me felt too good. She wouldn't hold me like this if she didn't feel at least part of what I felt. She wouldn't have smiled when she realized that her watch had always worked, that my desire had been for her. She wouldn't have loved my green dress, or touched my cheek, or kissed my palm and pretended it was an apology, or have grown suddenly distant and cold when I said I loved Aden. She wouldn't have made me a promise. My memories were clear, and what I hadn't understood before now seemed obvious.

I knew she would leave me. She had always said she would.

Whatever she felt for me wouldn't last. But I wanted it for as long as it did.

She got her key into the front door of the house. We went up the soundless stairs, the steps so quiet it was as though they were dreaming beneath our feet.

Sid pushed open the door to my bedroom. A draft tugged open the balcony doors, which I hadn't properly shut. The glass panes rattled in their frames. The wind lifted and swirled the sheer curtains. A breeze skimmed over the bed, swinging the tiny tassels on the creamy toile covers. I turned and shut the bedroom door behind us. The wind died.

Sid's back was to the bedroom door. I curled my fingers into her undone white collar, hooking down, the heel of my hand against the rise of her breast beneath the stiff jacket, her skin hot to the touch, her pulse fast against my palm.

"You're half asleep," she said.

"I'm awake."

Her hand lifted to cover mine and press it against her chest.

"I owe you a yes," I said.

Her dark eyes were shadowed. My palm was flattened now, the tips of my fingers against her throat, her hand firm on mine.

I said, "Ask me to kiss you."

She kissed me. Her mouth was hungry on mine, on my neck. Her hand fisted in my hair. I pushed off her jacket, found the jut of her ribs beneath her shirt, the sweep of her belly, the leather strap of her dagger belt. I tasted her mouth. My heart was thrumming in my throat, and I was greedy for her. I loved her gasp, her teeth on my lower lip, her thigh hard between mine. I tugged her by her belt toward me. I wanted the bed; I wanted her to press me down into it.

"Wait," she murmured. "Too fast."

I felt flushed all over. "You like it fast."

"Not like this." She pulled away. Her hair was wild, mouth swollen. She looked down at me, at her disheveled shirt. She rubbed a hand over her eyes.

"Sid." My voice was full of yearning.

She straightened her shirt and tucked it into her trousers. "You have a life here. One that you want to keep. One that doesn't involve me."

"It already involves you."

"Not this way."

"But why?" My voice cracked.

"You'll regret it."

"I won't."

"I will," she said, and turned away, shutting the door softly behind her, leaving me alone, my breath quick and harsh with hurt in the rising light.

41

WHEN I WOKE, THE SUNLIGHT was a hot blade on the bed. The hour was late and the still air felt like wet fur. I had cast off the sheet in my sleep.

Faintly, from downstairs, came the scrapes and clinks of someone busy at a task. There was the burnt scent of that foul eastern drink Sid liked so much.

I turned my face into the pillow. The pillow didn't smell like Sid anymore. It smelled like me, and I was glad, because it was painful enough to want her, painful enough to remember exactly the shape of her mouth beneath my tongue, without having the specific scent of her perfume and skin pressing against my face.

Would there have been any words that could have made her stay last night?

I could have said, I know it's not forever.

I could have said, I still want this, even if it vanishes like sugar on my tongue.

But I didn't, and maybe even if I had, it wouldn't have made a difference.

———

The second time I opened my eyes, the house had an empty silence. I was relieved.

I went through my Pantheon winnings, dumping them onto the bed. I set aside all the money for Raven, the jewels and the box with the meowing cat for Annin, and a little knife for Morah, mostly because it reminded me of her. It had a strong and appealingly simple blade, with an edge to reckon with, and a hilt so intricately wrought with gold over steel that it was difficult to follow the path of the pattern. I uncorked the little metal vial, noting the slosh of its contents, and sniffed. It smelled like water. I didn't see why anyone would bother to put such a small quantity of water in a vial—this was no canteen or flask. It fit in the palm of my hand. After encountering silver wine and pleasure dust at the party, I wasn't about to taste anything I couldn't identify. I took it to the bathroom and dribbled some of the vial's liquid into the sink. It was a faint pink.

I remembered where I had seen something like that before.

I glanced into the mirror. The faded burn on my cheek had returned. It wasn't a cream or the dressmaker's mirror that had made the burn disappear for a night. It had been Madame Mere's pink tea.

———

"Well?" she said when I entered her shop. "Was it a triumph? Which dress did she like best? Was it the final dress, right before it came off?"

I held out the little metal vial. "Is this yours?"

She looked at it, then at me quizzically. "No."

"Is what's inside yours? What is this liquid?"

She took the vial, opened it, and sniffed. "Oh, that," she said, and smiled.

"Why are you smiling?"

"Because if I didn't already know before that you were Half Kith, I would know now."

My pulse stuttered. My face must have betrayed me. Madame Mere said, "Only someone raised behind the wall or a traveler like Lady Sidarine would ask about elixir."

"You knew?" Fear coursed through me. "Why did you pretend you didn't?"

"My little kithling. I run a business."

"You're saying that you stayed silent in order to keep Sid as a customer."

"No. I have plenty of customers. I turn many away, and dress only those who intrigue me."

"Do you intend to blackmail me? I have nothing to give you."

"I know you don't. That is why I said nothing, and never will. Have you not noticed that most High Kith do not work, and that I do?"

I felt foolish for having thought she was blind to the obvious—that I was Half Kith—because of her assumptions. *I* had been the one to miss what was in front of my face.

"I work because I enjoy it," Madame Mere said. "Everyone loves beauty, but what I love more is *making* it. I like to map out someone's desires in pattern and cloth. I like to stitch them together. And if some of my kith think it's strange for me to do it, they overlook my strangeness for the privilege of wearing my clothes. You, my dear, want more than what life has given you. What is so wrong with that? This is what I want, too. It is what everyone wants."

"So you won't tell the militia?"

"That would be a very boring outcome to your unusual situation."

I was not at all reassured. "That doesn't sound like a good reason to trust you."

"I disagree. You have been to one of our parties. Surely you saw how, beneath all the finery, everyone is hungry for something different, something new. *You*, my dear, are exactly that. Why would I give you up?"

"So I am . . . your entertainment."

"You are a story whose end would come far too soon in prison." She busied herself pouring pink tea. "Would you like some? I can't tell you what the elixir in that vial does, but it'd be best to pour it out if you don't know. It could make you weep golden tears, or make what you imagine come to life, though usually only for a brief time. My elixir is very benign. It heals. It repairs scars, as you've seen. It fills in the cracks left by age."

I realized that I had never seen a truly elderly looking High Kith. If I had thought about it, I would have assumed it was because I had been to places only young people frequented, but it seemed that no one here needed to look their age.

I refused the tea. The burn would return anyway. This elixir didn't strike me as healing, but as an addictive respite from the truth. "Did you make the elixir?"

She took a sip from her cup. "No. It is supplied by the Council. There are many varieties. The price is high, but most are willing to pay, through either gold or pledges."

"Pledges?"

"Yes. Many parents pledge one of their children to the service of the Council, which is always in need of new members. Few people actively want to serve the Lord Protector, though there are always some who enjoy the thrill of being close to the center of power and voluntarily induct themselves into the Keepers Hall."

"Why is it called that?"

She shrugged delicately. "I suppose because they keep and control the supply of elixirs. And they keep order in the city. They oversee the militia, who are Middling, and appoint members of the Council to be judges. But I don't really *know* why the hall is called that. It has always been called that."

I was startled to hear these words coming from the mouth of a High Kith, uttered in that same blank tone I had heard Morah use, and Annin, and even myself. I had always assumed that only people behind the wall talked like that, and that everyone who lived beyond it had the answers to all our questions, just like they had everything else, even the ability to defy age.

"It is as it is," said Madame Mere, settling her empty cup in its saucer.

But nothing is as it is. Everything comes from something. There is nothing and no one without a past. I thought about the fortune-telling tree. It had not always been a tree. Once, it had been a sapling that threaded greenly out of the dirt. Once, it had been a seed.

"I don't believe you," I told Madame Mere, not because I thought she was lying, but because I wasn't sure that anyone in Ethin knew the truth.

Sid looked tired when I returned to the house. She wore a marigold silk dress as she busied herself in the kitchen, taking no care to protect the delicate cloth from the oil she rubbed into a shank of lamb, or the spices she liberally shook all over it, or the fresh red currants she plucked from their frail stems. It was as if she secretly—or not so secretly—wished to ruin the dress. Her face was drawn and unhappy, her eyes avoiding mine.

"Where have you been?" she asked.

"Upholding my end of our bargain."

"Oh." She looked at her oiled hands, at the mess on the table.

"You left the house first," I pointed out, since she seemed inexplicably dissatisfied with my answer. "Why are you wearing that?"

She looked down at the stained dress. Her mouth curled in distaste. "I thought I should."

"Why?"

"'Why?'" she repeated. "You are asking none of the questions I thought you would."

But I didn't want to talk about last night. I didn't want to talk about how the only way I'd been able to sleep was to keep my hands beneath my pillow, so that I wouldn't be tempted to touch myself, which would only remind me of how I wanted her hands, not mine.

She said, "I am wearing this dress because I thought it would be an appropriate choice when I attempted to use my status to get into the Keepers Hall."

"It didn't work," I guessed, based on her general mood.

"No." She glanced again at the seasoned meat. "There's only enough for one."

Affronted, I said, "I don't expect you to cook for me."

"I mean, we will have to share." She looked up at me. "I thought you weren't coming back. I found the house empty when I returned. I thought you had left for good."

"I'm not going to do that."

"But *I* will."

"I know you will."

She got very quiet. "I didn't like the thought that you had left. I was afraid I had made you go."

"But I'm here," I said. "You are here."

"For now."

"Everything is for now," I said, and didn't know how to explain to her the feeling I had always lived with, which was as old as the memory of the cold orphanage box: that anything could be taken from me at any time. I said, "We want the same thing."

"Do we?"

"We want answers," I said, because it was true but also because I wanted to turn the conversation to the reason we were in this house together to begin with, and away from last night and her rejection, which she seemed to be trying to explain, with an awkwardness unlike herself, and which I didn't feel needed any more explanation. Things were clear. She would regret taking me to bed. She was trying to explain that anything between us would bring me pain, because she was not someone who stayed. That she cared about me, which I could see, plain on her worried face, and which was a bitter comfort. I didn't want her to worry. I put my hand on her oiled and blood-ied one, the grit of the spices and salt like sand against my skin. "I haven't changed my mind," I said. She looked at me, and I faltered, because I didn't want last night to happen all over again, to ask for what she didn't want to give, or to think about how her wet mouth had skimmed my neck. I said, my voice clear, "I haven't changed my mind about our plan."

She nodded. "All right."

"And I have some information for you."

She lifted a brow. She looked more like herself. "Do you?"

"Doesn't it embarrass you to find that a lowly underling has discov-ered something a queen's spy hasn't?"

"You are not a lowly underling."

"Dodging the question as always, I see, which must mean that I am right."

"You are wrong. I am not embarrassed." Sid turned her hand, which lay beneath mine, and held my fingers. "I am impressed. But not surprised."

"Why aren't you surprised?"

"You're resourceful. Strong."

"Resourceful . . . ," I said. "Maybe. Strong?" I shook my head. "Sometimes I miss the wall. I miss being behind it." I knew it wasn't safe there, but it was my home. Even an unsafe home can feel safe.

"But you're *not* behind it," Sid said. "You're here. You are at risk, so much more than I am, yet you keep risking yourself. I wish you could see yourself like I see you."

"How do you see me?"

"You're like those flowers that grow along the walls. The indi flowers. The ones that freeze and come back to life. They dig themselves into any little crack."

"They're destructive."

"Yes. And beautiful."

I slid my hand from hers. I didn't like how warm her words made me, and how they felt, again, like bitter comfort, like the wound and the balm at the same time. She was trying to console me after she had rejected me, which was the very thing I had done with Aden the first time I broke things off with him: told him he was handsome, he was resourceful and talented and as good at capturing hearts as he was at catching people's images on a tin plate. So many girls in the Ward loved him. He just wasn't right for me.

"Your scar is back." She lifted a finger to touch my burn, but then didn't. "Where did you get that? You never said. You didn't have it when we first met."

"An accident," I said. "Let me tell you what I discovered today."

"I am not the only one who dodges," she said, but she didn't press, only listened to what the dressmaker had told me.

"We need to infiltrate the Council," Sid said.

"You have used your status in so many ways. To get us out of prison. To live here and get invited to High-Kith parties. To get dresses made. Why can't you be invited into the Keepers Hall?"

She shook her head. "The fact that I'm close to the Herrani queen will, in this case, make them only more unwilling to give me access to a place that might house what seems to be a state secret. And I can't sneak inside, because I look like one of the very few foreigners who have been to this island. Nor do I have the right documents. Councilmembers have an extra page in their High-Kith passports that has a special Council stamp to show their status."

"I could sneak in. I look High Herrath."

"No. I don't want to risk you. And we'd still have a problem regarding the documents."

"Well," I said, "not really."

She gave me a narrow look. "Would the person who forged your Middling passport be able to get you access to a Council stamp?"

"That person," I said, "is me."

"You," she said.

I explained how I used my skill at memory to forge passports. She stared. "Surprised?" I said.

"Yes, at how blind I've been. Why haven't you told me this before?"

"I didn't trust you."

"And now you do?"

I thought about last night. How worried she had been a moment ago that I had left for good. Her flat dismissal of the idea of me sneaking into the Keepers Hall. "I trust that you wouldn't denounce me to the militia. I trust that you don't want me to get hurt."

"I don't," she said. "You can't. It would hurt me if you got hurt."

"You are kinder than I have sometimes thought you to be."

"Ah, yes. You did accuse me once of being heartless." She studied me, then said slowly, "Is your forging . . . connected at all to Raven? She was entirely too anxious about losing you for a month. There was all that talk about a project you were working on. Was this it? I thought she was just being manipulative. That she was making excuses to control you and keep you by her side."

"She isn't manipulative. She was worried about how many people would have to wait for a passport because I was leaving the tavern. You're right: we work together to give forged passports to people who need them. She has a good heart. She has helped so many people. Aden has, too."

"Oh." Her face closed. "Right. Your young man."

"If you knew how much good Raven does—and Aden, too—you wouldn't be so cold about them."

"You might have decided that I'm kind enough to trust with your secret, Nirrim, and I suppose I am, but don't expect me to warm suddenly toward your handsome young sweetheart."

"I could forge a document that would let me into the Keepers Hall," I said, "if I could see a councilmember's authentic passport."

"No," she said flatly, "because then you'll want to use it."

"I recall you promising adventure."

"I don't want you to endanger yourself."

"It's too late for that."

Sid persuaded me that we didn't have to go into the hall, necessarily, to learn how the Council made that elixir, but that we could continue to attend parties to collect clues from the High Kith, as I had with the vial that contained the elixir. "And the Council is hosting a parade in two weeks' time," she said.

Two weeks. I thought about how short a month is, how little time I had with Sid, how quickly it would run out.

The parties—at least at first—showed us nothing but excess. A masked ball where, at the stroke of midnight, dancers ate their lovers' sugar masks while I looked awkwardly on, Sid standing stiffly beside me, her own mask still on her inscrutable face. Probably at least in part to make no matter of how people around us were licking each other's sugared lips, Sid busied herself as a pickpocket, filching a High-Kith passport from someone's pocket and slipping it to me. I paged through it quickly, committing each part of it to memory. Sid then returned the booklet to its owner, who thought he had dropped it, with a slight bow. Later, at her house, I carved a block of wood to re-create a High-Kith stamp, taking care that it would make the exact impression on paper as the stamp I had seen. Sid brought me dyes and scraps of leather. I cut the heliograph from my Middling passport and set it into my new High-Kith one. I didn't have the right stamp that would let me into the Keepers Hall, but having a High-Kith passport was a start.

The new passport gave me a sense of security, though Sid was right: no one at the parties demanded to see my documents. It was enough that I was with Sid, and dressed the right way. The High Kith were focused on their own pleasure, and certain no one could or would dare infiltrate their quarter.

There was a fountain party in a home where water gushed up out of the floor at unexpected moments in unexpected spots, catching glamorously dressed people, soaking their clothes to visible skin. Sometimes I saw furniture or decor that had been made in the Ward, which made me miss it. Once I found an entire library filled with books that bore, on their spines, a mark that showed that they had been made by Harvers, and I felt homesick for his workshop and the smell of ink-damp paper.

Every so often I looked at the trinkets I had saved for Morah and Annin: the knife, the boxed cat, the jewels. I missed Morah's stern care and Annin's sweetness, and I wished I could tell them everything that was happening. But the pile of gold and silver I had set aside for Raven made me feel an uncomfortable relief to be away from her. Her love could so easily sour. I never knew when I would anger her. In the tavern, I'd had to watch her as closely as I watched the militia, for fear of doing something wrong. I found that I did not miss her, that I avoided thinking about her. This made me feel guilty, and reminded me of all that she had done for me, and how ungrateful I was. Then I *did* miss her, and remembered her voice calling me *lamb* and *my girl*.

Sid took me to an outdoor party that had an intricate flowering labyrinth all too easy for me to solve, since I mapped its turns and blind ends in my mind and never made the same mistake twice. When I claimed the prize at the center—a simple gold bangle on a pedestal—a trapdoor opened beneath me, dumping me into a vat of pleasure dust. I sputtered, trying to get the dust out of my mouth, but the voluptuous, wild taste clung to my tongue. The dust glittered on my skin even after Sid helped me out of the trap. Partygoers laughed, and laughed harder as she brushed me off and dust got on her skin. Then her black eyes widened and got very glossy, and I knew dust had gotten in her mouth, too.

That night was hard, with me feeling enchantingly free, enamored with everything, each slight touch an intense caress, laughter liquid in my throat even as Sid dragged us both into a fountain that washed us clean but couldn't rinse the bright taste from my mouth.

"You're beautiful," I told her. The fountains' jets bubbled around us.

"You're foxed," she said.

"You stare at me sometimes, too. I see you sneaking glances." Later, when I was sober, the memory of this made me cringe.

"I don't."

"You are lying. You're a liar. You *told* me that you were one. But!" A new thought occurred to me. "If a liar says she is a liar and she *is* really and truly a liar then she has just told the truth. Which makes her not a liar. Or not always a liar."

"Please," said Sid, "keep drinking the water. It will clear your head."

She sounded so distraught that I did what she said until my whole body felt like lead and I wanted to crawl home.

"I'm so sorry," I said later, when I was cold and the world had stopped gleaming.

"Don't be. It wasn't your fault. You weren't yourself."

"You swallowed some."

"Yes." She sighed.

"You were normal."

"I didn't feel normal."

"You were able to act like you were."

"Maybe I'm getting better," she said, "at controlling myself."

I shuddered all the way home. I began to despise the parties, how they lured me with their beauty and then left me feeling sick with it, as though I had gorged myself. I was ready, with or without Sid's help, to find a councilmember's passport to forge access to the Keepers Hall, when finally one party was different from the rest, because I saw someone I recognized, someone who had taken something from me and owed me an explanation.

42

WE WERE AT A HOUSE called the Inverse, which was entirely underground. We entered via a trapdoor in the grass and found ourselves inside a slick marble-walled hall where everything was upside down. The chandelier was brightly lit prickles of crystal shaped like a tiara growing out of the floor. Its candles burned, the flames giving light to the delicate shoes everyone wore. The wax dripped upward, rising in tiny blobs toward the ceiling, where furniture was fastened near a fireplace that crackled in the upper corner, blazing green and purple despite the night's heat. Downstairs—which looked like an upstairs, complete with balconies that jutted out into cleared pockets of earth eerily lit with green glowworms—a Middling servant offered us crystal glasses of what looked exactly like Madame Mere's pink tea. I hesitated to drink it, fresh from my experience with pleasure dust and mindful of the dressmaker's warning not to drink the elixir if I didn't know what it had been brewed to do.

"You would think," I murmured, looking at the glass in my hand, "that different versions of the elixir would look different." We watched as the guests around us sipped their drinks. Then one of them gasped, floating lightly to the ceiling, which had been tiled like a ballroom's dance floor. She dropped her glass in surprise, and it followed her, careening toward the ceiling, where it broke and scattered above like rain that never fell.

"Do you want to drink?" Sid glanced at me over the rim of her glass, which was raised to her lips.

"People are *flying*," I said in wonder.

"Are they really? Or have we taken a drug that alters our perception? Maybe we have already sipped from the elixir, and it has changed us, and we believe the glasses to be completely full."

I eyed my pink-filled glass with mistrust. I tipped a little of it out. It flowed upward, where dancers had begun to find partners.

Sid said, "I suppose you don't want to risk a repeat of the pleasure dust incident."

"Definitely not."

A man with icy-blue hair in braids floated past us. His hair had changed, but I instantly recognized him.

"That man," I said to Sid. "He tasted my blood in the night market. He acted so strangely afterward."

"He did *what* to you?"

I drank the glass to its bottom.

"Nirrim, wait."

But I was already floating up toward the ceiling and its swirling dancers.

43

I FELT SICK WITH VERTIGO when I glanced below my dangling feet, Sid growing smaller below. I saw her hurriedly drink from her glass and knew she wouldn't be far behind, and then I had to stop looking, because as I neared the ceiling my body turned, my dance slippers pulled toward the ceiling, my head toward the ground where I had been standing with Sid.

The world reversed itself. I was upside down, but everything looked right side up, so I no longer felt upside down.

"This is boring," said the blue-haired man who had tasted my blood. "I must tell my brother so."

"I need to ask you something," I said.

"The flying was fun. But this ballroom is blah. I didn't come here to feel *normal*."

"Do you remember me?"

He squinted at me. "Did I bed you? Was it on Illim Beach where we flew kites until they tangled together and everyone slept in an enormous magic sand castle with little crabbies that pinched our feet until we squeaked but it also felt good?"

"No. When you met me, I was disguised as a Middling."

"Slumming it, were you?" He grinned. "I see, I see." But his eyes were still vacant. He didn't know me, and probably wouldn't remember me tomorrow morning.

"I asked whether you knew where I could find Lady Sidarine."

His gaze went over my shoulder. His eyes widened. "That is some good magic. You made her appear! Is she an illusion, or the real thing? May I try your elixir? I want to make people come to me, too. This party is already so old! It needs more floating."

Sid was just gaining her feet beside me.

"You *do* know the right people to have a good time," he said conspiratorially to me. "The foreign lord-lady from the country no one knows! She can stay awake for days. Eat pleasure dust until dawn. Always sweet-talking her way into the sheets. Her list of conquests! As long as my arm!"

"He's exaggerating," Sid said to me.

"Did you see her fight with Lord Tibrin? She pulled a knife on him."

"Dagger," Sid corrected.

"She killed him *dead*."

"A mere scratch," said Sid. "He's fine."

"They say she's cousin to the Herrani king."

"That's not true," Sid said to me. "This is all gossip."

"Including the bits about your conquests?" I asked.

"Well, I suppose there are seeds of truth to any rumor." She saw my face and said, "I'm joking! Mostly. I like pleasing women. What is so wrong with that?"

I turned back to the man, who was excitedly wrapping a blue braid around one finger. "You met me in the night market in the Middling quarter," I said. "I was dressed as a Middling. For fun. For a break from being so bored and so High."

He nodded understandingly.

I said, "You tasted my blood."

"Oh." He released the braid. It unspun from his fingers. "That was not fun. Not fun at all. Why did you do that to me?" Tears welled in his eyes.

"*You* did it to *me*. You insisted. You said you would help me if I gave you three drops of blood."

"My brother told me it was my own fault. He is on the Council, you know. He always warns me to never taste strange blood. But he thought it wouldn't *do* anything to me."

"Why not?" I said. "What did it do to you?"

"Because you were Middling. But you are actually High! That shouldn't work either. Oh, this is so confusing."

Sid said, "You're not answering her questions."

"Don't glare at me. I can fight, too, you know. I was trained with a sword, on my family estate outside the city, where the sugarcane grows. I would cut the cane down with my little sword like so, and like so, and all the other High-Kith boys trembled at my grace, and the Un-Kith in the field couldn't even look at me, I was like a tiny god."

"But what did the blood do?" I said. "You acted so strangely afterward, like you were made of stone."

"It made me remember," he said.

"Remember what?" Sid asked.

"I will not tell you, rude boy. It was *my* memory. But I had forgotten it, until this one's dirty blood ruined everything. I did not *want* to remember it. She *made* me remember it." He sank to the floor, crying into his hands. "Oh, where is my brother? Why can't councilmen come to parties? This is a horrible party. I have no more dust and the floating was too short and you mean ones are making me sad and I have no way of getting dow-ow-n." His last word ended on a sob.

"He's right, you know," Sid said. "We're stuck on the ceiling until the elixir wears off, and honestly I don't know what will happen when it does."

"Will we fall?" I asked.

"I want to float!" wailed the blue-haired man.

"Usually these parties don't end dangerously," Sid said.

"Usually?" I repeated.

She crouched down next to the weeping man and pinched his ear. "Ow!"

"Pay attention. Stop crying. Answer her questions."

He wiped away his tears. "It was not a normal memory. It was like I was there again. The smells. The tastes. Everything was so real, so *now*. Please don't make me say what it was."

"All right," I said, though Sid cut a disapproving look my way.

"The memory hurt," he said.

A sick feeling had been growing inside me. I turned over his earlier words in my mind. "You said that Middling blood doesn't work, and neither does High-Kith blood. You're taking it from the tithes, aren't you? From Half-Kith prisoners. What does Half-Kith blood *do*? How does it work?"

"Maybe three drops was too much," he said.

A realization seized me. I looked at Sid. "The elixir isn't pink tea. It's watered-down blood."

44

"I WANT YOU TO TASTE IT," I said to Sid when we returned to her house after the party's end, when Middlings filled the floor below us with velvet pillows. A dancer detached from the ceiling like a petal and sailed down, landing in the pillows with a whump. Eventually, we did, too, as did the blue-braided man, who had cried himself to sleep after our conversation and continued napping on the pillows below, one hand tucked beneath his cheek.

"No," Sid said. She stalked up the stairs to her room and shut the door behind her.

I followed her, shoving the door open. "You have no right to be angry. Nothing was done to you. The Council took *my* blood. They have been stealing from the Ward. Hair for wigs, limbs for High-Kith surgeries, blood for magic. They have been taking *children*, and I don't even know why. *I* get to be angry. Not you."

"Fine," she said. "I don't get to be angry." But she looked furious. "Now let me be. Go away. I am not tasting your blood."

"Is it because he said the memory hurt?"

"No." Her dark eyes were wide, her face paler than usual, the freckle beneath her eye stark against her skin.

"It's not like you to be afraid."

"You have no idea who I really am."

Frustrated, I said, "I know only what you let me know."

"Yes, I am afraid," she said, "but that is not why I don't want to do it. Maybe I don't have the right to be angry, not like you do, but I *am* angry. I am angry because of what's been done to you. I am angry because so much has been taken from you and you are asking me to take something else."

"But I want you to. I need to know."

"Ask someone else. Ask your sweetheart."

"I want it to be you. I trust *you*."

A defeated, worried look stole over her. She sat at the edge of her bed, which was plainer than mine, narrower, and impeccably made. She yanked the hem of her tunic out of her trousers, exposing the dagger, which she dragged from its sheath. She offered its hilt to me. "I keep the edge very sharp."

When I sat next to her she let herself fall back against the mattress with a strangled, frustrated sigh. "I have gotten myself in over my head," she said. "This trip was supposed to be fun. The whole idea behind running away is to *escape* responsibility." She screwed her eyes shut. "Do it, then. Quickly. I don't want to watch you hurt yourself."

The dagger's hilt was chased in gold. Now that I could see the weapon up close, I noticed that its intricate decoration included, at the pommel of the dagger, the same sign as on the card Sid had taken from her queen. "Did you steal this, too?"

She groaned. "Please just get this over with."

I nicked my finger on the dagger's edge. Blood instantly welled. She opened her eyes. "Gods," she said.

"Just one." I held out my hand.

She lifted herself onto her elbows, her head tipped back, her short hair bright in the rising sun. She gripped my wrist and lifted her face to my hand, licking my finger like a calf. I shivered. The cut stung, but I loved the feel of her tongue on me. I couldn't look away from her dark eyes, her mouth on my hand. Then her eyes glazed over. Her fingers slackened around my wrist. She dropped back down, heavy as wood, rigid, and staring.

She lay like that for a long time, long enough that I grew concerned, trying to tell myself that the blue-haired man had tasted my blood and survived, and his brain had seemed addled well before.

Sid's chest rose and fell with steady breaths. Her lower lip was pink with my blood.

I curled up next to her on the bed. I waited. I breathed in the scent of her smoky perfume. I closed my eyes.

Finally, I felt her stir beside me. She made a soft noise deep in her throat. Her hand reached out and found my thigh. She pulled me close, then turned onto her side to face me, her eyes wide, blinking rapidly. Then she burrowed into my arms and pressed her damp face against my neck.

"Are you all right?" I asked.

She nodded. I felt a tear slide down my neck.

"Did it hurt?"

"Yes," she whispered.

"I'm so sorry. What can I do? Tell me what to do."

She shook her head. "Nothing. It hurts inside. It's because I remembered something I don't have anymore."

"But it was real?"

"Yes," she said. "It was. It used to be real."

"Can you tell me?"

"I don't want you to see me like this." She started to pull away.

"Stay."

She relaxed a little but kept her face buried against me. "It was like that man said. It was not a normal memory. I was living in the past. I didn't even know I had forgotten it." She was speaking softly, her words little breaths against my skin. "I remembered my mother holding me. I could smell the cypress trees waving against the sky. We were on the grass outside my home. An irrielle bird sang. The wind made the grass shimmer. I was small, unsteady on my feet. I didn't know, then, that I had nearly killed my mother with my birth. My father raged at the doctors. He practically lost his mind with fear. I didn't know, when I was a baby, that I would be the only child my parents would have. I didn't know that all their plans would rest on me. I didn't know what plans *were*. I didn't know that anything would ever be more or less than it was at that moment. I fell in the grass. My mother lifted me into her arms. Her hair is similar to mine, but much longer. I pushed it aside and said, *Away*, so I could press my cheek against the smooth skin of her chest, just above her heart, and I felt so sure that she loved me more than anyone or anything in the world."

"But," I said, "this is a *good* memory."

"Yes."

"Yet it hurts."

"Yes."

I was confused. I didn't understand how a memory so loving could pain her. I had believed both of Sid's parents to be alive. "Did she die?"

"No. But things are different between us now."

"Why?"

"Maybe I was easier to love then."

"I don't believe that."

"It's hard to remember something you no longer have," Sid said. "My mother caught me with a girl when I was seventeen. She cried."

"Why? Is it against your country's law to be with a woman?"

"No."

"But she doesn't like it."

"It's not that, exactly . . ." Sid paused, considering, and when she spoke I saw that it was only because she had been thinking about this for years that she was able to speak clearly. "She has friends like me. I don't think she would care about me liking women if it didn't interfere with her plans. She cried because she was going to force her plans on me anyway, and she was sad for what it would do to me, and guilty for herself."

"What about your father?"

"I think he hopes the problem will solve itself." She got quiet. "I don't want to be a problem."

I stroked her hair. "You're not."

"I don't want to marry."

"You won't."

"He's as bad as she is. Just more passive."

"I don't understand why it's so important to them that you marry."

She shrugged. "It's expected. They want grandchildren. They want me to marry their friends' son. That family will be angry if I say no."

"They would rather lose you than lose their friends?"

"Let's just say they hope to get everything they want."

"But they risk losing everything."

"I guess they must be comfortable with that possibility."

My anger, which had been steadily growing, came out in a rush. "I hate them."

Sid looked up at me.

"They're selfish," I said.

"They want what they believe is best for me."

"But it *isn't*."

"No," she said softly, "it isn't."

I shook my head. "What about that girl?"

Sid sat up. She ran a hand through her hair, trying to get it to settle. She stood, walked to the window, and opened it. The salty harbor air drifted in. The rising sun burned through the dawn. The sky was a thin blue, with a sheen like hammered metal. "She grew up," Sid said. "Last I heard, she was engaged to a man."

"Does that bother you?"

She shrugged. "It's not like it was true love written in the stars."

"She probably wishes she still had you."

"Well"—she smiled, but her heart wasn't in it—"who wouldn't?"

"I would."

Slowly, she said, "Is that what you want?"

"What do you mean?"

"To think about me while you're in that young man's bed."

I stared.

"People want all sorts of things," she said. "It's not the strangest desire to want to be with one person but imagine another."

I left the bed and came to her. "I don't want to be with him."

"No?"

"No. I don't love him. I just said I did. He expected it, and I worried what he might do if he didn't get it."

She leaned one shoulder against the wall, looking down at me, her brow furrowed, her hands stuffed in her pockets.

I said, "I want you."

Her expression changed. It deepened with decision. Her mouth slipped into a slight smile that looked almost self-mocking. "Do you?"

"Yes."

"Nirrim, I can't be good to you."

"Then be bad."

Her hands still in her pockets, she leaned to brush her face against my neck. She kissed my throat. The heat of her mouth was everywhere except on my mouth, her body nudging me up against the wall. Her tongue found my quick pulse. "Touch me," I whispered.

"Not yet."

Her mouth seared through my thin silk dress, her tongue dampening it. I felt her gentle teeth.

"Kiss me," I said.

"Not yet."

I touched her cheek. She turned to glide her mouth over my fingers. "Please," I said, and pulled her toward me, my mouth hungry for hers. I kissed her. Her lips opened beneath mine. She made a low sound in her throat, and then her hands were on me, finding the shape of my body, its delicate spots, its needy ones. She unbuttoned the top crystal button of my dress, and moved slowly to the next one. Impatient, I began to undo them myself. She stopped my hands. "Let me," she said. Her tongue lightly touched my lower lip, and I knew I would let her do anything.

She undid all the buttons, her fingers dipping lightly beneath the silk to touch my skin, until the dress fell from my shoulders and slid to the floor.

"I'm not sure," I said, and her hands stilled. She pulled slightly away, her eyes hesitant, and I saw that she misunderstood. I said, "I'm not sure how."

She smiled. "I am."

She knelt before me, her lips and tongue on my belly. "Please don't stop," I said.

Her mouth went lower.

My hands twisted in her hair.

45

I LOVE THIS BED, I thought when I woke.

I loved how narrow it was, how close the scanty space made me to Sid, who slept on, her limbs tangled with mine, mouth relaxed and full, her lashes startlingly black, skin damp in the heat.

I loved the pillow, how it dented beneath her head, her blond hair messy against the cotton.

I loved the sheet that had slipped from her bare shoulder.

I loved the burning day, how soon it would pour honey over everything, the light getting golden before it dimmed.

When I shifted, Sid tugged me close. "Stay," she muttered, and kept sleeping.

I loved that my mouth still tasted like her.

There was so much that was mine in that moment. I counted everything I had, at least then, and all that I was allowed to love.

This was not like the poem in Harvers's book, where dawn came like a thief. Nothing had been stolen from me. Maybe it never would be.

Sid sighed in her sleep. My eyes got heavy again. I nestled into everything that was mine. I let it cover me like downy feathers and pretended it would always be like this.

⁓

When I woke again, the light had the glow of a late afternoon. Sid slept on.

I remembered my last thought before I slept: the poem from the book I had printed in Harvers's workshop. I remembered his stamp on a book in a High-Kith library. I thought about this, about the Ward, about the tavern. I thought, reluctantly, about Aden.

I started to slip from the bed.

"No," Sid moaned, her eyes still shut. "Don't do that. Why would you do that?"

"I need to go back to the Ward."

Her eyes opened in alarm.

"Not for good," I said. "Just to talk to somebody."

"Which somebody?"

"A printer."

She frowned in a sleepy pout. "You are abandoning me for a *printer*?"

"I'll come back. I won't be long."

"May I come with you?"

I thought about Aden. "No."

She turned her face into the pillow. After a moment, her muffled voice came. "I'm afraid you won't come back. You'll change your mind."

Gently, I said, "I'm not the one planning to leave."

She nodded into the pillow.

"Go back to sleep," I said.

"And that's all right with you, that we can do what we did, and one day soon I'll leave?"

I wanted to say, I would rather have you for a little time than no time at all.

I will remember you perfectly. My memory will touch your skin, your lips. The memory will hurt, but it will be mine.

She turned, her black eyes no longer sleepy, but searching. "Will you let me do it again?"

That question I could answer easily. "Yes."

She reached up and pulled me down to her, her mouth nuzzling my throat. "Then go," she murmured against my skin, "and return soon. I will miss you."

"It's only for a few hours."

"I will miss you the moment you leave."

She loved exaggeration, loved to flatter. It was her way. Still, my breath caught as though what she had said was real. "Will you?"

"I will be so lonely for you."

I played along, because it felt so good to believe she meant what she said. "And what shall I do to console you upon my return?"

"You know."

"Do I?"

Her hand slid up my thigh, and in fact I did not leave her bed, not right away, not for some time.

It felt wrong to put on my rough, stone-colored dress, to feel it scratch against me in a way that felt like home. Ever since I had come to the High quarter, I had worn fluid silk and cotton as soft as air, and at first it had felt like a costume, but now everything I used to wear felt like one, like I was impersonating someone I used to be.

It was frightening, to realize how far away from my old self I had grown.

Exhilarating.

I pulled off the dress, which I now knew to be fully horrible. I knew it in a way that I couldn't have known when I wore the dress practically every day. I knew the dress to be dead of any comfort or beauty, and promised myself I would never wear it again.

⁓

Morah smiled at the knife. "It's nice that you remember your friends."

"How could I forget?" I said. Annin was exclaiming over all her little treasures, spread across the tavern table.

"People do," Morah said, "when they find a better life." She touched the silk shoulder of my cyan dress—not with awe, I thought, or jealousy, but meaningfully, to prove a gentle point.

"I'll be back for good soon." My chest clenched with sadness, because when I came back for good, it would be when Sid left Ethin.

"No militia stopped you in that dress," Morah said. "No one accused you of breaking the sumptuary law."

"I forged a High-Kith passport," I said after a moment, and was astonished when she simply nodded.

"But it was a secret," I said, "that I forge documents."

"Raven wanted you to believe that Annin and I didn't know, probably so that you would feel special."

"Why?" I said, feeling stupid.

"So that she could better *keep* you. Haven't you ever wondered why she is called Raven? She collects things, just like the bird. She steals them for her nest."

"That doesn't make sense. This is my home. I wouldn't leave—not for good."

"She has tricked you into believing this is your home."

"What is so wrong about her wanting to keep me? If you love someone, you don't want them to go."

"I love you," she said, "and I want you to go."

Tears pricked my eyes. "Why are you so cruel?"

"Because it's time." Morah gnawed her lip. "I wouldn't have said anything earlier, but now . . . you have the chance to escape. A good, true chance. You have the right passport. You look High Kith. So *become* one."

"I can't leave you and Annin."

"Yes, you can."

"I can't leave Raven."

"You must."

"Where is she?" I held the purse of gold, rubbing the leather with my thumb, feeling the ridges of the coins.

Morah shrugged. "She comes and goes. She always has. Probably she is in the Middling quarter."

I gave her the gold. "This is for her."

Morah weighed the purse in her hand, then gave it back. "Keep it."

"She needs it."

Morah snorted. "She does not. Do not expect me to help you help *her* take advantage of you."

It was a complicated sentence to untangle. "I am not helping her take advantage of me."

"Find her and give her your gold yourself, if you believe that."

Uneasily, I realized that I didn't want to find Raven. I was relieved she was not home, and dreaded what she would say if she saw me dressed so High. She would reprimand me. She would make me feel like a traitor.

I looked down at my dress, its hue the vivid color of light through blue glass. I tucked the purse into my fist. I remembered happiness bursting all over my skin as Sid kissed me. I thought of Raven's painful grip on my chin.

I *was* a traitor, for being happy when Raven wasn't . . . and worse, for being happy at her absence.

It took Harvers a moment to recognize me. "So it's true," he said. "You even look like one of them." He didn't say it with resentment or reproach, which I would have understood, but with a kind of gentle wonder.

"I have seen you print books of poetry, botany, music, medicine," I said. "I have seen your printer's device on the spines of books in High-Kith libraries. But I have never seen books about the history of Herrath, or this city. Why?"

He blinked, startled. "History book?" He said it as if the term were entirely new to him.

"Yes. A book that explains why things are the way they are."

"But things have always been like this."

Frustrated at the blankness of his expression, I said, "That's not true. Why is there no book about how the wall was built?"

"The wall has always been there."

"A wall isn't a mountain. It isn't the sea. Someone made it."

Harvers's aged face looked helplessly bewildered. "I don't know who made it. I don't know how."

"Have you never printed a history book?"

"I print what the Middlings ask for, and what they can sell to the High Kith. I have never been brought a manuscript that contained Herrath's history."

"Why not?" I pressed.

Flustered, he rubbed his knobbed hands together. "I suppose it wouldn't sell. I suppose it's not interesting. I suppose no one would know what to write."

I thought about my dream of the god of discovery. "What about the gods? Have you printed books about them?"

"There are no gods. They don't exist."

"Then what harm would it be to print a book about them?"

"No harm," he said. "But it's not allowed."

"Who says so?"

"The Council."

"Why did the Council ban books about the gods?"

"It is not a *ban*. It would simply be a waste of paper and ink."

"But why?"

"The Lord Protector says so."

"Why does he say so?"

"He has always said so."

"He has not been alive for hundreds of years. He cannot have always said so."

"I mean," Harvers said, "that each Lord Protector has always said so. When a Lord Protector dies, and a new one is named, the law remains the same. The laws about books. The sumptuary law. The kith laws."

"There must have been a first Lord Protector who established the laws."

"Well, yes, of course," Harvers said reasonably, but as if he had been dozing, and although he was now awake, sleep clung to him. He rubbed his forehead. It looked like he was straining to recall something about the Lord Protector.

I placed my hand on his. My blood could make someone remember . . . but not a memory that I specifically wanted—or if it could, I didn't know how to make that happen. I wished that I could give Harvers the ability to remember a specific thing.

It occurred to me that all the rules that mandated we live behind the wall had one purpose: to make the Half Kith forget how to wish for things. We had been taught not to want more than we had. I realized that wanting is a kind of power even if you don't get what you want.

Wanting illuminates everything you need, and how the world has failed you.

I wanted Harvers to remember. It was one thing for him—and everyone else in the Ward—to talk as if someone had emptied their minds of the past, had scooped it out like flesh from a fruit. It was another, even more sinister thing that no one seemed to question what had been taken.

Harvers frowned. I felt his hand grow warm beneath mine.

He said, finally, "One of my ancestors was commissioned by him to print a book."

"What kind of book?"

"A story of the first Lord Protector's life. It is passed from one Lord Protector to the next. It is housed in the Keepers Hall."

Harvers looked exhausted.

"Thank you," I said. "I'm sorry. I didn't mean to tire you."

He patted my cheek. "I am always glad to see you. And look at you now! So fine, so High. Radiant. You are a credit to the Ward, my child."

I *did* feel radiant. I remembered the warmth of Sid's body against mine, her murmur as she asked me to stay, the quirk of her smug smile when I finally dragged myself out of bed and into clothes. I liked the thought that all these memories burned inside me like a flame and glowed through me.

Into Harvers's dry, cracked, ink-stained hands I placed a pot of skin cream whipped as thick as butter and scented with jasmine. When he lifted the lid and looked uncertain, I explained how the cream would soften his skin. He tried it, smoothing it over his rough hands. His expression grew faraway. "Is this what it's like in the High quarter?"

Everything rough made smooth. "Yes."

"You shouldn't have come back." He placed the lid back on the pot. "I haven't been good to you."

"What do you mean?" He had always been quietly benevolent, never minding when I read books not fit for my kith. It was because of him that I had learned that kindness sometimes means to do nothing, to make no mention of what is obvious, such as me sneaking glances at his printed pages. It can be a kindness to let a secret remain a secret. I had learned so much from his print shop, from books that gave me words I might never have heard in the Ward, that showed drawings of instruments I had never heard played, constellations the High Kith had named, with stories to explain them, which for the Half Kith were merely random stars, bright and distant and meaningless.

"Leave my shop," he said, his voice suddenly sharp. "Leave the Ward and don't come back. You don't belong here. You never did."

"*No one* belongs here," I said. "No one deserves to be trapped behind a wall."

He shook his head. "You don't understand. You don't even know."

"Know what?"

He rubbed an old, gnarled thumb over the glistening path of softened skin on the back of his hand. "Everyone in the Ward knows you had something to do with that soldier's death."

I sucked in a hurt breath. "Aden told?"

"Child, you were running along the rooftops under a full moon during a festival. You were seen by several people. Everyone knows you caught the Elysium bird and surrendered it. The gossip is that a soldier tried to drag you to your death, and you kicked him to his."

I rested a hand against a printing press to steady myself, gazing at the ink-darkened woodblocks of frontispieces, the collections of little letters collected like pulled teeth in the compositor's tray, and wondered what else I had been blind to, what else should have been so obvious, such as that any secret in the Ward spreads like a giddy fire, so hungry the Half Kith are for anything that is not ordinary.

"No harm will come to you," said the printer. "Not if the Ward can help it. We will protect you."

The lowering sun carved through the workshop and illuminated the ink-wet pages hanging to dry.

"You've helped so many people escape," he said, "and never sought anything for yourself."

"Of course. No one here has anything to give. It helped me to help. It made me feel good to forge passports. Special."

"You are. Anyone can see it. It's in your face. Your kindness. I have wanted to say this to you before. The Ward is grateful, and we won't forget it."

I shook my head. "You should be grateful to Raven. I would be nothing without her."

His expression tightened. "I suppose it is true that she raised you to be selfless," he said carefully. "But you need to demand something for yourself. Everyone in the Ward will miss you if you go, but it's nice to think of you somewhere else, beyond the wall. Comforting."

I had had no idea that people in the Ward were watching me, that they knew so much about me and they would miss me if I never returned. That they could even *want* me never to return.

It was a new thought to me: that you could take heart when someone escapes the trap that trapped you.

And yet it shouldn't have been a new thought, since I had already felt this whenever I forged a passport. I had simply not realized that this was what I had felt.

I *had* put love into each stitch in each passport's binding. I just hadn't known that was what it was, because the only love I had recognized as given to me was the kind that clutched tight, and never let go.

⟶

"I can't marry you," I said.

Aden's face looked as though I had slapped it. "You don't mean this."

"I thought I could marry you," I said. "I thought I should, that it was enough that I care about you and that we are friends. But it's not enough."

The fading light, as it always did around Aden, lingered on his skin, sifting in from the window of his home to touch him lightly, to brighten his wounded eyes, to gild his shocked mouth. "I'm not enough for you?" he said. "Who is?"

"I don't think you want to marry someone who can't love you."

"Answer my question. Or do you think you don't even owe me the truth? Who *are* you? What is this?" His fingers twitched the blue silk at my shoulder. "Of course you think you can break the law and never pay. Of course you think you can break my heart. That foreign woman has made you believe it."

Once, I would have said, She has nothing to do with this.

I would have lied because I was afraid. I would have hidden the truth because I knew it made him angry.

"I don't want to break your heart," I said, "but it's either yours or mine."

"So selfish," he hissed. "I should have known. You killed a man, and I bet you don't feel bad at all about it, just like you have no guilt whatsoever about hurting me."

"You're right that I don't feel guilty about killing him. Not anymore. He would have dragged me to my death to get what he wanted."

"What are you suggesting? That I am like him, that I intend to *drag you to your death* when all I want is to make you happy, to build a life with you?"

"I didn't say that."

"It's what you mean."

"Well," I said, "it's true. You are a little like him."

"Listen to yourself! How can you be so cold? How can you say such a cruel thing to me?"

"*You* said it." I remembered my earlier thought about how it wasn't wrong to want, how it was necessary. But of course nothing is as simple as that. Wanting something doesn't always mean it is owed to you. "I know you love me, but that doesn't mean I have to give myself to you."

"Let me guess. You've given yourself to *her*."

"Yes," I said.

"That's disgusting."

"I disagree."

"It's against the law."

"Then I'll continue to break it."

"You have been seduced," he said. "You don't mean what you say. She has twisted your thoughts. She has tricked you with gold and glamour. She has promised to take you away from here."

This time, his barb shot home. "Sid has never made me any promises."

"I will tell," he said. "I will denounce you as a murderer. A deviant."

"Do it, and the moment I am in prison the Ward will turn against you."

"Because you are so special?" he sneered. "You are a fool. You think she loves you. All she wants is to get you between her legs. She will use you and cast you aside."

His words were corrosive because they were exactly what I feared.

I saw, from the acute gladness in Aden's face, that he knew his words burned through me.

He pressed his advantage. "Can't you see that I have only ever wanted what is best for you?" His voice dropped low. "You might think you love her, but that's only because you don't know what love is."

I was afraid to think about whether I loved Sid. Aden was right about one thing: if I loved her, I would suffer for it.

I did what Sid always did. I dodged the real question by addressing the easiest part of what he had said. "Of course I know what love is."

"Do you really? You love Raven."

"What does she have to do with this?"

"You think she loves you."

"She does." I believed he was just trying to seek revenge, to stab me where it would hurt most, but my heart grew tight and shaky in my chest. "She says so all the time."

"She *says* so. You are like a child, Nirrim. You can't see the truth for what it is."

"Yes, I can," I said, though inside I retreated to the insecurity I had felt for so long, before I realized that the visions I had were true glimpses of the past. "I know what's real and what's not."

"You are deluded. You have been so sweet, so biddable, so stupid."

"Tell me what you mean."

"You've been forging those passports for years."

"So?"

"Nirrim, the little do-gooder, helping the less fortunate."

"What's wrong with that?"

"Nothing, I suppose, if Raven weren't milking her buyers for everything they're worth."

"Buyers?"

"You see," he said, satisfied. "You have no idea whom to trust. You thought she was giving them away."

"But," I said, "she is."

"She takes their life's savings. She makes them give all they have for a means to escape."

"But," I stammered, "but that can't be true. Look at how we live."

"You think she'd share with you? Look at how *she* lives."

"She lives simply. Her clothes. What she eats. She has a few little luxuries, it's true, like a mirror, a gold necklace, but——"

"That's what she *lets* you see. She squirrels all her money away into her house in the Middling quarter."

My stomach turned to stone. "She has a house in the Middling quarter?"

His smile was narrow and mean. "Go see for yourself. You think she loves you? Go see what her love looks like."

"That's too big a secret," I protested. "A whole house? So much money?"

"Everyone's heard the rumor."

"People would tell me."

"*I* didn't."

"Why? Why would everyone keep such a secret from me?"

"People had different reasons. Some feared Raven's reprisal if they told. She could denounce them for crimes, or refuse to sell them a passport. Others worried you would stop forging if you knew. As for me, stupid me, I didn't want to hurt you."

Devastation must have been written on my face. My eyes stung. My breath failed me, and I couldn't speak for a moment, so certain was I that anything I could say would sound broken, a pathetic denial of what I fully, terribly believed.

46

THE HOUSE WAS AS ELEGANT as a Middling house could be. It didn't break any rules. The trim under the eaves was as delicate as lace yet restrained in color, painted in a silvery green like the underside of an olive leaf. Bay windows bulged out like pretty blisters, yet with no stained glass. The hardware on the green door was iron, not brass, and the flower boxes held simple sea violets in shades of cream and powdery blue and lavender. The window frames were a freshly painted black, and although no detail broke a law, it was nonetheless a more beautiful house than any on the street: daring in its aggressive newness, in its sparkling windows and slick paint and flowers carefully plucked of any imperfect petals. It was a house that proclaimed itself as loudly as was allowed. Before I had left the Ward, I couldn't have dreamed that such a house existed. Even if I had seen drawings in one of Harvers's books, I would have thought it was a fantasy.

The door had no knocker, but a little iron button studded into its center. I had never seen its like before, but I pressed it and heard a musical, muted chime echo behind the door. My heart welled with a sick, poisonous hope. Aden had lied to hurt me. Or if he had told the truth, it could be explained.

I was Raven's girl. Her lamb.

This house must belong to someone else, a stranger, who would ask why I was there.

My mistake, I would say.

The door opened. A relieved breath fluttered from my lips.

"Oh." The woman's eyes widened. Nervous fingers straightened her pale blue dress and tucked black tendrils of hair behind her ears. "Forgive my appearance, my lady. I didn't expect—"

"Never mind." I smiled, practically giddy to have my worst fears proven wrong. "I must have the wrong address," I said, although Middlings on the street readily recognized Raven's name, and all of them had pointed me to this house. Since the woman at the door clearly thought I was High Kith, I tried to think of what someone of my supposed rank would say. "Forgive me for having disturbed the peace of your home."

"*My* home?" She looked at me blankly. "This is my mistress's home."

It hadn't even occurred to me that the woman could be a servant. My shoulders hunched. I felt the worn grief that comes when you deceive yourself into thinking that what you fear isn't true, and then are struck with the fact that it is.

"Please," she whispered, "don't tell her I answered the door looking so unkempt. She is very particular. I had no idea she was expecting someone of your kith."

"Take me to her," I said, and she led me through elegant rooms to Raven, who was drinking a pot of pink tea, her skin smoother than I had ever seen it, her hair a rich dark brown. A porcelain plate bearing sugared flowers rested on a frail table. She had just placed a flower in her mouth when she saw me enter the room. Her face slackened in surprise. A hand went to her throat, touching the gold chain of the necklace that disappeared beneath her batiste dress fringed with simple lace. She looked caught in the middle of a crime.

"Oh," she said.

"You used me," I said quietly.

She ordered her expression into one of delight. "My dear Nirrim!" She stood and embraced me, kissing my cheek, and pulled me down to sit beside her on the lilac jacquard sofa. "I have no idea what you're talking about. Never mind. We will sort it all out, you and your ama. So that arrogant foreign lady has released you from her service, has she? Well, good riddance! I never liked her. But what a fine dress she has given you. This blue makes your green eyes so brilliant. You are not allowed to wear such a hue, you know that, but here"—she leaned forward with a conspiring whisper—"we can do as we please, you and I. You there," she snapped at the maid. "Why are you standing about? Leave at once. My daughter and I wish to speak in private."

"Daughter?" I said numbly as the young woman scuttled from the room.

"Well, *no*, not really, but in a manner of speaking, are you not? Didn't I raise you and make you everything that you are? Look at how lovely you are. High living suits you, I must say. It would suit *me*, too, with a bit of your help. But no more of that! Pleasure before business! Have some of these sugared flowers. I know my girl has a sweet tooth. I've kept these on hand, just for you, for the day that you would finally see your new home. I wasn't quite prepared for today to be the day, but no matter."

Feeling as though I were made of stone, I put a flower into my mouth. Obedience was a familiar act in a deeply unfamiliar situation. The flower crumbled and melted. I felt an urge to spit it out, to vomit it onto my lap, but Raven was looking at me so expectantly, so proudly. "Thank you," I managed.

"That is my good girl. I don't suppose that High lady gave you what she promised me."

"Promised?"

"Now, Nirrim, don't be daft. The *gold*, my girl."

"I have this." I offered her the small purse of gold. "I won it for you."

"This is but a fraction of what she promised! That sneaking foreign cheat. She had best have left Ethin already, or we shall have our revenge, shall we not? No need to tell me how it was in her service, my lamb. I will never ask. No, no. I respect your privacy. I understand what we must sometimes do for money. If she made you do things you did not want, why, how could you refuse? Forget it all. You are with me now. I will take care of you."

"You will?"

"Of course! Nirrim, what is *wrong* with you? You are acting like someone has knocked all the brains out of your head. Do try to keep up."

"You lied to me," I choked out.

"Lied? I did no such thing."

"You told me we were helping people."

She spread her hands in helpless impatience. "We *did* help people."

"You took their money."

"Well, of course. I have to live, don't I?"

"You don't have to live like *this*."

"I don't like your tone. Who are you to judge me? You never had to worry about anything. Without me, you would have become Un-Kith. Who raised you? Me. Who put food on your plate? Me. Who saved you from the orphanage? Me. I didn't expect such a lack of gratitude from you." She placed a hand on her heart. "It cuts me to the quick."

"Stop," I said. "Stop it! You're acting like you didn't make me believe for years that we were forging passports only out of kindness."

"It *was* a kindness, and we got paid for it. I see no wrong in that."

"There is no *we. You* have been taking the money."

"Oh, I see. You want a cut of it. Well." She busied herself pouring a cup of pink tea. "I can't say that I am pleased by your greed. My plan was always to share everything with you. There is no need to be so demanding. Here." She offered me the cup.

I dashed it from her hand.

"Nirrim!"

"That's *blood.* You are drinking someone's blood!"

"You are completely hysterical. Calm yourself right now, or you will answer to my hand. Blood! Nonsense. It is simply a drink that will make you prettier. I am being *nice* to you, and this is the thanks I get."

"I am telling you the truth."

She sighed impatiently. "Need we worry about everything? Am I supposed to never eat, out of pity for all the poor animals and plants that must die to feed me? Am I supposed to give everything I have to people who have less? Am I supposed to work for free? If there is blood in the tea, it surely can't be much, given the color. It's not as if someone *died*."

"I don't want any."

"More for me, then." She poured herself another cup. "Why don't you lie down in your bedroom, dear? The sheets have been laundered with that soap you like, and I'll have the maid bring you a cup of cold, honeyed milk. You'll have a nice rest, and when you wake we will plan our future together."

"My room," I said.

"There you go again, repeating things like one of those pea-brained ithya birds. Yes, *your room.* Nirrim, I always planned to bring you here one day. You are my best girl."

"Why should I believe you? You have done nothing but lie."

Her smile was small, hard, appraising. She set aside her cup. "That is the question of someone grown. Not a child anymore, are you? Follow me, and you will see what I've done for you." She took my hand. Hers blazed with heat. Mine must have felt like a block of ice as she led me upstairs and unlocked a door with a porcelain handle painted blue, in a pattern of one of my printed breads. She pushed open the door.

The bed was sweetly made, the counterpane embroidered with sprays of roses, a flower I had never seen before I left the Ward. The wardrobe, when I opened it, was full of dresses tailored to my size, the cotton soft. A beveled mirror set inside the wardrobe door showed my pale face. There were sandals, the leather stiffly new.

"And see." Raven opened a jewelry box that sat on the vanity. Inside was a necklace of seed pearls. She lifted the strand of tiny beads from the box and strung them around my wooden neck. The pearls were luminous drops of moonlight, but all I could think of was the tortoises I had skinned for their nacreous shells, their thick bodies trying to blunder out of my grasp.

"There," Raven said, satisfied. "And we shall have better than that, when we come up in the world."

I touched the cool little beads. Pansies nodded at me from the green window box. This room was all I could have wanted. It was a room not for a servant, but for a daughter.

"Nirrim, I understand that you are surprised, but my generosity warrants some thanks, I think."

"What about Morah and Annin? Do they have rooms here?"

"That's hardly necessary, is it?"

"So you want me to live here with you."

"Of course, my girl."

"Without them."

"Someone must manage the tavern." She saw my face and leaned forward to clasp my hands. "You have always known that you were my favorite. Look at everything I have built for us. Imagine everything we can do together. Why do you think I allowed you to go to the High quarter with that imperious foreigner? Because I trusted my clever Nirrim. I knew you would gain access to a High-Kith passport and forge one perfectly, and you have, haven't you? If I turned such a tidy profit on Middling passports, just think what I could get for selling High passports to Middlings. And you'll forge one for me, of course."

I understood, then, why she had had Aden make a heliograph for her, the one I lost the night I was arrested. She continued, "Eventually, we will move to the High quarter. We shall live like queens!"

"No," I said.

Her nails dug into my hand. "I'm sure I didn't hear you. Speak again, Nirrim, with the respect due to your loving ama."

"No. I won't forge any more passports for you. You don't care about me any more than you do about Morah and Annin. I'm just more useful to you." Her nails drew blood. I tugged my hand away.

"You have me all figured out, do you?" she said. "Then tell me, girl. If you won't forge for me, what good are you? I'll denounce you to the militia. It will break my poor old heart, but your selfish ways force me to do it. You are a criminal. It was *your* hand that forged those documents. Do you think the Council will be pleased to learn that someone has disrupted the most important law that governs this country, the strict lines that keep our kiths in place? The Council will relish your punishment. They will torture you until you show them exactly what I will tell them you can do: copy perfectly. They will break every bone but the ones in your hand so that you can show them how you sign their names with the exact flourish. They will cut out your tongue yet leave your eyes so that you may see the stamps you will need to copy. They will discover my truths in your performed skills, and they will tithe you until you are whittled down to the bone, dear one, and you will weep at your lost chance to be with me."

"You won't do that."

She smiled. "Will I not? We know each other quite well, after these many years. One way or the other, I always win, and you always lose."

"There is nothing you can accuse me of that doesn't also implicate you. I will drag you down with me."

She waved an annoyed hand. "You have no proof."

"I will tell the militia about your heliograph."

She lost her smile. "What heliograph?"

"The one still in the lapel of the coat taken from me in prison." I was bluffing—I had no solid knowledge of where the original heliograph was, but I remembered how anxious she had been about its loss.

"You found it in the cistern. You gave it back to me."

"I gave you a different heliograph, which, if you look closely, will show that you weren't wearing the same beaded earrings you wore on the day you requested the one that was lost from Aden. Once the militia finds the original heliograph in the coat, it will be proof that you sought a passport even if it's no proof you were involved in forging them. You'll be punished."

Rage snaked across her face. "You are a wicked, deceitful girl."

"Then don't cross me, or I will cross you. I am not who I was. You expect that as soon as you threaten me, I will do what you want. No more."

"It's true," she said after a careful pause. "You are not who you were. But tell me, my lamb: Who are you, really? Little Nirrim, come from nowhere. Another orphan left to dirty herself in the box. No one special. But *I* know where you come from. *I* know just how special you are."

My heart kicked against my ribs. "What do you mean?"

"You have changed, I can see that. But would the girl I raised truly betray her kin? No, she would do anything for her family. I suppose I won't denounce you, even if you deserve it. After all, you are my own flesh and blood."

I stared.

"I named you," she said. "I pinned your name to your swaddling clothes. I placed you in the orphanage box."

"You . . . are my mother?"

"Such a little lamb! So eager for mother's milk! Me, your mother? Wouldn't you love it if it were true. Your mother is dead, girl, and you killed her."

"You must tell me what you mean."

"Oh, must I? Do I have something you want now? Let's make a bargain, my lostling. I will tell you the beginning of a story, and you will tell its end." She withdrew the gold necklace that had been tucked into her dress. From its frail chain dangled a crescent moon carved from a pale jewel that shone even though no light was near, even though the windows had darkened.

My bones felt tightly knit, my arms crossed over my chest as though I were again in the baby box, my body swaddled, the scrap of paper that must have been pinned to me while I slept quivering under my breath. Babies see badly at first, their vision blurry. They can see only what is right in front of them. I remembered that necklace wavering in and out of focus when my mother nursed me.

"Where did you get that?" I demanded.

"From my younger sister, my joy. You look like her, though she was far more beautiful. She never recovered after she gave birth to you. You drained the life from her. Yet she made me promise to take care of you, and so I did."

Shock settled over me like a heavy cloth. "You *abandoned* me."

"Oh, come. It's not as if I exposed you to the elements to starve. I left you in good care at the orphanage. They fed and clothed you. I kept my promise. And I continued to keep it. I was informed on your progress through the years. When the headmistress said you had a gift for writing and art, I knew I had been right when I named you after a cloud that predicts good fortune. You certainly made mine! I came to the orphanage to reclaim you. I took you in. Now I am giving you everything you could ask for. And what do you do? You spurn me. *Me*, your aunt, your only living relation, who has always taken care of you."

My eyes stung. "You let me believe that I was alone. That I had no one."

"You had *me*."

"Why didn't you tell me?"

"Did you deserve it? Wouldn't my sister be alive today, had you not come tearing out of her, killing her with your greedy little life? If she hadn't given birth to you, she would still be mine."

"It is not my fault I have no mother. You have been punishing me for my own loss."

"I warned her," Raven said, looking not at me, but into the past. "I told her she would regret her dalliance. But no. She would have her way. If people would only listen to me, everyone would be better off."

"Who was he? Who was my father?"

"Nirrim, it is time to uphold your bargain. You have some moral horror, it seems, at helping me build my business. But won't you, dear girl, do it for your family, now that you know who I am?"

"I always loved you. I always thought of you as family." Tears spilled onto my cheeks.

"Now, don't cry. There is no need. Why, I love you, too!"

I pulled away from her. The pearl necklace felt like a thin snake around my throat. I snapped it beneath my twisting grasp. Beads sprinkled the floor.

"How dare you," Raven said. "After all I've done for you."

I made for the stairs.

"Don't you leave me," she called. "If you do, you will never see me again."

My feet gained speed, rattling down each step. I heard her following behind me.

"You will never know anything more about your mother. How you were born. Who you are! You will be nothing to me. Is that what you want?"

Yes, I thought, and shoved my way out the front door.

The sun had set when I returned to Sid's home on the hill, and although I had mastered my tears, when I saw her sitting on the steps and how her face eased into gladness to see me, they came rushing back.

"What is it?" She drew me down to sit beside her. Duskwings flurried in the sky like black confetti. I buried my wet face against her. "Tell me," she said, and I felt the words vibrate through her. "Tell me who has made you like this, and I will kill them."

I laughed a little, the sound garbled by a sob, because of course Sid would try to lighten the situation by saying something extreme and obviously not meant. But then I pulled away from her to wipe my eyes and saw her hardened face. Her black eyes were cold with fury. "Say that you want me to," she said.

I had never seen her use her dagger, but I had touched her rangy body. I had felt the muscle that spoke of work despite the luxury she lived in.

Was a queen's spy trained to kill?

I believed, suddenly and surely, that Sid was ready to make good on her threat.

"No," I said. "Don't." I still loved Raven. I couldn't strip the habit of years from me.

In a halting voice, I told her everything. I told her about Aden and Raven, about the heliographs and the crescent-moon pendant, about the Elysium bird and everything that had happened that night. About the smashed lantern and the burn. My words unraveling, I explained how I used to think Helin was right that I couldn't understand the truth before my eyes, and then I changed my mind, and found strength in a newfound belief in myself. I told her how arrogant that belief was, because in the end I didn't know anything at all. My mother's sister had made me her apprentice, and I hadn't known. I had seen glimpses of the necklace at her throat for years, and although the pendant had been hidden beneath Raven's dress, it had nonetheless reminded me of my mother's necklace, and even then I didn't guess. I told Sid that I was a murderer, a criminal, a fool, a fool, a fool.

"You are not a fool." She kissed my tear-wet mouth.

I tightened my fingers in her shirt. "You warned me that you are a liar."

"I am not good with the truth. But I am not lying to you now."

"Promise you won't deceive me."

Softly, she said, "I won't deceive you."

But she already had.

47

ON THE DAY OF THE COUNCIL PARADE, perfumed blue vines with heavy blossoms lined the edges of the main thoroughfare through the High quarter. The vines seemed to have sprung up overnight. Muslin canopies covered the walkways as they had in my visions of the long-ago Ward: brilliant patchworks of color glowing with the setting sun, embroidered moons and stars that released a refreshing, cool mist that made my skin shiver.

"I see that," Sid said. "Don't make me jealous of mist."

"You, jealous? Never."

"Not of mist," she acknowledged, "though that little shudder of yours looked uncannily like something I did to you this morning, and I confess I am feeling challenged right now, to be so easily usurped." She purchased a spun-sugar bird's nest from a Middling vendor and passed it to me. It had a pink egg that hatched, an illusion of an Elysium bird coming wet from the shell. It trilled, hopped to my shoulder, spread its wings, and vanished. Sid put a shell fragment in her mouth. She made a face. "Too sweet. But you will like it."

I shook my head, remembering all the sweets Raven had given me and how happy they had made me. "Not anymore."

She raised a querying brow but said nothing at first, merely passed the bird's nest to a Middling boy who was tagging along behind a High family, apparently hired for the purpose of carrying the children's purchases from Middling vendors. He already carried several toys for the High children, who were pulling their parents toward the next stall. When the Middling boy saw the nest, he immediately crammed it all into his mouth, his eyes closing in delight.

Sid turned to me. "Why don't you like it anymore?"

"Sugar reminds me of Raven."

"I don't want her to spoil things that bring you pleasure."

"My memory is too good."

"Yes," she said. "I see. Maybe with time."

"People say that only because for them time softens their memories. They forget. I can't." Nothing would soften my memory of Sid when she left.

"I *was* jealous," Sid said. "I was jealous of Aden. The jealousy was how I knew I was in trouble." She saw my startled expression and added hurriedly, "If you didn't see what I felt, please don't think you are somehow blind or broken. I didn't want you to see it. I am good at hiding things. Everyone, even without your history, can miss what people desperately wish to hide."

"Oh? Desperately?"

She rubbed the nape of her neck, casting me a look both sheepish and sly.

"You saw when *I* was jealous," I said.

She grinned. "Of Lillin? Mmm, yes. But I shall tell you a secret." Her soft cheek slipped against mine as she leaned forward and touched her lips to my ear. "I saw you the moment you arrived at the party in your silver dress, my serious little moonbeam, and I thought"—her mouth brushed delicately over my stuttering pulse—"how can I make her mine?"

"Poor Lillin."

"I'm afraid I was a bit bad."

"You went out of your way to make me jealous."

"Did it work?"

"You know it did."

"I do, but your honesty in admitting it demands a reward." Her mouth glided down my neck. Her teeth nipped my throat. Her hand slipped into my dress pocket and traced patterns through the thin lining against my thigh.

I whispered, "You are trying to make me forget about the sugar."

"Am I?"

"You don't want me to be sad."

"Never sad. Not you." She kissed me. I tasted her mouth, sweet from the bird shell, and as I kissed her I yearned for more.

It was true that I couldn't forget. But maybe, I hoped, I could make new memories.

A painted pony trotted past us down the thoroughfare, its hide blue and red, its hooves gold, a chariot clattering behind. High-Kith children in their finery bounced inside the chariot, waving streamers. The horse threw back its head, but instead of neighing, cried eerily in a human voice, "Make way for the councilmen!"

"Have you gotten the maps for the Keepers Hall?" I asked Sid.

"My mind has been on other matters." Her fingers whispered against me.

"Sid."

She slipped her hand from my pocket, looking at me as if she were utterly dignified and *I* had been up to something indecent. "Yes?" she said innocently.

"Are you paying attention?"

"To you? Always."

"The maps?"

"Ah, yes. Well, the easiest way to acquire them would be through Lillin, and I am not her favorite person at the moment."

A lord with glitter smeared on his eyelids tried to pluck one of the large crimson blossoms from the vine, but it could not be broken off its stem. He shook it. It rattled. Excitedly, he called, "There is something inside!"

"The Council gifts!" someone cried, and dozens of High Kith descended on the flowers, trying to pry open their red petals, which were hard as shells. When that failed, they tapped the flowers, breathed on them. They put the blossoms in their mouths and tried to crack them like nuts with their teeth. Finally, one of the High Kith, an entranced expression in her eyes, sang something I couldn't quite catch. I heard only fragments, words like *hundred* and *grace* and *devote*. Yet, although I could not hear the song well, I heard enough pieces of it that it began to assemble in my mind and match, at least in the few words I heard, with a hymn to the gods in the book Sid had stolen from the piano.

All at once, the blossoms opened, and trinkets dropped from their petals. The High Kith scrambled to scoop the gifts off the ground: sapphires as large as eyes; cunning little mechanical birds that told dirty jokes; a perfect miniature tree with sand-colored bark and soft tiny leaves; a crystal egg filled with pleasure dust. Some of the flowers bore ugly fruit. One spat out a bony finger. I recoiled in horror, but the High-Kith woman who found it just laughed and stuck it in her swan-shaped hat.

I snagged the man with glittered eyes. He was looking at a handful of what appeared to be polished toenails. "What did you mean, 'Council gifts'?"

He squinted at me. "Are you from the plantations?"

"Yes," Sid said smoothly, "she is. Her family wanted her debutante party to take place in the city."

"Oh," he said. "That's why you don't know."

"And I am a curious traveler," Sid said. "Is this a local custom?"

"Every year during the parade the Council offers gifts," he said. "As thanks. It's fun. We never know exactly how we will receive our presents."

"Thanks for what?" I asked.

He shrugged, and he had that slightly blank look in his eyes that I had come to associate with a foggy memory. "I don't know."

Could it be that elixir or pleasure dust damaged people's memories? But no, because the Half Kith suffered from it, too, and they had no access to such things.

And it was always about the city's past. It was as if something—or someone—had wiped history away, so all of us were performing roles whose origins we didn't understand. We celebrated festivals without knowing why. We followed rules whose reasons were unclear.

I touched the man's hand as I had with Harvers, and poured my wish into him.

Remember, I thought. Tell me.

"It's . . . an anniversary," he said, blinking.

"Of what?"

"The building of the wall. The first Lord Protector commanded it, and promised gifts in return." Then he glanced down at my hand on his and frowned, shaking it off. "I don't know you," he said suspiciously. "Mind yourself." Then he turned on his heel and disappeared into the crowd, his grisly gift scattering like small shells from his hand onto the paved road.

Flutes began to pipe, and the thoroughfare cleared, everyone thronging by the ivy. A tendril curled around me, almost like a creature's tail, and I shuddered, ducking its touch.

A host of councilmen in red robes began to march up the road in formation, their faces ranging from bored to serious to intensely focused, but all of them hot, sweat dripping from their brows.

The Middling merchants, with furtive, worried looks at one another, began to pack up their stalls.

Then I heard a pure trill curl over the crowd. The call dipped and ascended, each note ringing as clear as a crystal bell.

It was an Elysium bird.

It flew over the awed crowd, its red wings shimmering green on their undersides, the iridescent talons tucked close to its belly. They looked like mother-of-pearl. It was the same bird I had captured the night of the moon festival. I knew that to be true by its green markings, the pink threaded through its plumed tail, which matched exactly with my memory. Most of all I knew it to be my bird because of how its song tugged at my heart.

The Elysium bird beat its wings, creating little currents of air that smelled as fresh as rain.

The formation of councilmen split in half, and one red-robed man walked between them to the dais at the square. I could not see his face, and his robe was not very different from his fellows', though dyed a deeper shade of crimson. But I knew from the deferential whispers that this was the Lord Protector.

He raised a fist. I thought it was a salute of some kind—a command of silence, perhaps, though we were already silent.

But his fist was intended as a perch.

The Elysium bird dove down from the sky to settle onto that raised fist. It opened its beak and made a full-throated call.

The bird I had captured the night of the moon festival didn't belong to an anonymous High-Kith lady. It belonged to the Lord Protector, the ruler of Herrath.

I thought, from the seriousness of his stance, that he might give a speech, that I might learn more about the building of the wall and why it was celebrated even if no one remembered its construction, but— even at my distance—I saw his mouth slide into a sneaky smile. "Enjoy," he called. "Take what you wish."

The crowd went wild.

As though possessed, people began to snatch at whatever was closest, whatever they liked. Children, screaming in joy and fear, were bounced from one set of hands to another. A man tugged at the ivy, wrapping it around himself. People tore clothes off each other. Laughter rose from the crowd, though the councilmen remained still, standing exactly where they had been.

Someone pulled the simple gold bangle I had won at a party off my wrist. "Hey!" I shouted.

The woman pouted. "It's just a game."

"It's a bad game," Sid said, and the woman rolled her eyes, tossed the bracelet back at me, and disappeared into the melee.

Then over the roar of the crowd came the warbling cry of the Elysium. It launched itself from the Lord Protector's fist. It circled above, predatory, and called again. It swooped above, growing closer to me.

Mine, it called, and some people stopped their thieving to clap hands over their ears, the sound of the bird pierced so deeply.

It *was* hunting for something, I realized.

Me.

The bird hovered above me, beating its glorious wings. *Mine*, it called again. The crowd went silent. They were all staring at me. Everyone was staring. Sid, too.

"Seize her," the Lord Protector said.

48

I RAN.

I heard Sid call, but I outran her, too, because if I was caught I didn't want her to be caught with me. I ducked under the screen of vines and dodged down narrow streets, weaving around startled people, thinking of the city as a labyrinth like the one I had conquered at the party. My feet clapped against stone and clattered the occasional metal cellar doors set into the streets. I knew, by now, almost all the twists and turns of the High quarter, but as soon as I found an alleyway the councilmen rushed past, a dark shadow fell over me. I glanced up. The Elysium wheeled above and sang in triumph.

Mine.

I flung myself into a cellar door outside a towering home. I hid among bottles of wine, sweat oozing down my back, my heart hard against my chest. I heard shouts from the alleyway above. The thin slice of light that fell from the crack between the cellar's double street doors broke and wavered as people ran past. Their footfalls pummeled the metal cellar doors.

As my breath eased, I wiped sweat from my mouth and considered going up into the house's kitchen, but it would be staffed by Middlings. I would alarm them, and they would have no reason not to alert the owners of the house, who would call to councilmen careening through the city streets in search of the girl the Elysium bird claimed.

But why? Why was the bird so interested in me, and the Lord Protector so interested in its interest?

I thought of my dream, of the murder of the god of discovery, and how a simple duskwing drank the god's blood and unfurled like a silk scarf into crimson and pink and green. If my dream was a vision of the city's true past, what did that make the bird? Could it, by drinking the god's blood, have absorbed some of the god's powers? Could it be that every Elysium bird that ever hatched thereafter had the gift of discovery?

Maybe the bird could sense magic in me.

I thought of all the different kinds of magic I had seen: the elixir that could make you float; the house grown entirely from plants; the fortune-telling tree; the visions of butterflies and birds; the tea that lent beauty. I thought of the blood that turned the elixir pink, the severed finger that fell from the red blossom.

The tithe wasn't only a punishment, and wasn't only a means to provide the High Kith with mounds of fake hair or organs for surgeries. It was also a way to collect magic from the Half Kith. I remembered how the blue-haired man who had tasted my blood had revealed that his brother, a councilman, hadn't expected Middling blood to have an effect, or High-Kith blood.

I thought of how the man I forced to give me a memory of the city's history had said that the festival and parade was a way to give thanks for the building of the wall.

What if it wasn't the case that the Half Kith were unimportant, lowly?

What if they were in fact the only source of magic in the city, and they were kept behind a wall to be harvested?

What if the gifted people I knew, like Sirah, who could predict rain, or Rinah, who could make anything grow, possessed magic but simply didn't know it?

What if, should the councilmen catch me, they took my whole body, and made my blood into tea, and found uses for every part and the magic it would give them?

The metal street doors squealed open. I heard someone come down the cellar steps. Panic sour in my throat, I shifted as far as I could into my corner behind the wine bottles. I heard gritty steps come closer, the scuff of light sand on the cellar floor. Heavy breathing, the pants of someone who has been running hard. Someone searching among the wine bottles.

My panicky heart ran wild. My ears roared with fear. I huddled.

The man turned down my row and saw me.

"Got you," he said, and rushed close to clamp his hands on my arm.

"No," I whispered in terror. "You don't." I spoke like a child, as though denying something would make it not true.

Surprisingly, his grip slackened. He looked at me strangely, as though uncertain.

"Please don't," I said, hopeful, though fear was still pouring off my skin. Did he pity me? Could he be persuaded to let me go? "You don't have to do this."

"Do what?" he said, clearly confused. "I know I was supposed to do something . . ." He looked down at me, as though I might give him an answer, then around the cellar.

I remembered how, in the Ward, I would sometimes pass the militia and think, Not me. I am unimportant. Forget me.

When I thought that, they always did.

I could make people remember. Could I also make them forget?

Could I do to their minds what I could do with vinegar on inked paper, and erase what I didn't want?

"You were supposed to leave this cellar," I told him. "You were supposed to let go of me and walk back up the steps onto the street." It wasn't so much that I was making him forget, I realized as I saw his face furrow in concentration. I was giving him a false memory. "You were told to tell the Council that I was not here, that you saw me nowhere near. You will tell them that I must have gone into the park, to hide among the trees."

"Yes," he said. "That was it. That was what I was supposed to do." He smiled at me gratefully, and did what I commanded.

⌒

I waited for hours in the cellar, until the rumble in my belly said dinnertime was nearing, which would mean that servants could come down into the cellar soon to fetch wine. Cautiously, I cracked open the cellar doors. The alley wasn't totally empty. Two women in frothy candy-colored lace were giggling and eating pleasure dust from their palms. Their lips glittered with it. But they paid me no attention. I glanced above. The twilit sky was empty of the Elysium bird—which, I hoped, had lost track of me long ago.

The thoroughfare was strewn with trash. The blue ivy had sagged into a heap, its blossoms blown wide-open and gone as brown as butcher paper. A few people stumbled through the street, drunk or foxed, but most people were probably sleeping until the parties began.

I turned to head back to Sid's house in the hope of finding her there, but before I took more than a few steps, I heard someone call my name.

It was the Middling boy, Sid's little spy.

He ran up to me. "You have to help," he said breathlessly. "I have been looking everywhere for you. Sid's in trouble."

"What do you mean?"

"I saw a man come up to her after you disappeared. He pulled her away from the crowd."

"A councilman?"

The boy shook his head. "No." His eyes were wide. "I've never seen a man like this before."

"Describe him. What did he look like?"

"A monster."

49

THE BOY SAID THE MAN had taken Sid in the direction of her house, so I rushed there, blaming myself for having brought the Lord Protector's attention to her. I assumed she had been seen beside me, that even if I wasn't easily identifiable in the crowd and the haste of the chase, someone had noticed Sid standing close to me and easily recognized the foreigner by her short blond hair, her large dark eyes, the way she dressed, and the reputation she relished. Home didn't seem like a good place for her to hide.

Unless it was a trap set for me, and she had been forced to set it.

The smart thing would have been to stay away, but my heart raged with fear at the thought of her in any danger. I couldn't leave her alone, captured by someone who sought me.

I remember clearly how I felt: my pulse quivering like a dragonfly over water, a glassy insect with a vivid green body. Easy prey, easily seen, its wings as transparent as how frightened I was for Sid—and for myself, should harm come to her.

When I flung open the door, I heard an argument in another

language: Sid's voice anxious in a way that pierced through me, and the man's voice alternately insinuating and forceful. It wasn't a language I recognized. It didn't sound like Herrani, with its rounded vowels and similarity to my own tongue. It had clusters of hard and harsh sounds. Sid said something that ended with a hiss.

I strode into the sitting room, where I expected to see Sid bound, or with her dagger drawn, threatened by the man who had stolen her. Instead, I found her impeccably dressed, drinking a green liqueur, and gazing up in worried affection at a tall man with no face.

At least, that was my instant impression of him. I immediately recoiled, sucking in my breath. His face had been mutilated. He had no nose and no ears. He looked like he had been made to pay a horrific tithe. He turned and took my measure, black eyes raking me caustically from head to toe with the gaze of someone who makes short work of assessing people. I felt summarized and quickly dismissed. He was old enough to be Sid's father, with gray in his closely cut black hair. His skin was far darker than mine, a rich brown. If Sid looked foreign, he looked more so: his cheekbones broad, his mouth very full, his liquid black eyes rimmed with green paint.

But most startling were his mutilations. The scar tissue was old, a lighter shade than the rest of his skin. I couldn't help staring. His mouth curled into a hard smile.

"Nirrim." Sid's grip on her glass slackened, her expression relieved yet still apprehensive.

The man spoke to her in a cool, amused, slightly mocking tone.

"Yes." Sid frowned at him. "She is."

"What is going on?" I said. "What did he say? Who is he?"

"A family friend."

"Why is he here?"

"His ship docked in your city's harbor today."

"That's not what I asked."

Hesitantly, she said, "I know."

I cut a glance at him. "Is he . . . safe?"

"Me?" he said in my tongue, his accent heavy. He laughed. "No."

I flinched in surprise. I had assumed he didn't know my language. I was growing angry at Sid for her silence. I said, "You are making me feel as though I know nothing."

In a slow, droll tone with the edge of command, the man spoke to Sid in the language they shared. She snapped at him. He shrugged.

Sid glanced at me but wouldn't hold my gaze. "Earlier, he asked if you were my lover. Now he says I owe you my honesty. Nirrim, there is something I need to explain."

"Swiftly, Princess," the man said to her in Herrath.

"Princess?" I echoed, sounding exactly like the stupid ithya bird Raven had claimed I was. "*Princess?*"

Sid closed her eyes, her brow furrowed in frustration and anger, and said something to the man that sounded like a terrible plea, a grieved accusation. Finally she told him, "Just go. Leave me, please."

I was flooded with relief, which made me realize how afraid I had been that sending him away was something she wasn't able to do, and that he was here to take her away.

"You have had your fun." He said the words to Sid, but they were meant for me to understand. "Now it's time to come home." With a scant glance at me, he left.

"What did he mean, *princess?*" I asked. "Was he teasing you? Was that a joke?"

Miserably, she shook her head.

"Who *are* you?"

"His name is Roshar," she said. "He is a prince of Dacra, the eastern land, and I have known him all my life."

"I didn't ask about *him*!"

She set the glass of green liqueur down on a small table with slow precision, like it was an act of utmost importance, her last act. "I know," she said. "I'm sorry. This is difficult to explain. Roshar—my parents—no one knew where I was for a long time, but he found out I was on this island after I made the prison officials contact his ambassador here to secure our release. He has always understood me in ways my parents don't, and I hoped he would keep what he knew to himself. Even if he chose not to, I accepted the risk because it didn't matter so much that he could track me down here. I planned to be gone long before he received word from his ambassador and his ship was able to arrive. But"—she twisted her fingers together—"I stayed."

"You're not a princess. You said you were the Herrani queen's spy."

"I *was* her spy." Quietly, she added, "I still am. I am also her daughter."

My throat was tight. "Why didn't you tell me?"

"In some ways, I did."

I thought of the sigil on her dagger that matched the one on the queen's card, the symbol of the Herrani family, and how she hadn't fully answered when I asked whether she stole it, which made me assume that she had. I remembered how when the blue-haired man at the party had suggested she was cousin to the Herrani king, she had denied it . . . which wasn't a lie, if she was the king's daughter. I remembered how she had described the queen, and how she had described her mother. Both women had seemed similar: intimidating, and alike in the power they had over Sid. Yet there had been no reason for me to guess that they were the same person.

"I was truthful about why I left home," she said. "I hated being a princess. I don't even like the title. Princess Sidarine." She cringed in disgust. "So . . . dainty. And so heavy. I don't think you can know what a burden it is, how hopeful my parents are that I will marry into Roshar's family, how my mother seeks to make me into herself. My father says nothing, and just lets it happen."

"You're right," I said coldly. "I *don't* know what it's like to be a princess. I *don't* know what it's like to have parents."

"Please let me explain."

"You tricked me."

She roughed up her hair, nervously, then jammed her hands into her pockets. "I had to," she said. "I didn't want city officials getting wind of the Herrani monarchy's interest in this island."

"I wouldn't have told anyone," I said, insulted.

"I believe you, but I didn't at first. Even after I trusted you, I didn't want to tell you because I didn't want you to look at me differently. I didn't want you to look at me like you are looking at me now. It was already hard enough, wondering what you thought. If I could . . . attract you. If I could make you want me."

"Of course," I said bitterly. "What would be the point in telling yet one more conquest?"

"You were never a conquest."

"You would think that a liar, caught lying, would be wise enough to stop."

"Nirrim," she said, "I love you."

My breath caught. My eyes stung. And then I couldn't look at her. I swore I would never look at her again, at her beautiful, worried face. "I don't believe you."

"I love you because you are true and kind, and curious, and clever. I love you because of how you kiss me."

"Stop it." My throat closed.

"The letter I wrote in the tavern was to you. I was trying to explain."

"In a language I couldn't read. On a page you never planned to give to me."

"I never actually told you a lie."

"What you just now *said* is a lie. You are lying to yourself about what a lie is. You deceived me. Playing games with words doesn't make you less a liar."

"You're right," she said miserably. "I'm so sorry. Ask me anything you want. I'll tell you the truth."

I refused to look at her face. I looked at her hands, which she had pulled from her pockets. She was rubbing one thumb against the palm of her other hand, her fingers nervous in a way I had never seen—not when she spread jam on a pancake or played a piano's keys. Not when she had touched me so deftly.

I didn't want the anger boiling in my chest. I didn't want my eyes to sting. I didn't want to have been made a fool, so easily deceived by her. I wanted to be a wall, to be stone and mortar. I wanted to clear the burn from my eyes. So I focused on that long, thin scar on her hand. It is ugly, I thought.

And dear. I loved its ragged line.

I asked, "Where did you get that scar?"

"From a tiger."

Which was what she had said before, though I had dismissed it as a joke. "Really?"

"Yes. I mean, I have other scars from weapons training with my father. But the big scar, the one you noticed, is from Roshar's pet tiger. It's mostly tame. Roshar brought it to a state function when I was twelve . . ." She drifted off, maybe because of the fresh anger that must have been plain on my face. I hated to hear the hope in her voice, as if she believed that she could distract me from her deceit by telling me a tale about a tiger among royalty, in a country I had never seen.

"Nirrim, please look at me."

I shook my head, my eyes brimming.

"Ask me what I thought when I first met you," she said. "Ask me how I felt when I first saw your face. Ask me how it is to stand in front of you and know how angry you are, how much I deserve it, how awful it is to have hurt you when I have only ever wanted your happiness."

I couldn't help it. I looked up. Her face was pale, stricken.

"You have my heart," she said. "I never knew I could feel for anyone what I feel for you."

She looked lonely. It hurt me to see her unsmiling mouth, how her body had lost its easy confidence. Sid hated to be serious but was so serious now, and so sad. My anger slipped away. I said, "I believe you."

The corner of her mouth lifted into a smile, but her eyes were still hesitant. She waited, but I couldn't say to her what she had said to me, even as I loved her bravery for saying it. I loved the freckle beneath her eye, the throat I still wanted to press my face against, how she loved her parents even when they failed her. How gently she sought my thoughts. How hard she held me when I asked her to. Her sly glances. Her laugh. I was a coward for saying none of this, but my throat closed over. My anger was gone, but I wished it weren't. Anger would armor me against the answer to the question I had to ask. "Will Roshar force you to return home?"

She thought for a moment, then shook her head. But her face was unhappy.

"Are you going to do it anyway?"

"Yes," she whispered.

"But"—I desperately cast about for the words that would make her stay—"we had a plan. You said a month."

"I can't."

"You promised. You swore on your life."

"I must ask you to release me from that promise."

"You said you wanted to bring the secret of magic back to your parents."

"That's not important now."

"You always change your mind," I accused. "You never want anything for long."

"Roshar says that my mother is very sick. No one knows why. It's a sudden illness and unlike anything anyone has ever seen. My father needs me. I don't even know if she will still be alive when I reach home."

Sid suddenly looked so small. I saw how utterly defenseless she was against this looming, enormous loss. I wanted to touch her cheek, to pull her into my arms, but if I did, I would never be able to let her go.

She asked, "Would you force me to stay?"

I bit my lip. I thought about what I had done to the councilman, how I had forged a fake memory in his mind.

I could do that to Sid, if I wanted.

Make her forget her parents. Make her stay in Ethin.

Maybe it would be a kindness. After all, if she couldn't remember her mother, Sid would never grieve her loss.

"No." I shook my head, horrified at my temptation, at how easily I could dupe her. I could force her to remember me as the only one she would ever love. I could make her always mine. "I would never do that." My eyes were wet. "Go, you should go. I will miss you so much."

Her expression changed, losing its hesitation. She reached for me, her lips touching my tears. "Don't cry," she said. "Come with me."

I went still. I drew slightly back.

"Won't you?" she said.

"What would I be there? A servant to the princess?"

"No," she said with a flash of frustration. "Have I ever treated you like one?"

"Then what?"

"My . . ." Her frustration grew as I saw that she didn't have any ready words to answer me. "My honored guest."

"Everyone will know exactly what we are."

"Let them. I want them to."

"So I would be there as your lover."

"Yes." Her voice was firm.

"In a country I have never seen."

"Herran is beautiful. You will love it as I do."

"I don't know the language."

"Your memory will help you. You will learn quickly."

"Your parents want you to marry a man. They won't want me there."

"*I* want you."

"I will have no place. I will know no one and nothing. I will have nothing to call mine."

"You will have me."

My eyes were dry now. They ached. I stepped away. Her hands fell from me, and she lifted her stubborn chin. She said, "You owe me a yes."

"No," I said. "I can't."

"Why?" she demanded. "You have been treated terribly here. One way or another, you have lived your life imprisoned. The people who should protect and care for you have failed you. I will never do that."

"Won't you? What will you do when your parents pressure you to marry?"

She hesitated, then said, "I will refuse."

She had reckoned with the lies she had told me, but even now I am not sure if she recognized the lies she told herself. You will change your mind, I thought. You have other loyalties.

As I do, I thought reluctantly.

"I think all the magic is coming from the Ward," I said. "I think the Council milks Half-Kith bodies of powers people don't even know they have. The children who have gone missing, where are they? Dead? Kept like calves in stalls, forced to give their blood? I told you I would find a way to give magic back to the Ward. I am going to keep my promise."

Helplessly, she said, "It's not your duty to change the world. It's dangerous to try."

You are dangerous.

"Be with me," she said.

Slowly, I shook my head at the impossibility of it, at the sure future I had seen written on the tree bark's inner skin. I saw how alone and friendless I would be in Sid's country. I would be her novelty. She loved me now. How long would it be before she grew tired of me, before she left me like she had left her own country, like she was leaving mine now, like she had left the Ward after one day when she had said she would stay three? I saw myself: abandoned in a land with unfamiliar birdsong, whose city never became suddenly encased in ice, where they did not salt bread, where I would never taste honey made by sea bees. I would hear the alien tones of a language I didn't know, and miss Morah's wisdom, Annin's hope, my only sisters. I would know no one there except Sid. I would depend on her for everything.

Her voice small, she asked, "Do you not love me like I love you? Won't you come with me?"

Yes, I thought. I love my blithe scoundrel. I love your good heart.

"No," I said. "I can't come with you."

"Oh," she said, the sound low and blunt. I realized I had unintentionally done to her what she had done to me so many times, which was to tell a misleading truth. She had asked two questions, I had answered one, and she thought my answer served for both.

"I see," she said.

"Sid," I said, and would have explained, but she lifted a hand to stop me.

She said, "An apology will make it worse."

"I don't want to apologize."

"Good. There is no need."

Then she left, quickly, even as I called her name, then stopped calling. I did not, in the end, want to share the truth, because the words of love inside me felt like the only part of her that could ever remain mine.

———

Night fell. There was no moon. The stars were painfully bright.

I stood on the balcony, looking at the harbor, the sea.

It was too dark to see her ship set sail.

50

MADAME MERE SHOWED DISCOMFORT at my request, but she was tempted when I promised her a rare elixir. "I haven't seen it used at any party." I offered the dressmaker the little stoppered vial I had won at Pantheon. This time, it was filled with my own watered-down blood. I'd had to guess at the ratio of blood to water. "I don't know how strong it is."

"What will it do?"

"It will make you remember something you have forgotten."

She gave the vial a wary glance, but curiosity eventually stole over her features. "Indeed, I have never heard of such an elixir," she said. "Fascinating." Her hand claimed the vial. She gave me the address, then said, "Councilmen have been asking about a girl who looks like you."

"Oh?" I kept my voice careful.

"Why don't you let me freshen your look? That black hair has a nice wave and shine, but really, my dear: it's far too natural. Even, I would say, *noticeable*."

"I can't pay you."

She waved an impatient hand. She led me into a back room, where she painted my hair with stripes of blue and green and purple. She dyed my eyelashes a shocking teal and patterned my cheeks with swirls of gold that she swore would last for days.

"There," she said. "No one will know you."

I was touched by her kindness. "Why would you help me?"

"Maybe it helps me, to help you." She smiled gently. "The gossip in the High quarter is that Lady Sidarine has left the city."

I bit my lip. I looked at the panoply of fabrics stacked along the walls, the brightly wrapped bolts, and tried not to think about her. I thought: Azure. Canary. Persimmon dotted with pink. Violet. I tasted blood in my mouth.

The dressmaker patted my hand. "The first heartbreak hurts the most. Every day it will be easier, and soon you will forget her."

But of course, I never could.

⌒

"Well," Lillin said imperiously, when her Middling maid showed me into the parlor. "Who are you, and what do you want?" She had exquisitely delicate features: an oval face, slender lips, gray eyes so pale and clear that you could see faint stars of blue around the pupils. I thought of her with Sid, and Sid with her, and wished I had never succeeded in convincing Madame Mere to give me her address.

"We both know Sidarine," I said, and Lillin's face flashed with understanding. "We saw each other at the party with the ballroom that rained."

"Oh," she said. "You. I didn't recognize you. Sid's not here." She brought the fingers of one hand together in a little flutter and then flourished them open, as if they had captured something invisible only to let it fly away. "Gone. Left the city for good, I hear. It looks like you have it bad for her, poor thing. She is the worst sort of rake. We are well rid of her. The worst is how she makes you feel special, for a time."

"She said you had something for her. Maps."

She narrowed her silvery eyes. "What do you want with them?"

"You don't have to give them to me, but I would like to look at them. I will trade you something for it."

She flitted a bored hand, gesturing at the pearl-and-gold parlor that surrounded us. "I have everything."

"I can give you a memory. Even if you think you remember something, I can make you feel it again, taste it again, as fresh as when it happened."

She was intrigued, I could tell. "Is this like pleasure dust?"

"More like an elixir."

"I've never tried such an elixir."

"I'll show you," I said, "if you let me touch your hand."

"Any memory I want?"

"Yes," I said, though I wasn't confident in my own control.

She lifted her little chin. "I'm not sure I fully believe you." She offered a cruel dare: "If you can really do as you say, make me remember my last time with Sidarine."

I touched her hand, and thought of how it must have touched Sid. As painful as this was, part of me also wanted it: to share Sid with someone, to know that I was not the only one who had wanted her.

Lillin's eyes slipped closed. Her hand twitched in mine. A breath escaped her lips. I hated this. I needed it. It felt like we were both trying to hold a ghost.

When it was over, she showed me the maps of the Keepers Hall that she had taken from her brother. She haughtily reminded me that they did not belong to me, but I simply glanced once at each page and took my leave, wondering what she had seen in her memory, and how it compared with mine. I shivered, to think of Sid falling asleep next to me. My heart clenched with missing her.

⟜

The Keepers Hall was less imposing than I had thought it would be, and more mercurial, with windows at oddly staggered intervals and riotous façades, rippling balconies that must have been made of stone yet looked as fluid as water. Turrets sprang from odd places and were jewel boxes of stained glass. The sun was hot on my head. My vision dazzled. The snakelike edges of the building seemed to bend, and when I glanced again, the windows appeared to have reordered themselves and were now shaped like stars where before they had been melting circles, the tops round and the bottoms deformed. Sometimes I saw the present and sometimes the past.

I slipped a hand into my dress pocket, where I ran a finger along the packet of poison Aden had given me. It rested against Sid's letter, which I could not read yet could not leave behind. The poison was the only weapon I had. I didn't know if it would be of any use, but it reassured me to have it, perhaps like Sid's dagger might reassure her, wherever she was now. I remembered how difficult it was to unstrap the belt, and how amused she was at my fumbling. She had slid it undone so that it fell heavily to the bed.

At the entrance, whose open double doors were slick with red paint as shiny as a mirror, dour militiamen stood. They barred my way.

"This building is reserved for councilmen," one of them said.

"Go prepare for your party," another said, his voice just careful enough not to be a sneer. I had always feared the militia and resented the power they had over me, but now knew that they were just Middlings who had been hired as all Middlings were to do work the High

Kith disdained. I saw that they must have had wishes and fears and resentments of their own.

"But I *am* a councilman," I said calmly.

Their brows wrinkled. They stared, then laughed.

"I will show you." I produced my High-Kith passport. One of them accepted it, sliding a look his partner's way, wondering where the joke was. I felt power prickle along my skin. It felt like panic, or pleasure. It felt the way the dark sky looks when lightning illuminates the clouds, giving the flat black sky sudden dimension.

"The last page in the booklet," I told the man. "The one you just saw held the necessary document for entrance."

"Oh," he said, flipping back to it. "I see."

"The person you saw," I said to both of them, "the one who just walked up to you. You might have thought, because of a trick of the light, that you saw a woman, but he was a young man from a good family, well known, well liked, dressed as he should have been in his red robe."

"Why, so it was," one of the men said to the other.

I took the passport back. "You let him pass, as you rightly should, and then no one stood before you."

They both stared blankly ahead. I went inside.

The entryway was dim, the walls painted red and green and pink in tight patterns, making the entryway appear as though covered with the scales of a wild, unknown creature.

Though councilmen passed me as I made my way through the building, following the maps in my mind, I did what I had done in the Ward, which was to wish that they didn't see me, to make them forget me . . . which, I realized, as I became more practiced in doing it, was not quite *forgetting* but rather giving them an invented memory of a moment so quickly passed that it came to occupy the present in their minds.

I made my way to the library, where green flames burned in oil lamps and the books were so beautifully encased in rich leather that each row of books looked as though it were a jeweled strip of vitreous enamel. Red-robed readers sat at polished wooden desks, drinking from pots of pink tea. When they looked up, I made them remember me differently, to be what they expected to see, but it felt harder. Their faces frowned, and their minds seemed to tug away from the thoughts I gave them, so that I had to be more forceful with my wishing, sterner in my construction of the vision of me they were supposed to believe. Eventually, their eyes fogged over and they went back to their books.

I approached a councilman who was shelving books and appeared to be in charge of the library. "I am looking for a book very special to the Lord Protector," I told him. "A history of the city."

His narrow eyes studied me, confused. "That book is only for the Lord Protector to read."

I replaced his memory of the person standing before him. "*I* am the Lord Protector."

"Oh, yes. Forgive me, my lord. Of course you are. I will fetch the book for you now. There is memory elixir for you while you wait, though I know my lord never needs it."

He set a glass pot of pink tea before me as I sat at a table. There were other, drained pots, and a little stack of glass cups that looked like a froth of bubbles. The man bustled away.

A memory elixir.

I glanced around the library at all the people reading, drinking their tea. Was that my blood in their glasses, drained from me when I was imprisoned?

I poured myself a cup and took a sip. It did nothing to me, probably because I already had any magic it could lend me, because I was simply giving myself back to myself. No wonder I'd had more trouble manipulating the memories of the readers in the library. They had drunk the tea, so what power I used on them had to work against the power they had already stolen and ingested in a diluted form. I set the cup aside. Then, after a thought, I slipped the packet of poison from my pocket and emptied it into the pot.

The librarian came back, bearing a red-bound book the size of a small child. He set it before me. Its front was embossed with a symbol I had seen on a card in the game of Pantheon. It was a grasping hand, the sign of the god of thieves.

"Will there be anything else you need, my lord?" asked the librarian.

"Yes." I cleared my throat, eager to begin reading, suffused with a feeling I was not at first able to name, because I had never felt it before.

Superiority.

I had never felt able to make people do what I wanted. Now it was so easy. If I wished it, it was so. If someone resisted, I needed only to twist their memory to make them obey.

"Clear the room," I told him. "And then leave. Bar the library doors. I wish to read alone, in peace."

"Of course, my lord," he said, and executed my order.

In the stillness that remained, I opened the book.

The gods once walked among mortals, read the first line. As I touched the page, a vapor rose from the printed ink. Specterlike, it drifted up to me. I inhaled, my gasp of surprise dragging the vapor inside me before I thought to resist it, and I fell into the story it told.

51

THE GODS ONCE WALKED AMONG mortals, charmed by their childlike ways, their lives as ephemeral as dew on grass. Most enchanting, however, was a mortal's ability to surprise. A god might bless a mortal, yet never know how the seed of such a gift might grow. Sometimes a frail human might glow with song, a pure melody shuddering from the throat, expressing a longing the god of music had never known, with an intensity that made the god, despite her eternal years, listen with wonder. And a mortal might suffer beneath a gift, extra eyes popping out all over the skin like weeping boils, such that the god of foresight could not help but laugh as she had not done since the birth of the god of delight.

Gradually, the gods left their realm, or left it for a time, drawn to a jewel of an island on the sea, its beaches dusted with pink sand, its inland lakes brimming with fresh water and fish brilliantly scaled. A city was raised on hilltops. The god of the sea carved a gentle bay from the coast into a natural harbor. Mortals chiseled marble statues in honor of the gods, and the gods were pleased, because worship was a relatively new pleasure. For certain gods, fear was equally pleasing.

The city was called Ethin, the word in the gods' language for the exhalation of praise.

A mortal's life is as fluttering and uncertain as a bird that flies into a lamplit hall filled with joy and argument, and then dives out a window into the unseeing night. A few of the one hundred gods came closer to certain mortals, enchanted by their beautiful brevity, their supple skin, their strangely warm mouths, their odd ways, their stumbling yet earnest efforts, their brilliance. Sometimes the gods would argue among themselves over a mortal. One might accuse another of blessing a claimed favorite. And a mortal might reveal a grace or intelligence marked by no god, causing the pantheon of the hundred to murmur among themselves, entertained—even, occasionally, concerned—that some mortals possessed skills due to no one but themselves, to human luck or labor.

One day, a mortal gave the gods the greatest surprise of all: a baby. The child radiated divinity. There could be no doubt that god-blood lurked inside her, though no god dared claim her as their child. She captured the love of most of the gods, who charmed sunbeams to her cradle, and cushioned her every tumble, and painted her skin with glorious colors to bear the sign of their favor.

Even the god of death stayed his heavy hand.

The god of foresight smiled her cruel smile. Death will come to the girl anyway, she said.

She will never lose a drop of blood, decreed the god of luck. She will never suffer disease, Luck said, nor the corrosion of age.

So may it be, said the god of foresight, who visited the girl in the night, and drew a blanket over her sleeping face until her breath grew slight, then smothered, and the small body was as cold as clay.

No god likes to be wrong, especially not this god.

I said it would be so, she told the mourning pantheon, and hear me yet. There will be more of her kind, to our everlasting misery.

The god of truth grew grim. His brother-sister god, the moon, whose great eye saw the dealings of the mortals' nights, shrank to a narrow crescent smile. The moon knew the sweet and salt of mortal flesh. This god had tasted mortal savor, and the incandescence of human love. Though sister-brother moon saw no reason to tell tales on fellow gods—at least, not when it was to no apparent advantage, and not when the moon sinned as other gods sinned—the moon knew that the god of foresight's words rang with truth.

Once tempted to taste a mortal kiss, many gods could not resist. Soon the bellies of mortals and gods alike swelled with hybrid fruit. Half-godlings slipped into the world.

They had gifts of their own—weaker but unpredictable, spectacular, subtle. The gods fought among themselves to protect the half-gods, or make them pawns in games against their god-kin. Most consternating, however, was that the little half-gods looked no different from humans. Sometimes divinity did not shine from them as with the gods' first half-child, but rather sank deep, undetected, like underground water.

Nor did all half-gods bear allegiance to the gods, or even fellowship toward humans. Mortals who suffered the devious machinations of half-gods begged for protection from them. Some half-gods, resentful of being chits in immortal games, bucked the authority of their undying parents. They stole secrets. They played games of their own. They thwarted the will of the gods and wrought unhappiness.

They will kill one of us, said the god of foresight.

Impossible, said the pantheon. But the god of death, their monarch, craved the god of discovery's aid.

Identify them, Death commanded.

Discovery ferreted out all the half-godlings and marked them with a sign on their brows that mortals and gods alike could see. For a time, there was calm, and the power of surprise was no longer a half-god's domain. For a time, all was well.

But a god took pity upon the half-ones. A god who had enjoyed the chaos they caused, who had chuckled with the god of games and wrought his own mischief in the chaos.

And it was this god who undid them all.

―――

"Do you enjoy what you read?"

The voice startled me out of my reverie, out of the world the book painted in my mind: the birth of Ethin with its sequined waters; the extravagant beauty of the gods, some of whom looked vaguely human, and others alien, with rose-colored skin or a snakelike form. Misty Death, who could coalesce into a solid weight greater than stone. The shifting Moon: sometimes a male, sometimes a female, sometimes invisible to all.

I glanced up from the unfinished book, my pulse high because I had been startled, but I wasn't truly afraid, not even when I saw who had spoken. I would twist his memory easily enough.

It was the Lord Protector.

He was sitting in a chair beside me, the Elysium bird on his shoulder. It called to me, its cry echoing in the empty library. The Lord Protector smiled. His face was resolutely plain, features so smooth and unremarkable that I found I had a hard time looking in his face. "Well?" he said. "It is impolite not to answer a question."

"No."

"Mend your words, child. After all, this is my book. Surely you do not wish to offend me. Why doesn't the story please you?"

Because he had made no move to hurt me and I was confident I could make him misremember me long enough to escape, I told him the truth. "Something bad is about to happen."

"Oh, yes. Something is. Tell me, little one, what is the appropriate punishment for someone who sneaks, who lies, who steals?"

Warm with my power, proud of using it, I said, "I didn't steal."

"Shall we put you in a barrel studded with nails and have you dragged by horses through the streets?"

I paused, staring. Expression mild, he waited for an answer.

"I am a councilman," I told him quickly, my voice high. "I have been your favored assistant for years. You were glad to see me when you entered the library."

"Or put your hands in the fire until the skin crackles and the flesh cooks off the bone? A punishment most worthy for a thief."

My heart beat hard and fast. I tried using magic again. "This book was always an ordinary book."

"It is too bad your foreigner is gone. I could take her from you. I could squeeze her body down to a pin. I would carry the pin with me always, and drive it through the tongues of liars."

I scraped my chair back, leaping to my feet. The bird shrieked. "I left already." The words spilled out of my mouth in a tangled stutter. "The library was empty when you arrived."

"Sit," he said, "or I will show no mercy in how I chastise you."

I sat. Fear crawled over my skin.

"A sneak may be a sneak," he said. "A liar a liar, a thief a thief, and yet still show courtesy."

"I—" I faltered, unsure what he wanted.

"Your name."

"Nirrim."

He waited.

"Nirrim," I said, "my lord."

"Ah," he said. "Better."

"May I"—the glass pot wobbled in my hand as I lifted it—"pour you some tea?"

He lifted his brows. I still could not quite tell the color of his hooded eyes. "How unexpected." He accepted a cup and sipped. "It tastes like I imagine you do." He drank deeply, and I tried not to show my relief. "It tastes like something else, too, but what?" He drained the cup.

I lowered the pot to the table, waiting.

"Poison." He licked his lips. "Good try, my child, but poison is no way to kill a god."

52

"THE GODS DON'T EXIST," I said, my mouth numb.

"I don't? And what do you think *you* are, half-one? I felt what you were trying to do to me. Tell me, Nirrim: What do you think *I* can do to *you*?"

I stood, ready to run from the room. He smiled, and the strength left my body. I slumped to the floor, banging my face against the chair as I went down. It clattered on top of me as I lay, and he stood to look down upon me, the hem of his red robe brushing the skin of my arm. I willed myself to move. I couldn't even twitch my fingers.

"I am being a good god," he said. "I haven't stolen your sight, for example."

Though my eyes were open, they went suddenly blind. I cried out. The bird answered my call. I heard its wings rustle.

Nothing was as dark as this. Not night, not the orphanage baby box, not even when I closed my eyes and light shone through my eyelids. The world looked entirely black and empty.

The fabric of his robe skimmed over me. I heard him walk around my prone body, pausing by my head. He could do anything to me. He could crush my face beneath his heel. He could do worse.

"Or I could steal your breath."

And it was suddenly gone. I strained for air. My heart panicked. I felt myself choking, dying, paralyzed and alone in the airless black.

"That's the fragile human in you," he said, and air came rushing back into my lungs. I sucked it in, my breath a horrible keening rasp.

"God of thieves," I said.

"Yes, little one."

"Let me up," I begged.

"No."

"Give me back my sight."

"No."

"Please, let me go. I'll do anything."

"Anything?" His voice was ripe with amusement. "Such a dangerous word. I haven't even yet caused you pain. I can slowly steal the blood from your body. The warmth from your skin. The tongue from your mouth. All the water within you, so that you desiccate into a tortured husk."

"There must be something I can do," I sobbed. "Something I can give you."

"There is," he said. "It happens to be the one thing that even I cannot steal."

"What? Tell me."

"You will lie there, and you will listen, and when I am done I will make you a bargain, my child."

One should never bargain with a god. But I did not know that then.

"Should you accept," he said, "you will leave here just as you were when I met you, save for one thing. Am I not merciful?"

"And if I say no? Will you murder me?"

His silence was thoughtful. "To whom do you belong?"

To Sid, I thought. Then I buried the thought, terrified that he might steal it from me.

"Perhaps you don't know," he mused. "Who bore you?"

I blinked against the blindness. I wished I could see his face. I had no idea what his expression was as he stared down at me. "I have no parents."

"Of course you do."

"I was abandoned," I said. "I am an orphan."

"If I give you to the god of death, there will be nothing left for me to steal. And to be honest, I am in trouble enough with my brethren without tempting their wrath by killing one of their favorites, whosesoever you are."

"Are there more gods hidden in this city? Where are they?"

"Gone," he said.

"But you are here."

"As punishment."

"For what?"

"I killed my brother."

"Why?"

"Nirrim, why did you wish to read my book?"

"Because I need to know what happened here."

"Why?"

"So I understand why things are the way they are."

"Why?"

I struggled to move my dead muscles. I strained to see. Yet, although blind to his expression, I sensed his curiosity, and sensed that this curiosity kept him, at least for now, from being cruel. It was hopeless to believe he would truly strike a bargain with me and let me go unharmed, but at least I could breathe; at least my life wasn't slowly dwindling out of me as it had been a moment ago, my lungs burning with pain. So I answered honestly: "I want to know where magic comes from. I want to know why the Half Kith are walled off from the rest of the city, and anything can be taken from them at any time." Like me right now, I thought, at the mercy of the god of thieves. "If I know, I can change things."

"How?" His voice was thoughtful.

"I will explain the city's history to the Half Kith so that we can seize the source of magic."

"Will you be believed?"

Slowly, I said, "I don't know."

"Revolution is a messy matter, and those who rebel may find themselves crushed under rebellion's wheels. *I* was. Ethin is as it is. I warn you—against my own best interests, I might add—to leave it that way."

I wanted to shake my head, but couldn't.

"No?" he said. "Then hear my bargain. I will tell you your city's history, and mine. But if you wish to leave this library with what you have learned, you must tithe something precious unto me."

At the word *tithe*, my skin crawled. "Will I be able to live without it?"

"Oh, yes."

"What is it?"

"Your heart."

I blinked rapidly against the darkness. "Impossible. I can't live without a heart."

"Not that lump of muscle beating in your chest. I mean what humans mean when they say *heart*: your delectable mix of worry and awe and love. I mean what makes you *you*."

"Why?"

"It is useful to me. With it, I may leave this wretched island, you wretched people. I have been cast out of the pantheon, Nirrim, for my sin. But I know of a god who would welcome me home, would help reinstate me among my kin, for the gift of a god-blooded human's heart."

"Me, god-blooded?"

"You."

"You mean . . . I am a god's child? Are we called the Half Kith because we are half-gods?"

He laughed. "The ignorant arrogance! Once, yes, the Half Kith were, before they were walled off and forgot their own powers. But that was long ago, and their god-blood has thinned since the gods forsook this island, and half-gods had children with pure mortals, and their children did the same. Now the Ward holds mostly ordinary humans. There are no true half-gods now, though the blood runs strong in you."

"If you take my heart, what will I become?"

Lightly, he said, "Who can say?"

As light as his voice might be, I heard eagerness beneath it. "Then my answer is no."

There was a silence. "No? I will force it from you, then."

"You said you couldn't steal it."

"I can hurt you until you give it willingly."

"Then why haven't you?"

In the silence that followed, the answer to my own question occurred to me. "Because that would damage it," I said.

"Yes," he acknowledged. "It would no longer taste so sweet."

"Tell me this country's history, and then let me decide whether it is worth it to me to accept your bargain."

"I could kill you," he said.

"Will my corpse be useful to you?"

The Elysium chirped. The god was silent.

"Tell me," I said, "did you give the first Lord Protector the idea for the wall? The tithes?"

The god laughed. Once he started, he couldn't seem to stop. The hem of his robe shuddered across my arm. "Nirrim. *I* am the Lord Protector. I have always been the Lord Protector. I was the first and the second and all the others that followed. When enough mortal years had passed that the city began to think I should be close to death, I pretended to die, and then stole the city's knowledge of my appearance. I have done this so many times it wearies me, like a joke told and retold. It was amusing, the first time. And yes, I had the wall built. I promised my acolytes that if they labored to build the wall, I would reward them and their children, and their children's children, and so I have. The people you call High Kith once worshipped me, and now they worship the things I give them, and if they have forgotten me, why, it is because I have let them."

"But why did you build the wall? Why do you tithe us?"

"The promise of a god must be kept. I promised my followers riches and delights. God-blood is delightful for them to drink. They revile your kith, of course, but oh how they love all the many parts of you. As for the wall, the half-ones deserved it, just as I deserved my punishment."

"Why?"

"Murder."

I remembered my dream of people in the agora killing the god. "The god of discovery."

"Yes," he said. "My brother."

I heard the rustle of feathers.

"He lives on in Elysium birds," said the god. "This one can sense the god-blood in you. It is drawn to you. I knew, when it called to you during the parade, what you were. You should see how it leans toward you. I must hold it back." The god sighed. "The murder is my fault."

"You killed your brother?"

"I may as well have. I, the pitying fool that I am, sought to help the half-ones. I admit Discovery irritated me. The tattletale. Always meddling in my affairs and exposing my schemes. Yet he was my brother, and though I sometimes loathed him, I loved him, too. And I was too clever. I had once stolen tears from the god of death. Take this, I told the half-gods, who had been marked by Discovery and thus had no freedom to scheme, to live, to hide, to be anything other than obviously what they were, and thus became the favorite playthings of the gods and hated and feared by humans. Anoint yourselves with it, and the tears of death will blind Discovery to you."

His voice grew quiet with intensity. "But one half-god, child of wisdom, took my gift and divined another use for it. He dipped a blade in the tears and thus made a weapon fit to kill a god. The half-gods spilled immortal blood in their agora, and the pantheon will never forgive them—or me—for it. Eradicate them, said Wisdom, or they will multiply through the ages, and one day bear someone fit to overthrow us all. Death lifted his hand. Then the weakest god, the least among us all in power, spoke. Still, the god of sewing said, they are our children. Death studied the Seamstress, whom he loved. The pantheon argued. It was decided that the gods would forsake this island . . . and that I, as punishment, would protect the rest of the world from it and its unruly god-children."

"I thought the Lord Protector was called that because he protected *us*."

"Lord, or nursemaid? Are you my subjects, or my wards? It was decreed that I must tend to Herrath. That I should clean up the havoc wreaked here, as if it were fully my fault that the gods could not help loving mortals, could not help giving them gifted children. And so I did what I do best. I stole. I stole the half-ones' knowledge of their gifts. I bribed my acolytes to build a wall around the half-gods, then stole the knowledge of what they had done even as I kept my promise to them. And for many years, all was well. For centuries, I labored in hopes that the pantheon would see my efforts and welcome me home. Eventually I realized that there is no one willing to take my place, and I can never atone enough to be forgiven. Most intriguingly"—his voice came closer, as if he had bent down to look more closely at me—"travelers began to find their way to this island, despite the spell I had cast around it. They began to arrive a few years ago—around the time, I would say, that you began to mature, little Nirrim. Your gift is memory, is it not? Or so the taste of your blood says, and the tricks you tried on me."

I thought of Sid. I wondered what I would be if she had never come here.

A stone, maybe.

A cloud, floating over everyone, part of nothing.

A gust of wind, trying to burrow into warm places.

I said, "Why did you let the travelers come?"

"I suppose," he said, "that I longed for something new."

"Let me see you."

"No."

"Please."

And suddenly, I could. I blinked my eyes, which were stinging from the light. The god had stooped beside me. His bland face looked remarkable now, for its sadness. I said, "I am alone, too."

"Ah," he said, "but not for nearly so long as I." The Elysium bird chirruped. "Well, Nirrim, do you agree to my bargain?"

The strength returned to my body. A little wobbly, I pushed myself up so that I was sitting beside the god.

"Will you release me?" he said.

"And if I say no?"

"Then I steal back everything I have told you. If I let you live, you leave with nothing. I will be Lord Protector until I pretend to die, and then I will be Lord Protector again, and the Half Kith will stay behind the wall and the High Kith will continue to feast on them and the Middlings will serve as go-betweens, longing to be just like the descendants of my acolytes, and relishing their place above the imprisoned children of gods and the stray pure humans unlucky enough to live among them."

"And if I say yes?"

"You might find," he said gently, "that it is easier to live without a heart."

I longed for Sid. I wished she were here to help me. She would say, No. Don't surrender yourself. Your goodness, your light, everything that makes me love you.

But she was not here. She never would be. And I would miss her always, would reach for her in my sleep, would weep for never having told her that I loved her with all my heart. I make nothing too heavy to bear, she had once said, and I wanted her to take my loss of her and make me able to bear it.

Time would heal nothing for me. Each kiss would feel fresh on my mouth.

What good was a heart, if it hurt so much?

"I want to make the city remember," I told the god of thieves, "and then I agree to your bargain."

His bland face became suddenly beautiful, suffused as it was with joy. "Quickly," he begged.

Could I make an entire city remember its past? I felt how the memory shared by the god filled me, how if I focused on it, it swelled large enough to spill out of me like blood. And I became afraid of it, of its trembling size, how it bulged against my insides. How maybe releasing it would take all of me away with it. But I remembered how I had thought my sadness at Helin's death was like a bowl always replenished, how my love for Sid was like that, too, how grief and love have a magic of their own because they can be never-ending.

I poured the city's memory out of me. I imagined it spilling out over its streets, its people.

The face of the god looked pleased, even proud. "Well done," he said.

Then he leaned toward me, placed his mouth on mine, and sucked all the breath from me.

EPILOGUE

I SEE THIS STORY PERFECTLY, its moments cut crystal in my mind. I remember how this story, like a great, sheer bowl, bore a sea of emotion—my guilt, my loneliness, my longing. I remember little rivulets of delight, the warmth of love.

But I do not feel it anymore. I feel light. Empty. Pure.

Sid's letter rests in my pocket, but it is mere paper. I carry its copy in my mind. I see its foreign script written in her hand, but what it might say, and how I will never understand it, is as meaningless as her absence.

The god is gone, too, to wherever gods go.

His bird is on my shoulder. I have no fondness for it, but I do not mind it. Its beauty enhances my own. Its talons pierce the skin a little, but when I hiss, it learns quickly to stop. It would be nothing for me to wring its pretty little neck.

I remember the people who once troubled me, who wrung my heart, who stitched me up tightly with little black threads of guilt, who made me wish and cherish and smile and weep.

I know they once touched me, but I no longer feel it.

Wonderful. It is almost as good as having no memory at all.

The Elysium bird on my shoulder, I walk through the stunned city. I stare back at the people who stare at me, daring them to cross me. None of them do. I wish they would. They call out questions as though it is evident by my face that I have the answers. Maybe they are not so stupid after all, yet none is worthy of my reply.

I make my way through them and into the Ward.

The Half Kith have come into the streets. They see me arrive and they are eager. Many of them know now what they are. I see Aden, sunlight dancing down his arms, ready to twist the light in his control and use it as he wills. I see Morah and Annin at the fringes of the crowd, how Annin starts toward me. Morah, wise to whatever expression is on my face, claws her back.

Even the god-blooded ones don't approach me. And I am not interested in the others, like Morah and Annin, who might as well be made from sticks and cloth. There is no power in them, not like there is in mc.

Finally a god-blood dares to approach me. It is one-eyed Sirah, creeping up on her feeble old legs. "Nirrim, child, look." She holds out her hand. "I can make it rain." A little thunderstorm erupts on her palm.

A nice trick, and it could be useful to me, but she is weak and worn. I need powerful allies for what I want to accomplish. I push past her.

"Nirrim," she says, shocked, "who do you think you are?"

I say it loud enough for all to hear: "I am a god," I tell them, "and I am your queen."

ACKNOWLEDGMENTS

THANK YOU TO MY STALWART writing group members, Marianna Baer, Anna Godbersen, Anne Heltzel, Jill Santopolo, Eliot Schrefer, and other dear friends who read drafts: Kristin Cashore, Morgan Fahey, Donna Freitas, Drew Gorman-Lewis, Sarah Mesle, and Becky Rosenthal. You gave vital suggestions and encouragement when things got hard.

This book wouldn't have been possible without them, or without the kindness and generosity of Cassandra Clare and Josh Lewis. Many thanks also to Robin Wasserman for her ever-keen perspective, Holly Black for plotting with me while we wrangled with the Aga, Elizabeth Eulberg for not letting me die on a tiny, tiny plane, and Sarah Rees Brennan, who always had a ready answer for my worries and wrote alongside me in our bower until the very end. Many thanks also to Renée Ahdieh, Leigh Bardugo, and Sabaa Tahir for giving me advice when I needed it most.

The poem Nirrim reads in the printer's workshop is (of course) by Sappho.

I love having FSG, and Macmillan at large, as a publishing home. Joy Peskin and Trisha de Guzman have been so insightful and supportive as my editors. I thank them and the entire Macmillan team, especially Jen Besser, Beth Clark, Molly Brouillette Ellis, Teresa Ferraiolo, Kathryn Little, Kelsey Marrujo, John Nora, Janine O'Malley, Taylor Pitts, Melanie Sanders, Janine Barlow, Anne Heausler, Mary Van Akin, Allison Verost, and Ashley Woodfolk. Lisa Perrin gave me a gorgeous cover. My agents, Charlotte Sheedy and Alexandra Machinist, have shaped my career and books in profound ways, and have always been there for me.

My readers impress me every day with their enthusiasm and open hearts. You are what made me want to write this book.

My last thanks are to Eve Gleichman, for everything you've given me. I am so grateful for you.